A big thanks to the Hong Kong and British police forces. Thanks to all my family and friends who have helped me in so many ways. I could not have written this book without you all. Admiration and thanks to the late Martin Booth, whose history of the triads, *The Dragon Syndicates*, has been my reference book. A huge thank you to Maxine and the team at Avon for all their support and help. And, of course, the man who made it all happen – a massive thank you to Darcey and his team of wonderful women – thank you for believing in me.

The journey is the reward

THE TROPHY TAKER

Lee Weeks left school at 16 with one O'level and, armed with a notebook and very little cash, spent seven years working her way around Europe and South East Asia. She returned to settle in London, marry and raise two children. In those 15 years, she worked as a cocktail waitress, chef, model, English teacher and personal fitness trainer. She now lives in Devon with her two children and her dogs. *The Trophy Taker* is her first novel. Please visit www.leeweeks.co.uk for more information on Lee.

Visit www.AuthorTracker.co.uk for exclusive updates on Lee Weeks.

LEE WEEKS

The Trophy Taker

A V O N

AVON

A division of HarperCollins*Publishers*
77–85 Fulham Palace Road,
London W6 8JB

www.harpercollins.co.uk

A Paperback Original 2008

First published in Great Britain by
HarperCollins*Publishers* 2008

Copyright © Lee Weeks 2008

Lee Weeks asserts the moral right to
be identified as the author of this work

A catalogue record for this book is
available from the British Library

ISBN-13: 978-1-84756-078-0

Set in Minion by Palimpsest Book Production Limited,
Grangemouth, Stirlingshire

Printed and bound in Great Britain by
Clays Ltd, St Ives plc

For my dad, Brian Davies Bateman, who gave me the gift of self-belief.

1

Hong Kong 2003

Glitter Girl crouched in the darkness. Sweat trickled down her back to the base of her Lurex halter-top and her denim miniskirt rode up around her waist.

She didn't dare move. She couldn't see a thing. She tried to rub away the melted make-up that sweated into her eyes and made them sting, but she couldn't – her hands were tied tightly behind her back. So instead she blinked as hard as she could and stayed absolutely still and hoped that it would come to her in a moment – something would tell her where she was and how she got there. So far, nothing. She did her best not to cry. She could hardly breathe as it was, through the tape over her mouth. She would definitely suffocate if she cried.

As her eyes searched the gloom, shapes began to appear, outlines to form. She looked down at her bare feet and saw that she was squatting on a thin mattress. Long ago it had had some sort of willow pattern, but now there were only dark-rimmed stains, bleeding into one another. To her right, two metres away, was the door through which she must have come, if only she could remember. She twisted around to her left to see what her hands were tied to and recoiled from what she saw. The wall behind her was covered in photos of women. They weren't nice pictures – not even porno ones like the sort that Darren had up in his garage. The women in these photos stared out, slack-jawed and cloudy-eyed. They were all dead.

2

Detective Inspector Johnny Mann stepped out of his car and straight into a sauna. In the half-hour he'd been driving, cocooned in air-conditioning, the morning heat had arrived outside, sucked all the moisture from the ground and left the air as thick as a wet blanket.

He put on his sunglasses, pushed his black hair away from his face and looked up at the sky. His dark eyes were swamped with blue. Clear – *good*. He scanned the horizon . . . *not for long*. A bank of clouds sat pregnant with rain and ready to drop. A typical Hong Kong summer – forty degrees and a hundred per cent humidity – the perfect time to go somewhere else. But Mann wasn't going anywhere. This was the end of a long night and the beginning of an even longer day. He had been on the first response team when they'd found the body. Hong Kong was used to murders, but not like this one.

He checked his watch and looked around the car park – one other vehicle – an unmarked police car. He was relieved. It meant he wouldn't have to hang about.

The autopsy was scheduled for eight. It was twenty to. The sooner they got going, the sooner they'd be able to get out. The mortuary was a place he'd never got used to. The bodies didn't bother him but the smell – dentist meets butchers – stayed in his nostrils like school dinners and old people's homes – there for life.

He took off his jacket and draped it over the back seat before reaching in and pulling out his briefcase. Then he slammed the door shut and strode across the gravel to the mortuary entrance. Mann had a tall, athletic English frame along with high cheekbones and a square jaw. He had hooded eyes: deep set, dark chocolate, and smudged with sadness.

His finger was barely off the buzzer before Kin Tak, the young mortuary assistant, appeared. He was smiling – enthusiastic as always – glad to see that Mann was early and eager to begin the morning's autopsy rota. Dressed in his off-white coat, Kin Tak had that permanently dishevelled look of someone who had never known youth and had spent far too much time caring for dead people. In the mortuary hierarchy Kin Tak was a *Diener*. He moved, handled and washed the bodies. He didn't get to do the technician's job of removing and replacing the organs or sewing up the bodies afterwards, although he was hoping to do that someday. He practised his stitching whenever he could and when no one was looking.

Mann shivered as he hit the wall of cold just inside the door of the once 'clinically clean' but now slightly grubby autopsy room. The room had to be kept below minus five to stop further decomposition on bodies awaiting identification and autopsies. He stood squinting beneath a flickering fluorescent strip-light.

'Full house?' He looked around at the stainless-steel fridges that ran along three sides of the room.

'All but two drawers. We had a gang fight come in overnight – twelve chopped – lots of needlework to be done. Lots of practice.'

Two men emerged from a doorway on Mann's left. He knew one of them well – Detective Sergeant Ng. They'd worked together at the Organised Crime and Triad Bureau. The other man – young and slight – Mann had never seen before.

'Good to see you again, Ng.'

'Hello, Genghis.' Ng came forward to shake Mann's hand warmly. Ng was portly, in his mid-forties and already losing his hair, but still a notorious flirt. His soft brown puppy eyes, quick smile and deep intelligence made him a magnet for women. He always seemed to find one to look after him. 'Thought they'd managed to lose you in the New Territories,' said Ng with a lopsided smile. 'I'm glad to see they didn't.'

'You know me, Confucius – easy-going type, can't think why some people don't like me.' Mann grinned. 'How's it going with you?'

'Not bad, not bad at all, thanks. Still working too hard for too little pay. We miss you down at the OCTB – things are really quiet there without you.'

Mann shrugged. 'Yeah, well, I didn't leave there willingly.'

'I heard. You irritated the wrong people too many times – that was your trouble. You need to be more careful, Genghis. You should know by now: *when you go up the mountain too often you eventually encounter the tiger.*'

'Yeah, but *you cannot fight a fire with water from far away* – unless of course you're *pissing in the wind*, which you do all the time. Then it's possible.'

Ng's face broke into a big crooked grin.

'Very good. Very good. But what does *pissing in the wind* mean?'

'Very old English saying. I'll explain it to you one day.'

'You've been swotting up on your proverbs.'

'Yep! Thought I'd give you a run for your money . . .'

Ng turned towards the officer just behind him. 'Have you met Detective Li?'

Mann looked at the young man who was grinning up at him and evidently itching to speak. He was wearing a brown, seventies-style pinstriped suit with the widest orange kipper tie Mann had ever seen. Mann never remembered going through that fashion stage, although he guessed he must have. He hoped it hadn't lasted long.

'I know! I know!' Ng rolled his eyes towards Li and put his hand up to his mouth to hide what he was about to say. 'They get younger every year! But . . .' he slapped the young detective on the back, 'he may be only twenty-two and wet behind the ears . . . talks like a Yank *and* he definitely hasn't found his dress sense yet . . . but . . .' Detective Li's anxious eyes flicked from one man to the other '. . . this guy passed with honours from cadet school. He can Kung Fu kick ass and he knows all about computers. He'll get there – eventually. Hey, Li?' Ng pulled him forward by the sleeve. 'Don't be put off by the look of this guy,' he said, gesturing towards Mann. 'He may look big and white. He may only be *half* Chinese but he's still the meanest cop you'll ever meet. Meet Genghis Khan.'

Clutching his laptop under one arm, the young detective stepped forward and stared up into Mann's face.

'Awesome,' he said. 'Truly awesome. Heard all about you, boss – honoured.' His eyes stayed fixed on Mann's face as he shifted his weight from one snakeskin boot to the other and grinned inanely. 'You're a legend – a one-man triad annihilator. Never heard you called Genghis Khan before, though.'

Ng thumped Mann in the ribs. 'I named him that because he is a tenacious warrior and he looks like a wild man.'

Li giggled nervously – high-pitched and girly. Ng put a protective hand on his shoulder and edged him further forward.

'And I have decided to call Li "Shrimp", owing to his peculiar resemblance to one.'

The boiled-sweet complexion; the random crests of over-gelled hair. Mann could see what he meant.

'Shrimp here is a regular Bruce Lee. Aren't you?' said Ng proudly.

Detective Li blushed a deeper scarlet and his eyes darted around the room. 'I wouldn't say that . . . but . . .'

Mann shook Li's hand with an extra-firm grip that left Li wincing and Ng chuckling. 'Good man – useful

7

to have around. Take no notice of Confucius. Good to have you on the team, Shrimp.'

'Thank you, boss . . .' Li beamed, his mouth showing more gum than teeth. 'Awesome.'

'We called in at headquarters earlier, Genghis. The place is heaving. There are people there I haven't seen for years,' said Ng.

'I know. This is big. The top brass want it dealt with super-fast, before we lose what few tourists we have.'

'Is it true it's a *Gwaipoh*?'

'Yes, a white foreigner. She was discovered sixteen hours ago, dumped in a bin bag on a building site out in the New Territories, near Sha Tin. A workman found her when he started moving some rubble. She'd been there a few days.'

'Anyone notice anything?'

'No. There's a constant stream of construction vehicles twenty-four hours a day. It's easy to get in and out of the site. She could have been dumped at any time – day or night.'

Kin Tak appeared beside them, ready to start the autopsy.

Ng turned to Li. 'You ready for this, Shrimp? You're about to attend the autopsy of a murdered white woman – a rare thing over here. We usually only get to see dead triads, don't we, Mann?'

'Yes, and the more we get of those, the better,' Mann said, and signalled to Kin Tak that they were ready for what was to come.

3

Morning finally arrived outside. Glitter Girl watched the faint rays of light squeeze through the cracks in the far wall. She watched them widen, soften and fill with spinning dust particles. She felt a little calmer. She loved pretty, sparkly things. She thought of home: Orange County, USA. It was a Saturday night and she was sixteen. It was her first 'proper' dance and her first date with Darren. Her mama said her dress was too tight, too revealing. She'd had to smuggle it out of the house in a bag and change in Darren's car. That had been the most special night of her life, spinning round and round in Darren's arms, showered with light beams from a rotating disco ball. Darren's strong arms held her so tightly that she'd thought she would faint. That was the night she knew he was the one for her. How wrong she had been.

And then it occurred to her – the room was the same size as the one she and Darren had started out their married life in – in the days before he'd started hitting her. *When* he'd started that, there had been no stopping him. *Oh sweet Jesus!* Why did it remind her of *that* room? Was it because Darren had beaten her so badly in *that* room that she'd thought she was going to die, and now she actually was? Her mama always said she'd come to no good and she was right. She was right about a lot of things – especially about Darren.

Glitter Girl looked at the photos of the women. Some of them were staring straight at her, but their eyes were blank. She'd seen eyes like that before. When she was a little girl on the farm she'd fallen on the dung heap and, as she'd struggled to get out of the muck, she'd turned and the dead piglet had been right there in her face. Its eyes were cloudy too, and although it wasn't alive it was moving with maggots.

In the dim light she tried to make out the room. On the far side, hanging from a hook beneath a row of shelves, she saw what looked like a piece of fur and strips of pale animal hide. On the shelf itself there were jars like the ones her grandma kept pickles in. She was trying to make out what was inside when she stopped, held her breath and looked towards the door. A key was turning. Someone was coming.

4

'Okay, gentlemen, shall we begin? It's a Jane Doe, is that right?'

Mr Saheed, the pathologist, had arrived. He was a tall, wiry fifty-five-year-old, originally from Delhi and now settled in the region. He had an abrupt manner, and a habit of grunting his reply, but it was just his way. He was a very good pathologist who never minded questions as long as they weren't too puerile. Mann had learned a lot from him over the years and on the several occasions they had met over a mortuary slab.

The detectives waited while Saheed rammed his feet into a pair of white rubber boots and pulled on a starched white coat and plastic apron. He looked over his glasses and raised an eyebrow at Mann.

'Yes. It's a Jane Doe, sir, and I'll be recording,' Mann said, in answer to Saheed's silent enquiry as to which of the detectives would be taking the role of assisting Kin Tak. 'Ng here is photographer, and that leaves Detective Li to do the dirty work. Scrub up, Shrimp,' he said, remembering the first time he had attended an autopsy. It was at the height of the invasion of the Vietnamese boat people. A pregnant woman and her two children had been washed up after spending a week in the water. It was an experience he'd never forget.

Kin Tak checked a number on a fridge door against one on his list, pulled out one of four drawers, slid a white body bag out onto the trolley and wheeled it over to the stand above a drain in the centre of the room.

Saheed began dictating into the microphone clipped to his breast pocket:

'The head of a Caucasian woman . . . late twenties . . . frozen after death. Bluish discoloration around the mouth . . . no obvious sign of injuries.' Mann looked over his shoulder as Saheed shone a light inside her mouth.

'She looks like she's had a fair amount of work done, sir.'

'Yes. She should have dental records somewhere.'

'Cause of death, sir?'

'Asphyxiation of some kind – we will have to wait for the x-rays to be sure. Let's move on. There's plenty more of Jane to get through. Wash her hair, please, Kin Tak. Sieve the contents and send them off for analysis.'

Kin Tak unzipped the bag along its length and lifted out a woman's thigh, dissected at the knee and hip. He weighed it in a set of scales suspended above the table, before placing it on the slab. Ng measured it and recorded its dimensions on his pad.

Saheed turned the leg over twice, examining it closely before lifting his head to address the policemen. 'Tell me what your observations are, Officer,' he said to Li, who had managed to avoid getting too close to the table so far.

Li stepped forward and stared nervously at the leg. 'Uh . . .' His eyes darted hopelessly around the room in search of an answer.

'And yours, Inspector?' Saheed turned to Mann.

Mann pointed to the knee joint. 'Pretty impressive, sir. Someone enjoys his work. Likes it to look neat.'

The pathologist grunted his agreement before addressing Li again. 'Do you cook, Officer? Ever had to joint or bone meat? No? Well, let me tell you, it's a skill. You need to be at least a competent surgeon or at worst a good butcher. You need a very sharp knife and you need to know where to saw, chop and cut. Like here,' he said, tapping the open knee joint with his scalpel. 'Now, let's see what else we have . . . Victim is approximately twenty-five years old, five foot five inches tall, and . . . what's this?' He paused to study a mark on the inside of the thigh.

'We have us a biter,' Kin Tak blurted out, unable to contain his excitement.

The pathologist looked up, nodded and smiled at his assistant. He allowed Kin Tak his little eccentricities and his almost Tourette's-like need to voice his observations. 'Yes . . . There is a human bite mark here on the inside of the thigh, made *after* death occurred. Within twelve hours, I would say.' Ng stepped forward to photograph the bite mark and measure dimensions in preparation for a cast to be made. 'She had been dead at least a week before being dismembered.'

'So, someone hung on to her after they killed her and before they froze her?'

'Why would they do that?' Li looked at Mann.

'All sorts of reasons, Shrimp. None of them nice.'

5

Reasons? He shrugged. She had made him feel good – reason enough. He hadn't wanted to let her go. He had a video of her death, which he watched often. He was watching it now – sat in his chair, remote in one hand, cock in the other. Ready to pause and rewind at his favourite bit. The look on her face when she knew this time was the last! He loved that bit.

He watched himself turn and grin at the camera, a length of twine in his hand. The girl, frantic, trying to get away from him. But she couldn't. She was tied tightly to the chair. Only her pretty little head moved in tiny shakes as she squealed into the gag. There was nothing she could do. Her fate was in his hands. *Wait . . .* It was coming to his favourite bit now. *Tourniquet in place. Turn it once, twice . . . turn and tighten. Hold it for longer this time . . . Yes! She knows this is it!* Her eyes bulged. Her body convulsed. The shaking stopped. Still he carried on watching. This was his favourite part of the film. She was dead but he wasn't finished with her. *Pause. Rewind. Pause. Rewind.*

6

Saheed waited for Ng to finish photographing the bite mark before continuing:

'The right arm of the victim has been cleanly dissected at the shoulder joint. Obvious signs of injury around the wrist: deep lacerations, residual debris.' He picked out some fibres enmeshed in the flesh. 'Rope fibres,' he said, holding his tweezers aloft for Li to take the sample from him. 'The hand is still attached, two fingers remain intact but lifted from the bone . . .' Saheed scraped beneath the nails, and tapped the scrapings into a plastic dish, 'which is common with bodies found in water.' He cut the lifted skin from the woman's finger.

'Found in water, sir?' Li spoke.

'They had been frozen, hadn't they? When they thawed they created a lot of liquid. Give me your hand,' he said, at the same time reaching over and taking it. He wrapped the woman's cut skin around Li's index finger before passing his hand to Ng to take a print. Ng rolled Li's finger, and the woman's, in the ink several times. Pressing hard onto the pad, he held it there to ensure a good print. Li's boiled face blanched.

'You all right, Shrimp?' It looked to Mann like he was about to throw up.

'Totally.' Li cleared his throat while managing a half-smile. 'No problemo.'

'Good lad.' Mann and Ng exchanged grins.

'Okay, gentlemen, let's move on, shall we?' Saheed peeled off his gloves and apron and pulled out a new set from the box above the sink. He indicated to Li to do the same and resumed his dictation:

'The torso is showing greenish-black discoloration on the abdomen – a sign of decomposition. There is a deep cut which runs directly across from one hip bone to the other, measuring . . . ?'

Mann stepped forward. 'Twenty-one centimetres,' he announced, holding the ruler while Ng photographed.

'A large-bladed knife with a sawing action made this wound, and it was made at least twelve hours after death.'

Li shook his head with disbelief. 'How do you know that? How do you know the size of the knife? Awesome!'

Saheed paused, looked over his glasses at Li, then, with a small upward jerk of the head, he beckoned him nearer.

He'll learn . . . thought Mann, as Li hesitated. *The hard way* . . .

'Come closer, young man. I want to show you something.' Mr Saheed guided Li's hands to the edge of the wound. 'Put your fingers in there and gently pull back the surrounding flaps of skin . . . Now what do you see?'

Li reached in gingerly.

'A pattern of straight and jagged cuts, sir . . .' he held his breath, 'along the length of the wound.' He stood up and turned his head away to breathe.

'Stay there!' Mr Saheed said as he held on to Li's retreating hand. 'Give him the ruler, Inspector.' Mann handed it over. 'Now . . . how long are the horizontal cuts?'

'Four centimetres, sir.' Li measured it with his free hand.

'How far into the muscle and flesh has the knife travelled? Fingers in, young man, get on with it!'

'Right through, sir. The cut goes past the fat and through the muscle.'

'As far in as the length of your thumb, would you say?'

'Yes, sir.'

'Okay. So the blade has to be at least that thick, doesn't it? Does that answer your question, young man?'

'Yes, sir.' Li stood up and backed away to safety. He looked like he was about to throw up.

Mann winked at him. You had to admire his guts – he'd just *had* to ask, and that was a sign of a good detective. You had to be a good listener and a great questioner. Of course, timing was also important, but Shrimp hadn't learned that bit yet.

Saheed moved his attention to the upper half of the torso.

'There is a cluster of small burns across the chest area – cigarette burns by the look of them.' He scanned the scatter of black dots, a centimetre in diameter, that were spattered across her chest and collarbone.

'They were made over a period of days and are at different stages of healing.' Li didn't ask, even though he wanted to. Mr Saheed hovered over her chest. 'And there is a tattoo here above the left breast. Can't make out what it is.' He paused, peeled off his gloves, and waited while Mann and Ng finished photographing and plotting the position of the tattoo. As he waited he was handed a slip of paper from a mortuary technician. He took it, studied it, picked up his file and flipped back over his notes.

'Something else, gentlemen. According to the results of these blood tests . . .' he checked his notes again and looked over his glasses at the detectives '. . . there isn't just *one* woman on this table.'

The video stopped. He sat back, satiated, weary. He closed his eyes. Then the crying started. Behind him Glitter Girl cowered in the corner of the room. Still sat in the chair, his head relaxed against the back of the seat. Still holding the remote. He opened his eyes and looked at her.

'Your turn will come – be patient. You just paint your pretty nails like I told you – make them sparkle.'

7

'All three Caucasian?'

'We may never know for sure, but the measurements, the forward curve to the femur, they tally.'

'We may get lucky with some IDs,' said Mann. 'We have one skull, in pretty good shape at least, and a tattoo.'

'And a fingerprint,' added Li. He wasn't going to let them forget that.

'We'll download these photos we've taken onto Detective Li's laptop – get them straight across to headquarters so that they can begin working on it,' said Mann. 'Let's hope it's enough to positively establish the race and identity of these women. One *Gwaipoh* is bad enough – three will start a mass exodus.'

'What about the texture of the skin?' asked Li. 'Would that help to give the ethnicity of the victim away, sir?'

'How?'

'Everyone knows that *Gweilos* have really rough skin and are very hairy.'

Mann looked at him, half-amused, half-appalled. 'Yeah, that's about as true as the one about all Chinese men having tiny cocks. Oh wait! That one *is* true!' He turned back to the pathologist who was suppressing a grin.

'Any theory about cause of death, sir?' asked Mann.

'We need to wait for the toxicology results to be sure about poisoning, but I suspect the cause of death to be asphyxiation again – manual strangulation or with the aid of a ligature. We're just waiting for the x-rays to come back; that might give us an idea of how it was done. Right, let's see what else we can find.' He pressed his fingers inside the wound again and eased it apart.

'We're quite lucky here – because of the freezing process we still have some organs left intact. However . . .' his gloved fingers disappeared inside '. . . some are not where they should be.' He looked at Li.

'Sir?'

'The ovaries and uterus are missing . . .'

'What does that mean?' asked Li, before he could stop himself.

The pathologist paused and looked at him. 'It means . . . young man . . .'

Li blinked back at him, ready for the worst, but before Mr Saheed could answer, Kin Tak exploded:

'We have a trophy taker . . .' and immediately smacked his hand across his mouth to silence his excited giggle.

8

Before the process of reclaiming land from the sea, Hong Kong Island was just a big rock. Now, the further up the Rock you lived, the more prestigious the address. At the top, the Peak represented the pinnacle of affluence. Its lofty head rose above the smog and heat, affording some respite from the stifling summers. Its wooded areas were a welcome contrast to the skyscraper world below. It was where the fabulously wealthy lived; where fleets of lucky-numbered Bentleys sat idling in air-conditioned garages. Up to two million US was paid in Hong Kong for a lucky number plate. Two stood for 'easy' or 'fast'. Three for 'living' or 'giving birth'. Six for 'longevity'. Eight for 'prosperity'. It wasn't just number plates and the numbers weren't always lucky. Four stood for death. Two and four combined – fast death.

Halfway up the Rock towards the Peak were the Mid-levels, a sought-after residential area populated by high-earning professionals. At the foot of the Rock was the business heart of Hong Kong: Central District.

Headquarters was situated at the top of Hollywood Hill, on the rise above Central District towards the

Mid-levels. It was a wonderful Victorian colonial legacy: big, white and smack-bang at the top of the hill. At one time Headquarters was a 'one-stop shop' where criminals could be held for questioning, interviewed, judged, sentenced and incarcerated all in one place. Now it was the centre for all serious crimes.

In room 210 Superintendent David White sat behind a heavy oak desk. On one side of the desk were photos of his grandchildren. On the other was an engraved cigar box and a small silver rugby ball on a stand – a trophy from his coaching days, awarded for surviving five unbeaten seasons and presented to him by his beloved police rugby team.

In the centre of the room a colonial-style fan hung down from the ceiling and whirred lazily at half speed.

Superintendent White was not only the senior officer in charge of the investigation but also Mann's mentor and an old friend. He commanded great respect in the force, one of the only non-Chinese senior officers to speak fluent Cantonese. Not that he needed to with Mann, who, with a Chinese father, English mother and educated in England, was fluent in either language.

David White was approaching retirement. He had given his life to fighting crime in the colony and now was being gently phased out under Chinese rule. He knew it was time to go but it didn't stop him mourning the end of an era. He had arrived in the colony in the sixties when the police force had been one of the most corrupt in the world. When the clean-up came in the seventies he lost many of his good friends. Accepting pay-offs from triads, even working with them to keep the crime level under control, was the norm at that time. Some officers admitted their guilt and did their time. Many more took the money and ran. David White stayed. He helped the Hong Kong police force to develop into one of the finest in the world. He wished he felt happier about leaving it to others.

'DNA?'

He didn't wait for Mann to sit down. He had the photos from the autopsy spread over his desk.

'No chance, David. The bin bag is a great place to rot – makes two days look like seven.'

'Any reports of missing foreigners?'

'Fifty in the last year, and those are just the ones we know about. They're the ones that someone cares enough about to report missing. We don't know whether there's a particular ethnicity he goes for. It could be black, Asian, mixed race . . . we have no idea yet. And I've asked to go further back than one year, David. I have a hunch the head we found is much older.'

'Bloody hell!' White rubbed his bald head with his hands – a sure sign he was stressed. 'Hong Kong can be proud of this one. It's all we bloody well need,' he moaned. 'We are going to have so much heat on our backs, Mann. Say goodbye to life as you know it till this is solved. This is going to be our home for the foreseeable future.'

The Superintendent got up from his desk and walked over to the window where he pulled at the louvre blind to observe the day. The morning smog was lifting and rapidly being replaced by rain clouds. 'But, on the positive side . . .' He let the blind go and turned back to Mann, smiling. 'At least you're back at Headquarters.'

Mann grinned back at his old friend. '*Ten months*, David! It felt like a lifetime,' he said, shaking his head with relief. 'I thought I was going to be forgotten in Sha Tin. Lucky for me they found the bodies out there. You have no idea how good it is to be back.'

'I can imagine.'

'I still don't understand why they transferred me. I'd only been at the OCTB for eighteen months. I expected to stay there for at least three years. I thought I was doing a good job – making some progress.'

'Yes, well . . . You *were* making progress, that was the problem. There are *some* people, Mann, and not just at the OCTB, who hoped they'd *never* see you again. You never know when to ease up on the triads, Mann. You could do with having a bit more respect for death. You might be a big lad, but there are still plenty of foundations out there that need filling. Sometimes I think you go looking for trouble.'

He paused, looked squarely at Mann and waited for a reaction. Realising he wasn't going to get one, he sat down heavily.

'I was just doing my job, David,' Mann replied. 'Since when did that become a crime?'

White shook his head and sighed. 'Your job, and a bit extra, Mann. You forget I've known you all your life. I knew your dad when we were both wet behind the ears – him just starting out in business and me just off the boat. I was proud to know him, proud to call him a friend. After his death I was delighted that you wanted to come into the police force. You've proved your worth many times. There are few policemen with your level of intuition for a case, Mann, but there are none so reckless of their own safety either. I know how you think. I've seen you on the cricket field. I've watched you on the rugby pitch. I was proud to be your coach for many years. You were the best player the police team ever had. I know what kind of sportsman you are: you give everything you have *and* a little more, and you hate to lose. But, more than that, good sportsmanship is paramount to you. And that's all right on the sports field, Mann, but not in real life. Right or wrong, black or white, there's no grey area with you. But there is in real life. Your father was just the same – a strong, upright and honest man – but it was his inability to see the grey that led to his death . . .'

White stopped abruptly. He wanted to say more, but one look at Mann told him he had already overstepped the boundary.

'My father stood up for what he believed in, David. He died because he refused to pay protection money to a bunch of thugs. Just because it's the norm doesn't make it right. My father died rather than compromise his beliefs.'

'I know. I know.' White held his hands up, calling for a truce. 'But it was such a great loss . . . Such a huge loss for you and your mother. For all of us.'

Mann knew that the Superintendent meant it – White missed Mann's father. He missed all the good men he had known in his life. He was coming up to that point when he looked back and reminisced more than he looked forward. The last year had seen the Superintendent shrink inside the uniform that he used to fill with such pride. His retirement couldn't come quick enough now, and yet it was the last thing he really wanted.

White inhaled deeply and shook his head, world weary.

'And now I begin to despair that anything will make a difference any more. Fighting against the triads is useless. They have moved north to do their business in China. It will be impossible to control them now.'

It was the first time Mann had heard him speak in those terms. It took him by surprise. He had never thought of his old friend as a quitter.

'I know things have been difficult since the Handover, but we *will* win in the end, David. Believe me, we will find a way to defeat them. I'm not prepared to give up. And you're right – I *don't* see a grey area when it comes to justice.'

'Mann – let's face it, you love to tread on toes. Since the Handover there are a lot of well-connected criminals that the Chinese government call *patriots* who we are supposed to accept as pillars of the community – when we all know them to be nothing but gangsters.' White shook his head sadly. 'And the trouble is, you don't know whose toes they are until you step on them too hard and it's too late to say sorry.'

'I'm not going to apologise for any of it, David. If people have nothing to hide then they shouldn't fear me. I didn't join up to allow the triads to run Hong Kong . . . I just don't get it – returning to China was supposed to mean tougher penalties on triads – they used to shoot these guys daily. But now the Chinese government is making deals with them. How does that work?'

'I don't know. It's hard to know who's pulling the strings these days in the government *and* in the police force – *especially* at the OCTB.'

'Tell me about it.' Mann pinched his thumb and forefinger together. 'I was *this* close to nailing that bastard Chan. I was getting really close to finding out *exactly* what he was up to, when *whoosh*.' He threw his hands up in the air. 'They virtually took my chair away from beneath me and posted me out to the back of beyond.'

The Superintendent sat back in his old leather chair, which had served him for the last thirty years but was now beginning to show its age, just like its owner. Then he sat up, looked hard at Mann and slammed his fore-arms on the arms of the chair.

'But, for now, I need this case solved – ASAP. And that's what we need to concentrate on, not the triads and *definitely* not Chan. I know how much you hate him, Mann. I am with you on that, but I want no personal vendettas played out now. His time will come, I promise you that.'

He paused for a moment as if he intended to speak further on the subject, but then thought better of it. Mann knew what he was going to say. He was going to say that Mann would be a better policeman if his judgement wasn't sometimes clouded by his hatred of all things triad and especially of all things Chan-related.

And that Chan was not responsible for the death of Mann's father. But David White didn't say it. He merely paused, and the pause said it all.

'Now, as for the workings of it all,' he said, businesslike once more and changing tack. 'I am to head the investigation. You will be my second-in-command. We will set up an operations room at the end of the hall downstairs. We have recruited officers from all over the district to help. Some are already here. The rest will be arriving tomorrow. Detective Sergeant Ng and Detective Li will share an office with you. It'll be a bit cramped and hot, but then you know what it's like at Headquarters – no such thing as working air-con.'

'Hot and sweaty – just the way I like it.' Mann got out of his chair and picked up his jacket.

'Remember what I said, Mann – be careful, but most of all be clever, and don't let that hot head of yours take charge.'

'You know me, David . . .'

'That's what I'm worried about. I promised your mother I'd keep you alive at least until I retire, and I've only got six months left. Please wait till I'm safely back home with my garden gnomes and Sunday papers before getting yourself killed, will you? Now, where are you going to start?'

'In the Sports Bar.'

'It's a bit early, isn't it?'

'Not for the person I want to talk to.'

9

Mann picked his way past the police officers on the stairs and paused in the entrance hall before passing through the heavy oak doors. He stood on the black and white tiled floor and breathed in the smell of lavender wood polish and Brasso and allowed himself a self-congratulatory moment. He had been given a reprieve, for which he was extremely grateful. Now he was back in the building he loved, working on a proper investigation instead of chasing traffic offenders. If he was lucky they wouldn't transfer him back when the case was finished. If he was lucky and very good . . . so not likely then.

He went outside, crossed the car park and walked the steep road down to Central District. The area was number one in the region for shopping and commerce, with its golden skyscrapers, plush shopping malls and one of the most prestigious hotels in the world – The Royal Cantonese. Many deals were struck by an elite few in its Sports Bar, past the Doric columns and just left of the foyer.

James Dudley-Smythe was propping the bar up as

Mann walked in. Originally from Cambridge, he had lived most of his life in Hong Kong. He was fabulously wealthy, with a large house on the Peak. He owned a fleet of Rolls-Royces and employed two full-time chauffeurs. But money *really* hadn't brought him happiness. Besides his massive drinking problem, rumour had it that he could only achieve an erection when indulging in rough sex. Pain was what did it for him, if anything did any more.

He picked up hostesses on a nightly basis, but half the time he couldn't remember whether he'd got what he paid for or not. Most of the girls were wise to it and knew that if they gave him enough drink he would pass out and they could get their money for doing nothing. Some weren't quite so lucky.

Mann sat down on the stool next to him. 'How's it going, James?' he asked, as the waiter brought him a vodka on the rocks.

Dudley-Smythe was, as always, impeccably dressed: sports jacket, cravat, pressed trousers and shiny brogues. He liked to say that you could always tell a man's breeding by the state of his fingernails. He never missed his weekly manicure.

'Rather well, thank you, Mann. And yourself? Married yet? I thought you were going to marry that pretty English girl?'

'No, afraid not.' Mann shifted his weight on the bar stool. 'Been too busy. Talking of which, I'm working on a big case at the moment. Maybe you can help me with it?'

James replaced his glass on the bar, a little unsteadily, and motioned to the barman for a refill. 'Shame that

... I thought she looked perfect for you. Feisty little thing, wasn't she?' James Dudley-Smythe took a sideways glance at Mann.

Mann said nothing – he'd let the old drunk have his fun a little longer. He waited while the barman finished pouring his drink.

'Still playing cricket? You're a damn fine bowler, you know, Mann. All those years in private school in England did wonders for you. Of course, it helps having an English mother – big-boned stock.'

'No time for cricket right now, James. Too busy – as I said.'

'Sorry. Do go on, dear boy . . . Big case . . . I'm all ears.'

Mann hailed the barman to refresh James's empty glass and thus ensure his concentration.

'Over the last twenty years, have you ever heard about either a *Gweilo* or Chinese who took his S&M way too far?'

James knocked back his newly arrived scotch and motioned to the barman to pour another. He looked visibly uncomfortable with the reference to his sexual practices. Mann had had to reprimand him once after a new foreign girl (who didn't understand the rules and didn't know to ply him with drink) had found herself handcuffed to a bed and at the receiving end of one of Dudley-Smythe's party games that involved a whip and a blindfold. She had to be briefly hospitalised. She made a complaint but didn't press charges and was miraculously recovered by the time the cheque cleared.

'Well, that was some time ago now, Mann. I explained about that . . .'

'James, bottom-smacking is one thing, torture is quite another. I want to know if any of the women have mentioned someone who goes much too far, someone who scares them? Has there been any talk like that?'

James took a large gulp of scotch and said thoughtfully: 'That's more of a Filipino thing. That's where you can get away with more these days – if you know what I mean. Haven't seen many Chinese indulging in that sort of sport, mainly Europeans. But then, you're not describing something that has to do with sex, are you, Mann? You're after a psycho?'

Mann had to smile at the wily old drunk – he still had his lucid moments.

'Yes, you're right, James. But he takes trophies from his victims, of a sexual nature. He enjoys inflicting pain on women. It might have started like that.'

'Can of worms, old boy. Can of worms.' Dudley-Smythe shook his head remorsefully. Mann wasn't buying it – he could see the glint in the old pervert's eye.

'Yeah, well let's keep it legal, hey, James? Over sixteen would be good.'

'Of course! Absolutely! Wouldn't dream of it, *certainly not*! You know, come to think of it, there is someone who might be able to help you. It's who we all go to . . .' he wetted his thin, livid lips with whisky, 'all of us who enjoy a spot of spanking. Club Mercedes – girl named Lucy – Chinese. She's the one to talk to. She's a specialist. One of a kind.'

Mann could swear he saw James shiver.

10

Glitter Girl was supposed to run – that was the game. It was always the same one. She was supposed to run and to hide and then he would come and find her.

She ran barefoot through the newly planted forest. The bark was rough beneath her feet and the spiky leaves scratched her face. She ran till her lungs burned, ready to burst. She ran till her legs wobbled like jelly. She knew she was running in circles and that there was no way out. When she could run no more she crouched in the vegetation and made herself as small as she could and stayed absolutely still. Listening hard, she prayed silently: *Sweet Jesus, save me. I'll be good – I promise. Save me, Lord . . .* She didn't hear a reply from Jesus. All she heard was, *Ready or not . . . I'm comin' . . .*

11

In the skies over Hong Kong, on a packed plane from Heathrow, Georgina Johnson prepared to touch down. She was tired. It had been a long journey and she hadn't slept at all on the plane. She looked around. People were returning to their seats to get ready for landing. One woman, sitting across the aisle to Georgina, had been doing her make-up for the last hour. All but two of the passengers were Chinese. Georgina had never seen so many Chinese people before. Sometimes, as a child, out shopping with her mother in their home-town of Newton Abbot, a medium-sized market town in Devon, she had seen small family groups of Chinese. There were never more than two noisy children at a time, happily chasing their parents' heels or pulling on their arms. The family only had eyes for one another – protected in their Chinese capsule. As if the rest of the world were a dream that they could choose to step in or out of, but in which everyone else was trapped. Every morning Georgina's mother, Feng Ying, walked the three miles from their home on the outskirts, into the town centre to the produce market next to the multi-storey car park. There she haggled and badgered the stallholders for the best vegetables, the cheapest meat. Then, content with her dealings, she allowed herself a social call – a brief visit to the Golden Dragon, the town's only Chinese restaurant. It was situated above the multi-storey and looked down over the market. The Golden Dragon was owned by the Ho family, a family of Hong Kongese who had come over with just enough money to open a take-away, which, within a few years, expanded to a restaurant. For Feng Ying, the Golden Dragon provided an oasis in the pasty-white town of expanding new-builds where she had lived since the day her husband Adam Johnson had brought her to Britain. Where she'd lived alone, since the day her husband had not come home. He had left for no apparent reason. From that day she'd set about making do without him. She lived on the small savings that her husband had put into an account for her and she crocheted decorative pieces of linen, bedspreads and tablecloths for the upmarket handicraft shop in town. At times, when they needed her, when they had a large function which required her artistic eye at decorating and table setting, she helped in the Golden Dragon. But Feng Ying's main job was to bring her infant daughter up as best she could. She was a foreigner in a country she barely knew but she found strength through her child. Every day she bundled her pink, washed and pampered baby into the pram and manoeuvred it into the outside world. She faced all life's obstacles for this child and forged a bond between mother and daughter that was dependence and love entwined. Now Feng Ying was dead and Georgina must make it alone – something she had never imagined in her twenty-two years that she would have to do.

After clearing passport control Georgina collected her case and made her way through the new airport, a massive high-ceilinged hangar on Lantau Island. Pulling her heavy case behind her, she looked anxiously along the line of names written on cardboard held up by eager-looking drivers. Most were written in Chinese. It took her a few minutes before she saw hers. *Georgi-na* written in red felt pen on brown card and held up by a leathery-faced old man. He greeted her in Chinglish, smiling and nodding profusely as he picked up her case. Georgina tried to explain that it had wheels and that he could pull it along if he wanted. But he didn't understand and it didn't matter. He hardly struggled with the weight. Small and wiry he might have been, but he was definitely strong.

As they stepped outside, the bright sun slapped Georgina in the face and the heat wrapped itself around her like cling film. By the time they reached the taxi, less than a minute's walk, she was sweating and couldn't wait to find shade inside the cab.

The taxi driver's name was Max, but it hadn't always been. A teacher handed out the English names in class. He had been allotted the name Maxwell, which he later shortened to Max on the advice of an American tourist. Fong Man Tak was his birth name; he preferred Max.

Max was not altogether sure what age he was: there was no definitive documentation. But he had counted the years from when he was told by his mother that he had reached the age of eight. So now he thought he was sixty, and his mother was long dead.

Max had been a taxi driver for the last thirty years, and most of the time it brought him a modest income. Taxis were thick on the ground in Hong Kong so he had to work long hours to make it worthwhile.

Georgina peered silently out of the window. She was mesmerised by the cars all around her. She hadn't envisaged Hong Kong looking quite so un-British. She'd thought, as a former British colony, that somehow it would mirror London in miniature. Or perhaps it would look like a Victorian seaside town with mock Tudor B&Bs, maybe with a dilapidated pier. She didn't know quite which, but she certainly hadn't expected it to look so completely different. It seemed to her to be a futuristic alien world of skyscrapers.

She tilted her head at the window and stretched her eyes upwards. 'Gods,' she thought, the skyscrapers were like gods' legs: perfected from glass and chrome, glinting gloriously in the sunshine. There were so many different kinds: some were honeycombed like rectangular wasps' nests; others were skeletal, jutting skyward as bony white fingers. And the strangest thing of all were the building sites that bridged the gaps between the buildings like gums between teeth.

All the time Georgina studied her new environment, Max studied her in the mirror. He was fascinated by her cascading curls and her pale, luminescent beauty. It was not the first time he'd had a foreign girl in his car. Many girls had sat where she sat now. They were strange, unearthly creatures, the Western girls. They didn't seem real to Max. They were images from a film: plastic, false. Sometimes Max thought about the other girls, the ones who had ridden in his cab. He wondered where they'd gone.

One of the girls who'd sat in the back of Max's cab, where Georgina was sitting now, had not gone far. Part of her now resided in a drawer of a mortuary fridge. The rest of her was still waiting to be found.

12

Max turned the cab into a narrow street – typical of the ones found just a stone's throw from the main tram line on Johnson Road. The road was so narrow that the washing hung from poles, jutting out from the overhead balconies and meeting in the centre of the street, hanging down like heavily laden tree branches, providing a canopy over the busy street. They trapped smells and dust, but afforded some welcome shade in the heat of the day.

The cab pulled up outside the mansion block on a side street in Wanchai.

Georgina thanked Max, took her case from him and wheeled it into the building. She checked her piece of paper, the one that Mrs Ho had written the address on, in both Chinese and English: fourth floor, apartment 407. She took the lift – a small oppressive space that only had room for her and her case. As she wheeled the case out onto the fourth-floor landing, she paused outside the apartment door to gather her thoughts. She had come a long way to reach this point. She hoped it would prove worth it. She took a deep breath, rang the bell and waited.

A young woman in a dressing gown opened the door. She looked like she'd just got up. She wore no make-up and her hair was a mess. Her face was as rounded as a full moon, while her nose was small and flattened, emphasising the largeness of her visage. Her eyes were set slightly wide apart, and then there was the mouth, like Georgina's, a family trait – lips that formed an almost perfect circle topped by a cupid's bow.

The woman grinned. She had a gold crown just behind one of her eyeteeth.

'You got to be Georgina, right?' Her voice was loud, deep and brackish. The words had a hint of American, but the accent remained pure Hong Kong staccato.

Georgina nodded. 'Ka Mei?'

'Yeah, thaz me. Call me Lucy – English name more easy. Come in, please. Let me help you.'

She pulled Georgina's case in and ushered her forward into the dimly lit flat. Immediately in front of them, as they entered, was a small lounge area. Beyond that was a fifties-style Formica breakfast bar. Behind it there was a one-ring cooker, a microwave and a decrepit water heater that appeared to cling to the wall by its fingernails. There were two rooms on the left, and a bathroom ahead. Lucy pulled Georgina's case into the middle of the lounge.

'Sorry. I expect you later. But no worries, huh?' She patted Georgina on the arm. 'You very pretty girl – so tall.' She laughed. 'Ka Lei!' she called. 'Come, meet your cousin . . .'

There was a screech from the bathroom and a young woman came flying out. She looked quite different from her sister. She was taller, but much slighter. Her features were also long and thin, accentuated by her hair that fell from a centre parting and divided into two shiny black sheets falling either side of her face. She was so excited. She had been on a high ever since they had known that Georgina would be coming.

She barged past her sister (falling over Georgina's huge suitcase, which filled the tiny lounge) and threw open the bedroom doors. Ka Lei squealed with delight as she pulled her cousin out of the room and dragged her around the tiny flat, pointing things out as they went. There was always something else she absolutely must show her.

'Here is our bedloom,' shrieked Ka Lei, as she dived into the first open door and jumped onto the bed in the centre of the room.

Lucy came behind her, scolding but smiling. Georgina squeezed past the bed to look at the view from the over-sized windows, more out of politeness than anything else. All she could see was the side wall of the adjacent building. By pressing her face against the pane and looking up she would have been able to see a corner of sky, and, looking down, people's heads would have been just visible below. But she didn't; she stood politely, staring through the never-been-cleaned glass at the blacked-out windows of the building opposite, which was so near you could almost reach out and touch it. Georgina was used to looking out of the window and seeing fields. Now she knew what it was to feel claustrophobic.

They eventually collapsed onto the bed in what was to be Georgina's room. It was identical to the sisters':

the same two lazy bamboo blinds hanging lopsided against the oversized panes, the same wallpaper peeling from the wall and the same air-conditioning unit droning away in honour of Georgina's arrival.

All three sat on the bed.

Ka Lei reached for Georgina's hand. 'We hope you happy here . . . wit us,' she said.

Georgina felt too overwhelmed to answer. It was all so strange. So many new things to take in. She looked around her. Had she left England for this – this scruffy, dark and damp-smelling apartment? Then she looked back at Ka Lei, sitting on the bed, waiting expectantly, smiling at her, and she knew it didn't matter what the flat was like – she had found her cousins and they were happy to see her.

'Ayeee . . .' Ka Lei looked at her watch. 'I late . . . muz go . . . I wor until ten o'clock, okay?'

'Okay,' Georgina mimicked, laughing.

Lucy moved forward to usher her sister out. She spoke sternly to her in Cantonese about being late. Georgina found she could understand quite a lot of what they said. The years of listening to the workers in the Golden Dragon had meant she'd absorbed a lot of the language without realising.

Ka Lei grabbed her bag, kissed her sister and her cousin, and flew out of the door amid uncontrollable shrieking. Her energetic presence diminished with the descending elevator.

Max was heading home. He lived with his brother and his father. The old man would be waiting for him now, dozing in his chair, waiting for the sound of his son returning. Max had been so exhausted before he picked up the young woman but now his mind was alert, jumping. He craned his neck to look up at the sky. A storm was coming. The electricity in the air charged Max's weary old brain. Now he had the girl to think about too. He would not sleep today.

13

Lucy went behind the breakfast bar to make tea.

'See Ka Lei later. She a student nurse. Works at the government hospital not far from here. One more year be qualify. Very good girl.'

As Lucy busied herself making tea, Georgina took the opportunity to study her. Lucy wasn't pretty. Her looks were brash, hard. Georgina felt a small pang of disappointment. Lucy looked very different from her mother, whose beauty had been subtle and soft. Then she was cross with herself. She hadn't come all this way to find fault with her cousins.

'So funny, when you write me, huh? My sister and me, we talk juz couple of weeks ago. We say: we wonder how old you are and if we ever meet you. Funny, huh? We never thin you come Hong Kong. It's pretty strange, huh – meeting like this for firs time? How you fine us?' Lucy asked.

'My mother left a list of people I should contact . . .'

Georgina felt sadness surge. She swallowed hard and tried to stay focused, not think about her mother for just a few seconds. She was jumpy and tired. It would be too easy to get over-emotional.

Lucy placed her hand on Georgina's arm. 'Very sat, about your mommy . . . very sat.' She turned back to wait for the water to boil.

'She had been ill for a long time. Four years,' Georgina said in hushed tones, more to herself than anyone else, as Lucy had her back to her and was busy washing cups.

Georgina thought about those years. She had nursed her mother through two relapses. She'd never really expected her to die. She never thought her mother would ever leave her. She wondered how she had survived those early days, after her mother's death. At the time she had felt so completely lost. She had gone back to work. The bookshop was just as she'd left it. Iris, her co-worker, was still wearing the same brown court shoes and pink blouse as she had always done, and the same coral lipstick that clung to the edges of her front teeth. Nothing was different, except Georgina.

Iris had never been good with emotions. The sight of Georgina's distress had made her uncomfortable.

'Have you *no* other family?' she'd asked. 'No one? Are you sure? You must have *some* relatives?'

'I have two cousins in Hong Kong but I've never met them,' Georgina told her.

'Maybe you should take some time off and go and visit them, Georgina. Hmm? I can cope here. I have to take on some temporary staff nearer to Christmas anyway. I'll take on somebody now, to cover for you, just until you get back. How's that?'

Then Georgina had sat down on one of the unopened boxes in the storeroom. 'I don't know what to do any more.' She had put her head in her hands. 'I feel as if I don't belong here, without my mum.'

'You may find what you're looking for in Hong Kong, Georgina.' Iris had knelt down beside her and smiled kindly. 'Who knows? You can only try. Life is a challenge. Sometimes it just throws up loads of shit at us, for no reason. It makes no sense at the time, but it makes us stronger, makes us grow. You need to grow, Georgina. You are twenty-two years old. You've been in this shop for five years now. You came in here with all sorts of plans. You were going to go to university. You were going to travel. You had a boyfriend. What happened to Simon?'

'It just didn't work out.'

'You did a marvellous job looking after her, but it's time for you to live *your* life now. It's time to find your wings and learn to fly.'

It made Georgina smile to remember how Iris always erred towards the theatrical. But it had stirred something within her, and that afternoon she'd gone to see the Hos. They sat at a table overlooking the market. Mrs Ho stayed with her while Mr Ho went to fetch her some of her favourite wonton soup. When he returned, Georgina told them she was thinking of going to Hong Kong.

'Good idea,' Mr Ho had replied.

'Don't be stupid!' Mrs Ho had retorted angrily in Cantonese. 'How will she cope out there, on her own? Look at her! Skin and bone!'

Mr Ho had stood his ground. 'But she's not coping here, is she? Better go where she has some family to look after her. New start for her.'

Mrs Ho had scowled at her husband, turned back to Georgina, and spoken to her in English.

'You better stay here, Georgina. You have friends here, don't you?'

Georgina pushed the wontons around her soup.

'Not really,' she answered. 'Most of my friends went to university when I stayed here. I have you and Mr Ho. I have Iris. That's it, really.'

'Better stay here with us then, huh?' It had broken Mrs Ho's heart to see her so sad.

Then Georgina put down her spoon and looked past Mr and Mrs Ho, down to the market below where the stallholders were shutting up shop, and for a second she thought she saw her mother. She looked away quickly.

'They are my cousins. But I've never met them. Do you think they would even want to see me?'

'Of course they would want to see you, Georgina. Why wouldn't they? But maybe it's not such a good idea to go there *right* now.'

'But I think, perhaps, I *should*.' For a few seconds she felt the sadness, which seemed to be cemented to her heart, crack and fall away and hope begin its return.

Mr and Mrs Ho had looked from one to the other. Then Mrs Ho had shrugged and smiled resignedly. Reaching over, she'd brushed Georgina's hair away from her face and kissed her cheek.

'Okay then. Maybe you should go,' she had said with

a sigh. 'Maybe you should go to Hong Kong, Georgina, and find your family.'

And now, for better or worse, Georgina had found them.

14

'I'm gonna make you some tea, okay?'

'Yes ... sounds good ... thanks.' Georgina yawned and sat down heavily on the stool.

'I hope I'm not stopping you from going to work, Lucy. I'll be fine here by myself, honestly.'

'Hey, no worry, right?' Lucy handed her tea in a chipped cup. 'Working later.' She smiled, turned away and began busying herself. 'Good, huh? Give me more time to get to know you, huh?'

'So you work when you want to?'

'For sure!'

Lucy turned away from Georgina and searched for something in a cupboard. 'And what kind of work do you do, Lucy?'

There was a pause, as Lucy pondered the question that she knew she would have to answer sometime. She stopped and turned and met her cousin's gaze.

'I work in nightclub.'

'You're a singer!' Georgina exploded. 'How cool!'

Lucy laughed. 'No ... but my mommy was a singer, did you know that? Ah! Juz a momen. I remember something I want to show you.' Lucy slipped out from behind the breakfast bar and shuffled into the bedroom. She stood on a chair and pulled down a box. 'Georgina, come see what I have here,' she called as she carried on rooting through the box's contents and pulled out an old tattered photograph. She held it aloft to show Georgina as she walked in behind Lucy. 'See anyone you know?'

Georgina sat on the bed beside Lucy. She took the photo from her and studied it. It was an old black and white print of a man and woman and two girls, all in traditional Chinese dress. They were posing in front of a painted backdrop: tranquil water and weeping willows. Georgina turned it over – there was writing on the back: *December 1950, Hong Kong*, and some Chinese script. Turning it back, it was her mother's smile she recognised first, then the shape of her face. Feng Ying was the smaller of the children, holding on to her elder sister Xiaolin's hand, and she was staring into the camera with her head tilted to one side.

'Nice picture, huh?'

Georgina nodded, transfixed by the treasure she held in her hands. 'So beautiful.'

'I'm gonna get you a copy, okay?'

As Georgina looked up and nodded her appreciation, Lucy saw that her cousin's eyes were watery. She jumped up. 'More tea! We need more tea!' And she scurried back out to the kitchen. 'Chinese tea, the best! Do you like it?' she called.

Georgina didn't answer: she was transfixed by the photograph. Lucy came in again, carrying a tray. 'Long time ago, this picture, huh? You know this picture was taken when our family first moved here to Hong Kong. See! There is father, mother, and two little girls. My mommy and yours, see? When our family came from mainland China, long time back . . . they had *big hopes* then, but . . .' she shrugged '. . . didn't work out so good, huh? But your mom, she did fine,' Lucy continued. 'She was good in school . . . learn a lot . . . worked in a bank. Really good how she manage to get that kind of job.'

'She met my dad in that bank.'

'Yes! Very lucky. My mommy not so lucky.' Lucy shrugged. 'Maybe she not so clever . . .'

Lucy poured out more tea. Georgina was still looking at the photo. 'Have you got any more photos?'

'No, shame, I have very little of our family. Now not many of us left, huh, juz the three of us now.'

'Lucy, I am very grateful to you for letting me stay. But what about you and Ka Lei? You have to share a room now?'

'No problem. We always share.'

'My room is always empty?'

'An American girl had your room. I don't know where she is now.' Lucy rolled her eyes and shrugged her shoulders. 'Nice girl, very pretty; blonde hair, long nails.'

He liked her nails. It was one of the first things he'd noticed about her. He liked women who looked after themselves. He had made her paint her nails especially, on that last day before he chased her through the forest. He'd made her paint them in stars and stripes, like the

American flag. She had painted her nails with expert precision, each stripe was perfectly in line. In the centre of each nail she had painted one red star and sprinkled it with glitter. He smiled to himself, satisfied. Now he would always know which finger was hers.

15

Max lived in Sheung Sai Wan, Western District. It was an area that, despite its name, was the least westernised district of all Hong Kong. It was also the place that the British had first settled in, then hastily fled from when malaria came biting at their heels. Industries in the area were small and family run. Life was as it used to be. Profits were small and everyone had something to sell. Traditional skills and oriental sundries crowded the cobbled alleyways. Bolts of silk that were rolled from one-hundred-year-old spools. Chinese calligraphy that was carved into ornate 'chops' made from ivory and jade. Snakes had their gall bladders removed and presented to the purchaser to drink, before being placed back in their wooden box – gall-bladderless. But Western District's days were numbered: new developments were poking their bony fingers out of the living decay and time-debris. The Fong family – Max, his brother Man Po and his father – lived on Herald Street. It was one of the broader, quieter roads at the lower end of the district. Most of the buildings on Herald Street had a shop front. Some shops were still in full use, merchandise spilling out and obstructing the pavement. Others had rusted-up metal shutters and decrepit doorways that had been a long time silent. There was a peaceful, dusty old quiet about Herald Street, but there was also a permanent smell of decay there: rotting, fermenting vegetation, cultivated by years of neglect. The Fong family lived in a four-storey building situated three-quarters of the way along the street. They had had a thriving business once. Father Fong had been a well-respected doctor. He had held his practice on the ground floor of the house, and the shop front had served as the dispensary. Queues had formed from the shop entrance and continued down Herald Street on most days, with people waiting patiently to see him. He was so respected that it was widely accepted he could perform miracle cures, and his notoriety spread in both Chinese and Western circles.

The shop was crammed with all manner of cures and herbs, dried skins and animal parts. It was all kept in perfect order. That was in the days that his wife was alive. It was she who had structured the day-to-day running of the surgery. Under her supervision, Max had helped his father, dispensing the medicine, weighing out the various herbs, bagging them up according to prescription. He had started to train in acupuncture and showed an aptitude for it. His mother spent a lot of time nurturing Max's abilities. Those were happy days in the Fong household – before his mother died suddenly. She was shopping for groceries when she was hit on the head by a piece of falling construction material being used to build one of the new tower blocks. The shock was too great for Father Fong. His world was shattered, and only the chore of looking after his twelve-year-old son and treating his patients kept him from ending his own life. The business would have gone to pieces, if it hadn't been for the employees who took over as best they could, keeping things ticking over. One of them, a young woman by the name of Nancy, who had been in their employ since the age of fifteen, and who Mrs Fong had not only trained but had been particularly fond of, came to the fore and did a good job of running the show. She proved herself to be more than just adept at running things – she set her sights on marrying management. It didn't take her long to work out the best line of approach, and in her attempt to seduce Father Fong she stuck to him tighter than a pressed flower and made it very obvious she was easily plucked.

Father Fong had panicked into marrying her – anyone was better than no one, and the boy needed a mother. But, once married, Nancy quickly grew discontented and let the business fall into decline. Then, as luck would have it, just as Father Fong's patience was stretched to breaking point, she fell pregnant and became so tired that she had to sit in the upstairs lounge all day, feeding the canary and eating buns. In jubilation at her pregnancy, Father Fong forgave her laziness and bought her a dog, a small white toy Pekinese. All you could hear all day long was the tap tap of the ping-pong ball and the yap yap of little 'Lucky', as Nancy played with her beloved dog.

That summer, when Nancy was pregnant and Father Fong too busy to see her cruelty, she poured pints of vindictive venom on her stepson, whom she hated with as much perverse energy as she loved the dog. Max was beaten and starved and locked in the store cupboard, which had no artificial light, just a tiny barred window. It had been summer and the storms had come, lightning illuminating the room for seconds at a time. The heat made his clothes stick to his body, so that he had to pull them off and sit naked, squashed up in the suffocating darkness, panting, breathless with fear and excitement, screaming as the lightning blinded him and the rain came lashing down.

That summer he became a man. He touched his body in the darkness and felt its yearnings and longings. He became a man, caged in that cupboard, howling at the storm.

One day, in the last stage of Nancy's pregnancy, while she was resting, Max found himself alone with Lucky. The dog sat watching him from its place on the leather-look sofa. Its pink tongue protruded as it panted in the heat. It kept its bulbous eyes on the bedroom door, patiently waiting for its mistress to wake. Max looked at the dog and gave in to an overwhelming desire to kill it. Taking Lucky by the throat, he shook and squeezed the little dog until its eyes bulged from its head and its body stopped running in midair. As Lucky collapsed, limp in his hands, Max jammed the ping-pong ball – Lucky's favourite toy – into the back of its throat to make it look as if the ball had been the cause of the animal's demise. Then, trembling, he ran to his bunk to hide and waited for Nancy to awaken and find her beloved dog. When she did, she screamed so loud that Max felt a spurt of hot pee shoot down his leg. The neighbours heard her screams and came down from the floors above to investigate; and Father Fong came rushing up from the surgery below to find the reason for her anguish. It was Father Fong who, after examining the dog, discovered the ping-pong ball. Max's trick had worked. He was safe.

Nancy produced a son that evening. Her pelvis was too small and the large baby had to be pulled from her like a calf. Consequently, the baby's head was misshapen and his look somewhat strange. Nancy didn't care for the ugly baby at all – she was still mourning for her dog.

She finally left the Fong household for good when Man Po was one year old.

After she left, the surgery dwindled until it became just an occasional knock on the shutter to ask for this and that. Then Father Fong would pull down the dusty jars and rummage through old boxes and tins until he put together a prescription, but his heart wasn't in it any more.

Now, the shutter outside their house no longer opened and closed; it was firmly shut. They continued to live in the two-bedroom apartment on the first floor. Old Father Fong slept in one room, while the brothers slept in bunks in the other. But Father Fong was mainly housebound now. Arthritis had crept into his joints and settled in the marrow, drying them up like abandoned riverbeds. His physical world had narrowed to just a few rooms, and every year saw him shrink a little more. His old slippered feet wore a path on the floor tiles as he shuffled painfully back and forth from kitchen to bedroom to sitting room, only stopping to make kissing noises to the bright yellow canary that twisted its head this way and that as it watched the old man from the confines of its bamboo cage. He spent his days preparing food for his sons and waiting for them to come home.

Man Po was fourteen years younger than Max, which made him nearing forty-six, but he would always look like a baby. He had a round face and large eyes and the hair on his head looked as if it had been hand-stitched like a doll's. He dribbled from the lazy corner of his mouth. The things he enjoyed in life were simple. He loved his work – driving his lorry. And he especially loved butchering the pigs.

16

Club Mercedes was Hong Kong's newest and most exclusive nightclub – for the moment. It occupied the top floor of the most prestigious shopping mall in Hong Kong, situated in the heart of Central District on Peddar Street in the Polaris Centre – a landmark in privileged shopping. On its seven floors were the pick of top European designers, jewellers by royal appointment and Rolex suppliers. Club Mercedes sat on top of all of it on the 'lucky' eighth floor.

The club was officially owned by a consortium of top businessmen. It was really owned by the Wo Shing Shing triad society and provided a useful way to launder money.

Over three hundred hostesses of various nationalities worked within its golden walls. Plenty of *Gwaipohs* for a murderer to choose from, Mann thought.

Mann decided to pay Lucy a visit that evening, while, at the same time, checking up on how many foreign girls were working there. He made his way past Dolce and Gabbana and Yves St Laurent and reached the foot of the conical glass elevator that would take him up to the top floor.

A stunning Asian beauty in a cheongsam greeted him as he stepped inside.

'Welcome to Club Mercedes,' she said, bowing and pressing the ascent button in one perfectly choreographed move.

Just as the doors were closing a Chinese woman stepped in. She stood at a discreet distance from Mann and kept her eyes floor-bound – except for the odd flutter of lashes and tilting of the head to see if Mann was still looking at her – which he was. Mid to late twenties, he reckoned. She had that 'been around the block look': black leather trousers, black polo neck and a gold chain snaking her collarbone. He surmised rightly that she was a hostess going to work.

When the elevator slid to a silent halt and the cheongsamed lovely had completed her farewell bow, Mann and the woman both stepped out onto a red carpet. A pair of solid gold crouching dragons met them (strategically placed according to feng shui), as did two impressively built doormen. As they made their way up the narrrow strip of carpet, a smiling woman in a red and gold cheongsam appeared. Mamasan Linda was a petite Chinese with an outwardly kindly nature but an inwardly frozen heart that could only be melted by money in her hand. She was a former hostess herself. When her appeal had begun to wane she was lucky enough to have made the right people happy over the years, and was rewarded for her services to mankind by being placed in a lucrative job.

'Aye! Good girl, back so soon, huh?' Mamasan Linda said to the woman from the lift. 'Customers waiting! Go change, quick-quick!' She ushered her past and into the club. Then she looked towards Mann, bowed and smiled respectfully. 'Can I help you, Inspector?'

Mamasan Linda had not met Mann before, but she had seen him and knew all about him. Even though Hong Kong was one of the most densely populated places on earth, it was still just a big village at heart. Plus, there weren't many six-foot-two Eurasian policemen around, and there definitely wasn't another like Mann. His reputation for tough justice singled him out. He had earned the respect of cop and criminal alike because Mann feared nothing, and in Hong Kong society, no matter what side of the law you were on, that was attribute number one.

'Good evening, Mamasan. I need to speak with the foreign hostesses you have working here. I won't keep them long – just routine enquiries.'

Mamasan Linda listened with a fixed smile on her face, then nodded and beckoned Mann to follow her.

He had plenty of time to look around the half-empty club as they made their way through; Mamasan Linda wasn't going anywhere in a hurry in that tight dress. It seemed funny, thought Mann, quaint even, all the money spent on the club: Italian lighting, rivers of red velvet, herds of black leather, yet there was still something else: the inevitable gold, red and chintz and those irrepressible 'lucky fish'. No matter what the designer had originally planned for the club, in Hong Kong you could never get away from the slightly tacky look. He loved his birthplace for it – that wonderful mix of East and West that never let itself be corrupted by ordinary style.

Mann was shown into a VIP room at the back of the club. Most of the rooms in the club were themed, and this one was traditional Mandarin and housed an impressive collection of antique black lacquered furniture inlaid with abalone shell, silk-painted screens and ornately carved wooden seats.

Mamasan Linda left him in the care of Mamasan Rose, one of the newest mamasans at the club. She brought the foreign girls to him one at a time. Eleven were in so far that evening, out of twenty-five, she explained.

One of three sunny-faced, robust-looking Australians came in to be interviewed first. Her name was Angela. She and her two friends were working and living together, sharing a flat in Kowloon. They'd been in Hong Kong for two months and were working their way around Asia. They'd already done the lucrative Tokyo circuit, missed out Thailand (where holidaying Westerners weren't interested in paying for white women and locals couldn't afford them), and had made a detour around the Philippines where there were a lot of lonely wealthy Westerners but no hostess clubs to work out of. Finally they had stopped in Hong Kong en route to Singapore. From there they were headed home to resume their jobs as dental nurses.

Mann asked Angela if she'd had any friends go missing unexpectedly. *What? Was he serious?* she answered. People were always moving on. What did he expect? Had she heard anything about a problem client? She shrugged. Nothing she couldn't handle.

Mann interviewed the rest quickly: the other two Australians, who were clones of the first, two Kiwis, three Brits, two Americans, and a tall Irish girl named Bernadette. They all said the same thing – they were used to people disappearing, it happened all the time. People came and went continuously. Hong Kong was a transient society. Girls came to work there from all over the world; they did their business and left. They brought with them a new alias, but their identity was always the same. Mann had seen it many times. They were game players looking for easy money – looking to turn their God-given assets into cold hard cash. But at the moment the game wasn't going all their way. Someone else was having fun making his own private collection of foreign dolls.

17

'Is Lucy working here tonight?' Mann asked Mamasan Rose when he'd finished interviewing the foreign girls. Mamasan Rose smiled curiously at Mann, said she was, and left to fetch her.

As soon as she entered Mann recognised her as the woman from the lift with the leather trousers. Now she was wearing a lilac-coloured figure-hugging evening dress that she didn't quite have the figure for, and an extra coating of lip-gloss. He waited while she sat and readied herself.

'Hello again, Inspector.' She smiled sweetly, a very practised smile, and adjusted her dress to show a flirtatious amount of leg.

Surprising, thought Mann. She was nothing special to look at; her sickly sweet smile was set into an over-rouged face. But then she didn't *have* to be beautiful. According to James Dudley-Smythe she was extremely talented in other ways.

She giggled, batting her eyelashes and feigning shyness under his scrutiny.

'Are you the only Lucy working here?'

'Yes, just me, Inspector. There's only one Lucy.'

'Well, it must be you I want then.'

Lucy raised an inquisitive eyebrow and pursed her lips into a 'butter wouldn't melt' smile.

'I have heard that you provide certain services for men who like something *special*.'

Lucy's face was a picture of surprise but her eyes betrayed her. Mann could see that she was as sharp and as calculating as they come – but most of all she was a survivor. She had seen right into the depths of men's souls. It may not have been a pretty sight, but boy was it lucrative.

'I mean that you cater to *certain* tastes. Men who like to feel pain, feel it *and* inflict it.'

Lucy held his gaze, kept the smile, and inclined her head in a small movement.

'Tell me, Lucy, have you had any problems with a particular client? Anybody go too far? Anyone scare you? Hurt you more than you wanted or were paid for?'

Lucy kept the smile, lowered her eyes and shook her head slowly.

'No, I don't think so. It's just fun – you know?'

She looked up from beneath her lashes with a hint of a proposition, as if maybe he *did* know and it was always worth her while testing the water.

Mann had the distinct impression she was imagining him with a whip in his hand and his pants around his ankles.

'What about the foreign girls here? Are you friendly with them?'

'*Quite* friendly. I rent some of them a room in my apartment, Inspector,' she said, moving to sit slightly to one side; her best side.

'Your apartment?'

'Yes, I live with my sister in Wanchai. We have a spare room which we let to foreign girls from the club. They pay more.'

'Any of the foreign girls talk to you about a bad experience they might have had?'

Lucy thought for a few seconds and then swung her head slowly from side to side while keeping her eyes pinned on Mann – still holding that sweet, simpering smile, which was beginning to grate on him.

'Any of the foreign girls gone missing that you know of?'

She gave an exasperated shrug. 'They're always disappearing, just leaving all their things and moving on,' she said. 'An American girl, Roxanne, all her belongings are at my flat at the moment. Such a nuisance.'

'Is it unusual for girls just to leave all their stuff and disappear?'

Lucy rolled her eyes. 'She's not the first. Guess it's just the way they are . . . *Gweilos*, they come and go. Do whatever they like, whenever they like. It's just the way they are.'

Mann let his eyes fasten hard on Lucy for a few seconds longer than she was comfortable with. He could tell she was curious about him. He had no problem with being mixed race, but others did. They didn't know whether to speak to him in English or Cantonese.

Mann liked feeding their insecurities. He belonged wherever he wanted to belong. Everywhere and nowhere. If Lucy was seriously trying to flirt with him she was wasting her time and his.

'Can you give me a description of Roxanne?' He poised, pen in hand.

Lucy's attitude changed. She knew she wasn't going to get anywhere with him. She had to accept defeat, at least for now. She covered up her leg, and shifted uncomfortably in her seat as if she were going numb from sitting so long.

'Curly blonde hair, bit fat, nice hands – liked to do her nails, manicures, you know?' She twirled her bright red nails in the air as she spoke and glanced towards the door.

'You say there have been other girls?' He looked up from his notes.

'Five or six maybe, over the years.' She straightened her dress in preparation for the off.

'You have no idea where they went?'

She shook her head.

'I will need you to give me details about these girls, physical descriptions, that kind of thing.'

'Of course, Inspector.' Lucy nodded sweetly, batting her eyelashes, but her smile had changed. 'Always happy to help the police. If that is all . . .' She slid off the chair, bowed, and left.

After she had gone, Mann was left with the distinct impression that Lucy was as mercenary as they came – a good Hong Kong girl if ever he met one. But, he couldn't blame her. In fact, he even kind of admired her. Hong Kong wasn't the most caring mother to her daughters. It wasn't so long ago that infant girls were left to die on the roadside. Now there was every type of brothel – floating, high-rise or underground – to keep a girl off the streets.

He'd done all he could. It was time to move on. He thanked the mamasans, said he would be back soon, and made his way out of the club, past the 'lucky' fish and the Taiwanese bouncers.

He was just about to step into the elevator when two men stepped out. One was a prominent elderly Chinese politician, Sun Yat-sen. Mann recognised him from some recent publicity shots. He was in Hong Kong promoting trade alliances – creaming off a few backhanders. The other man was the same age as Mann. He was shorter by six inches but made the most of his slight frame with expensive suits and well-tailored jackets. He carried himself with authority. His hair was very neatly cropped, smoothly side parted. His face was narrow, angular with a sallow complexion. His eyes were dark-rimmed and hooded and larger than his triangular face could cope with.

Chan and Mann eyeballed each other for several seconds before exchanging places in the lift. They had not always been enemies. They had been friends once, brothers almost. Mann had even saved Chan's life when they were at school together in England on a school trip to the Lake District. Chan had wandered too far out in the water and a hidden shelf took him unawares. He couldn't swim, and Mann had saved him. From that day on they had been best friends, shared their hopes and dreams and supported one another through the years of a sometimes-lonely exile at boarding school in England. In the last year of school the boys had come back to spend their summer vacation in Hong Kong, as usual. They had spent the evening together and parted company at Mann's house. When Mann went inside he found his father held captive by triads and being tortured and beaten. Mann was seized, held, and made to watch his father's execution. The boys had vowed to be united forever in vengeance against them. But only one of the boys had kept that vow. The other had joined forces with the enemy.

Mann stood rigid now. His tall, muscular frame tensed as his body willed him to take action against the man he hated. But Mann knew that hurting Chan would only give him momentary satisfaction. Okay, maybe it would last for an hour or two. But it wouldn't destroy Chan in the long run, and Mann *definitely* wanted to do that. Because Chan hadn't just joined forces with the enemy. He had become the enemy. Mann watched them walk away and saw Chan glance back.

Keep looking behind you, Chan, because I'm going to be there.

18

After her interview with Mann, Lucy went back to the Dressing Room to wait for her number to be called. The 'home from home' for the girls was a large rectangular space about fifty-five metres long and twenty wide. It was sparsely furnished with lockers and chairs down its left-hand side and starlet-style mirrors arranged in rows down its right. In front of the mirrors were broad shelves used for eating, doing make-up, sleeping. There were stools and chairs scattered around, but never enough.

There were girls everywhere, descended flock-like to roost, at least two hundred at any one time, dressing or undressing. Their glamorous frocks were semi-draped over smooth shiny skin or poured intestine-like from lockers where they had fallen from hangers or been hastily discarded.

The noise of excited girls greeting one another, of locker doors bouncing off their hinges, was deafening, but the camaraderie was touching. Lucy threaded her way through.

'Hey, Lucy, what's up?' The distinctive American

tones of Candy could be heard above the racket. 'You late?'

'Nah . . . been out already . . .' Lucy sassed over her shoulder as she made her way through.

Candy feigned amazement. 'Jesus, Lucy! You're gonna be rich!'

Lucy giggled, then screeched as she heard her number called over the tannoy:

'*NUMBER 169, MISS LUCY . . . NUMBER 169, MISS LUCY . . .*'

She doubled back and squirmed through the waiting girls to meet her mamasan on the other side of the velvet curtain.

'You must be good girl now, Lucy.' Mamasan Linda held on to Lucy's hand and trotted ahead like a mother escorting a naughty child to receive judgement from a waiting father.

They wound their way through half-full tables, past the Filipino band singing the Police song 'Don't stand so close to me' *quite* earnestly, considering that a consignment of blow had arrived that day from Manila, past a man from Taipei who was on the dance floor clinging pathetically to the pencil-thin, Lycra-slippery hips of his young date while the changing light patterns on the dance floor stole his drunken feet from beneath him. And past Bernadette, who was leaping from foot to foot in a frenzy of chiffon. Her hair sat rigid on her head like deep-fried roadkill, while the rest of her body hopped madly around the dance floor. Lucy remembered going out on a double date with Bernadette. What a nightmare! She recalled Bernadette straddling a diminutive Taiwanese, his face exploding like a bull-frog on heat at every squeeze of those massive white thighs. Lucy had had to drag her off at the end of the evening with her screaming, *But I haven't feckin' come yet!*

Mamasan Linda stopped in her tracks and turned back to talk to Lucy. She lowered her voice.

'He's a good customer. He's come back many times and asked for you. Look after him, okay? Be a clever girl, huh? Big VIP. He owns all this.' She swept her hands in the air theatrically.

Lucy gave her a 'teach grandma to suck eggs' look and fell into a trot behind her again, following the red and gold cheongsam swishing hypnotically from side to side. They approached a booth that was situated to the back of the club, in the VIP section, overlooking the semicircular dance floor.

'Here she is.' Mamasan Linda let go of Lucy's hand and pushed her forward. 'Here is Lucy.'

Lucy smiled and slipped in behind the round table until her thigh made contact with her client's. She studied him but her eyes were still adjusting to the gloom and it took time to recognise him as the man who had bought her out a couple of weeks before and a few times before that. It took time to place body with face – to transcend the gap between leaving the club and leaving the Love Motel. Then she placed him and a surge of adrenalin went through her as she remembered his peculiar tastes that had taken some time to heal.

Chan spent his evenings doing the rounds of the

hostess clubs. He was son-in-law to C. K. Leung, the Dragon Head of the Wo Shing Shing triad organisation – the most powerful society in Hong Kong. It was Chan's job to oversee some of the Wo Shing Shing's many business concerns and, at the same time, he liked to cherry-pick any new young hostesses who had just come on the market. Chan had a bent towards pubescent girls. He liked his girls to be girls. Surprising then, that he had asked for Lucy, she wasn't really his type – too fat and certainly, at twenty-four, too old. But tonight he had come looking for her. He had need of her quite extraordinary talents.

'So, Lucy, how's things?'

'Good evening, Mr Chan. Everything is good, thank you. It's nice to see you again.'

Lucy smiled, met his eyes, and began her usual routine. She feigned 'coy mistress' mixed with 'sure bet' in as few seconds as she could. The act was wasted. He was busy signalling to Mamasan Linda that he would be buying Lucy out and he was ready to leave.

'Go change, quick-quick,' she said, appearing beside the table.

Lucy stood up and left the two to negotiate.

'See you in a minute, Mr Chan,' she said. He didn't answer. He was already busy with his wallet.

On the way she met Candy en route to one of the VIP suites at the back of the club. Her tall figure – broad shoulders, stiff hips and straight back – dwarfed the two Chinese hostesses with her. Her eyes widened in mock disbelief as she glanced at Lucy. Lucy grinned. Candy had no need to worry. She always did well. She lived in an expensive apartment near Tsim Sha Tsui and came to work in the evening to recruit customers for the next day instead. Moving from table to table, she never wanted to be bought out – preferring to make back-to-back appointments for the following day. She was sending the money home to an Italian boyfriend who wanted to open a deli in New York.

Chan dropped Lucy back at the club afterwards. She smiled sweetly and thanked him for his patronage. He wasn't listening. He was anxious to be rid of her. He was always the same afterwards: curt, cold and callous. He had hurt her, but he didn't care. He had overstepped the mark, crossed the boundaries, and ignored the signal to stop. Now he couldn't even look at her. Not because he felt any guilt, but because she repulsed him. Easing herself out of the car, Lucy turned to wave goodbye, but he had already pulled off erratically into the stream of traffic. Lucy wouldn't be able to work again that night.

19

She packed her evening dress away in her locker, put her leather trousers back on and said her goodbyes to the handful of girls left in the Dressing Room. She had done enough work for one night. It was only when she reached the line of taxis that she decided she wasn't in the mood to return home just yet – she deserved a little fun after her ordeal. She caught a cab to the Macau ferry terminal, just a short distance away, and boarded the waiting ferry.

The journey would take nearly an hour, but tonight she didn't mind. Usually she was impatient to arrive; but this time she knew it would give her the time and space to mull things over. Mostly she thought about Georgina, who had just arrived – landed, almost – in their lives. She smiled to herself. Those big hands! That innocent face! She brought out the maternal instinct in Lucy. God knows, that was funny, feeling maternal to a girl just two years younger than herself. But why not? She could take care of them all.

She sat back to take stock of her surroundings and to enjoy the anticipation and the rush of pure adrenalin and excitement that only Macau gave her. Gambling was a need that had grown in her over the last few years. She had become addicted to its thrills, its uncertainty – knowing that she could lose everything she had, or simply win the world. It was a thrill second to none. But it was a deadly game to play. Macau was run, ruined and ruled by triads.

She looked out of the window to see the lights flickering on the horizon. They would be docking soon. She shifted in her seat and smiled to herself. Her buttocks were raw – it had taken her time to get used to it: the pain, the fear. But she had to cut herself a niche in the hostess market. There were just too many pretty Chinese girls out there.

She'd started young – she'd had to, when their alcoholic mother was found floating among the boats in Aberdeen, just another piece of flotsam. Then Lucy had to provide for herself and her little sister. She was twelve when she sold her virginity to a Taiwanese, and when that money ran out she went to work in the clubs. She might not be the best-looking girl but she was one of the smartest. She cottoned on quickly to a dark sadistic side to men that they so desired but never dared ask for. Lucy let them have their heart's desire – as long as they paid, and paid well. It was a lucrative market. There wasn't a Caucasian she'd met that didn't like to inflict pain. Not the Chinese so much, except the ones who were educated abroad like Chan. Middle Eastern men wanted that and nothing else, and the Japanese? Don't ask! Not only could Lucy perform almost any act of self-degradation, in truth she quite enjoyed it.

The sting of smarting flesh, the power of perversity. She liked to look into their eyes at that point of abandonment and steal a part of their soul. But Chan had gone too far tonight, and not for the first time. In Chan she had met her match.

Lucy sighed to herself. It would all be worth it one day, maybe even *this* day. Perhaps tonight would be the night to change everything. She looked around and sized up her fellow passengers. No one she recognised, which was a relief. A bunch of Americans, over-sized and over-dressed. The men wore a uniform of Farah slacks and club ties. The women dressed too young, had sharp features and orange skin, and ridiculously over-dyed, back-combed hair. That's not beautiful, thought Lucy. Much better to have a good Hong Kong girl than *that*!

Apart from the Americans and a few Portuguese returning home, the ferry was practically empty. She stared at the Americans and tried a smile. She might still be able to catch herself a *Gweilo*. An American passport, that would be the one! Canadian or New Zealand would do very well too. She would even take British if she could get it! At the age of twenty-four she would be happy with any ticket out for her and Ka Lei.

It didn't work this time, though. The men's wayward attention was refocused and held in a mental headlock by their eagle-eyed wives.

Lucy gave up and stared out at the lights coming from Macau. They were gliding on the water, on its skin, like oil. Her thoughts returned to the future. Lucy wondered what difference her English cousin's arrival would make in the grand scheme of things. She and Ka Lei were like twins separated at birth, now reunited. They were so innocent, so young. Both of them were like children: laughing, playing, running around the apartment. And Lucy was like their mother. Something told her that whatever it was that lay ahead, her newfound cousin would feature in it.

She shifted in her seat again: the sitting was beginning to irritate her and concentrating was becoming more difficult. Anyway, that was enough speculation. She didn't like dwelling on things to come or things gone. '*Now*' was what counted. Bernadette had told her that life was like driving a car – you just needed to look in the mirror now and again to see what was behind you. The rest of the time, keep your eyes on the road ahead.

Tonight all roads led to Macau, and one big win would take care of them all: Ka Lei, Georgina, all of them. Lucy knew something big was coming – she felt it.

But, while it was true that tonight would change her life irrevocably, that all their lives would never be the same from this night on, it was not in the way that Lucy hoped. Not at all.

20

Macau was busy – always busy – twenty-four hours a day. Hong Kong didn't allow casinos, but Macau did. The smartest one was the newest: the *Royal Palace*. A floating, multi-floored casino that was moored alongside its sister ship, the *Portuguese Queen*. It had opened only a month previously and it was the first time Lucy had seen it. It was as she was about to enter that she saw Chan. She recognised him from behind: his flat arse swivelled like a woman's when he walked. Funny, she thought, they had been together just hours before, having sex, and now they were both here! How alike they must be in some ways.

Chan was keeping an eye on things for the Wo Shing Shing. CK was one of two partners in this new casino; the other was a prominent member of the Chinese government. Money was becoming the new Communist ideal, and Hong Kong was more than happy to wet-nurse. The milk of capitalism flowed freely from her bosom – enough for everyone.

CK had been cultivating friendships with state councillors and prime ministers for some time. He'd been working his way up the ladder over the years and had built himself an impressive network of influential friends. He finally nailed it after the Tiananmen Square massacre. He was the only one of the prominent Hong Kong businessmen to step forward and support China's stand.

Lucy thought nothing of seeing Chan there: he was a VIP after all, and she knew that he was probably involved in many ventures. She watched him walk into the casino and wondered what made him tick. It remained a mystery to her why he had chosen to buy her out on the occasions he did. Surely two concubines and a wife were enough 'face' for the man with an erect penis the size of a middle-finger salute? He had weird tastes even by Lucy's standards: the pretend-virgin thing wasn't the normal, it was more rape than seduction. And 'Daddy', as he wanted her to call him, could certainly inflict pain, but could he take it? No way! 'Daddy's' S&M games were strictly fun for one. Knowing when to stop was a definite problem.

At the entrance to the casino Lucy caught the doorman's eye and slipped him one hundred Hong Kong dollars. She always over-tipped the doormen. They had helped her out many times, if just to jump the taxi queue, and it was worth it. She paused for a second or two to admire the casino's flamboyant foyer, and, as she did so, Chan turned and noticed her. He acknowledged her presence with a slight incline of his head and a curious smile, before passing through the carved mahogany doors into the *Royal Palace*.

That night Lucy moved from blackjack to roulette

and back to blackjack with losses that were inconceivable. Nothing stemmed the tide of money lost and the speed with which it disappeared. So strange was this catastrophic losing streak for Lucy, who, as a rule, always gained as much as she lost, that she read into it signs of the wrong kind. She began to believe that some huge win was coming her way – she only needed to keep playing – she just needed to stay in the game. But it wasn't coming, and Lucy eventually took a loan from a triad, a massive loan that she would never be able to repay.

It was Chan who came to her aid when her money ran out. It was Chan who gave her the loan. It was Chan who moved in on Lucy like carrion on roadkill.

21

'I'm comin'!'

Glitter Girl had run out of places to hide and he had found her. The more she struggled against the rope around her neck, the tighter it became. In the end, only her body continued the fight. Her mind said:

Let me go ... Let it be quick ... And please, sweet Jesus, let someone find my body ...

Strangely enough, her last thoughts were of Darren, in the days *before* he'd started hitting her. In the days of disco balls and hot, salty, stolen kisses, fevered embraces and love that should have been forever. She had never truly managed to hate him. She still loved the man she wished he could have been.

Now her photo stared out from the wall, with the others, and her index finger bobbed in a jar of formaldehyde, just like the one her grandma kept pickles in. In certain lights it still glittered.

Tonight he would start his hunt again.

22

Lucy stumbled off the Macau ferry in a daze, right at the start of the morning rush hour. The bright sun stabbed at her eyes and the car fumes caught in the back of her throat. The walk home was tortuously slow. All she could do was keep her head down, shuffle along the crowded pavement, and pray that soon she would find some respite from the raw guilt she felt. One minute her heart beat so fast she couldn't breathe, and she thought she would pass out; the next it slowed down so much that she thought she must be walking in a dream.

Lucy was in shock, in mourning. She had squatted in the gutters of Macau and aborted all her dreams, and not just hers . . . All the years she had protected her sister from harm and kept her off the streets, made sure she could follow her dream and become a nurse. Now all those dreams would be shattered. Both their lives would be ruined if she couldn't think of a way to pay back what she owed – a triad debt was a family debt. The pain of retribution would be shared. In fact, Lucy knew that it would be Ka Lei they would come after first, just to teach Lucy a lesson.

After an hour of shuffling along pavements she finally reached home. She turned the key to the apartment door as quietly as she could and crept inside. There was not a sound in the stagnant gloom of the flat except the *plonk plonk* of the leaky kitchen tap. Ka Lei had already gone to work and Georgina was still asleep. Lucy listened to the droning of the air-conditioning unit coming from her cousin's bedroom.

She tiptoed into her room and sat on the edge of the bed, scared to move, frightened to make a sound in case she woke Georgina and then she might have to tell what she'd done. She couldn't do that. *She definitely couldn't do that.*

As the hours passed she stared at the blacked-out windows of the adjacent building, seeing nothing, reliving the events of the previous evening. The light in the room changed hue. Shadows lengthened and altered shape. Somewhere outside, the sun arced in the sky, the earth turned, the universe existed, the day completed its rota. Inside the room Lucy went over the process of self-recrimination countless times. She relived the events that had led to her destruction over and over until she became quite exhausted by the process. She hovered above herself and watched herself lose and lose again. *Why had she continued?* She knew why. She just couldn't leave, not then, not when she was so down. She just needed to stay in the game, like she always did. It had happened that way so many times before: lose a lot, win a lot more. She had always come out on top – but not this time. Lady Luck had stabbed her in the back last night. Now Lucy must find a way not just to bear it, but to end it.

Gradually, over the course of the following day, the shock subsided, until, by reworking the events in her mind, they changed shape and became something of far less consequence. She began to reassess the situation. She had survived worse – she would survive this. But now her survival was out of her hands. Lucy had unwittingly made a pact with the devil.

23

She waited in the Dressing Room for two hours before her name was called. She knew when she followed Mamasan Linda past the dance floor that they were heading to Chan's favourite seat. She knew he would be watching her walk the length of the club, his eyes fixed on her. She knew she had to try every trick in her book to make this work.

'Hello, Ka Mei, how's things?' His cold eyes fixed on her face.

It was the first time Chan had ever called Lucy by her Chinese name. It did not bode well. She was momentarily startled into letting her guard down. In the half-light she could see he was sneering rather than smiling. She looked downwards at her lap, trying to compose herself. *Stick to the plan,* she told herself, just as rehearsed: slightly submissive, slightly flirty – *humble yet brave.* She had been over this meeting a hundred times in her head.

Chan was sprawled in his usual place, and as Lucy sat down he extended one arm so that his hand rested on the nape of her neck.

'Good evening, Mr Chan,' she said, and waited for an answer. She felt the electricity in his fingertips commute to a burning sensation as he rubbed the same spot at the base of her neck repeatedly. He was a tightened band that threatened to snap at any moment. 'I have been a bit worried, Mr Chan,' she said, tilting her head sideways to look at him.

'Worried?' He played along, and carried on stroking her neck. 'Worried about what, Ka Mei?'

Lucy summoned up all her courage. She locked her gaze on his. 'About the money I owe you, Mr Chan.'

Chan nodded his head slowly, deliberately, like a judge considering the gravity of the situation before passing sentence.

'Yes, Lucy. You did borrow a lot of money. I hardly remember how much it was now.' Lucy caught a glimmer of hope and looked up from her lap to see him still nodding. 'But it was more than is prudent for a girl in your position.'

She would do the '*what a silly girl I've been*' act if that's what it took.

'I do have *some* money to return to you, Mr Chan.' She smiled sweetly. 'But I do not have it all . . . at the moment.'

Chan raised an eyebrow.

'How much do you have for me . . . *at the moment*?'

'I have thirty thousand dollars. My savings, everything.' She pleaded silently, trying every trick in her extensive book to find that deeply buried corner of Chan that cared.

Chan switched from nodding his head to swinging it from side to side. 'Not really enough, is it, Lucy?'

Lucy felt the fluttering of panic begin in her gut. Chan slipped into his soliloquy:

'You know you borrowed a lot of money from me, and not just from me, from the Wo Shing Shing. And you say to me, "Sorry, Mr Chan, I can only afford to repay you a measly thirty thousand dollars *at the moment*", when you owe ten times that amount. Do you think that is fair?'

Lucy shook her head, feeling the blood drain from her face. The actual sum she had borrowed was being inflated as she sat there. Suddenly it seemed insurmountable. She hadn't reckoned on such calculated cruelty. He couldn't really expect her to pay all that, could he?

'So, Lucy, what do you think I should do?'

There was a pause and Lucy returned to staring at her lap and shaking her head miserably.

'Have you no one to help you?'

Lucy was puzzled. What could he be driving at? He was waiting to spring a trap on her, all her instincts told her so.

'I know that your sister – Ka Lei, isn't it? I know that she works at the hospital. She relies on you, doesn't she, Lucy?'

Lucy's eyes flitted back and forth across his face, searching desperately.

'You live with your sister, don't you? She's young, isn't she? She is training to be a nurse. Is that right? There's just the two of you?'

Lucy nodded her head almost imperceptibly while twisting her hands as they lay in her lap.

'Not just the two of you at the moment, is there, Lucy? Your English cousin is staying with you. She's a very attractive girl, I hear. Maybe she can help you? She can't live off you forever, can she? Plus, she's family – and this debt is a family debt. You didn't just borrow from me personally, you borrowed from the Wo Shing Shing. You understand the implications of that, don't you, Lucy?'

Lucy nodded her head miserably.

'Maybe she can help you?'

He knew everything. Every small detail of her life. She was doomed. They were all doomed.

'Georgina's parents are dead. My sister and I are her only family. I don't see how she can help, Mr Chan.' Lucy looked up, suddenly sensing an awful point to Chan's questions.

'She can come and work here. We are always in need of good foreign hostesses. Chinese girls are as plentiful as grains of rice; a good foreigner can bring a lot of new customers. Bring her in tomorrow and I will wipe a quarter of the debt away immediately. Then I will see what else I can do to help you. Because . . .' Chan placed his hand over hers, 'I like you, Lucy . . . really, I do.' He moved his hand to her thigh and squeezed it hard. Lucy winced. 'But *Daddy* has to be strict sometimes.'

24

'Anyway, juz be for a little while. You like to work with me, huh? Family, huh?' Lucy put the suggestion to Georgina over breakfast the next morning.

'I've never done any waitressing or anything like this before. Are you sure I can do it?'

'You got to believe me, it's perfec job for you,' Lucy assured her.

'Is *no*.' Ka Lei stood with her arms folded across her flat chest. Her English wasn't as good as Lucy's. When she was trying her hardest to find the word she wanted, her hands flitted in front of her face in expressive gestures and her head tilted to one side, then she lifted her eyes skyward and twittered like a starling. Now, she stamped her foot and dug her hands deeper into her sides, and looked much younger than her seventeen years as she blocked Lucy's way, preventing her from reaching Georgina.

'Club no goo for Georgie. No goo place. She petter do nudder job.'

They quarrelled in Cantonese. Lucy looked past Ka Lei to Georgina.

'Juz want show off my beautiful cousin from England. Juz for few days. That's all.'

'What would I have to do? . . .'

'Juz sit an talk. Drink a little. If the client like you, he buy you out of club for a few hours – take you to dinner, nice expensive restaurant. No problem, huh? Goo money. Nice place.'

With a sigh and a smile Georgina gave in. 'Okay, Lucy. I'll give it a go.'

Ka Lei also eventually agreed. After all, hadn't Lucy always made the decisions for her? And now she would make them for Georgina too. It seemed only natural.

She would start on the coming Saturday. That gave her three days to find a dress.

While Ka Lei was at work, Lucy and Georgina began their search of the shopping malls. It was no good. They were never going to find one to fit. Georgina was too tall, too curvy. One had to be made.

Lucy took her to a tailor in Western District. The tailor stood on a chair to measure Georgina's chest. After much wrangling and deliberation between Lucy and the tailor, a dress was decided upon. It was black with spaghetti straps and a split up one leg.

The next day she went for a fitting. On Saturday they picked it up. Georgina tried it on for Ka Lei.

'So beautiful . . . you be mos beautiful girl in club.'

Georgina stared at herself in the mirror. Her breasts – two white mounds sitting proudly above the neckline of the dress. *Not sure this is what Iris meant by 'finding my wings'.* Georgina looked at the unfamiliar image in front of her and felt a feeling of panic.

Ka Lei smiled reassuringly.

'Be okay, Georgie. Lucy loo atter you.'

That night Georgina and Lucy left for work at eight. They had no need to hail a taxi, as Max was waiting for them.

Lucy explained to Georgina that Max was a friend of sorts. He liked to look after them. He always took her to work as it marked the start of his night shift. All through Lucy's explanation Max nodded and grinned at Georgina in the mirror. Max was very good to them, Lucy said, and not just her. He had been very kind to all the girls who had lived in Lucy's apartment. He had looked after them all over the years, and there had been several. He was getting on now and would have to retire very soon.

'Shame,' said Lucy. 'We will miss him.'

Max shook his head sadly and shrugged resignedly. No one would miss the job more than him.

Georgina sat in the back, peering silently out of the window while Lucy and Max chatted. She didn't bother to try to understand the conversation, it was too fast for her and she had other things on her mind. She was nervous about starting work at the club. She needed a few minutes' peace to prepare herself. As much as she loved her cousin, Lucy's voice was pitched at a level louder than comfortable, so Georgina was glad it was directed at someone else for a few minutes.

There was a halt in the conversation and Georgina's attention was required.

'Max say how you like Hong Kong? He say when he pick you up you look so frighten that day. You remember?'

Georgina remembered it well. 'Yes, I do. Tell him I *was* scared. Hong Kong wasn't as I imagined it would be.'

Max spoke and Lucy laughed again, loud and hoarse. She turned to Georgina and pointed at Max as if he were mad.

'Max say you remind him of his mother!'

Max glanced fleetingly into the mirror at Georgina and smiled, embarrassed.

'Me?' Georgina said, unsure how she was supposed to react.

Max spoke again and Lucy translated.

'His mother die when he was twelve year old. He have photo. He say she was a beautiful woman from north of China. Very tall. He say you look like her.'

'Thank you,' Georgina said, embarrassed. 'Does Max live here on the Island?' she asked, struggling for something to say.

'Max live in Sheung Wan, Western District. Not too far. Very old part of Hong Kong. I'm gonna take you there. You see many sights. Old traditional Chinese skills. You can drink snake blood there. Have chop made with your name on it. Buy ivory, silk. Max live there all his life. His daddy was Chinese doctor – herbs, acu pun ture, you understand?'

Georgina nodded. Max looked suitably proud, understanding enough to know that his family was being talked about.

'Is his father still alive? Is he still a doctor?'

'He alive yes, but doctor no. Max say he very ill in his bones. He just stay at home, look after Max and his brother.'

'Just the three of them?' Georgina asked while Lucy translated. Max glanced curiously at Georgina in the mirror. *So many questions!*

'Max say his daddy did marry another woman, but she not nice. She left after give birth to his brother, Man Po. Not even feed him. She juz left him for Max and his daddy to bring up. Ah, here we are. We arrive at work now,' Lucy said, stopping the conversation abruptly and sliding across to help Georgina with the door, which wouldn't open. She shouted something at Max and turned to Georgina.

'He forget to unlock door. So stupid!'

Max giggled nervously and apologised profusely.

Lucy pushed Georgina gently from the cab.

As Georgina took her arm and allowed herself to be guided towards the Polaris Centre, she looked back and saw that Max still sat there, his window down and the engine running. He did not pull away. He was watching them.

25

They made their way up in the elevator, past the band warming up, and through the club to the Dressing Room. It was moderately busy: about one hundred and fifty girls. Georgina stood just inside the door, over-awed by it all.

Lucy took her by the hand and led her through to the mid section of the room where her locker was. She showed Georgina which locker was to be hers and they changed into their evening dresses.

Candy came over to introduce herself and speak to Lucy. She wanted to know if there had been any news about Roxanne. Lucy couldn't tell her anything. Candy shook her head sadly; she'd really liked Roxanne, she would miss her. Then she shrugged her shoulders. Candy was hoping not to be here too much longer herself. Her boyfriend had put a deposit down on a deli premises in Little Italy, and just needed a couple more months' money to stock it.

While they waited for their names to be called, Lucy caught up with the gossip and did her make-up. Georgina was given a bowl of rice and vegetables to eat. Bernadette turned up, looking the worse for wear after a heavy drinking session. She came over, pulling up the arms of her dress. It was layered chiffon, in all the colours of the rainbow.

'You new?' Bernadette asked.

Georgina nodded.

Bernadette sat down next to her and started applying her make-up. 'Where are you from?' she asked, pulling her mouth into a lipstick grimace.

'Devon.'

'What you doing in this place?' she said disparagingly, as she moved on to hair arranging, which involved jamming it all into a bunch on the top of her head and securing it fast, before it escaped.

'Just thought I'd give it a try.' Georgina turned and gestured towards Lucy, who stopped her chatting to acknowledge Bernadette. 'Lucy's my cousin.'

'*That* Lucy?' Bernadette pointed. '*Jaysus!*'

'*NUMBER 169 – MISS LUCY.*'

'*NUMBER 305 – MISS GEORGINA.*' A voice came over the intercom.

Lucy jumped to her feet with a screech and yanked Georgina out of her seat. 'Aye! Our number. Come on!'

'Good luck' came from the direction of Candy and Bernadette. Georgina followed Lucy nervously through the velvet curtain. Lucy held her back for a second as they were making their way out. She whispered:

'Don worry, huh? Be okay. Juz sit, talk, laugh. But easy on drink, okay? Just water or Coke, okay?'

Georgina nodded that she understood but her face didn't reflect it. Mamasan Linda took Georgina's hand

and Lucy followed behind as they trotted off in the direction of the cheaper seats. They were going to sit with a group of three well-dressed office workers on a very expensive night out. The eldest of the three, Don, sat with Georgina, while Lucy sat between the other two.

It was all pleasant enough; not Lucy's usual kind of punter. Mamasan Linda must have wanted her to help her cousin on her first night. Lucy knew she was wasting her time at the table. They would not be buying her out. They did not have the money. But never mind, she also knew that Mamasan would hoick her off at the first sign of a decent client.

It didn't take long. Mamasan appeared and excused Lucy. She had a visitor. Someone very important wanted to see her again.

Bernadette passed Lucy on her way to sit with James Dudley-Smythe. Bernie was surprised to see him. He must not have realised that she'd helped herself to the contents of his wallet the last time they'd met – emptied it while he slept. There was obviously something he liked about her. He was an odd old fecker! But Bernie could handle him. It would be a case of him and whose army.

'All right, James?'

'Grand, thank you, my sweet. Just super. Fancy a nightcap back at mine?'

'Sure. Why not?' Bernie laughed. *Like taking candy from a baby.*

At one a.m. Georgina was back in the Dressing Room. There was no sign of Lucy, just a dozen girls sitting around chatting. Most of the girls were already at tables or out with customers. Mamasan Linda came to find her.

'You go home now. Very good girl. Come again tomorrow.' She patted her on the arm.

Georgina took off her evening dress and put it away in the locker. She changed and walked back through the club. The doormen smiled politely at her as she passed. The woman in the cheongsam stared at her as they descended in the conical elevator.

Ka Lei was still up, waiting for her.

'Okay?' She rushed to the door as she heard Georgina open it. 'Okay?'

'Yes. It went fine.' Georgina went into her room to change.

'Sure, they all love you, so beautiful!' Ka Lei called to her, and then handed Georgina some tea as she re-entered the lounge wearing a sarong.

Ka Lei rubbed her cousin's shoulders. 'Cole?'

'No, I'm fine, really,' Georgina laughed.

'Okay?'

'Yes, Mum!' Georgina teased.

'Me? Loo lie your mum?'

'I didn't mean it . . . but maybe a little bit,' Georgina said, after seeing Ka Lei's delighted expression.

'You have photo?'

'Yes, wait here, I'll get them.'

Georgina returned holding the small photo album. She turned the pages and Ka Lei held the album.

'Here is my father, holding me.'

'Such a big man, thaz why you so tall. Who tis one?'

Ka Lei pointed to the next page. 'Tis one is you?' It was a picture of a baby in a high chair, eating a biscuit, chocolate all over its face. Ka Lei laughed. 'Chocolate baby!'

'Yep! That's me.'

The next photo was of Georgina as a young teenager, standing with her arm around Feng Ying's shoulder.

'Tis is your mommy?'

'Yes, we were on a trip to the seaside. We went with the school.'

Ka Lei held the picture closer to her face to get a better look.

'It make you sat, looking at photos. I am solly. You sat about your mutter?'

'Yes, I am sad, sad about a lot of things, but I am getting happier.' Georgina smiled to reassure her. 'I am getting *much* happier. Coming to Hong Kong is the best thing I ever did.'

He surveyed his hunting ground. Even the knowledge that he was out there murdering women just like them didn't stop the girls from working. That was the way they were – greedy little whores.

He looked around the club. Candy was there. He would like to add her to his collection but she had a boyfriend. That meant she had family. The Italian boyfriend might not care for her, but he certainly cared about the cheques she wrote him. He might come looking for her.

Bernie? He'd seen her leave with the old drunk. Bernie was tempting. He had yet to add Irish to his list of nationalities. He was also missing a black girl – English or American would do. Still, he had his eye on one of those already, and it *would* happen when the time was right.

But tonight he had seen something that excited him greatly. A new girl. A mixed-race girl. Another first on his list – a Eurasian. He'd watched her walk out alone. *Just off the boat*, he thought. She hasn't even been paid for sex yet. That thought thrilled him. He would be her first customer.

26

Lucy hadn't needed to worry. It wasn't Chan waiting for her – Big Frank was in. Big Frank was a good customer. He was a sixty-three-year-old six-foot-five Texan who liked to tell people he'd made his money from selling shit, but really he'd made it from fertiliser deals. Although he was originally from Texas, he had his retirement home at Dolphin Key, in the middle of the Florida Keys. It was a once-beautiful bird sanctuary that had been completely ruined by the invasion of condos and resorts. Most of which Big Frank, through his myriad of business interests, had been indirectly responsible for.

Big Frank loved it at Dolphin Key and had bought himself the biggest and best penthouse available. It had marble floors and a gold-plated bidet, four-poster beds and an original Norwegian sauna. On one side was the ocean. Imported beaches were on the other.

He loved to open his French doors every morning and stand on his balcony, inhaling the sunshine. He loved to watch the magnificent ocean – alive and dancing – as it slid apologetically into the marina. And even though one boat melted into another, until it all became a jumble of money and yachts, Frank's keen eyes could always spot it. There in the middle sat the biggest, the most beautiful of all of them – the *China Doll* – Frank's baby.

When Big Frank wasn't fishing and felt in need of a new challenge, he took off on a business trip. At the moment he was dabbling in import/export. Mainly he imported sexual favours and exported Hong Kong dollars for them, and Lucy was his biggest supplier. She had captivated his soul. She had introduced him to a new world of pleasure and pain infliction – and he found he had a taste for it; couldn't get enough of it; could hardly get through a day without it.

They took a taxi to a decent love motel. It was the upmarket kind: warm towels and fountains. It had a brochure full of various themed rooms: Haiwaiian, Parisian, rubber, wet. Lucy giggled dutifully while Big Frank pontificated over the list of extras. His fingers, like blanched sausages, turned the laminated pages and ran down the menu as he read the items aloud: five-speed waterbed, pulsating Jacuzzi and a fruit basket.

Gotta have me one of those, honey.

Eventually he picked the most expensive room, with all the extras – the Paradise Suite.

Lucy didn't like wasting time like this. She was just about to get started when, from the corner of the room, above the plastic palms, came the offbeat soundtrack of a porn flick starting up. The TV screen came to life with close-up flesh and lurid colour. Big Frank took off his polo shirt and his buff-coloured slacks and stripped to his underwear. He unstrapped his reinforced girdle and left it standing to attention on the rattan chair before flopping onto the waterbed – which tsunamied beneath him – and propping himself up with pillows, ready to settle down and watch the movie.

Lucy had seen it before. She went into the bathroom, slipped out of her clothes and had a shower. Wearing only a towel, she re-entered the room just as the housewives' fantasy was starting. She stood, blocking Frank's vision, and let the towel slip. But instead of appreciating her warm, rounded body, he craned to look past her as rabid panting came from the direction of the television.

She threw the towel onto the chair, where it hung draped over his corset like a magician's trick. Then, lying down, she rested her head on his stomach and traced his triple-bypass scar down to his navel hair, which she proceeded to wind around her fingers. His wheezing grew louder and his heart thumped in her ear.

'You know what, honey, I bet you have a girlfriend we could call to come over?' he wheezed.

'Oh I *sollleeee . . .*' She exaggerated her Suzie Wong voice. 'All busy tonight.' Lucy had no intention of letting some other girl in on the act. Frank was all hers. 'Never mind, Flank.' She moved onto her hands and knees and turned her bottom towards him. 'We gonna have fun. Okay?' She slapped her hand against her right buttock and said 'Spanky!' over her shoulder. Big Frank's chest hair bristled. 'Coz I think I bin . . .' she sank onto her elbows, 'I think I bin naughty girl.'

27

Johnny Mann was heading east from Lan Kwai Fong, the nightclub end of Central District, and working his way along towards Causeway Bay, when he decided to pay another visit to Club Mercedes. He didn't intend to stay long. He'd come back to the club in the hope of talking to Lucy and taking some more details from her about the foreign women who had stayed in her flat. When he got there he found out from Mamasan Linda that Lucy was out with a customer and that there was a new foreign girl working there – Lucy's cousin. So he asked to interview her.

It wasn't busy. He was given a table at the front of the club. It was an area far enough from the band that you could talk easily and be heard, but it didn't afford the privacy of one of the VIP booths around the dance floor.

He was deep in thought when pink toes and gold strappy sandals appeared in his line of vision. Then there were long legs, smooth rounded thighs, a tiny waist and small full breasts to get past. *But* it didn't even end there . . . *Shit! That was a face to die for . . .* It was heart-shaped with high cheekbones and large amber-coloured eyes. She had pale skin, a splatter of freckles across her nose, a long, slender neck and espresso-coloured hair that cascaded around her shoulders in pre-Raphaelite curls. She was not just pretty. She was breathtakingly beautiful.

'Miss Johnson . . . is that right?' he almost stuttered.

She nodded and a small anxious smile flitted across her beautiful face. As it did so, Mann saw that her mouth formed an almost perfect circle, topped with a cupid's bow complete with a small turn up at either end – perfect.

'Please sit down.'

She did so in a slightly uneasy fashion, as if she were neither used to the dress nor the heels. She seemed very young, thought Mann, and very out of place.

'Mamasan says you've just started at this club. Is that right?'

'Yes, tonight is my first night.' She perched on the edge of the seat.

'Did you work anywhere else before here?' He tried a smile to relax her.

'No.'

'When did you arrive in Hong Kong?'

'Two days ago.'

'And what reason did you have for coming to Hong Kong?'

She paused, reluctant to answer, then blurted: 'I came to find my cousins.'

'Cousins? Ah, yes, Lucy! Have you any other relatives here?'

106

'No. Just Lucy and her sister Ka Lei.'

'You came all the way here to find them? It's a long way.'

Mann felt a pang of pity. He wondered why someone so obviously inexperienced in life had come to the other side of the world, and at the worst time possible?

He paused for a moment and studied her. 'How old are you?'

'Twenty-two.'

Yes, she could be twenty-two, he supposed: she had the face of someone much younger but the body of a grown woman.

'Why did you choose a job in a nightclub?'

Georgina looked uncomfortable.

'Do your parents know you are working here?'

'I never really knew my dad. My mother died two months ago.'

Her amber eyes clouded over and she turned her face away. He instantly regretted asking the question. He knew what grief was like. Just when you thought you had it sorted and you could cope with people's questions – BANG! The emotions came at you from behind like a tidal wave suddenly appearing over your shoulder. From a young age, from the time his father had died, Mann had learned how to cope by turning grief to rage – anger made a much better survival tool than pity. He learned to read the signs, to know when it was coming. So when he knew the wave was just about to outrun him he turned and faced it, waited for the spray to hit, then he jumped on board and rode the mother all the way to the beach.

'Here in Hong Kong?'

'No, back in England.'

'I am very sorry to hear about your parents.'

'Thank you,' she said, with a flicker of a smile.

'That's your home – England? London?'

'Devon, in the countryside. Do you know it?'

'Not well. I was sent to school in England, in Hertfordshire. I went to Devon with the rugby team. We got hammered. They were all enormous – farmers' sons.'

She laughed and sat forward in her chair, animated. 'How did you end up in a school in England?'

'My father was Chinese but my mother's English. It was her idea.'

'So you're Eurasian, like me?'

Mann was struck by the strangeness of her childlike naivety as she beamed at him. This new knowledge had instantly bonded them in her eyes. It was like a secret handshake between them. 'Now I can see it,' she said. 'You have Chinese eyes.'

Mann laughed. 'Chinese eyes, a Celtic chin and ears like Mr Spock from *Star Trek*. See!' He turned his head to the side and brushed his hair back with his hand.

'They are a bit pointy,' she admitted. Her laugh was young and spontaneous. There was more to her than met the eye. 'Did you go to university in England?'

'No.' He hesitated, unused to divulging his life history to a stranger, but if it was putting her at ease it was worth it. 'No, my father died. I had to come home to look after my mother. I wanted to,' he corrected himself. 'Then I ended up joining the police force.'

'Is your mother still here?'

'Yes, she is. She lives in a flat out at Stanley Bay in the south of the Island. I go over for Sunday roast when I can, take her some washing, keep her happy. Have you been to the market out there? Although we are not supposed to encourage the sale of counterfeit goods, it's a great place to buy every type of fake T-shirt or Armani watch.'

'No, I haven't done much sightseeing yet. I've just been sort of settling in.' Her voice trailed off again.

'You haven't been to the Peak?'

She shook her head.

'You'll have to do that. Take your camera, there are some fantastic views. You can see all over Hong Kong.'

He held her gaze and smiled reassuringly. She was a little girl lost in a big world. He just managed to stop himself from offering to take her sightseeing.

'Do you ever go back?' she asked, searching his face – looking for answers of her own.

'To England?'

She nodded.

'No, I haven't been back there since I left in the sixth form. Hong Kong is my home. It always has been. What about you? How's it working out here?'

'I think I'm going to like it here.' She beamed with a mix of conviction and bravado. 'It's a great place.'

'Good. I'm glad you like it here. Hong Kong *is* a fantastic place. But the nightclub world is a dangerous one. You need to watch yourself here – be careful who you trust.' He opened his wallet and took out a card. 'On the back is my home number . . . just in case you need it. Don't hesitate to call. If I can help you, I will.'

She smiled and thanked him.

'And please inform your cousin Lucy that a Detective Sergeant Ng will be in touch tomorrow to take a statement from her.'

Georgina got up to leave.

'Remember what I said, Miss Johnson – I don't want to see you here the next time I come.' He leaned closer, out of earshot. 'This is not the place for a nice Eurasian girl like you.'

Once he got outside he checked his watch. It was one a.m. He stopped just round the corner from the Polaris Centre and pulled out a list of places he had to visit and decided where he would start. Tonight he was on a mission to cover as many hostess bars, karaoke bars and general 'girly' bars as he could get through. He wasn't doing them in any particular order. They just had to have one thing in common – they had to have foreign girls working in them.

It was as he paused to push up his shirtsleeves and sling his Armani jacket over his shoulder that he felt a cooling breeze pass over him and prickle the hairs on his arms. He turned his eyes towards the starry sky and sighed gratefully. *Thank God for that – clear – no rain.* Summer's one hundred per cent humidity and searing heat were coming to an end at last: the 'cool season' was on its way.

He took a diversion to the waterfront. It wouldn't hurt him to take a few minutes out from his bar trawling. He needed to pace himself, keep himself fresh and alert. A bit of cool sea air would help him focus. He loved the water: it had a centring effect on him. Luckily, in Hong Kong it was never far away.

He rested his hands on the waist-high harbour wall. Dipping his head forward, he pushed against the cold stone to stretch the muscles in his neck and upper back. Releasing his stretches, he sighed heavily and took a few deep breaths. Lifting his weary head, he looked across the bay to mainland Kowloon. In the day the skyscrapers stood like gold-capped teeth crammed together, strong and immovable – the mouth of the harbour. At night they were transformed into illuminated beacons of delicate beauty. They shone their laser lights heavenward into the fuzzy-edged, tarmac-black sky, and bled pure primary colour into the deep still water of Hong Kong's harbour.

Mann inhaled deeply and smiled to himself. He never got tired of Hong Kong; never got bored. Six years ago, in 1997, he had stood on this spot and gazed across this harbour and wondered how Hong Kong would survive the Handover and in what form. On that wet night Old Man China marched in at midnight. *Britannia* sailed home with a very wet Prince of Wales on board, plus the whole distraught Patten family. Old Man China had stood over his decadent daughter and stripped her of her colonial make-up. He had issued a new set of house rules, none of which was aimed at giving more freedom. He had allowed the triads to spread more freely than ever and he had made the police's job a lot harder. There was still no witness protection scheme in place, so no one wanted to testify, and when they did manage to bring someone to court they did not have the power to seize their assets. How was that ever going to work? But, fundamentally, Hong Kong was the same wild girl she'd always been. She was strong, pushy, and a little dirty. Whereas the rest of Asia was famous for its nubile maidens lying on their backs saying 'take me', Hong Kong was renowned for being a gaudy old whore, opening her legs wide, saying, 'It'll cost you but there's plenty of room.'

Mann wouldn't wish to be anywhere else. He would live and die in Hong Kong's arms. Which probably wouldn't be difficult or take very long, the way that he was going. He knew it was a fault in him. He was too reckless. He had no conception of self-preservation – he recognised that. He never thought twice about a situation; he was always the first man in. But then, he hadn't found a reason *not* to risk his life, and he didn't want to find one either. The day his father was murdered, Mann's dreams became distant memories. From boy to man in those few seconds. The boy died; while the man emerged damaged and burdened. His life, from that day forward, was spent trying to make recompense for that day.

28

Mann looked around – a few courting couples, small groups of overawed tourists enjoying the skyline – nothing untoward. He sat down on a bench, suddenly weary from the kind of tiredness that doesn't so much creep up on you as hit you like a bus from behind, when you least expected it. His heavy head rested back onto the polished granite seat. He closed his eyes for a few minutes and his aching body relaxed. The cool breeze brushed across his face, and, before he could stop it, his mind drifted away.

His thoughts turned to England. He didn't know why he thought of England so often. It must be the 'cool season effect' – autumn in Hong Kong was so like spring in England, with hot days and cool nights. Or perhaps, and more likely, it was because the time he had spent in England had been a precious time of care-free youth. But they were bittersweet memories – Chan was always part of them.

Mann shrugged off sleep and sat up. He instinctively touched the scar on his cheek. It was the scar that Chan had given him when they were boys. After a summer spent running with the street kids, Chan had brought a 'throwing star' back from Hong Kong. It was a triad street weapon, designed to maim rather than kill. He'd been showing off, demonstrating it to a group of boys, and had thrown it as Mann walked past. It had spun across Mann's face, slicing a groove into his cheekbone where the skin was tautest, and left a scar shaped like a crescent moon. It had been impossible to make the wound neat with stitches. The school staff had been horrified. Chan had been sorry. But, in real terms, a scar never hurt a lad, and Mann wore it with pride. It left his smooth face with a touch of ruggedness, and the girls loved it.

Mann still had the star. It was part of a collection he had made of triad weaponry. He'd taught himself to use them – the stars, the throwing spikes. He had become an expert over the years. Combined with his martial arts training it meant he hardly needed to carry a gun.

He settled back onto the bench and made the mistake of closing his eyes again. Just for a few minutes he allowed the memory of summer rain, mown grass and humming bees take him spiralling back. Then, BANG. He saw his father forced to kneel. He watched a man swing a meat cleaver and strike the chopper hard into his father's strong frame. He saw his father's body judder and lurch as the chopper snagged, caught in muscle and bone, before it was freed by the assailant's boot against his father's back. His father remained upright until the last blow that split his skull.

Mann jolted himself upright. Sweat was pouring

down his face and back. He stood up, shook his head and wiped his brow. The nightmare of his father's death would never go away. The worst part was watching it, not being able to stop it – not being able to reach him in time; not being able to save him. It would haunt Mann forever. But he had been just a lad, and had been held back by three strong men. He had been made to watch in triad-style retribution, a warning to Mann and to others – what happens when payments are not met. He was just a boy, but still Mann blamed himself for not being a superhero, for not saving his father.

He looked about him in a panic, relaxing when he realised where he was. The courting couples had progressed slowly on their promenade and the tourists were still there. He leant against the harbour wall and steadied himself for a few seconds. He looked across to Kowloon. The stars were out. The laser beams were shining into the liquorice sky. The water was still. He shivered as the breeze cooled the sweat on his back, then he pulled out his list of nightclubs.

The Bond Bar would be next.

Lucy slid into the centre of the waterbed and flipped onto Big Frank's stomach like a wet fish. They lay panting together for a few minutes. Lucy could hear his heartbeat through the wiry carpet of silver-grey chest hair. She lay there, smiling to herself. Big Frank was getting more adventurous every time. It wouldn't be long before he was hooked. He could be the answer to all her prayers. God knows, she deserved it! He could get her out before Chan had any chance to look for her. Big Frank had big bucks, Lucy could tell – she was used to men with money – she'd known many. He was generous and eager – that was a good sign. Lucy would work hard on him, devote everything to winning his heart and soul. But she'd better hurry up: the clock was ticking and the debt was mounting.

29

It was gone two a.m. when Mann arrived at the Bond Bar in Wanchai. The area was number three on his list, and probably the same number in order of importance in the nightclub world. It used to be number one, but the smarter clubs across the water, in Tsim Sha Tsui, Kowloon side, had taken that slot.

The bar's theme was Bond girls: Honey Ryder, Holly Goodhead, Plenty O'Toole. It was in the guidebooks as one of the 'must see' bars and was described as 'intimate'. It was certainly that: small, cramped, and with a definite exchange of body heat going on. But it didn't matter what the place looked like. The fact that it had half-decent, half-naked girls in it was all that mattered.

The doorman, Sam the Sikh, was in his usual position – a genie in the shadows in his red silk – guarding the entrance to the club. He stepped forward and greeted Mann.

'Good evening, Inspector.'

'Hi, Sam. How's it going?'

Sam screwed up his face and rocked his hand in the air. 'So so. Business is not bad but I've seen better.'

'Not like the old days, huh?'

Sam clapped his hands together and laughed. 'The old days – before the Handover. Before we all changed into Chinese.'

'This place hasn't changed, that's for sure – still as disreputable as ever. Still, I'd better make an inspection, Sam – see if it passes the health and safety regulations.'

Sam laughed. 'Very good, Inspector. Say hello to her from me.'

Mann passed the wall of famous faces – an array of framed and signed photos of those well-known visitors who had been caught – some off-guard and obviously regretting it, others past caring. A few looked almost grateful. No new ones, though.

He scanned the room as he entered. There were about thirty punters in. It should have been busier than it was, but Hong Kong was still reeling from one global catastrophe after another. It had only just emerged from the SARS epidemic and, before that, the stock-market crash. Visitor numbers were down. The punters were distributed around the room, according to their preference in women. They sat at individual bar stations and were served by a topless Bond girl who sat or knelt at eye level in the centre of their bar on a raised rotating island, a metre in diameter.

All eight podiums were up and running that night.

Mann passed a group of nervous-looking Japanese who were hovering just inside the door. They'd probably wandered in looking for something more explicit and were too polite to move on when it hadn't materialised. Across the room there were a few Indonesians around Honey Ryder's station. They were probably dignitaries back home, now getting their first glimpse of a semi-naked white woman and trying not to giggle. The rest of the podiums had small groups of Europeans and Americans, just getting going for the evening. They wouldn't be staying there for long. The Bond Bar was just an appetiser – pure titillation and completely harmless by Hong Kong's standards – *nothing* like the real deal. In Hong Kong, money could buy the darkest of desires and everything and everyone had a price.

On the way through, Mann passed Honey Ryder entertaining the Indonesians – she looked up and gave him her endearing gap-toothed smile. She was dressed in black rubber hotpants and sported a cute blonde bob. She had an expectant look on her face and he was tempted to say a quick hello. She looked like she was waiting for him to come over. They'd had something going a while ago but it had never quite got off the starting blocks. It would be worth another shot, but it would have to wait. Now was not the time. He was here to see one of the others, Pussy Galore and, although Honey might be, Pussy wasn't the sharing kind.

He spotted her at her usual podium at the right-hand side of the room. Her station was the busiest – he wasn't surprised. He walked over and sat down on the fake leopard-skin stool, sat back and waited for her to notice him. It didn't take long – she was good at her job; she'd been doing it for long enough.

Mann had known her for five years. They had provided mutual comfort for each other on several occasions and were fond of each other in their own way – on a part-time basis.

'All right, Johnny?' she said in a strong cockney accent. 'Long time no see.'

'Hi, Pussy. How's it going? Business good?'

'It's always good in here, Johnny, you know that,' she said, with a big false smile that she flashed to the dozen or so punters around her podium. Then she added, under her breath, 'And don't call me Pussy, you wanker . . .' before spinning away from him.

Mann was amused by her show of frostiness. He knew she was angry that he hadn't called her in a while, but he also knew it wouldn't last long – three minutes max. She never could keep her feelings or anything else under wraps. Nor had she mastered the art of suspense.

She slammed a vodka on the rocks down in front of him before twirling around to flirt with an over-weight loud-shirted tourist on the opposite side of the podium. Her electric laugh was mesmerising to the group of men who sat less than a metre from her, watching every undulation of her beautiful black shiny body as she turned on the rotating table. They didn't attempt conversation between themselves. They weren't incapable, but they hadn't come here to think of anything else except Pussy Galore.

Two minutes later she swivelled back to Mann. He was playing with the ice in his glass, clinking it against the side.

'You're looking good, Johnny,' she said, taking his glass to refresh it.

There! Knew she wouldn't make it past three minutes.

'You too, Kim. You missed a spot with the oil, though. Just there on your right buttock.'

'You've lost weight,' she said, ignoring his jibe and sitting back on her heels to look him over. 'Lean and mean – it suits you.'

'I've been doing a lot of running. Helps me think. Gives me energy.'

'I thought you was doin' it to keep your stamina up for the next time you take me out.'

'That too,' he grinned.

She stretched out her hand and moved aside the crow's wing of dark hair that always fell over Mann's left eye, before running her finger along the scar on his cheek. She was a lover of scars – emotional and physical – he knew that much about her. That's how she'd ended up working on the other side of the world serving drinks dressed in a g-string.

She tilted her head to one side and softness crept into her eyes. Mann tried to avoid that these days. He liked her but he wasn't interested in taking it further, and neither was she if she was honest.

He turned his head from her hand.

She drew back as if she'd been smacked in the face and twirled angrily away from him. He knew she wouldn't like that. But she'd be back. She was a creature of habit – a boomerang. She always went full circle and ended up back where she started. She couldn't even leave the Bond Bar. Sometimes she managed to stay away for a few days, even a few weeks, but she couldn't hack it. She always came back with one excuse or another. Really she missed the adoration and the easy money.

Mann gave an inward shrug. He wasn't one to judge or cast stones. Everyone had their buttons. Kim's were complicated and yet simple – she looked for love but never wanted to find it. She didn't think she deserved it. Mann's buttons all merged into one big fat one, and it had a T for triad etched on the top.

30

Kim spun back to him and sat pouting. He was amused by her hurt expression. She was extremely easy to read. She had a catalogue of expressions and Mann had seen them all, even the ones that she didn't know she had at certain moments. This one was number six – the 'pretend to be hurt' one.

'You're stressed out, Johnny. I can see it. You should learn to relax more. You should get yourself a girlfriend – someone you can trust.'

'How do you know I haven't?'

'Coz I know *you*.'

'Got anyone in mind, Kim? Does she work in a bar and spend her evenings in a spangly g-string?'

'Might do.' She pulled her hand away and resumed quarter turns on her island. 'Anyway, it's just a thought,' she said, but fighting a smile.

She was a lot like him – Mann knew that. They might have come from different places, but they had arrived at the same point. He was a 'love shy' commitment-phobe. She was a 'grass greener' sort – always looking over her lover's shoulder to the guy behind. But when she got it, she couldn't wait to get rid of it. And the thing Mann knew about greener grass was that it still got weeds and it still needed cutting.

'Anyway, Johnny, I might not be here much longer. I'm thinking of leaving this place.'

'Really?'

'Yes. And don't look at me like that. I mean it this time. I've had a good job offer.'

'What?'

'Can't say. Not yet, anyways.'

Mann could see she was itching to tell him. He smiled to himself. He could tease it out of her if he wanted, but then what was the point? The job wouldn't last five minutes. Then she'd be right back where she started – serving drinks in the Bond Bar in her smalls.

'Maybe you'd like to come and work for me? I need a personal assistant.'

She laughed and spun away. Pausing with her back to him, she shifted her weight from buttock to buttock and stretched forward to serve some new punters. Mann smiled to himself. He knew the show was just for him. It was appreciated.

When she finished flirting, she spun back.

'The thing is, Johnny – you pay me enough – I might just consider doing it.'

'*Money?* I was thinking *perks.*' He held on to her table and stopped her from moving. He wheeled her back to him. 'I need to talk to you, Kim . . . it's serious.' He lowered his voice. 'I need to ask you something.'

Her smile disappeared and she frowned at him.

'What?' She glared at his hand holding on to her table. Even that much control pissed her off.

'We're looking for someone at the moment. Has there been any talk among the girls of anyone they're worried about? Any punter overstepped the mark?'

Kim thought for a minute before moving her head slowly from side to side. 'No more than usual.' She arched herself forward as close as she could physically get to Mann without giving the loud shirt behind more to look at than he'd paid for. 'But then, you know me, Johnny, I don't do that kind of thing – I'm a good gal.'

'I haven't forgotten,' he said. 'How many foreign girls are working here, Kim?'

'Seven at the moment. Different shifts. Why?'

'All of them been here for some time?'

'We had to replace a couple recently.'

'What's the turnover of girls like in here?'

'Fast . . .' she laughed, 'and furious.'

'Why?'

Kim gave a derisory snort. 'It ain't the kind of job you give notice to, Johnny. They don't bovver showin' up, then we know they've gone. Sometimes they turn up again 'cross town. Sometimes they come back after a month, just need a rest, a bit of head space.' She leaned forward to whisper in his ear again. 'You know, Johnny, you need to ask me more questions you could always buy me dinner?'

'Are you on the same number?' he asked, getting out his wallet to pay for the drinks.

'Yeah, but you better hurry up, Johnny,' she breathed

into his ear, her heavy breasts resting against him. 'I might get a better offer.'

'Than me? Impossible.'

'Mmmmm.' She closed her eyes for a few seconds. 'You're a bastard, Johnny. But a lovely one . . .'

'I'll be seeing you, Kim . . .' He pulled away. '. . . Very soon, I hope. Meanwhile, don't take any risks. Watch yourself. I mean it.'

She recovered her composure, spun away once more and blew him a kiss over her shoulder.

'Don't worry, Johnny. I'll be careful. And Johnny –'

He hovered.

'Don't wait too long. I get very fidgety.'

'How could I forget, Pussy?' he grinned.

At the top of the steps Sam was having trouble with a group of rowdy British holidaymakers.

'Need a hand, Sam?'

A lairy drunk in a Manchester United shirt turned round and found himself two inches from Mann's chest. He looked up, then stepped back.

'Thank you, *Inspector*.' Sam puffed himself out. 'There's no problem here. Is there, gentlemen?' he said, forcing the suddenly well-behaved men into order. 'One at a time. One at a time, and remember . . .' he wagged his finger at the sheepish line, 'all nice girls in here – the best – no touching titties.' He flashed Mann a big smile. 'Be seeing you, Inspector.'

'Be seeing you, Sam.'

Mann stopped at street level, stepped out of the stream of people, and took out his list again. He scanned down it and then looked up again to get his bearings. He was reluctant to move on. He glanced back at the Bond Bar. *It didn't feel right...* He didn't feel good about leaving Kim and the others. They were all at risk, but there was no point in worrying every foreign woman working in Hong Kong. Besides, Kim wouldn't listen to him anyway, and Mann was under strict instructions not to start a panic, a stampede out of the region – not to do any more damage to Hong Kong's vital tourist trade. Not that Mann seriously cared about orders. If it would have helped, he would have told them all – but it wouldn't help. Wrong place, wrong time... any one of them might just be the chosen one. The killer was definitely out there somewhere, sat at some girly bar, watching and waiting.

Mann looked at his list; he had several more places to visit that night. He needed to get to as many as possible. He needed to find out how many foreign girls there were, and where they worked – so that the next time one turned up dead, dismembered and dumped in a black bin bag, he might have a chance of putting a name to a head.

Bernadette was surprised at the old drunk's nastiness. Hadn't she just tried to give him what he wanted? He'd turned on her in a flash – had her handcuffed to the feckin' bed before she knew what had hit her. Then he'd kept her tied up there for eight feckin' hours while he snored his head off!

She stood with her back to the mirror and twisted round to look at the damage. Feckin' bastard! He had marked her good and proper. Thinking about it, she hadn't got him pissed enough. Ah well! He'd paid her for it – sent his maid to get his stash from the safe. She'd emptied his wallet while he was talkin' to the maid. Served the nasty old fecker right . . .

31

Just as the early-morning traffic was beginning to build, and the Tai Chi enthusiasts were finishing their salute to the sun in the parks and on the rooftops, Mann stepped into the cool of the underground station and took a train home. He'd worked through the night and could do no more for a few hours until it all kicked off again. He needed a shave and a shower. He boarded a train for Quarry Bay, on the north-east side of Hong Kong Island. He lived in a great location: it was served by the wonderfully efficient MTR and was just a short distance from Central and Headquarters. But it wasn't a community. It was a vertical village – fifty tower blocks with a shopping mall in the centre – affordable housing for the young executive classes.

Mann lived in a two-bedroom apartment on the fortieth floor in one of the older blocks. Built in the early nineties, it had wooden floors, white walls, and very little else. Mann didn't do the homely look. He had cutlery for one, crockery in single units and a solitary armchair that he'd positioned opposite a massive plasma TV in the lounge.

But his apartment hadn't always been so Spartan. It had been a proper home once. Not long ago someone had stood in his home and in his heart. Helen had been there.

She was long gone now. He wished he didn't think of her so often. He missed that spontaneous laugh of hers, that optimistic view of life – so different to his cynicism. He missed the little things she cared about. He missed her. But he didn't regret her going. She deserved more than he could give. He had never seen himself pushing a baby's buggy or having friends over for dinner. He hadn't wanted anything or anyone else – just her. But she wanted the whole package, and he just didn't have it in him to give.

He flopped onto his bed. He knew that he would sleep for a week if he didn't watch it, so he dozed, waiting for the alarm clock to sound. In that last hour, just as he was dreamless and heavy as lead, it started ringing and ringing as if from some faraway planet, dragging him into consciousness. He hit the clock first, then hit the floor running. He checked his watch – noon, time for a quick shower; the colder the better.

He stepped out of the MTR half an hour later and cut through the park. It was a ten-minute walk up the hill to Headquarters. The midday air was scented with the smell of lush vegetation. The traffic noise was momentarily lost in a pocket of wilderness and replaced by the sounds of insects – as loud as pneumatic drills.

He cut across the road, up the cobbled alleyways, past skinny kittens and makeshift kitchens, until he hit Soho, an area of fusion restaurants and fancy artefact shops. In the evening it was given over to partying *Gweilos* who loved its European feel. Cafés spilled over pavements and noisy Italian waiters touted for business.

Mann nodded to a cleaner sweeping the front of a Malaysian restaurant. The man paused, leaned on his broom and inclined his head a fraction Mann's way. Mann would speak to him later – he was one of three undercover officers working the street.

Mann crossed the packed car park and walked up the well-trodden steps of Headquarters. It took him ten minutes to get past the people waiting to talk to him on the stairs. Finally, he made it to David White's office.

The Superintendent was alone. He looked harassed. He hadn't slept more than a couple of hours, and it showed.

'The post-mortem report makes for gruesome reading, Johnny,' he said, as Mann walked in and sat down opposite him. The Superintendent was holding the report in his hands. 'Trophy taker? A torturer? He must hang on to these women, Mann. Where is he holding them? We need to get as many officers out there asking questions as we can. Get some undercover officers into the clubs with foreign hostesses. But for Christ's sake, make them understand we need discretion.'

'Don't worry, David, we're on to it. But, if he is murdering *Gwaipohs*, it's a clever choice. Many of these women work under aliases. They have no family here. He must have picked them quite carefully. We have hundreds of matches for our Jane Does. *However*, if this man moves in the nightclub world, he must have frightened a few women along the way. There must have been some who got away without even realising it.'

Just then Ng knocked on the door, followed closely by a very agitated Li. 'Genghis – this just came in from Scotland Yard.' Ng handed him a file.

Mann flipped it open and scanned it before reading it out:

'The fingerprint belongs to Maria Jackson. Born in 1963. British. She had form for drug dealing in the UK. She was given a one-year probational sentence in May 1989. Came to Hong Kong in April 1991. Last known place of employment – the Rising Sun in Wanchai. That was in November 1992.'

'Interpol are trying to trace any family at the moment but have come up with nothing so far,' said Ng, handing the photo of Maria to the Superintendent. It was a mugshot taken at the time of her arrest.

'The pathologist put the woman's age at mid to late twenties. She'd be forty now. That means she's been dead ten to fifteen years. So, our murderer has been around a long time,' said Mann.

'There's also victim one . . . the head . . . belonged to twenty-eight-year-old Beverly Mathews,' said Ng.

'When did she go missing?' asked Mann, scanning the second page of the file Ng had handed him. He pulled out a grainy photo of a woman with big hair and a big smile.

'Seventeen years ago – July 1986.'

'You were right to extend the search so far back,' said Superintendent White.

'How did you know, boss?' Li asked, looking very *Saturday Night Fever* in his wide white-collared shirt and his slicked-back hair.

'She had nothing but metal amalgam fillings in her mouth, Shrimp – every one of them. Most people over thirty have at least a mixture of new and old – she didn't.'

Superintendent White left his desk, took the report from Mann, and went to stand at the window to read it.

'I worked on the case. I remember it,' he said.

'Was she a resident here, David? Do you remember?'

'No. She was a tourist. She'd sold the most Renaults in Reading – she won herself a holiday to Hong Kong.'

Superintendent White picked up the old shot of Beverly Mathews taken at a cousin's wedding a few weeks before she disappeared. 'She failed to turn up at her workplace back in England. It was then discovered that she hadn't returned from her holiday.

'We searched the area. We found nothing. The case was left open but it was generally believed that she'd decided to jack in her job and her life back home and had probably headed off towards Bali or somewhere similar on the backpackers' trail.'

'When was she last seen?'

'At a party in a local's house out at Repulse Bay. After a night of heavy drinking she decided she needed to get back to her hotel. She was staying in Causeway

Bay. Apparently she couldn't be persuaded to call a taxi from the house, said she needed to get some fresh air and promptly left.'

'What time was that?'

'It was about six in the morning when she was last seen. She had to walk down a remote road to get to the bus route. No one ever remembered seeing her in Repulse Bay itself, and I think they would have if she had made it that far – she was wearing very little and it was early in the morning. At the time, it was our guess that if anything untoward had happened it must have happened on that walk – someone picked her up there.'

'That means our killer has been around for two decades. He's at least thirty-five, probably over forty.'

'It also means he could have killed a lot of women in the last twenty years – we could be finding a lot more bodies.'

'Count on it,' said Mann.

'What about the reports of missing foreign women, Ng?' asked the Superintendent, going back to sit behind his desk. He spread the photos from the autopsy neatly across his desk.

Ng shook his head at the enormity of the task. 'Sir, Interpol have come up with hundreds of women who are unaccounted for and who fit the profile. Even tracing the people who reported the women missing is proving very difficult.'

'And attacks on foreign women?' White picked up the photo of Beverly and the mugshot of Maria.

'Attacks do not usually involve local men. It's nearly

always between two foreigners. Just a drunken disturbance,' replied Ng.

'Similarities between these women, Shrimp?' asked the Superintendent, studying the photos in his hand.

'Foreigners. Young women. He likes young foreigners.'

'Likes, or maybe *hates* all foreigners, and he certainly doesn't *like* women,' said Mann. 'He enjoys inflicting pain.'

'Age, sex, ethnicity? Basic similarities? Marks on bodies? What have we got, Ng?'

'Victim one.' Ng read from his notes. 'Beverly Mathews – no evidence of torture. Victim two – a bite mark on the thigh . . . rope fibres on the wrist. Victim three – many small burns and sexually mutilated.'

'What about the way they have been killed and dissected?' White asked Mann.

'Probably asphyxiated. We're not sure yet. All three were dismembered in the same manner, though – with precision, neat, surgeon style. The process is important to him. He takes his time over it. He enjoys it.'

White scanned the report. 'He leaves the bodies somewhere cold, the pathologist said?'

'He leaves them for long enough for the lividity to settle, then moves them to somewhere else where he takes his trophies and dismembers them. Some of them he freezes,' answered Mann. 'Which is useful for us because some parts have been less affected by decomposition than others and some of the surface injuries are still visible.'

'Like the bite mark that was made after death,' said Ng.

'That's so weird! Why would he do that?' asked Li.

'Part of his fantasy. It's a common trait with serial killers,' said White. 'And to return to the body several times before finally disposing of it.'

'Ng, what did you get from Lucy, the S&M queen?' asked Mann.

Ng took out his report, flipped open the page, and shrugged dismissively.

'She gave me a description of six women who had lived in her flat at various times over the last five years. They were all in their twenties. All white. One American, three Europeans, two Antipodeans. According to Lucy, one of the Europeans had a strong accent. She didn't know where from. None of them had any distinguishing characteristics. Nothing that stuck in her mind, anyway. She seems to have known very little about them. They kept themselves to themselves, she said. She seemed to think that most of them were on their own – no families, no ties. None of them gave reasons for leaving. They just left. She didn't consider that strange.'

'Not much help then, was she?' said Superintendent White.

'She wasn't trying.' Mann took the report from Ng and looked at Lucy's statement. 'Leave her to me, Ng. Li – get me photos of those women. Find out all you can about them. I want a name for them all. They deserve that much – and Shrimp . . .' he handed Li a photo from the autopsy on victim three, 'that tattoo. What would you say it was?'

'A fish?'

'Possibly – but I'd say it's more likely to be a mermaid. Find out all you can about it. I want to know where she got that tattoo, look into the ink used – it differs in different countries. And the design – see if you can trace the artist . . . And remember, Shrimp – these women could have been somebody's girlfriend, wife. They could have been somebody's mother if they had had the chance. Real names and faces – I want to see them. And – before you go – a name for this perpetrator. It's up to you.'

Li didn't hesitate. 'The Butcher.'

'The Butcher?' The Superintendent looked questioningly at Li.

'Yes, sir. You need to be a good surgeon to be able to bone and joint a piece of meat, or at least a good butcher – the pathologist said.'

'The Butcher it is then.'

Just then an officer opened the door with a message. A second bag of bodies had been found.

32

Mann and his team were the second squad car to arrive at the New World restaurant in the New Territories. Two young policemen had cordoned the site off as best they could and were in the process of trying to keep a group of people away from an object buried beneath builders' rubble at the far end of the car park.

As Mann's car went to turn in, an open-backed meat lorry carrying pig carcasses blocked their path. The driver had slowed down to see what was happening, and was contemplating turning in to the restaurant car park but changed his mind when he saw the police car in front of him. Instead, he pulled out of the way and parked across the road, and stuck his large, gormless head out of the cab window to see what was going on.

As his vehicle turned in, Mann looked into the back of the truck. Pig carcasses were thrown haphazardly into the back of the lorry, forming a mangled jigsaw of puffy white flesh.

The police car headed for the far end of the car park, trying to avoid contaminating the area even further or covering the killer's tracks. They swung round to park.

'Anything?' asked Ng, following Mann's gaze and pointing towards the lorry.

'Not sure. Take down the plate number for me, Li. Now, let's get a move on – looks like chaos over there. Put these over your shoes.'

Mann handed Li two plastic bags and rubber bands. Li looked at him.

'So we know which prints are ours. Although, I seriously doubt anyone else is wearing winklepickers.

'What the fuck are they doing?' Mann pulled the bags over his shoes and marched off in the direction of the rear of the building, where an extension for a new dining room was being built. 'They're trampling over everything.' He pointed towards a crowd gathered around a mound of smashed masonry, then shouted to the crowd to stand back. They chose not to hear and continued to form an ever-shuffling yet impenetrable ring around the source of a stomach-churning smell of putrefied meat, which grew more intense at every step. As they neared the police officers could see a black plastic bag partially hidden among one of the slabs of broken-up concrete paving.

Mann shouted again. This time some of the crowd turned to watch the three policemen marching across the car park, but they didn't all pull back. Some of them were transfixed to the spot, rooted in disgust and repulsion, with bulging eyes and hands clasped over mouths. Others ran back and forth like demented yoyos – not able to stay with the offending object and not able to leave it.

No 3D High Definition could prepare the men for

the reality of what they saw and what they smelt. This time Mann shouted to one of the young policemen, who, in his attempt at restoring order, was taking names of some of the people present, and making the mistake of turning his back on the rest.

'Stand back!' Mann shouted. He turned to Ng. 'Fuck! The bag looks fit to burst.'

'There must be a hole in it – look at the flies!' said Ng.

'We better get there quick and stop that crowd touching it before it's too . . .'

At that second, and fifteen metres out of Mann's reach, one of the restaurant workers became ever more brave with a metal rod he'd found amid the rubble. He dug a little deeper into the stretched plastic than he intended. The black bag ripped from one end to the other and spewed up its rotting treasure in volcanic style. The restaurant worker screamed and jumped back several feet, where he stopped, frozen to the spot and staring wide-eyed as a wet curly-haired head, carried by a viscous stream of melted body fat and water, slid onto his foot.

Mann moved forward to get a better look: wide-jawed, big-mouthed, perfectly even teeth . . .

Shit! An American, that's all we need!

Meanwhile, the pig lorry pulled noisily away and started its ascent of Monkey Mountain.

33

Man Po forced his lorry into first, slammed his foot onto the accelerator, and laughed out loud as the lorry shuddered, belched diesel, nearly stalled, then lurched forward to begin its long and slow ascent, leaving the commotion at the restaurant behind.

He liked making his meat deliveries on these fresh sunny days. Days when the forest buzzed and the birds sang. The cheeky monkeys ran alongside him, screeching from the sides of the road. He made faces at them, daring them to come within arm's reach, but they didn't. They were frightened of his deathly cargo. They screamed at the dead pigs in the back of the lorry, at the black throats gaping and trotters shuddering. They shrieked at the smell of death. But Man Po didn't care. He laughed at the silly monkeys and stuck his large head further out the window at them. Dribbling from the corner of his mouth, he sucked the saliva back up spaghetti style before banging his hand on the side of the cab to scare the jittery creatures even more.

He loved his job because it allowed him to drive his lorry all through the countryside, visit all sorts of places, and talk to lots of pretty girls. But, most of all, Man Po loved it because of the pigs. He loved scratching the coarse hair between their ears, patting their broad rumps and touching their wet snouts. He made special trips to the pig farms to take them treats. He liked to watch them fight over the tasty morsels he brought them. He liked to watch them being killed. They squealed and squealed as they were forced into a pen, then trussed, ready for slaughter, and hung while their throats were cut. Man Po liked to stand close enough to be hit by the spray as the blood spurted from the pigs' throats. He delighted in watching the last twitchings of the dying animal, its muscles keeping on moving long after it was dead. But his favourite thing of all was cutting up the carcass.

A look of panic came across his face as he remembered that he would have to look for a new job soon. He couldn't bear to think about it. Sometimes it just popped into his head and he was forced to imagine it for a few minutes until he could chase the thought away. His brother said he mustn't think about it. He mustn't worry. It would all be all right. He would find something else. But he did worry. What would he be without the pigs?

Curse the owner for selling up. What did he expect Man Po to do? If he wasn't a delivery man, if he couldn't truss up the carcass, carry it on his strong back; if he couldn't carefully, so skilfully, cut it up? What was he to be? But then Man Po smiled to himself and laughed out loud. His brother was right – he didn't need to worry, Man Po was much more than that. He was a very important person, and one day people might find out just how important he *really* was, and the things he had done. He chuckled to himself. *If only they knew . . .*

He thought about the New World restaurant and reprimanded himself. He should have found out what it was about, all that commotion, all that fuss at the restaurant and that smell! He knew that smell all right. One of the fridges at work had packed up once, and no one had realised until it was stinking the place out. But he couldn't find out what the fuss was about. He had wanted to, but he hadn't been able to; that car had been in his way and he couldn't turn in. Otherwise he would have done so. The restaurant workers knew him – he often delivered there – they would tell him what was going on.

Now he must *make up* a story ready for his return home. It would have to be a good one to entertain his old dad, Father Fong. He had time: he was in no hurry. Father Fong would be dozing in his chair right now, crouched over like a tortoise. He slept for hours every day waiting for his sons to come home. Then, when they did come back, Max would have to tell him of the streets he had travelled in his taxi – the fares who had sat in his cab – and Father Fong would imagine himself sat next to his son, driving along forgotten roads and half-remembered streets, transported back in time; back to the Hong Kong of his youth and the happy times when his first wife was alive. And Man Po would tell his father of the pigs: their funny habits, the slaughter-house, the squealing, and about the people he met on his deliveries.

Father Fong was greedy for his stories. He eagerly awaited each instalment. *Has she got the sack yet, the new one who's related to the chef?* Or, *Does anyone know who the father of the quiet one's baby is?* But it took Man Po so long to tell his account of other people's lives that his father became so excited and impatient that he pecked at Man Po – *and then and then and then . . .* – until he forced the gossip out of Man Po's mouth like regurgitated food from a gull.

Max was still dozing when his brother came in that evening, making the most of his rest before his shift began. The two brothers shared a room. They slept in bunk beds in one of the bedrooms while their father slept alone in the other. But Max was so weary he felt nauseous and too tired to sleep properly. There was a brooding weight in the atmosphere, a heavy charge in the thick air. The summer was hanging on. Max wanted the 'cool season' more than most. The summer heat and the incessant rain drove him mad. The thunder and lightning made him agitated.

Today he felt that breathless claustrophobia as he lay in the heat and dust in an airless flat, trying to breathe in a small space, and he thought his lungs were about to collapse – and, something else – that his world was about to implode.

The chatter of the two men and the noisy canary, trying to make its small voice heard above everyone else's, woke Max up from his fruitless, fitful nap. He lay on his bunk for a few minutes, straining to hear what the clamour was about. It would be the usual nonsense, he supposed. Man Po would be talking tittle-tattle, anything to punctuate the old man's day with a little excitement. But then Max heard the mention of police cars and tape and crowds and commotion.

He waited by the door, until he heard the sound of Father Fong's slippered feet shuffling away across the linoleum towards the kitchen to prepare his sons' dinner. Then he emerged.

Man Po was sat on the edge of the sofa, his legs apart and his stomach hanging between them like a sumo wrestler's. In front of him he had a collection of photos. It was Man Po's hobby, photography. He spread the photos out onto the coffee table, picking them up and rearranging them – placing them in order. Max stood behind him, looking over the top of his brother's misshapen head.

Man Po turned and grinned up at his brother as Max placed a hand on his shoulder and smiled forgivingly down at him. Max looked at the line of photos, laid edge to edge so neatly. He thought about the cupboard again and his stepmother's cruelty and he smiled to himself. He smoothed his brother's misshapen head. They had certainly made her pay for what she did to him, there was no doubting that.

34

Mann called in at the mortuary. He knew it was late but he also knew that Kin Tak would still be there. His finger hadn't even touched the reception bell when the assistant burst through the plastic curtain to meet him.

'Ah, Inspector! Good news! We have a complete victim. All we're missing is a finger.' He ushered Mann forward and through to the autopsy room. 'There are two new victims,' he said, while opening one of the heavy fridges, sliding a bag out and unzipping it. 'This is one: two legs, dismembered at ankle, knee and hip. Been frozen.'

'What does the pathologist think? Caucasian?'

'Forward curve to the femur, length of limb. Yes, Caucasian.'

'Any marks?'

'Around her ankles – at first we thought it was where she was dissected but it isn't – there's evidence she was tied tightly at the feet and then dragged and hung, by the ankles, after death. There are abrasions also, on the back of her legs, from where she was dragged.' He turned the legs over for Mann to see. 'We have sent the debris off for analysis.'

Mann looked at the feet. Her toes were beautifully polished. Someone had taken the time to give her a pedicure before killing her, but her legs were thin, the skin slack.

'Now,' Kin Tak said, moving Mann on, 'there's not much to see on this one, but the other . . . now, that's very different . . .' He zipped the first bag back up and returned it to its slot in the fridge, slid out another, wheeled it further into the room and unzipped it.

'This one's in good condition.'

Mann helped him lift the body out, first the legs, arms, torso, and then the head of a Caucasian woman. She was small-boned with curly blonde hair and freckles.

'Not frozen?'

'No.'

Mann looked at her hands, perfectly manicured like her feet. But the index finger on her right hand had been amputated neatly at the knuckle. The soles of her feet were dirty, and she had scratches on her arms and legs.

'Was she wearing anything?'

'Just a crucifix. But she did have traces of animal hide on her body, we haven't identified what yet.'

'How long had she been dead, do you think?'

'Twenty-four hours.'

'Cause of death?'

'Strangulation by ligature. A thick rope, with a knot to the side.' He illustrated graphically. 'Possibly killed by hanging. She was almost decapitated by it.'

'Was she moved after death?'

'Yes. Laid out somewhere cold for at least six hours, then moved.'

'What else?'

They turned her torso over. 'Extensive bruising and a burn made by a branding iron on her left buttock.'

Mann examined it. 'It looks like an F. Anything else?'

'Needle marks.' Kin Tak turned her arm over to show Mann the puncture marks on the inside of her elbow. 'We're waiting for the results from toxicology, but it looks like she'd been taking heroin. And guess what else we found?'

Mann could see that this was the bit the assistant had been dying to tell him, had been patiently waiting to tell him for the last hour. 'This killer, this man . . .' The assistant's small hands were shaking and he was showing more gum than teeth as he grinned up at Mann, a happy puppy. 'He likes his women *dead* receptive,' he said, giggling manically. '*Dead* receptive, get it? Get it? He likes his women with a touch of rigor mortis . . .'

'I get it. DNA?'

'No chance. They were cross-contaminated in the bag. But look, your detectives just faxed this through . . .'

He handed Mann a photo. The woman in the picture smiled provocatively out from a poor-quality modelling shot, permed blonde hair and pink pouting lips, hotpants and a crop top, and a big mouth.

Underneath, Li had written: '*Roxanne Berger from Orange County, USA. (One of the photos you wanted of the women in Lucy's flat – the most recent occupant.)*'

Mann glanced back and forth from the dismembered head on the slab in front of him to the photo in his hand. SNAP.

Mann turned to see Kin Tak was busy taking photographs. 'Do you need to do that? They'll have taken a load at the autopsy?' Mann asked.

'I thought while she was out, I might as well take them. They are before and after shots. I am making a reference book of my own. Building up a portfolio – showing my work.'

'You must have quite a collection of photos by now. How long have you been working here?'

Kin Tak stopped what he was doing. There was something about Mann's tone that he didn't understand – a hint of mistrust tinged with disgust.

'Ten years. I've seen all types,' he said, too excited to be embarrassed for long. 'Don't often get *Gwaipohs*, though.' He went back to photographing, almost oblivious to Mann's presence. 'Mr Saheed says he's never seen stitching like it – takes me ages. But I like to do a good job. I'm working my way up the ladder. I'll get there. No one loves the job like me.' He looked up and grinned. 'I like to make them look pretty again.'

35

Mann headed for the bars and restaurants of Soho. This area catered for every taste. It would be the ideal hunting ground for the Butcher.

He looked up and down the street. It was time for the *Gweilos* to come out after work. Their existence in Hong Kong was never lonely – they belonged to an exclusive club of well-paid Caucasians, and, like the Chinese, they tended to stick together in their ethnic groups. Most serial killers killed within their own races – black on black, white on white. That was why, if this was a lone serial killer, he was most likely to be white. But nothing was certain. Rules could always be broken.

Mann walked into the Havana – a long, thin bar with a raised section to the left dotted with round tables and stools, an intimate section at the back with sofas and cushions, and a rowdy bar at the front. People stopped drinking and stared as he walked in. He was used to it. All his life he'd had to fight the prejudice of being mixed race.

Most went back to their drinks after a minute, but

three white men carried on staring. The tallest one was bald. He had 'LOVE' written on one hand, 'HATE' tattooed on the other. *Should have written 'UGLY' and 'FUCK' instead*, Mann thought. He would present the least problem, he decided. The second man, slightly shorter, also bald, looked like ex-army. He was muscle-bound; obviously still went to the gym every day – didn't look like he ever got on the running machine, though. The third man, with a grade-two hair cut, was shorter, slighter, meaner, more damaged by life. He had plenty of chips on his shoulders and probably a knife pouch hidden on him somewhere.

They watched Mann walk up to the bar. He looked at them with a practised stare, then ordered a large vodka on the rocks.

Chip on his Shoulder stared straight at Mann. 'Hey, banana boy? Your mama slip on a banana skin? She really got fucked over, didn't she?' His friends laughed. 'Who was your daddy? GI? Squaddy? Who was your mama? Suzie Wong?'

Mann looked away.

'Hey, banana boy – I'm talking to you.'

You're going to be the first. Musclebound second, Ugly Fuck last.

Mann looked back and smiled. 'Hello boys. Here on holiday, are we?' He glanced around the bar. He could take all three out and cause minimum damage. He would do it as a last resort, though.

He leaned his elbow on the bar. The barman brought him his drink, a look of concern on his face. Mann smiled at him and gave him a reassuring look.

Mann made sure he stared equally at each man – made sure they all took responsibility for what was about to happen; what they were about to get themselves into.

'What's it to you?' Chip on his Shoulder's eyes were gleaming – he knew he had the two baldies to back him up. He thought he could be as antagonistic as he liked. But then, the one thing he didn't know – he didn't know Johnny Mann.

Mann grinned. 'Educational trip, is it, boys?'

'Depends what you mean by educational . . . banana boy.'

The three men laughed. They didn't take their eyes from Mann.

Mann smiled, studied each man, gave them the chance to back down before it was too late.

'I can't abide rudeness, racism, ignorance or base stupidity. And, guess what, boys? You tick all those boxes. Thought you might be here to learn some manners.'

The big bald duo shifted their bulk, took a small step towards him and flexed their muscles, ready.

Mann picked up his drink and walked past them.

'Manners are my speciality. But I'll have to teach you some other time.'

Someone had caught his eye, and she was smiling at him.

The barman leaned across to the three men.

'You were very lucky. Keep out of Johnny Mann's way for the rest of your holiday, unless you want to go home on a stretcher.'

''Avin' fun with your friends, Johnny?' said Kim,

reaching up for a kiss. She was sitting at one of the small tables on the raised section. 'Thought it was goin' to kick off. Never was much of a fuckin' negotiator, was you?'

Mann laughed. 'Sorry – bit wired. How's it going, Pussy – night off?'

'Can't decide whether to go in tonight. I'm definitely quittin' the Bond Bar.'

'Glad to hear it. What are you going to do instead?'

'I used to be good with figures – accounts, that type of thing. I could go back to it. I'm always dreamin' of doin' somethin' different.'

'To believe in one's dreams is to spend all of one's life asleep, Kim. *Make* it happen if you want it to.'

'I love it when you get all philosophical on me! Let's go back to my place and discuss the works of Nietzsche, Plato, and who was that other guy? Aristotle Onassis . . . ?'

He laughed. 'Believe me, I'd love to – but I have to take a rain check.'

She frowned. 'You look knackered. Ain't you gettin' any sleep?'

'Not much. It's a big case. Do me a favour, Kim. Take a couple of weeks off, at least. Stay home. Don't work at the bar until we catch this guy. It isn't safe. If you need money – let me know. Just stay away from the bar.'

'Awww, Johnny – that's so sweet. But I'm a big gal. I can take care of myself. You know what happens if I have to stay in? I turn into a caged animal!'

He kissed her cheek. 'I love it when that happens.

Okay, Kim . . . I'll leave it to you – just look after yourself . . . call me if you need me.'

Mann got up to leave. Kim held on to his arm.

'Thanks, Johnny. I miss you. Would be nice to talk more.'

'Sure – call me.'

As Mann walked out, he couldn't resist one last grin at the three men.

36

The call from Mamasan Rose came as Mann was on his way back to Headquarters. Bernadette hadn't been seen for three days. He went straight round to her flat.

She lived in a prestigious complex in the Mid-levels, which she shared with a load of bankers. It was the sort of accommodation that most of the foreigners on contracts lived in. The flats were spacious, had communal swimming pools, a live-in maid, and afforded a standard of living that none of the occupants had ever seen before – nor would again. The experience might be short-lived, but the imbued arrogance would stay with them forever.

Mann stood in the lounge, watching the maid clear up the previous night's revelry. A half-dressed Filipina came out of one of the rooms, saw Mann, giggled and darted straight back inside.

He stopped the maid as she passed him with another tray of empty beer bottles.

'Tell them if they're not out here in three minutes, they'll spend three days in the cells.'

That did the trick. Three men stumbled out, blinking

away the beery blur, and told him what they knew. They all had the same story – they had known Bernadette for a couple of months and they regretted giving her a room. She had proved a belligerent house guest – anti-social towards them most of the time and a huge party girl who had a temper when drunk. They had been drawing lots as to which one would tell her she had to go, when she'd disappeared and saved them the job.

Mann had a look at her room. Despite the attempts by the maid to keep up with it, it was a mess. It didn't look as if she spent much time in there.

He rummaged through her belongings and quickly found her passport. Within five minutes of Mann phoning in the information, Ng had found a match. Bernadette was the wayward daughter of an Irish MP. She had gone AWOL shortly after her father had been elected. This time the killer had chosen the wrong woman to kidnap. This woman would bring them all a heap of trouble.

Mann headed back to Club Mercedes. It was early evening and the club was just warming up. The band were playing 'Hotel California'. There was a group of mamasans giggling at the bar. A few of the larger tables in the centre were occupied by several groups of Koreans on a works bonding outing. It looked like they were forming a kitty to get one of them laid.

Mamasan Rose escorted Mann to a booth. She ordered a Diet Coke. Mann accepted the offer of a double espresso. He needed all the help he could get. He was surviving on a few snatched hours of sleep.

They went over the particulars of Bernadette's working life. Mamasan Rose told him what she knew. Bernadette was a good girl. She always came to work. It was unlike her to miss even one night at the club. She loved it: the sex. Yes, she could be difficult when drunk. *Yes*, she had a short temper, but she had a kind heart and was well-liked by everyone. She didn't really have any special clients, and, so far as Mamasan Rose knew, she had not been invited to go on holiday with anyone. Apart from that there was little else she could tell him. Bernadette didn't mix with anyone except the foreign girls, and none of them seemed to have socialised with her outside work. On her rare night off she frequented the foreign bars, especially the Irish ones, but she worked most nights anyway. She loved it. He got the point.

'Anyone see her leave that last evening?'

'The doormen. They saw her. She left alone. One of the men left at the same time, went down to the taxi rank with her. He saw her get into a cab.'

37

He arrived and slid clumsily into the circular seat, the way that overly big men do. He was a former Taiwanese wrestler of some television notoriety. He was as wide as he was tall. His neck, which spilled over his collar, was bigger than his head. His hands were like shovels. The wrinkled skin on his bald head reminded Mann of a Ferengi.

Christ! Was everything in life going to come back to Star Trek?

The wrestler sat there uncomfortably and recounted the last time he had seen Bernadette. From what Mann could gather, the wrestler was quite partial to her.

'I saw her get into a cab.'

'Why? Were you leaving at the same time?'

'Yes. I didn't feel well – gut rot.' He clutched his stomach – although the pain had long since gone, the memory was obviously lasting.

'So you decided to leave at the same time?'

'The boss told me to go. Just happened to be when Bernie was walking past. We went down in the elevator together, that's all.'

'Then she got in the cab . . . alone? You didn't offer to see her home?'

'It wasn't like that. Anyway . . . the gut rot . . .' He screwed up his face, which transformed him from 'hard man' to 'baby' in one frown. 'Not that she would have wanted me to . . . Well, maybe she might . . . I don't know . . .' He blushed like a teenager.

'Which driver?'

'I saw her get into a cab with one of the older drivers that hangs about here . . . Max. He drives a lot of the girls. Small old guy.'

'Okay, that'll do. Thanks for your help.'

Mamasan motioned to him that he could go.

'I hope you find her. Real nice girl . . . lovely . . . perfect.' The big wrestler extricated himself from the narrow seat and waddled back to his station.

Mamasan Rose apologised that she couldn't be more helpful about Roxanne Berger, but she was new to the club herself and hadn't known her. Mann would have to interview one of the others for that. She did fetch the work record for him, and it stated that the last time Roxanne Berger had worked was three months ago, in early June. He was just about to ask Mamasan Rose where she had worked before, when he caught sight of Georgina walking across the floor, on her way to sit at a table.

'I need a quick word with the English girl, Georgina Johnson. I won't keep her long.'

He stood up as she approached. As she walked across to him she was smiling, but she had lost the youthful flush to her face – she looked drawn and tired. Just as stunning, though maybe a little more practised at arriving at men's tables in heels and a revealing dress.

'Hello, Miss Johnson, please sit down. Are you okay?'

'I'm all right, thanks, but is it true that Bernie's gone missing?' Her eyes fixed anxiously on his face.

'Yes, I'm afraid it is, and I have some bad news about another hostess who used to work here.' He waited for her to sit. 'We have found the body of an American woman named Roxanne Berger.'

Georgina looked from Mann to her mamasan. She was visibly shocked.

'She had the room in Lucy's flat before me. Her things are still there.' She stared wide-eyed at Mann.

'Don't worry. But, if it's all right with you, we'll go to your flat now and get her belongings. I need to take them back to the station. I'll bring you back here after-wards, of course.'

Georgina agreed. Mann explained what he needed in Cantonese to Mamasan Rose, and she consented to losing Georgina for an hour. Georgina went to get changed.

Five minutes later, she came back. She was wearing a long skirt and a sleeveless top, her long curly hair cascading around her shoulders.

They left the club, took the elevator down, and stepped out into the hot evening air. Warm outside, cold inside, that was Hong Kong. As she walked beside him, Mann noted that now she was wearing sandals she walked properly: long strides, athletic gait. It was not something he saw often and she would lose it soon. Hong Kong's pavements were too crowded to allow for big strides. It struck Mann that it was a shame that soon she would have to learn to shuffle like everyone else.

As they passed the waiting taxi ranks, Georgina glanced towards one of the cars and raised her hand in greeting.

'You know one of these drivers?' Mann scanned the line of cars.

She pointed to the third taxi from the front. 'Max. He brings me to work in the evenings. He knows Lucy.'

'Just wait here for a moment please. I need a quick word with him.' Mann turned and started towards the cab. But, before he could reach him, Max sped off.

Mann returned, shaking his head.

'Never mind, I'll catch up with him soon,' he said, making a mental note of Max's cab number.

38

They drove in silence along the narrow back streets of Wanchai. Mann glanced across at Georgina a couple of times and she returned a half-hearted smile, but he could see that she was anxious. It wasn't nice to find out that the person who'd last slept in your bed was now sleeping in a drawer at the mortuary.

'It's here.' She pointed to the front of a small supermarket. Mann pulled up outside. As they opened the car doors they were hit by the unmistakable smell of rancid dairy goods. It was a supermarket that tried to offer something for foreigners: milk, cheese and yoghurt specially imported from New Zealand. But dairy had a habit of going bad in the unpredictable world of Hong Kong's electricity supply and broken fridges.

Next to the supermarket was a door to the residential block above. It was typical of the old residential blocks in Wanchai, Mong Kok and Kowloon. Ripe for development: scruffy, rat-infested and generally authentic old Hong Kong.

Mann followed Georgina inside. They took the lift, which was always a risky thing to do – brownouts were common – but Mann wasn't worried about being stuck in a lift. The one thing you couldn't have in Hong Kong was claustrophobia. Everything was designed small, compact and space-saving. It left Europeans feeling uncomfortably large. Anyway, if they took the stairs they'd have to negotiate whole families who lived on them, and the overwhelming stench of urine. Plus, Mann wouldn't have minded being pressed into a tiny lift in the dark with Georgina with nothing to do for two hours.

But Mann wasn't going to get that lucky. The lift came to a stop without a hitch, and they alighted to a well-lit landing with four doors leading off from the front and left. To the right were old metal-framed French doors leading to a balcony beyond. One of the tenants was hanging out her washing. The woman turned and stared but didn't speak.

Georgina unlocked the door to the apartment and led the way inside. Mann looked around. All was quiet, just the sound of a dripping tap. The flat was shabby, although there had been some attempts to make the place homely. It was dusty and airless and devoid of any natural light. It was crying out to be gutted. It smelt of damp washing and rotting linoleum. There were a few stools around the breakfast bar and a couple of chairs to the left of the entrance: straight-backed, holes in the rattan – definitely not meant for sitting in. Past the chairs were two doors. Georgina opened the second one. She walked in and hastily pulled the sheet across the bed. It amused Mann to note that she was messy.

In the centre of the tiny room was a single bed. On

the right-hand side was a single pine wardrobe and a cluttered chest of drawers. The room was dominated by two oversized windows on the far wall. Even at night the room was light – the neon glare flooded in from the street. He thought how hot it would be in the day. The flat had been designed all wrong. It was back to front. Where you needed light, in the living area, you got none. Where you wanted cool and dark, in the bedroom, you got heat and light. *Fucking Feng Shui.*

'Sorry about the mess,' Georgina said, head down, picking up scattered items of clothing as fast as she could.

'Don't worry about that. Never could stand tidy women. Makes me feel inadequate.'

She looked up and smiled gratefully at him. For a second he felt himself give that look of affection that he was so used to getting, the one that says – I care.

Shit, he thought. *Better watch that. That's definitely not what I need.*

Then it occurred to him: maybe he was just feeling paternal towards her. That scared him just as much.

She turned her back to him and bent over to retrieve the last item of discarded clothing, a size 34C balconette bra. He'd already checked out the label. *Definitely not paternal then . . .*

'Nice place,' he said, trying not to make it sound sarcastic.

'It's okay.' She stood up and opened the wardrobe, pulled out a carrier bag and a small pink suitcase. 'Bit noisy at night. All the construction work. Does it ever stop here?'

She was still jittery. She set the bags down on the bed in front of him.

'No, afraid not. Hong Kong never sleeps. Buildings go up overnight. You'll get used to it.' He picked up Roxanne's belongings. 'Okay, I have what I need now. Let's get you back to the club.'

It was as he looked at her, standing in the lurid light of intruding neon, that he felt such an urge to hold her. It took him by surprise. The feelings he had for her were not the usual. The feelings he had for Kim were straightforward – honest in their limitations. They didn't pretend to be anything other than affection and sex. It would never be love. Looking at Georgina now, he had to concede that he felt a small pang of something he didn't even want to acknowledge: an affinity; a bond. Not since Helen had he felt like this about anyone. He wasn't sure he welcomed it.

39

Georgina turned, looked at him, and hesitated, as if she felt it too and was waiting for him to say something – take charge of her destiny. But, even if he wanted to, Mann couldn't do that. He had far too much on his plate right then. He felt something more than just his job when he looked at her. He saw someone who needed him.

He stopped at the flat door. 'You know, I was hoping not to find you still working at the club, Miss Johnson. Bernadette's missing and we don't know who killed Roxanne Berger. We have found other bodies. I'm not allowed to say too much, but I want you to understand the gravity of the situation. This person killed a woman eighteen years ago, and he killed one just a few days ago. He's a very dangerous man who has managed to elude detection and capture for many years. That makes him more than lucky: it makes him clever. He picks his victims. They tend to have no family, be in their twenties, may or may not have some connection to the nightclub world . . . Does that sound familiar? I'm not saying this just to scare you. But he hand-picks these

166

women and he watches them. You should change jobs straight away. We think he strikes either very early in the morning or late at night. If you do nothing else, then at least vary your routines. Don't let him see a pattern to your movements.' He stopped abruptly. 'I am sorry I've scared you, but I'd hate to get a call about you.'

'No, don't be sorry. It's kind of you. I will start looking for something else straight away.' She stepped nearer to him and her eyes stayed on his face as if he were her salvation.

Mann could smell her perfume, feel the heat of her body. He stepped back.

'I could ask some people I know. I'm sure we could find you something else. What kind of work would interest you? Can you type?' he said, drumming his fingers in the air.

'Yes, not bad. I'll try anything, I don't mind.'

'Give in your notice and I'll ring you as soon as I hear anything.'

The drive back to the Polaris Centre was a quiet one. He knew she must be frightened. She was out of her depth and treading water but he could only do so much. He would throw her a life raft but it was up to her to paddle it to shore. She wanted something from him that he couldn't give. She wanted to be rescued. She wanted a hero. He wasn't it. He didn't want to be it for anyone.

He pulled over to let her out. She thanked him, and the smile that lit up her face returned, albeit briefly. He watched as she turned reluctantly into the centre and back towards work. She glanced back at him, her eyes still focused on him. She looked like a rabbit caught in headlights. He would have a new job for her within days. He would get the life raft inflated, sea worthy, and there his responsibility ended. Anywhere she worked would be better than Club Mercedes.

As he watched her walk away from him and back into the Polaris Centre, he felt a small sense of relief that she had listened. Then he felt uncomfortably anxious. Helen came into his head. The day she'd left would haunt him forever. He had watched her pack her suitcases. Was there nothing he could have done? He had asked himself that question hundreds of times, but the answer was always the same. Yes, probably. But, she had chosen to go, and that was something he had to live with. And he had chosen not to stop her.

He watched Georgina until she was swallowed up by the crowd. Maybe he just needed to get laid. It had been a while since that had happened. He would give Kim a call. It was early. She wouldn't be starting work yet. She'd have time to see him for a couple of hours. After all, she might have some new information for him, and undercover work was vital to the investigation.

But first there was someone else he needed to speak to.

40

The Albert was a lively pub in Central, established in the sixties. It was somewhat of an antique by Hong Kong terms. It was laid out in three bars of differing sizes and functions. The pub appealed to all ages of expats, but the younger ones stayed mainly in the middle bar, which was big, open and noisy, and difficult to get served in on a weekend. The staff were mainly British, as was the forty-year-old manageress, Mandy. Mann signalled to her as he walked in. She was right in the middle of the dinner trade. She put down her tray of accoutrements: Colman's mustard, HP sauce and Lea & Perrins.

'Hi, Mandy, how's it going? Got time for a chat?'

'A chat? Doesn't sound like you, Johnny? What's up?'

Mann smiled. He liked Mandy: she was tough, but fair. He admired her strong character. She had been dumped by a banker boyfriend ten years previously and, rather than run home, she'd made a good life for herself in the region.

'Need to talk to you for a few minutes.'

'Sure, follow me.'

She led him through the bar to the kitchen beyond

and out to the staff smoking room, which doubled as the back alley. There were two stools and a pile of cigarette butts.

'Sit down, make yourself at home,' she said, pulling her stool nearer so she could hear him over the noise of the extractors. 'But, before you start, Johnny, I want to know why you haven't been in here for ages, and, even now, you turn up without a woman?'

She was grinning but he saw her eyes searching his, knowing that it was a sensitive subject and wondering if she had gone too far.

He smiled reassuringly and shook his head. 'You know me, Mandy, career comes first.'

'Rubbish!' she snorted. 'Just because she hurt you, Mann, doesn't mean they all will.'

Mann was beginning to feel uncomfortable. Any mention of his ex always made him feel like someone had just pushed him off a cliff.

'I need to find myself someone like you, Mandy.' He grinned.

'Huh!' She laughed. 'I'm too old.'

'You can't be *much* more than fifty.'

'Cheeky bastard! Anyway, I'm far too bolshy for you. We wouldn't last five minutes – one of us would be jumping off the sixtieth floor. But thanks for the offer anyway. I'm serious, though, Johnny. It's been more than two years now – about time you moved on. Did you ever hear from her?'

'I watched her go, Mandy.' He shrugged sadly. 'She definitely wanted out. Anyway, can I please get back to the reason I came here?'

'Okay. Go on.'

'We found some bodies – five altogether – dumped out in the New Territories.'

'Is that all? Christ! I wouldn't be surprised if there weren't dozens of them out there. Triads killing other triads. Hopefully that'll get rid of a few more.'

'This is different, Mandy. All the victims were women, women like you.'

'What do you mean . . . *Gwaipohs*?'

'Yes. All foreign women. We think they were mainly workers in the entertainment industry, nightclubs, but we are only just beginning to put names to faces here, Mandy. *And*, we have no idea how many victims there are, how many more will turn up. This man's been around a long time, we're sure of that. His psychological profile is all over the place. We have to assume he could be anybody . . . He could be a regular of yours, sitting at your bar every night. He could be Foxy, Toad . . . whatever their stupid names are. Have a think.'

'All right, Johnny. I'll be careful and I'll be vigilant . . . I promise.'

'Another thing. Have you got any jobs going here at the moment? I need to get this young Englishwoman out of a club. She's a nice girl. You'll like her.'

Mandy raised an inquisitive eyebrow. '*And?*'

'There's no *and*. Just wanted to help her, that's all.'

'Help get her horizontal and naked, you mean?'

'Maybe, but preferably not on a mortuary slab.'

'Tell her to ring me. I have an Aussie guy returning home next week. She can take his place. She'll have to work various shifts, some evenings, some days, but I'll keep her on earlies.'

Mann leaned over and kissed Mandy's cheek. 'I owe you, Mandy. Ring me if you suspect anything,' he said, getting up to leave. 'And be careful.'

'Okay, I will. Come again soon, Johnny. You don't visit often enough any more. But remember what I said,' she called after him as he disappeared up the alleyway, weaving his way past the piles of dumped rubbish. 'I want to see you with a new woman.'

'Yeah, yeah. Maybe,' said Mann, with a backward wave.

He called Georgina and left a message on her phone, telling her about the job in the Albert and leaving Mandy's number. He felt a sense of relief. He'd done all he could.

Kim was waiting for him when he got round to her place. He was late. She had started getting dressed for work. He told her to take it all off again.

Two hours later he was back at Headquarters, sorting through Roxanne Berger's belongings. The place was heaving. Police officers were arriving from everywhere to help with the case. Ng was on the phone when Mann walked into the office. Li was out chasing the path lab results. Mann began emptying out Roxanne's possessions onto his desk. There wasn't a lot worth looking at. A few items of clothing, cheap jewellery, lots of make-up. Inside a handbag he found her passport, but there was little else of any significance. He had the impression that someone else, probably Lucy, had been cherry-picking through her things.

Ng got off the phone as Mann was putting everything back in the bag.

'They've traced Roxanne Berger's only relative, her husband, Darren. Guess what?' Mann waited. 'He had already remarried. He's facing a bigamy charge now. And that, coupled with the assault charge his new bride is bringing against him, should see him locked away in a small room without a window for some time.'

41

Mann finally made it back to his apartment. David White had said he looked like shit, and that he needed a shave and a shower and a few hours in a proper bed. Mann had argued, then given in. He didn't much like going home. It wasn't a home. Since Helen left he'd felt more and more uncomfortable there. It was where he kept his stuff, crashed, showered and watched too many DVDs. It would be better to sell it, but he couldn't be bothered. It was a good investment, after all, even if he didn't like living there.

He switched on the air-con, washed his face, tore off his shirt and fell onto his bed. Within seconds he was asleep.

He woke up feeling worse. He sat on the edge of his bed, reeling from tiredness, unable to focus for a few seconds. Then he checked his watch. He'd been asleep for three hours. That would have to do. He rang in to work, and Li answered.

'I've been waiting for you to ring in, boss,' he said, unable to curb the high-pitched excitement that had crept into his voice.

He'd never make a poker player.

'What is it?'

'We've got some results back from the lab. It's been confirmed that there were traces of heroin in Roxanne Berger's blood. She'd had sexual intercourse several times in the last few hours before she died, and after. The traces of animal on her turned out to be calf skin. So, this is what I think . . .' Li paused to draw breath. 'I think someone dressed her up as a cave girl, raped her, branded her and then hanged her. Then they came back later, dragged her off somewhere and had sex with her again after she was dead.'

'Yeah, well, hang on to that theory, but keep working on it, Li. Get on to the pathologist. I want to know if Roxanne Berger's tongue had been bitten.'

'Why? Do you think the Butcher did it?'

'No, I think she did it herself.'

'Why? How?'

'Just do it, Shrimp. If I'm right I'll tell you why, and if I'm wrong I'll tell you anyway. Also, I want a biopsy done of the tissue around the nipples on victims three and five. Run more tests on all victims. I want to know if any of the others had heroin in them. He must be giving it to them for a reason. Research it, Li. Any fingerprints from the bag itself? And find out for me how many stages of fly larvae we have on each of the victims. If there's more than one, can the pathologist identify if one set was laid before they were frozen and if it had developed past the first stage? We want to be clear about how long the bodies are being held somewhere before being frozen. And Shrimp . . .'

'Yes, boss?'

'You're doing a good job.'

'Awesome.'

42

Lucy was slumped on a stool in front of the Dressing Room mirrors. She had no idea what she was going to do, the problem just kept getting worse. She had been pulling in every punter she could – too many. Mamasan said the clients were beginning to notice Lucy looking over their shoulders and had told her off for being greedy. And now Georgina had left Club Mercedes and was about to start work in the English pub! Chan would not be happy about that.

Lucy had no more money to give him. She had already parted with her entire savings. But none of that would matter to Chan, Lucy knew that much. He would want his money in some form or another. It remained now to find out what 'another' would turn out to be. Georgina had given her a few hundred Hong Kong out of her wages towards her keep, but that wasn't going to go far. It was as much as Lucy could expect to get now that Georgina was working at the pub and earning a lot less than she was at the club. And Ka Lei was still a student. What was Lucy going to do?

She held her head in her hands and groaned.

A hand on her shoulder made her jump.

'Come, Lucy! Big American look for you!' Mamasan Linda interrupted her thoughts.

There! thought Lucy. *Just when things seem darkest, Big Frank comes in! There's always hope.*

He could be her chance to solve all her problems. She tried a smile into the mirror, turning her head to view it from all angles. She stood and smoothed the creases from her dress . . .

Perfect.

That evening Georgina started her new job. Ka Lei wrote 'The Albert' in Chinese on a piece of paper for her before she left for her shift at the hospital. Georgina couldn't risk being late, or getting into a cab with a driver who wasn't about to risk 'loss of face' and admit that he couldn't understand where she wanted to go, so would take her somewhere completely different. That happened a lot in Hong Kong.

She arrived with thirty minutes to spare. Mandy looked up from cleaning tables as Georgina walked in.

'Ah, you must be Georgina. Welcome to the Albert. Have you ever worked in a pub before?'

'No, I worked in a bookshop back in England.'

'Don't worry. Just keep smiling and you'll be perfect for this job. But there are a few rules: don't drink too much, be polite at all times, don't rip the customers off, and don't charge for sex. Give it away by all means – the place'll be packed – but don't charge. Okay?'

Mandy laughed as Georgina blushed crimson and shook her head vigorously. 'Don't worry, I don't mean it. I know you're a decent girl. Mann says so and Mann should know, he's had enough of them. Okay, sorry. What I mean is that Mann's a good judge of character. Still, it's good to see him taking an interest in someone again. You're a lucky woman. Johnny's one of the good ones.'

'He seems nice, but I don't really know him very well. And we're not *together*.' Georgina looked uncomfortable.

'Not yet, anyway.' Mandy laughed. 'Believe me, he never used to be so slow off the mark. It's a case of "once bitten" with Johnny. He let the last one slip away. Dumb bastard should have put a ring on her finger – commitment-phobe like the rest of them.'

'What happened?'

'She was great, Helen – funny, bright. Everyone liked her. She was a hostess when he met her, gave it up when she got serious with Johnny. Then she worked as a PA for a local firm. They seemed very happy. They were together for five years, but they didn't progress on to the next step. Helen got tired of waiting for him to commit. He carries a lot of baggage, does Johnny. Anyway, she was going to try leaving him to see if he came after her to beg her to come back. See if he would finally realise that she was *the one*. So, she left, and by the time he realised that *the one* was exactly what she was, she'd gone for good. He's been moping ever since. Come on, I'll introduce you to the rest of the inmates.'

Georgina followed Mandy and met the other workers. They were a mixed bunch: a Scottish chef, an Irish barman, a barmaid from New Zealand and two big surfer types from Oz who worked as a double act behind the main bar, and several more kitchen staff. They were an interesting mix, very energetic and friendly.

The first night flew by and Georgina found herself enjoying it immensely. Mandy told her what she would be doing. She would be working shifts, six days a week. She would start by bringing the food orders out and progress to serving behind the bar when she was ready. The pay was pretty appalling but the job was fun. She had forgotten how nice it was to be with people whose sole aim in life was to have a good time. It reminded her of her late teens, a time of boyfriends and parties and no worries, before her mother got ill. She hadn't realised how wonderful that time had been until now. Two weeks went by so fast. The Albert opened up a whole new world, not just for Georgina but also for Ka Lei. Whenever her shifts allowed, Ka Lei came to meet Georgina from work and joined in with the socialising that went on after hours. They were invited to parties and picnics and endless barbecues. Life was beginning to feel like fun. But not for Lucy.

43

Lucy was glad to see that Frank was waiting for her one evening. She was working long hours every night and coming back to an empty house. She slid in beside him.

'Good evening, Flank,' she simpered. 'Why you no come see me long time? What matter, Flank? You no love your little Hong Kong girl no more?' She looked at him curiously. He was a mess. 'You okay, big man?' He didn't smell so good either and his left eye was twitching uncontrollably. 'Wha matter, Flank? You sick?'

'Just lovesick, honey.' He patted a bag next to him on the seat. 'Got some toys for us to play with.'

'Oh learly? Got sometin nice for your goo little Hong Kong girl?'

'Got something *really* nice for my *naughty* one.' The twitching moved to the other eye.

They wasted no time in finding themselves a love motel, where Big Frank unzipped his bag and pulled out an assortment of whips, leather apparatus and ponytail attachments. Lucy laughed out loud at the peephole leather, but Big Frank was too excited to be in the mood for laughing. He had some *serious* fun in mind.

'Was these, Flank?' Lucy pulled out some leather chaps.

'Those are what I wear when I'm out herdin' up steer.'

'Steer?'

'Cattle. Cows. Moo Moos.' He pulled her to him, crushing her with a bear hug. 'I'm gonna herd you. But first . . .' he reached into the bag '. . . I've gotta catch you . . .'

And he brought out his lasso.

44

Johnny Mann walked through the lobby of the Peninsula Hotel. It was prime cocktail time. He was looking for James Dudley-Smythe. Mamasan Rose had remembered that he had bought Bernadette out a few days before she disappeared.

People watched him walk through. Mann was used to getting stared at. He didn't slot neatly into any pigeon hole – which suited him. Being a Eurasian he was at ease in both worlds but belonged to neither.

The pianist was playing Sinatra songs. Mann headed for the corner of the lobby bar where he knew James liked to hold court. James still had enough clout and enough money to call in a few friends to drink with most nights. They were the same sorts – lonely old drunks that had made their money and were now spending it on drinking themselves to death.

James saw Mann coming from some distance. His stare was fixed on the Inspector. He was more alert than Mann had given him credit for. But then a pretty young blonde passed in front of Mann and he saw James's eyes refocus on her. The two other red-faced, white-haired paunch bellies looked up as Mann reached them. They stared at him as if he were a bad smell.

James smiled: thin, wet-lipped. 'Johnny, dear boy. Come, come. What is it now? Need my help again?'

The other two tittered nervously.

'How did you guess? Want to talk to you about some Irish connections, some business transaction you might have made. Do you mind?' Mann pulled up a chair and sat between James and his friends. 'Won't keep him long, gentlemen.'

They lumbered out of their seats, grumbling disdainfully, and went to find someone else to buy them drinks. James looked like he was just getting into the evening.

'You bought out a girl the other night . . . Irish . . . from Club Mercedes . . . Ring a bell?'

James was shaking his head before Mann had even finished asking. Then he looked at Mann's face and his head switched to nodding. 'Actually, dear boy, now that you mention it – I think I did. Big girl – broad accent. Lovely hair – that the one? Bernadette?'

'That's the one. She's gone missing. You were the last client she went out with.'

'She left in the morning,' he said, a little too hastily. 'I paid her and she left. You know how it is, dear boy – my memory is not so good these days. As far as I remember we had a lovely evening –'

'Okay, James.' He'd probably passed out early, Mann thought. He seemed to be better at remembering the morning more than anything else. 'If anything comes back to you, let me know.'

'Count on it, dear boy. I will search the innermost

crevices of my pickled old brain and see if I can remember anything to help you.'

Mann left him to it. On his way back to Headquarters he had the urge to call in at the Albert. Georgina had been working there for nearly three weeks now.

She was chatting to some regulars at the end of the bar as he walked in. She didn't see him. He stood watching her, smiling to himself. She seemed so settled. It looked as if she had always been there. She was a changed woman – confident and sexy in her T-shirt and jeans – and she looked happy. He was glad. She must be safer in here than in Club Mercedes. Plus, now that he saw her in different surroundings he knew there was definitely something about her that he liked. Strong, cocky women usually did it for him. At first he thought that Georgina might be the exception, but now that he was watching the way she talked to the customers, joked with the other members of staff. The way she moved – strong and confident, maybe that's exactly what she was; she just didn't realise it yet.

She still hadn't seen him and she disappeared behind the bar to pour some drinks. As he watched her he realised, *God knows why*, that he was proud of her. Maybe it was because she had thrown herself in the deep end by coming to Hong Kong. She had shown guts and determination. He admired her for that.

Mandy came through from the other bar and caught sight of him. She followed his eyes to Georgina and was about to alert her to his presence when Georgina disappeared into the other bar.

'Hello, Johnny. Come to check up on her?' said Mandy, walking over.

'Just checking on all foreign staff, that's all.'

'Especially Georgina?' She laughed. Mann started to leave. 'Won't you stop and say hello, now that you're here?'

'I wish I could, but I'm up to my eyes at work at the moment. You say hello from me, okay?' He was backing out of the door.

Mandy wouldn't let him go. She followed him as far as the door.

'She's a really nice girl, lots of men have been asking her for a date, so you'd better watch you're not neglecting her.'

'I wish I had the time to come in, but I've been working on this case. Anyway, I told you, Mandy – I'm not looking for romance at the moment.'

'Yes, well, sometimes it comes looking for you, Mann. Remember that. Love is not a sign of weakness, Johnny.'

'You're just an old romantic at heart, Mandy. I never knew that.' He laughed at her.

'Less of the "old", and I never knew you were a quitter.'

'Sorry, Mandy. Can't hear you. Bye.' Mann was already out of the door.

'Catch you soon, okay?' Mandy stood, hands on hips, with a 'don't mess it up again' look on her face that women seemed to be born with.

As Mann stepped out onto the street he caught sight of Max pulling away in his cab.

45

Max had only just got up from his daytime sleep and was running a few errands for his father before starting work, when Mann shouted to him to stop. Mann could see that, just for a second, Max contemplated ignoring him and driving off. Mann shouted again and stepped into Max's line of vision; he wasn't going to let Max get away twice – he'd have to run him over or stop. Max stopped. Mann walked around to the driver's side and leaned into the cab.

'I've been looking for you, Max.'

'Huh?'

'You're a regular taxi driver for the hostesses at Club Mercedes, aren't you? I need to talk to you about one of the girls – Roxanne Berger. You knew her, I understand?'

'I gave her a lift to work, that's all.'

'Where do you live, Max?'

'In Sheung Wan.'

'Alone?'

'No. I live with my father and brother.'

'What does he do – your brother?'

'He's a meat delivery man.'

'For whom?'

'The Ho Young Dim Sum Manufacturers.'

'They're closing down, aren't they? Selling up?'

'Yes. Yes.' Max was sweating. He fiddled with his keys and looked nervously into the mirror as if their conversation was causing a massive traffic jam, which it was. He started the engine and prepared to drive away.

Mann leaned further in and placed a hand on the steering wheel. He had seen something on Max's arm. 'Looks nasty.' He pointed to a bite mark, the edge of which was just visible beneath the cuff of Max's shirt-sleeve. The skin, angry and inflamed, bulged around the puncture marks. Max hastily covered it up.

'You should get that looked at. Human bites carry a big risk of infection.'

'It's nothing, nothing. It's not human – it was a dog.' He put the car into gear.

'What time do you finish your shift?'

'About eight a.m., sometimes earlier, sometimes later. I never know.'

Mann released his hold on the steering wheel. 'See you at Headquarters at five past eight. Don't be late. Ask for Detective Sergeant Ng.'

As Mann stepped back from the taxi and watched Max speed away, he realised that something was bothering him. Somewhere in his memory bank a series of images were searching for each other and trying to find their match. Among those images was Max. Just as Mann thought he was about to get it, it was gone.

His phone rang. It was Li.

'Are you ready, boss?' Li's breathless voice screeched into the phone.

'For what?'

'Ever been to Poland, boss?'

'No.'

'They have this awesome legend about two mermaid chicks. There's a statue of one of them, with a sword and shield and stuff, defending Warsaw.'

'And . . .'

'There is one tattooist in Warsaw who specialises in drawing this mermaid. I emailed a photo of the tattoo to him and . . .'

'Go on.'

'He recognised it straight away. It's a one-off. He said he only ever drew it once, for one person – his sister. After that he changed it, made some modifications, gave it a boob job, so that the mermaid looked less like a fish and more like Pamela Anderson. Victim three – the torso – *has* to be the tattooist's sister.'

'Well done, Li. What else could he tell us about her?'

'Not much. They fell out years ago. He said that, the last he heard, she'd been working her way round the Far East. She could have been in Hong Kong. He didn't know. Basically, he couldn't give a shit.'

'Did she have any other family?'

'Nope.'

'What's her name?'

'Gosia Sikorska. I looked in the file. She lived in Lucy's flat in Wanchai two years ago. She was one of the women Lucy mentioned in her statement – the one with the strong accent – but she never said anything about a tattoo. She worked in Club Mercedes for six months.'

Mann hung up and checked the time before calling Lucy's mobile. It was six thirty, she wouldn't be going to work for a couple of hours yet; she'd have time to see him first.

He caught the Star ferry across to Kowloon side. This part of Hong Kong didn't have the charm of the cobbled ladder streets on the Island, or the colonial mansions, or the Peak, but Kowloon had Tsim Sha Tsui, second only to Central for business, and bird markets, jade markets and night markets. Best of all it had the the New Territories. A precious wilderness with fantastic beaches and glorious picnic spots. Where it was possible to find space and freedom and, in the last month, bags of bodies.

The evening was cool and the ferry was quiet. It had deposited its business-suited customers on to the next stage in their journeys home, and it had taken the tourists back to change for dinner. Now it glided across the water, serene and unhurried, making the most of the respite.

Mann walked briskly up the gangplank and off in the direction of Nathan Road; a road that ran vertical from the harbour, long and straight – the Golden Mile. It was *the* place to buy watches, perfumes and electricals. It was awash with Indians selling fake anything. Every square inch of Nathan Road screamed something: *try me – buy me – you can't live without me . . .*

The neon made Mann sweat and the thumping bass

made him deaf. At every doorway a different song was spat out then batted away and replaced by another at the next step. Every doorway multiplied to five and the pavement disappeared as people fought for every inch of retail territory. He gave up trying to walk down it and took off on a side road, cutting across until he came to the Excalibur Hotel, halfway up Nathan Road, eight hundred metres down a side street. The Excalibur was an 'old school' type of hotel whose rooms were slightly shabby but well soundproofed. It had a small pool on the roof and its coffee shop was renowned for the fine pastry chef. It was a hotel that most foreigners were familiar with because it specialised in offering not-too-cheap package holidays to Brits and was always full. Helen had loved going there for a late breakfast. It was nice to walk to it along the harbour.

He was thinking about Helen again. Maybe the thing with Georgina had got him thinking *What if*? What if he'd tried harder? What if he'd been prepared to give it a chance? What if he'd wanted the things she'd wanted? *What fucking if?*

ENOUGH!

Mann walked through the lobby and past the lounge bar, where a pianist was tinkling away forgettable tunes for the cocktail lounge clientele of post-shoppers and pre-diners to chat over. He walked down a short flight of stairs to Oliver's Bar in the basement.

Oliver's Bar was overdone in 'Old English Stylee'. It was dark red, oak-panelled and tartan-infested. Straight ahead of the entrance was a hexagonal bar. Tables and chairs fanned out from it on two levels, all in regimented restaurant fashion. Further to the right of the entrance was a lounge area, with a brick fireplace and a living-flame gas fire that gave out no warmth. Above the fire was a decorative arch and an oak bookshelf dotted with mock-leather faux Dickens first editions.

Mann gave an involuntary shiver as he hit the wall of air-conditioning that sat waiting for him just inside the entrance. He scanned the bar. There were just a few customers. It was happy hour, but the lure of cheap drinks had proven easy to resist. It wasn't the most atmospheric of bars, but the good thing about it was there was usually space to sit and chat and at least you didn't have to compete with a piano.

A few locals were ensconced around the far end of the bar, obviously hailing from the 'snifter' brigade where one drink always turned into seven. There was a young couple at one of the tables, as far away from the bar as they could get, gazing intently into each other's eyes. And then there was Lucy, sitting side-saddle on a stool at the bar and wearing her trademark leather trousers, black-ribbed polo neck and gold chain. She was snacking on peanuts and drinking Coke through a straw.

When she saw Mann she slid off her stool, picked up her drink, and followed him over to a table near the fire. Mann signalled to the barman that he would have his usual. As he did so, one of the snifter brigade looked up and held his gaze. Mann stared back. The man was white, early fifties, silver-haired, well-groomed. He looked like he had money and looked after himself. As Lucy left the bar, she nodded to the man.

'Good evening, Inspector,' she said, setting her drink down and positioning herself in the armchair opposite. Then, as she smiled at him, Mann saw the only similarity between her and Georgina – a mouth that formed an almost perfect circle, topped with a cupid's bow. Hers was painted deep red to match her nails.

'Do you know that man?' He nodded in the direction of the bar.

'I met him once. He's a surgeon.' She giggled softly, looking Mann over. 'Lives in a nice apartment. Loves his clothes. Smart dresser, like you.'

Mann looked over. The surgeon was once again talking to his colleagues.

'Do you always wear Armani? You look very handsome.' She tipped her head to one side, picked up her Coke, searched for the straw with her tongue, and flicked it into her mouth.

The barman arrived and set down his drink. Mann looked hard at Lucy. She was full of games. She certainly had balls.

'No, I don't always wear Armani.'

'Always wear designer, though? Not fake, made in Hong Kong. You wear genuine Paris, Milan. Am I right? Last time I saw you, you were in Valentino – very expensive – very nice.'

Mann smiled. She was definitely bold. This woman could handle herself and just about anybody else. She was one of Hong Kong's survivors. You never got to see the ones who didn't make it. There was no place for them in Hong Kong.

He picked up his attaché case and unzipped it. 'You

have a good memory, Lucy – impressive. Strange you didn't remember this then . . .' He threw the blow-up photo of Gosia's tattoo in front of her. 'Do you recognise it?'

Lucy glanced at the photo casually. 'No, I don't.'

'You never saw Gosia Sikorska's tattoo?'

'This is Gosia?' Lucy's jaw dropped.

'What's left of her . . . yes. And you never saw the tattoo before?'

'I knew she had a tattoo but I never saw it. She was very modest.'

Yeah, right . . .

'. . . And you gave descriptions of other girls who lived in your apartment. Thanks for that. But they weren't terribly detailed, were they, Lucy? I expected you to remember something about the women you lived with. You could be describing any foreign women, any place, anywhere. You lived with these women. You must have known them better than this?' He rattled her statement.

Lucy shrugged. 'You know how it is. When I first started to take in the *Gwaipohs*, I got to know them, made friends. But, after the first few, when they came and went so fast, I couldn't be bothered any more. Mostly they kept themselves to themselves. They preferred it. I didn't like to pry.'

You have to be kidding – you're a woman – you never get tired of finding out about other people's lives. That's what made the female detectives so good at their job.

'Well, if any more tattoos, birthmarks, glass eyes or wooden legs come to mind, you'll let me know?'

'Of course, Inspector. Immediately.'

'And Lucy . . .' Mann leaned forward and tilted Lucy's chin upwards. 'If you are hiding *something*, protecting *someone*, in the hope of getting something *out* of it, I should warn you, you may get more than you bargained for.'

Lucy called his bluff and raised him some.

'I completely understand, Inspector.' She pursed her lips around the straw and sucked.

Mann looked back at the bar – the surgeon had gone.

46

Mann took the MTR back to the Island. It was quicker than the ferry and there was something refreshing about it. So different from London or Paris, where you descended into darkness and depression that made so many want to finally seek that last resort and jump under an approaching train. In Hong Kong, after descending from the infernal noise, heat and crowds above, you found bliss: cool, air-conditioned, clean, white-walled, wide passageways, and hardly any people. Bliss . . .

He got out at Wanchai and cut across Johnson Road to the Bond Bar.

'All right, Sam? How's business? Plenty of punters?' he asked as he came down the steps.

'Very good, sir, and yours? Plenty of bodies?' Sam grinned.

'Word's out, huh? Thought it wouldn't take long. Enough bodies to keep me busy, thanks, Sam. Is Kim working tonight?' he asked as he stepped inside.

'Kim's gone, Inspector.'

'Gone where?'

'She said she'd found a better job. Left today. She brought me this. Look . . .' He extended his arm, and beneath the red satin sleeve was a diamond-encrusted fake Rolex. 'It's a really good one – keeps perfect time.'

'That's nice. Where did she go?'

'Sorry, Inspector, she wouldn't say.'

Mann went inside. There was a new girl at Kim's station. She was auburn-haired, pretty, with a small muscular frame, pert breasts and nipples like pencil tips. She was dressed in lace knickers. Mann was just about to go over for a chat when he caught Honey Ryder looking at him from across the room. She was entertaining a couple of Chinese middle management who were escorting some visiting Americans and showing them a good time on the company account.

He made his way across to her. She looked up and beamed her beguiling gap-toothed smile at him as he approached. She'd exchanged the French knickers for a black thong and a laced red and black corset that ended beneath her small round breasts, pushing them up and emphasising them perfectly – like pink tennis balls. The corset would have looked tacky on anyone else, but on Honey it just looked like she'd been rifling through her mum's 'Saturday night' drawer and was about to get found out any minute. There was always something about Honey that begged to be spanked.

'Good evening, Johnny. The usual?' she asked, wiggling like a child wanting the toilet.

'Thanks, Honey. How's things? I see you've got your convent outfit on.' He perched on the suede-covered stool.

She giggled shrilly and spun away to make his drink. She dropped the ice noisily into his glass and overfilled it before spinning back round to face him.

'Everything's super, thanks, Johnny,' she said, flicking her long fringe away from her eyes with a shake of the head.

He had forgotten how pretty Honey was: her green eyes and a sprinkling of freckles over her nose. She *looked* and *was* still a little girl, not woman enough for Mann. Whenever possible he tried to avoid the 'fucked-up little girl' ruined by some man or other – *probably her father* – who was still trying to make herself into a beguiling child to get love, even from strangers.

She leaned towards him and Mann wondered if she had freckles everywhere.

'But I'm sure you want to know something else,' she said, setting his drink down.

'You're right, Honey.' Mann glanced towards Kim's station. 'Just curious. Where did she go? Did she say?'

Honey tilted her head to one side and twiddled with her hair, rocking back and forth on her heels. 'She said you wouldn't like it if you knew, Johnny. She said I wasn't to tell you. But . . .' She stopped rocking and sat up straight. 'She's not here and I am.' She giggled, then looked up at him from beneath her fringe. 'Remember that, Johnny. When you get lonely, you can always give me a call. I'll bring my teddy bear and we can sleep over.'

'That's very sweet of you, Honey. I will certainly do that, and tell Teddy to wear stockings.'

She giggled again.

'Where did she go, Honey?'

Honey rolled her eyes. 'All right, you win. She went to work for some bloke – I don't know who. She was offered a lucrative job, in-house somewhere.'

'Where?'

'All she said was that she didn't actually know where it was going to be, that it might not even be in Hong Kong. She said she'd call as soon as she could. But she hasn't.' Honey pursed her lips into a tight, small smile and cocked her head to one side. 'And you know how it is, Johnny . . .' She wiggled again – playful and eager. 'Out of sight, out of mind. Here's my number in case you've lost it. And remember – any time, don't hesitate, Teddy and I will be waiting.'

Mann walked back up to join Johnson Road, one of the main roads leading down to Causeway Bay. It was heaving. Every square inch was in motion. Intrusive neon flooded the street with false light and created day when it was night . . . Sam was having his usual banter with a few loud-mouthed tourists. Around the corner a scuffle was breaking out. Mann almost ignored it. There were plenty of coppers around patrolling the streets, they would deal with it in a minute. He *almost* turned and walked away, until he heard a familiar sound:

'Hey, banana boy?'

The three men from the Havana Bar were walking his way. Mann turned and smiled. 'Come for your lesson, boys?'

'We heard you were some martial arts expert. We were in the Marines. We reckon we're a match for you, banana boy . . .'

They fanned out – the two baldies to Mann's right, the small one to his left.

Mann moved towards the passageway at the side of the Bond Bar, where the rubbish was dumped from the restaurants that backed onto it. He held up both his hands in a peace gesture then he stepped forward and put his arm around the shoulder of Ugly Fuck.

'I can see you just want to have a good time: get drunk, get laid. Let me tell you where's the best place to go for that.'

The big guy grunted his agreement. He was the most used to fighting and the most keen to avoid it when he could. Mann looked past him to the other two and saw Chip on his Shoulder nod, roll his eyes Mann's way, and reach for a knife pouch he had hidden in his waistband.

Mann gripped Ugly Fuck hard and swung him round. The man took a heavy blow to the side of his head, delivered by Musclebound and meant for Mann. Ugly Fuck staggered back, hit the wall behind and sank into the piles of rotting veg waiting for collection. The punch had off-balanced Musclebound and Mann was right in thinking he didn't have the speed in his feet to get out of trouble. While Mann's left hand delivered a punch to Musclebound's throat, his right hand snapped Chip on his Shoulder's wrist. There was a sickening crack and a bestial scream as the smaller man dropped the knife and staggered off clutching his arm.

Mann walked away. 'Hope you enjoyed your lesson, boys,' he said over his shoulder.

47

Chan sat in the back of his car. He was early. He wanted to be there first. He had set up the meeting on mutual territory. It was in a small restaurant in Kowloon. It would be easy to guard. Privacy was paramount.

His driver drove past once. Chan peered inside. It looked dead. He had instructed the owner to shut it for the evening.

He drove past the restaurant again. The owner had closed it, as instructed. The place looked empty – dark. He saw the owner come nervously to the door of his restaurant and make last-minute checks to ensure all was as it should be. This was a big moment for him. It was a big moment for all of them. Chan was about to carve his own name in the triad world. He knew he wasn't going to get promotion from his role of legal advisor, Paper Fan, to Incense Master and Deputy Mountain Master. They were dead men's shoes and he couldn't wait for that. So, if he couldn't kill them off, he would spread sideways within the Wo Shing Shing and create his own society. He would use the cloak of the Wo Shing Shing to hold the men's allegiance to him. CK would know nothing about it. Their loyalty would be to Chan. When he had collected enough powerful allies he would be in a position to oust his father-in-law. The promises of wealth and power would be enough to convert several prominent Chinese officials.

Chan parked up. He left the driver in the car and took three men with him. One of them was his second-in-command – Stevie Ho. Stevie held the rank of Grass Sandal. His role was one of collector of debts, organiser of meetings. He was a stocky man, taller than average, with a goatee beard and a bald head. He had sustained an injury across the right eye, and one side of his face didn't match the other. He was an ex-policeman.

Stevie had joined the force at the same time as Johnny Mann. They were cadets together. After he graduated, Stevie was given the opportunity to go undercover and infiltrate the triad gangs. He'd accepted it gladly, and before three years was up Stevie was a fully fledged member of the Wo Shing Shing. The temptations proved too much. It was a common problem with undercover work. There was no middle road to walk. The other two men with them, Chan's bodyguards, were ordinary members, the lowest ranking in the triad world.

The restaurant owner met them at the door. Bowing continuously, he stood back to let them pass.

'Show us the room where it is to take place,' said Stevie, and shook his hand with the secret handshake.

The owner led them through to the back room. It

was barely lit and clouded with the pungent smell of incense. In the centre of the room an altar was laid out, with two brass single-stemmed candlesticks, three red stones, a brass bowl for burning paper, a jug of wine and five wine cups, a pot of tea and three tea bowls, and a small thin-bladed knife. To the right of the room, on the wall, was a mock gateway, above which was a piece of yellow paper.

'Good,' said Stevie, and nodded his approval in the direction of the owner, who bowed repeatedly and wiped the sweat from his head with his apron.

Stevie and the others were all dressed in simple cotton suits. He handed Chan his robes – a red Buddhist-style monk's garment. The restaurant owner announced the arrival of the new recruit. Stevie went out to meet him and led him in. He was a short man, in his late sixties, wearing glasses. He had thinning hair and a large round head. He was an important minister in the Fujian Province in China.

The man stood at the doorway and opened his shirt to reveal a bare chest. Then he removed his shoes and stood barefoot. It was tradition that he should make himself appear poor and dishevelled. In his hand he carried a yellow piece of paper, on which he had written his name and his pledge to Chan and the Wo Shing Shing.

Stevie led him forward and stopped beneath the symbolic gateway of the east lodge, over which was hung the sheet of yellow paper.

'Swear to your identity,' Chan said.

'I swear I am Sun Yat-sen.'

Chan took the man's hand and shook it with the new secret handshake that he must use. His index outstretched to press into Sun Yat-sen's palm, his middle and fourth finger tucked away, and with his little finger he tapped the outside of the minister's hand three times. The two bodyguards picked up the swords and held them aloft to form an arch. This would represent the mountain of knives which had been part of the triad initiation since the beginning. After leading the minister beneath the archway, Stevie lit the two candles on the altar and handed the minister three red stones, which he held in his hands as he began to read the thirty-three oaths.

I shall not disclose the secrets of this society, not even to my parents, brothers or my wife. I shall never disclose the secrets for money. I will be killed by a myriad of swords if I do so.

I will offer financial assistance to sworn brothers who are in trouble. If I break this oath I will be killed by five thunderbolts.

I must not give support to outsiders if so doing is against the interests of any of my sworn brothers. If I do not keep this oath I will be killed by a myriad of swords.

If I should change my mind and deny my member-ship of this society I will be killed by a myriad of swords.

And so on.

The oaths done, Stevie handed Sun Yat-sen a small bowl of cleansing tea, which he drank. Then Stevie filled the bowl with wine and picked up the small knife from the altar and handed it to the minister. Sun Yat-sen pricked his middle finger and squeezed two drops of blood into the wine. He sipped the wine first, then he handed it to Stevie, who took a sip before passing it to every man in the room to drink from, ending with Chan. Each man sipped from the cup so that the oath of secrecy was shared. Then Stevie smashed the cup on the floor. He handed the list of oaths and the yellow paper, on which was written the man's name and his pledge, to Chan. Chan burnt them in the bowl on the altar. Chan then took a new cup of wine and spilled his own blood into it before addressing the minister:

'From this moment on your old life is finished. You are reborn in this room as a triad brother. Together we will make this society the most wealthy and the most powerful ever known in the world. I will give to you the opportunity to realise your dreams. You will have your heart's desire – whatever it may be. In exchange I expect your absolute loyalty to me. Until death we are joined.'

He passed the cup around. Each man repeated the oath: *Till death we are joined.*

48

The next morning Johnny Mann arrived at Headquarters as Max was leaving, having just finished giving his statement to Ng when Mann passed him on the stairs. Police stations were obviously not his favourite places, and 'rat out of a barrel' came to mind as Mann watched Max's small wiry frame slip elusively past the men in the hallway and disappear.

Only Ng was in the office, deep in files. The room was sweltering. The men's three desks were set out along each of the three walls; the door and a filing cabinet took up most of the fourth. There was so little space in the centre of the room that the three men's chairs clashed if they all chose to stand at the same time. Their office was originally part of a fine Georgian room with high ceilings, ornate coving and a marble fireplace. It had been subdivided and partitioned to create several smaller rooms. That meant that the only Georgian feature left in there was one large sash window.

As soon as he entered, Mann stripped off his jacket and threw it over a chair. Ng looked up and nodded his greeting, deep in thought.

Mann went around behind his desk to pull the blind down. The sun was blasting in – *thank God for the breeze*. He opened the window as far as it would go. His eyes were dark-rimmed, aching with tiredness. Just as he allowed the blind to slip through his fingers he caught his reflection in the window and thought of Helen. She'd have told him to get some sleep, that he was getting the look of a trapped animal about him. She'd have made him close his eyes, sit down, whilst she rubbed his shoulders and soothed his brow. She always showed him how much she cared, always told him how much she loved him. He wished he'd been able to return that love in the way she wanted. Wherever she was, he hoped she knew that he missed her.

He scanned down towards the harbour and felt the presence of the sea. His eyes closed for a second; he was calm again. He smiled to himself, and in his head he saw Helen smile back. Then he saw Georgina. He snapped his eyes open. Shrimp came in, grinned at Mann and headed for his desk. Shrimp's desk was the most untidy – littered with files, sticky drinks cans and hair products. Ng's was the tidiest – everything in neat, chronological piles. Mann's desk was as empty as he could make it – he hated clutter. Mann looked over Ng's shoulder. Ng had started writing up the interview he'd had with Max.

'Any good?' Mann asked.

Ng saved his work and looked up. 'Max, or Fong Man Tak is his real name, has been a taxi driver for thirty years. He says he doesn't really know the girls, he just gives them lifts. Lucy always does all the talking. His English isn't brilliant – so that part must be true. But he's nervous, shifty, couldn't look me in the eye. I don't know what it is he's guilty of, but he's done something he doesn't want us finding out about. Somehow I don't think it's murder. He's not young any more, either, can't see he'd be able to do it. He's shorter than most of these women, and he's slighter. Bernadette must be at least twice his size. He's much smarter than I thought, though.'

'Any form? What's his history?'

'He has no previous. Never married. He lives with his father and brother. The brother works for the Ho Young Dim Sum manufacturer. His father is Doctor Fong. He was a well-known medical practitioner. The family had money once.'

'What happened?'

'The practice went into decline after the death of Max's mother. The old man remarried but the business collapsed, and then the new wife seems to have disappeared. He has family connections, though.' Ng looked up and grinned. 'You're going to like this. The doctor's first wife was Chan's mother's sister. That makes Max and Chan cousins.'

'It also makes Max a fully paid-up member of the Wo Shing Shing, whether he likes it or not. I wonder what he has had to do for them? Shrimp – go and find out all you can about any new developments in the New Territories. Our women are co-connected with the area somehow. The Butcher knows it well. He always dumps the bodies out there. Maybe he has some business concerns there. Find out if anybody's been buying up land, Shrimp. Any new business going on.'

Shrimp reappeared two minutes later, popping his head around the door.

'That was quick,' said Mann.

'Just to let you know, boss, the Super's on his way back.' Shrimp disappeared again.

Superintendent White came straight in – he didn't knock.

'Have you seen these headlines?' He threw the *South China Morning Post* onto Mann's desk. BUTCHER CARVES HIS WAY THROUGH HONG KONG . . .

'They even know what the investigation is called. They've got some facts spot on. Some of it is rubbish designed to cause panic. They're even suggesting that people shouldn't come to the region right now. No woman is safe, it says. Bloody hell, Mann! We'd better sort it fast. Get hold of the papers and put out a state-ment telling people there's absolutely no need to panic.'

'You mean unless you happen to be young and white and female?'

'You know what I bloody mean. Tell them we need the public's co-operation on this. Tell them we need to know if anyone's acting suspiciously, that kind of thing. It seems we have no choice. We may as well throw it open, get people involved. Now let's get something positive to tell them.'

49

Bernadette sat at the dressing table staring into the mirror. She was arranging her hair. It hadn't been the best feckin' start to this new life. She'd been there a week already. But things were definitely looking up. She looked over at the costume hanging above her bunk. A kimono. Japanese shite. She hated wearing it, and the stupid shoes, the white make-up *and* that feckin' irritating black wig with the dangly bits that smacked her in the face. The way those men sat around her in a circle with a box of tissues, a razor and that feckin' flannel! Weirdos! They could feck right off!

Bernadette looked disdainfully at the outfit. Well, this was the last time. She'd been offered a *real* acting part – costumes, director, the works. She'd made some influential new friends through the club. Soon she'd be starring in her own film. The director and the rest of the cast were on their way to the club right now.

50

During the following two weeks Georgina and Ka Lei set up home together in the tiny flat. They made it their own. Sometimes they cocooned themselves and didn't step outside all day. They painted each other's nails and brushed one another's hair. They were twins: not identical, but matching. They slotted into each other and made a complete person. That was their secret; they were in each other's souls. They said they would never be parted – all they had to do was look in the mirror and find the other one.

Two was a magical number, but three didn't work. They were usually asleep when Lucy came in and they went out before she got up. They walked through Hong Kong's streets, window-shopping. They went down to the harbour to watch the boats, or they picnicked in the park, people-watching. They went to the malls and markets to look at clothes and took pictures in photo booths, and pasted them all around the flat.

When Max picked Lucy up for work in the evenings she was glad to get out of the house. She was beginning to feel like a stranger in her own home.

On Friday evening Max picked her up as usual. He watched her in his mirror. She was checking her make-up, busy adding a highlight here and a touch of gloss there. She looked up and caught him staring.

'You all right, Max?'

'Of course.' He turned his attention back to the road, adding, 'Make sure you take care tonight, Lucy.'

'Oh, I think I'm pretty safe.' Lucy smiled sweetly, grateful for his concern. 'Whoever it is seems to be targeting *Gwaipohs*.' She snapped the compact shut and met Max's eyes in the mirror. 'Or so the police think.'

'Have they been to see you?' he asked, his eyes flicking from the road to her face.

'Yes.' Lucy stared out of the window. 'I'm surprised they haven't asked to interview you, Max.'

'I had to make a statement this morning. I don't know why.'

'Because they're speaking to everyone who knew Roxanne. You knew her quite well.'

Max shifted uneasily and was just about to object; but then instead he just shrugged.

Lucy continued: 'Well, you did. When you think of all the times she got in your cab, you probably knew her as well as anyone.' Lucy hid her smile behind the compact mirror, as Max started to shake his head in denial. 'Oh well, we all need to help them find this madman, or madmen. Who do you think it could be, Max? Any ideas?' Lucy laughed. 'Don't look so worried, Max, they can't think it's you!'

Lucy was in a good mood, and Mamasan Linda was

212

pleased to see her. She greeted her outside the Dressing Room. She was always happy to see her best girl arrive at work.

'Has the big American been in?' Lucy asked.

Mamasan Linda thought for a moment. 'Big Flank?'

'Yeah, Big Flank, has he been here?'

'No.'

Lucy was disappointed. She still held out hope that one day she would be able to get herself and Ka Lei out of Hong Kong. Then they could put all this bad luck behind them – get back to being just them again. Lucy had felt Georgina coming between them. She felt her sister slipping away from her little by little. Lucy needed to get back on track – get a passport – get out – find a good husband for Ka Lei. Big Frank was her latest hope.

Lucy walked into the Dressing Room, momentarily deflated by the disappointing news about Big Frank. Candy sauntered over.

'Hey, Lucy, how's things?'

Lucy screwed up her face and shrugged. 'No bad. And you? Deli in New York ready now?'

'Yeah, almost, shelves are goin' in, stock is ordered.'

'Good, huh? You pleased, huh?'

'You know, Lucy, I am pleased, just somethin' inside tells me I need to be careful. It's hard to trust in this business. I really hope Giovanni is getting the right stock in. I told him I want those big fat silver anchovies in those ornate little jars. Don't get those cheap shitty little ones in salt – nobody classy eats those! Oh well . . .' She shrugged. 'What the fuck! I just have to trust, right?'

'Right!'

Candy looked about her to make sure no one was listening and whispered: 'I'm working my butt off, trying to get me as much money as I can. I wanna get outta here. Christ knows who's gonna get killed next. It's scary!' she said, with her eyes wide and her mascaraed lashes like squashed spiders. Then she looked around. 'Still no Georgina?'

Lucy shrugged.

'She's not coming back or what? She's scared about the murders, isn't she? First of all, no one wants to tell us anything. They want to keep it quiet. Now everyone's talkin' 'bout it.'

Lucy sat down in front of the mirror and began retouching her make-up. An amah brought her a bowl of food. Candy sat down next to her. Lucy picked at her food, placing each morsel at the end of the chopsticks and depositing it carefully inside her mouth so as not to disturb her lipstick.

'Did you hear about Roxanne?'

Lucy nodded.

'And then there's that other woman. God knows what they found of them! I couldn't make it out, body *parts*. They were talking about *parts*, not *wholes*! And because some of the bodies were found near a restaurant, people are sayin' that they have got into the food chain – that they've been made into some kind of dumplin' thing. Like what you're eatin' now!'

Lucy spat her food out into the bowl and went back to applying her make-up. 'What about Bernie, huh? Any news?' She looked up from pencilling in her eyebrows.

'Nope!' Candy shook her head dramatically. 'Christ, Lucy! It could happen to any of us! *We* could be next!'

'I know, I know, we better make money now, huh? Maybe soon too late!' She chuckled as she zipped up her make-up bag. Secretly smug that for once in her life it paid not to be white.

'Yeah, you're right. Hey, what about her stuff – you know, Roxanne's things at your flat? You said you were going to bring them in for Mamasan to look after.'

'Oh yeah – police took them. Sorry, huh? But don worry, I save you manicure set. Hundred Hong Kong, okay?'

Before the two had time to strike a bargain, Lucy was called to Chan's table.

Chan waited till Mamasan Linda left them alone. Lucy's heart hammered in her chest. She dreaded what was to come.

'So, Lucy. I thought we had a deal? No cousin? That's disappointing to me.'

'I am sorry, Mr Chan. I did my best. I am working very . . .'

He held up his hand for silence. 'And *I* am under a lot of pressure, Lucy, to recover the debt. Your sister Ka Lei must come and work here instead of your cousin.'

Lucy gasped. 'Please, Mr Chan. Not Ka Lei. She is innocent. She is so young. She . . .'

'Innocent? With a sister like you?'

'I promise you, Mr Chan, she is a good girl. She's never even had a boyfriend. Please don't make me do it to her.'

Chan sat back. He smiled smugly. He was enjoying this game immensely. He had all the information he needed. An innocent – perfect.

'Okay, Lucy. Because I am fond of you I am willing to compromise.'

In the gloom Lucy saw that his eyes were alight with malice.

51

Lucy stood beside Ka Lei in front of the mirror. Everything inside Lucy told her that it was wrong, but she had to ignore it – she had a job to do. It had to be done and she'd better get on with it. She busied herself in the preparations. It took time to choose an outfit: young but not too girly, sexy but innocent.

Lucy placed her hands on Ka Lei's shoulders and assessed the result of her preparations. Ka Lei looked like your average department-store worker in her smart clothes: neat blouse and tight pencil skirt.

Ka Lei stared numbly back at her reflection and said nothing. She had said nothing for two hours, since Lucy had told her what she had to do. She was about to sell her virginity to a man she'd never met. She was to become just another commodity on the open market. She needed Georgina so badly, but Lucy had tricked Georgina into leaving early for the pub, and now Ka Lei must face it alone.

Lucy smiled into the mirror and squeezed her sister's shoulders while her eyes filled with floating tears.

'It will be all right, Ka Lei, I promise.' She couldn't

217

hold her sister's gaze and looked away briefly to gather her courage. If *she* fell apart they'd have no chance of going through with it. 'Believe me, I only did it to try to make enough money so that we could be happy. You know that, don't you, huh? I would suffer anything for you. Please believe me, Ka Lei. I would die rather than see you hurt, but tonight is just one night out of your whole life. You are brave, strong, you can do it. He will be gentle with you. He gave me his word. It won't hurt.'

Lucy got no response. Ka Lei seemed to have accepted her fate without question. It was as if she faced an execution for which she was prepared. She scooped her hair up and tied it back into a ponytail at the nape of her neck – baring her neck for the block. All her dreams were shattering around her. She said nothing. She *was* nothing.

Man Po was in the front of the taxi with Max. He turned to leer at the girls. Max talked to him sharply and told him to keep his eyes front and stop dribbling. His large head tried to fix itself forward but it kept being drawn back. Lucy was in no mood and glared at him, while Ka Lei stared at her lap and felt the shame of his lechery as Lucy gave her sister instructions.

'We go in together, but we separate in the lobby. I will wait for you there. I'll show you where in a minute. You come and find me when it . . . you are finished. You must go straight to the lift, don't look at the reception desk, just get straight in the lift and ask the attendant for the tenth floor. Give him this.' Lucy handed her some money. 'Go to suite number one hundred and four. Mr Chan will meet you there, okay?'

Man Po turned to grin at Ka Lei. Lucy smacked him on the back of the head and he thought better of looking back again.

They reached the hotel.

'Do you need us to wait?' Max asked.

'No, we will manage.'

The sisters left the taxi and walked towards the hotel entrance. The concierge held the door open for them, and Lucy discreetly handed him a tip. Ka Lei looked like a frightened rabbit. Lucy took her arm firmly and they walked to where Lucy would be sitting and where Ka Lei could find her later.

For a second Lucy thought her sister was going to run – she could feel the tension in Ka Lei's body – but she held on to her fast. There would be no turning back now, not now they had come this far.

They reached the place where they would separate and Lucy steered her sister towards the lifts. She watched Ka Lei's slim frame being swallowed up by hotel guests, in elegant evening attire, making their way to the cocktail lounge to relax over their Martinis and catch the harbour views before dinner. She looked again towards the lift and watched the doors start to close. She was half-expecting Ka Lei to come running back out. She did not. She was gone.

Lucy sat down on one of the lobby chairs to wait. She heaved a big sigh, a monumental sigh that caught in her throat and came out as a groan. Although Lucy felt full of remorse for what her sister was about to go through, she also felt a glimmer of hope inside her. The debt was almost dealt with – three-quarters of it was gone, or as good as. It was a small thing, in the end – virginity. Lucy had sold hers to a Taiwanese when she was much younger than Ka Lei. She had sold herself to feed them both, when their mother's money had run out. What else could she do? Hong Kong wouldn't look after them, they had to do it for themselves or die. 'Virginity' was just a word. Inside was what counted. Time would heal; Ka Lei would forget.

Lucy cut the mental process of self-recrimination short as she caught sight of a likely punter. She wondered how audacious it would be to proposition him in the lobby of such a great hotel.

At the same time as her sister was being raped, Lucy was giving her number to an Australian businessman.

52

Lucy expected to see Ka Lei reappear from the lifts at any time, but instead she got a call from Chan telling her to come and collect her sister.

The door to the suite was ajar. She walked through the lounge and into the bedroom where she discovered Ka Lei alone, sitting on the edge of the bed.

'Ka Lei?' Lucy tried to steady her sister as she rocked back and forth on the edge of the bed. 'Ka Lei, I've come to take you home.'

She was a mess: her hair hung over her face and her nose was running.

Lucy went into the bathroom to fetch tissue and tried to wipe her face for her, but Ka Lei pushed her hand away. Instead, she wiped her nose with the back of her hand.

Just when Lucy was beginning to wonder how she was going to manage the situation, Ka Lei stood up, her fists tight to her sides. Her head was bowed.

'Are you ready to go?' Lucy asked, as she smoothed Ka Lei's hair and pulled the creases from her blouse. Ka Lei nodded. Lucy tried to check her face to make sure she wasn't looking too horrendous, but Ka Lei pulled away from her and Lucy decided it was probably best just to go.

Ka Lei followed her sister, shadow-like, out into the corridor and into the lift. She walked through the lobby, head down, taking small steps, following in her sister's path, staring at her sister's heels.

Outside, they hailed a taxi and travelled home in silence. Once or twice Lucy tried to whisper some consolation into her sister's ear, but Ka Lei wasn't listening. As soon as they entered the flat Ka Lei walked straight into Georgina's room and closed the door behind her. Lucy sat in the kitchen and listened to her sister sobbing.

Lucy phoned Georgina. She didn't know what else to do – the door was firmly shut in her face and yet she knew how deeply her sister was hurting, and how much she needed to be helped by someone. *Better Georgina than no one*, Lucy surmised, although she wished it could have been different. Georgina had known nothing about the deal. Lucy knew she'd never be able to do it otherwise – two against one and Lucy would have lost. But neither of them could understand the importance of paying back the debt. Their view of life was very different to Lucy's. They lived in a more innocent world. Lucy knew that whatever it took, it had to be done.

She waited for Georgina in the lounge, hoping to talk with her when she returned. But Georgina burst through the door and cut Lucy off mid-sentence as she strode through to the bedroom to find Ka Lei.

They talked for hours. Lucy sat in the kitchen listening to them, straining to hear what was being said. Occasionally she heard Ka Lei start sobbing again, and as that subsided the whispering would start. Eventually there was silence, and Lucy went to bed knowing that she had a lot of reconciling to do. She would have to make it up to her sister somehow.

53

Chan left the hotel room with a new spring in his step. He felt like such a man. The smoothness of her skin, the way her black silky sheets of hair fell over her tiny shoulders when she slumped forward trying to hide her nakedness from him. The sound of her whimpers as he had entered her. He was on a high that gave him a hard-on several times a day. He would have to own her. He would have to have sole access to her. From this moment on she would know no other man but him. Perhaps she would even bear him a child? God knows he was sick of waiting for his wife to produce one. Not that he ever saw her much. She spent her life in the tennis club or the shopping mall with friends. Luckily for Chan, she had no idea what his life was like.

But Victoria Chan knew more about her husband's affairs than he realised. She knew all about his concubines – 'the old faithful' and 'the young greedy'. It wasn't that she kept tabs on him. His infidelity was never in question. It was rather that it didn't concern her.

Victoria was beautiful and sophisticated. Her flower

arrangements were second to none and she could estimate the number of bottles of Bollinger needed for any event down to the last magnum. On the surface Victoria seemed to be perfectly happy with her marriage. She had her own life and her own room. With immense wealth, the cloak of matrimony about her and an absentee husband, she could do as she pleased. She made sure she was the first to carry the latest Fendi bag, be seen at the chicest restaurants, and the one who always beat the good-looking tennis coach, game set and match. And she made sure her husband knew nothing about her. She was saving herself. She had put her life on hold until something better came along. Chan passed over her life like an unwelcome gust of wind over a new hairdo.

Chan would not be headed home that night. He would ring and leave a message for his wife on the house phone – she was probably down at the tennis club, working on her backhand again. He had schemes to hatch and people to see that night. He had thought of a way to get what he wanted. If he pressurised Lucy enough then she would have no choice but to comply with his demands. And Chan knew just how he would do it. Someone would have to get very hurt. Then Lucy would be *really* scared. Then she would agree to anything.

54

The next morning, Lucy was up before the others. Today was a new day. She was determined that it would be a new start for them all. Lucy's guilty secret was out and aired and nearly dealt with. In time, Ka Lei would realise it wasn't so bad.

Lucy tidied the flat and then she went out and bought some cakes for their breakfast and small gifts for Ka Lei and Georgina – a peace offering – a bracelet for Georgina and a hair ornament for Ka Lei. She made tea. She sat and waited. She heard Ka Lei start sobbing again. She heard Georgina – still comforting, whispering. Lucy made tea and she waited.

She took the gifts from their bags and placed them on top of the breakfast bar. She leaned her head against the wall behind and waited. It was a new sensation to her – loneliness. She and Ka Lei had always dealt with things together. How had she ended up sitting alone?

Now she was waiting for a chance to say sorry. She looked about the flat. It was true, it was a mess, but it had a dingy homeliness that she had always found comforting. The evenings they had sat together in this flat, planning futures that now seemed impossible, all those times she had taken for granted. That one day Ka Lei would stop loving her? That was something she'd never thought would happen. Now, the flat was turned into a strange place, full of unfamiliar things – Georgina's things. It was all so changed. But she had to face the facts: they blamed her for everything and she deserved it. She stared at Georgina's bedroom door. It was covered in photos of Ka Lei and Georgina. Lucy thought about the nights she had slept huddled with her sister and the comfort that she had taken for granted.

She sat and cried. She let go of tears that she had been holding inside for more than a decade. She had looked after Ka Lei since she was a baby. Ever since their mother had stopped coming home every night. Sometimes Lucy was hungry. Sometimes the baby seemed to cry forever. Lucy had gone to the old man in the shop below and asked for some food for the baby, and the man in the shop had told her how to feed her sister with a bottle. The tiny baby had felt so heavy that her arms shook with the strain of holding her, but she never let go. She spoke to her all the time, and sometimes the baby stopped her suckling to listen to what Lucy was saying. Sometimes she stopped to smile and the milk spilled from her mouth, which made Lucy laugh.

By the time Lucy was ten she had taken full charge of Ka Lei. Their mother came and went, sometimes disappearing for a week at a time. When she returned she was always very tired, and so Lucy had two babies to look after. Her mother would sleep for days, but she could not stay once she was rested.

At first Lucy pleaded with her to stay, but it was of no use. In the end, Lucy only welcomed her back for the money she left on the table. Sometimes it was a lot of money. Lucy hid it, saving it away so that the baby would never be hungry again.

When Lucy was eleven and Ka Lei was four, their mother was found drifting facedown among the boats at Aberdeen. By then Lucy had saved enough money to last the sisters a year.

Lucy's thoughts were suddenly interrupted by the click of a door handle, and she wiped her face hurriedly. Georgina came out to make some tea for her and Ka Lei. She didn't look at Lucy.

'I boug you tese.' Lucy pushed the gifts towards Georgina. Georgina glanced at them then went back to making tea.

'I am sorry, Georgina. I had no choice. I owe too much money. I lose it gambling. So stupid. I am sorry. Had to pay it back. There was no other way. Had no choice.'

Georgina stopped and turned towards Lucy. Her eyes were swollen with crying and her hands were shaking with anger.

'You had no *choice*?'

'Believe me. I feel so bad but . . .'

'You had no *choice*?' Her voice was breaking with rage. 'You sold your sister to pay off your gambling debt.' She shook her head and lifted her palms towards the ceiling at the horror of it all. 'How could you do that?'

228

Lucy attempted her explanation again. Georgina wasn't listening. She shook her head in disbelief. 'What is the going price for virginity these days? How much did you get for your sister?' She turned to glare at Lucy. Her eyes burned as they filled with tears. Lucy looked away. She didn't like the hatred that she saw.

'Mr Chan say the debt is nearly finish now. I can work off the rest.' She lied as much to herself as anyone else. No final settlement figure had been reached. She could only hope that this would be an end to it.

'Yeah, right.' Georgina picked up the tea and turned back to Lucy. 'You can never repair the damage you've done to Ka Lei, Lucy – never.' Then she went back into her room.

Lucy was stunned. She realised that, for the first time in her life, she was in danger of losing her sister. That thought hit Lucy like a punch in the stomach.

Ka Lei was curled into a ball. She lay on the bed and stared at the closed bedroom door, knowing that her sister was sitting on the other side. Her world was crumbling. She didn't know how to maintain her balance. She only knew she must hang on to Georgina. Georgina was both her trapeze and her safety net. Lucy was the missed catch. Georgina was the person Ka Lei wanted to be with – she was her future. Somehow Lucy had blurred in Ka Lei's mind to become someone else – a deceiver and a stranger. Now she was mourning the loss of her sister.

'You all right, Ka Lei?' Georgina sat down beside her. 'I don't understand why she did those things – bad things – hurt everybody. I don't understand any more. But she is my sister. It is Lucy. It's very hard for me. I love Lucy – but it's so difficult now.' She shook her head, confused, and stared at the door. Then, turning to Georgina, her eyes full of panic, she said: 'Please don't leave me, Georgina. I will die if you leave me.'

Georgina took her hands. 'Look into my eyes, Ka Lei. What do you see?'

Ka Lei peered into them and smiled.

'I see me.'

'That's because we are in each other's souls – you and me. I am in you and you are in me. That will never change. Never. I belong here in Hong Kong. I belong here with you. I never realised how lonely I was until I came here. You are my best friend and my sister all in one.'

'For me also. When I tink sometin – you say it! It very funny.'

'I know! It is strange and wonderful. It makes me so happy to know that I have you and that we will always belong to one another. Everything will be all right – you'll see.'

55

The next morning was one of the rare occasions that Mann, Ng and Li were in the office at the same time. The Superintendent joined them. Mann placed the autopsy photo of Beverly Mathews' decapitated head next to the old one taken at her cousin's wedding three weeks before her death.

'He seems to have a thing for good-looking women,' said the Superintendent, who was looking over Mann's shoulder as he added the pictures of Gosia and Roxanne. 'He has a clear type that he likes.'

'Not precise . . .' said Ng.

'No, you're right. Some serial killers narrow it down to the colour, length and centre parting of the victim's hair. Not our man. He just likes a good-looking woman of a certain age and ethnicity,' said the Super.

'Which fits a lot of women in the entertainment industry here in Hong Kong,' added Mann, 'and since we asked for information we've had lots of new leads to follow. We have missing women being reported at the rate of one a day at the moment. Most of them turn up within forty-eight hours.'

'I wish we knew more about him,' said the Super.

'All we are certain of is that he lives here in Hong Kong and has for the last eighteen years. He knows the terrain well. He has some medical or butchery skills. Because of his treatment of women – he bites – it would indicate an infancy problem. The profilers say that he has missed out on a whole section of maternal, feminine nurturing. All that shit. So, they're saying he has no mother, either she left or she died, and that unhinged him,' said Mann.

'Do they think he lives alone or with someone who knows what he is doing?' asked the Superintendent.

'They suspect someone within his family knows about the bodies. The way he holds on to them – he has to keep them somewhere. Someone else has to know. He might have an accomplice.'

'He must be wealthy enough to have his own transport, unless it comes with his work. Wealthy enough to be able to get close to the girls – they're not likely to follow some tramp back home. These girls cost big money,' said the Superintendent. 'And, these women stick out like sore thumbs. It wouldn't be easy to kidnap them off the streets – possible, but not *easy* in these crowds.'

'Yes. You'd have a hard job persuading one to go quietly without attracting too much attention. He must have a clever way of gaining their trust, or he must have mega bucks,' said Mann.

'Where is he storing them? It must take up a lot of room, keeping these bodies on ice? He has to have a lot of freezer space,' said the Superintendent.

232

'He doesn't have to own the freezers – maybe he has them at work,' answered Mann.

'But why get rid of them now?'

'He is being disturbed in some way,' said Ng.

'We are not ruling out triad involvement,' Mann added.

The Superintendent looked at him curiously. 'Can't see what the angle would be. They make their money from drugs, prostitution, gambling and people trafficking. I don't think it is a triad – too messy, too careless. Not their kind of thing. They invest in mainstream entertainment, restaurants, clubs, taxi firms, legit businesses. Anyway, keep me informed.'

The Superintendent left. Two minutes later Li got a phone call. He listened intently and scribbled notes onto a pad on his desk. He turned to Mann as the call ended.

'That was forensics, boss. You asked whether Roxanne Berger had bitten her tongue. She had.'

'Did you work out why?'

He looked at his scribbled notes. 'Electrocuted during the torture?'

'Correct. Anything else?'

'Gosia too. A biopsy of her nipple showed that she had tissue damage from an electrode. No nipple damage for Roxanne, though.'

'He probably used a cattle prod. What about the fly larvae?'

'Two sets – unhatched – one set before they were frozen, second set got in the bag.'

'Means they were frozen within twenty-four hours.'

'Except Beverly, she had pupae, not far from hatching, the pathologist said.'

'So, she was different. It was at least a week before she got frozen, or disposed of.'

'Why's she different?'

'Because she was the first.'

56

Mann was headed to the bars in Tsim Sha Tsui east. On the way he passed the Albert. It wouldn't hurt to call in – see if Mandy had any information for him. He might even catch a glimpse of Georgina.

He joined the noisy groups of office workers desperate for that first drink – that first slug of ice-cold Chardonnay, or gulp of San Miguel – all filing into the Albert ready to start their evening. He man-oeuvred his way past them to the front of the bar.

Georgina was polishing glasses and listening politely to a couple of old colonials – Foxy and Badger. He could see that she wasn't really listening. She was smiling when required, but her thoughts were elsewhere.

She looked up from her glass-polishing and beamed as she saw him approach. She looked pleased to see him, thought Mann, even if her eyes had a distance in them.

'Hello, Miss Johnson. How's it going? Everything all right?'

'Hello, Inspector. Not bad, thanks.'

'Call me Johnny or Mann, I don't mind, anything

so long as it's not rude. Settled in?' He nodded in the direction of the old colonials – who grunted a greeting and looked decidedly uncomfortable in his presence.

'Really well. Thanks for getting me this job. I love it here.'

That bit was true, Mann could see. Her face brightened. She didn't hesitate.

'And *we* love having her here.' Mandy came up behind her, put a protective arm around her shoulders and gave them a squeeze. 'All right, Johnny?' she said as she walked on past on her way to the middle bar to take the first meal orders of the evening.

'Yes thanks, Mandy,' he called after her. 'Thought I'd see how Georgina was getting on. See if she wanted to file any complaints against the management, lecherous locals, that sort of thing.'

Mandy was almost out of sight. She turned and winked at him and waved a reassuring hand to Foxy and Badger to say that Mann wasn't meaning them – when he obviously was.

'She gets Tuesday off, by the way,' she shouted back over her shoulder, before disappearing into the next bar.

Mann grinned at Georgina and nodded in the direction of Mandy. 'She's an old friend; she knows me too well.' His phone buzzed just then. He checked the screen – there was a message from Li. 'I have to go. But I'll call back to see you soon. Then I'll take you on a sightseeing tour – as soon as things calm down.'

'Sounds great.'

He paused. 'Is there anything worrying you? Anything I can help with?'

She hesitated, then shook her head. 'I'm fine – really. Come and find me when you've caught the Butcher. I'd love to come out with you, when you have time.'

'Look forward to it then.'

As he walked towards the door he saw a man he recognised. It was the surgeon from Oliver's Bar. Mandy was serving a customer. Mann nodded to her and she came over.

'What's up?'

'That man over there – the silver-haired one?'

'Peter Farringdon. He's a surgeon. Really nice man. Comes in here about once a week.'

'Does he ever come in with a woman?'

'Hmmm.' She thought for a moment. 'No, I've never seen him with one. Although, I have heard that he buys the odd service. Girls talk, you know.'

'What type of girl?'

She looked at him incredulously. 'Never had you down for naive, Mann. The kind who sells it.'

'I mean, what nationality?'

'Foreign. Always *Gwaipoh*.'

Mann got outside, checked his messages and rang Shrimp. 'What's up? You left me a message?'

'The lab report has just come back. We've got a new link between these women.'

'Go on . . .'

'They all have soil debris on them that's contaminated with pig blood. There are even pig hairs in the residue from Beverly Mathews' hair. Plus, the abrasions on the back of victim four's legs – where she was dragged – clogged with pig hairs.'

'So, they have all been dismembered in a place that's been used to slaughter pigs. Good work, Shrimp. Get Ng on to it. I want him out looking at all the slaughter-houses in the New Territories, all the farms. Tell him he can close the lot down if he needs to. Anything else?'

'You're going to like this. The knife he uses has a nick in it. It leaves a distinctive shape in the cut.'

'Shit! Well done, Shrimp! Good lad. Anything else?'

'There are sixty-eight cigarette burns on Gosia's chest.'

57

Ng and Johnny Mann took the ferry across the harbour to Kowloon. The evening rush was just beginning to slow down. It gave them time to talk and a change of scenery to do it in.

'I get this niggle in my head about the Butcher, Ng. The inconsistencies in his profile just don't add up. No clear idea of age . . . only that he has to be over forty. In some ways he seems very organised. He plans these girls' abductions very well. He waits for his chosen victim. That would indicate someone of a high level of intelligence. Someone sociable and probably well-liked. He might even have a family. He could easily be a prominent member of society. But then he is disposing of the bodies in a hurry. In a careless and disorganised manner. That would indicate a loner, a man of low intelligence. Why take all that care to kill them and then leave their remains around for us to find?'

'Nothing is clear. This butcher has one knife, but many sides to his blade.'

They disembarked and headed up Nathan Road,

before turning left onto Peking Road. The road opened out to an area swarming with gap-year kids and young locals. Along the street was an Irish pub, two Aussie bars, a Kiwi place and a steak house, all within spitting distance of each other and all nestled between traditional Chinese girly bars. In front of them was the largest and most notorious of Hong Kong's backpacker hostels. It was an area where young kids were constantly hassled to part with their money. After a few drinks they could buy a fake watch, sign up for a trip to China and get laid – all by the same person.

Shrimp was waiting for them. He looked like an extra from *Miami Vice* today. Mann sent Ng on to O'Reilly's to get what he could from the local Irish expats about Bernadette. They would meet again in forty minutes and work their way up the street in tandem.

Mann and Shrimp crossed the street and pushed through the swing doors of The Western – a saloon-themed pub with sawdust on the floor, dead animals on the walls and an impressive collection of spurs.

A rotund middle-aged Filipina named Annie was in the process of collecting glasses as they swung through the doors.

'Watcha, Johnny,' she drawled, and nodded in the direction of Shrimp.

'How you doing, Annie? Meet my colleague – Li.'

Her eyes lit up and she gave a wet-lipped smile. 'Hello, handsome.'

Li stood rigid, panic-stricken, gave his girly giggle

240

and looked to Mann for help. Mann grinned and wagged his finger at her.

'The older you get, the worse you become, Annie.'

She laughed like a full-strength smoker who can never quite clear her throat, pushed her Stetson to the back of her head and pulled down her fringed waistcoat. Then, swinging her hips into action, she shimmied over. 'Always had a big appetite for life – you know me, Johnny, can't seem to grow out of it . . .'

Mann watched her and marvelled how she still had *it*. She'd been wearing the same cowgirl suit for at least twenty years. When she'd first put it on the gun belt had hung at a lazy slant from her nubile hips; now it was wedged around her midriff. But she moved those hips like a belly dancer. She was still a very sexy woman.

'You got a licence for those?' He leaned forward to kiss her cheek and pointed to the two antique guns she had in the belt. She gave a deep-throated giggle and reached up to kiss him. She loved the same old joke, and Mann always obliged her.

She put her hands up in the surrender position. 'You just gonna have to take me in, Johnny. You'll need cuffs, though,' she purred. 'I should warn you – I aint' goin' quietly.' She reached out and ran her finger down the buttons of Li's pink shirt. 'I might promise to behave for your friend, though – just keep it to a whimper and it'll be his choice – with or without the cuffs.'

Li blushed scarlet. Annie laughed and coughed at the same time.

'Same old Annie. The only way you know how to behave is badly. Get me a drink and I'll think about it.

He could do with educating.' Mann winked at Li, who hadn't understood all the patter, but he'd seen the exchange of looks and it was enough to petrify him.

Annie winked back as she went behind the bar to pour their drinks – two vodka tonics. She turned back from the optics, set their drinks down, and leaned over the bar, squeezing her breasts into an impressive cleavage.

'You're looking good, Annie.'

'Thank you, Johnny,' she said, keeping her eyes on Li and rocking from one cowboy boot to the other.

'How's it all been going?' Mann asked.

'Dandy. Just dandy. Never better.'

'Yes, and really?'

'Crap.' She turned back to Mann and the smile disappeared.

'Don't worry, it'll pick up now. The high season is on its way. It already feels cooler out there. People will be pouring in here soon.'

'I hope so. I hope so. Ain't gonna afford bullets for these here guns else . . .' She patted her holster and gave a wry smile. 'But . . . as much as I love to see the best-lookin' cop in Hong Kong – you're here on business, aren't ya? What is it you want to know?'

'I wanted to ask you something about the old days.'

She looked perplexed. 'What old days?'

'Before you took this bar on.'

'Huh! You must be jokin', Johnny. I can't remember that far back.'

'I mean when you were a working girl, Annie.'

'Ahhhhh. I see! Okay, what do you wanna know,

apart from the fact I was the best there was.' She ran her tongue around her lips and grinned at Li, who shuffled nervously over to study the spurs collection.

'Anyone that was around *then*, who's *still* around? Anyone who was a regular of yours?'

'A couple. Of course, I don't know whether they're still into the same action. But then it's a hard habit to break – so I should think they are. Let me see . . . I haven't seen him in a while, but there's James Dudley-Smythe. He was a really good customer of mine. Liked his booze a bit too much, and most of the time he needed help to get anything going. You had to know how to handle him, though – give him half a chance and he could get nasty. He had quite a collection of mean-lookin' whips in that cupboard of his. But . . . if you knew how . . . he was easy. Some of the girls used to get him drunk first. I used to insist that *he* wore the handcuffs.'

'Anyone else?'

'I had several clients who came regularly from abroad. I still see them around town. They look older now, of course. I remember their faces, and certain other things about them, but not their names.'

'Any more locals?'

She shook her head. 'Can't think of any.'

'Any word on the street about someone getting nasty? *Really* nasty?'

She shook her head. 'No one's spoken to me about it. If one of the girls had been hurt I would have been told. Hang on a minute! There was some talk recently. I heard these young lads talkin' in here. They'd been buyin' films off a stall on Nathan Road. One of them got taken round the back and shown weird stuff. Apparently there are some dodgy films going around.'

'What kind of films?'

'Not your usual. This young lad was shaken up. He'd only seen a clip. He said it looked like a snuff movie.'

58

Mann, Ng and Li were stood in room 210, telling David White about the film Annie had mentioned. The Superintendent looked seriously in need of sleep. His eyes were rubbed sore, his face was ashen and he was irritable as hell.

'It was probably some twenty-year-old spotty-faced virgin who mistook a blow job for death by suffocation. Whatever it was, you didn't find evidence of it, did you? You didn't find evidence of any snuff movies for sale? I don't think we'll find that these films have anything to do with the death of our women. Now, let's get back to what we know. Any leads on Bernadette?'

'She went to the area, mainly to O'Reilly's, about once a fortnight – on her night off. She picked up men sometimes. I was given the names of a few people that she used to talk to. I've already contacted a couple on the list. I'm waiting to hear back from the others,' said Ng.

'Good. Okay.'

The Superintendent sat back in his chair and rubbed his head. 'How many pig farms have been located?'

Li flicked through his notes.

'There are two hundred and sixty-five pig farms, sir. Mainly concentrated in the northern New Territories. They are small, family-run concerns.'

'The government's trying to phase them out. Apparently they're unhygienic and they are taking up land that could be used for residential development,' added Ng.

'The samples from the victims? Does it narrow it down at all?'

'We checked the rope analysis and the bags that the victims were found in. Both are common to ninety per cent of the farms,' said Ng.

Superintendent White laid the photos of the victims out on his desk. 'Tell me about the torture. Is it always the same?'

'No, it isn't. Two were electrocuted. One was burnt with cigarettes. One was branded. Excessive bruising, small cuts,' said Mann. 'It varies a lot. He's not sticking to the rules here – most serial killers have their trademark way of torturing – it's part of their fantasy. He doesn't.'

'And the way they died?'

'Asphyxiation by various means. Some with the aid of a ligature, some not.'

'Other similarities?'

'He gave heroin to at least two of the victims. Maybe to numb the pain? But why would he care?' mused Ng.

'Maybe because he could do worse things to them if they couldn't feel it – make it last,' answered the Superintendent. 'Or maybe just to keep them quiet while he held them hostage. Some showed signs of substantial weight loss, didn't they? He obviously kept some of them hidden for a long time.'

'Yes, and I think he needed help to do that. I think we're looking for a double act.'

Mann paused as an officer knocked and stepped inside. 'What is it?'

'We've found some more, sir.'

59

'Let's go. Shrimp . . . Ng? Let's move. The helicopter's waiting. The SOCOs are on the way, they will be there before us.'

The helicopter circled over Headquarters before heading north. It would take them thirty minutes to fly, two hours to drive. Mann had an anxious feeling deep in his stomach. He didn't mind helicopters. It was the thought of what they'd find at the other end. He sat back and let the rush of cool air clear his head, watching the scenery unfolding beneath him.

They crossed the harbour. Large freight ships and small fishing vessels dotted the water below – gleaming in the sunshine. They passed over Tsim Sha Tsui and the banks and multinational corporations. Past the commercial districts and over the housing estates and market streets of Kowloon and Mong Kok. As they flew over the New Territories, villages, walled cities and patchwork rice fields embroidered the ground beneath them. From the ultimate in modern design in the business district they came to oxen tilling the rice fields. It wasn't long before they were flying over a country park and a vast area of water came into view. It was Plover Cove. Not actually a cove, but a reservoir, manmade with water brought from China.

The place was quiet – as you'd expect on a weekday – no families, no kids – tranquil. The water sat idyllic and inviting below. The area was green and lush. The pilot pointed out some activity to Mann. It was on the edge of a wooded area to the right, below them. Mann could see the SOCOs at work. Two police vans and a squad car were there. About ten policemen were standing around outside the cordoned area; just three white-suited SOCOs inside. The less people who walked over the actual crime scene, the better.

Mann indicated to the pilot where he wanted to set the helicopter down. They landed twenty metres outside the exclusion zone. Mann, Ng and Li stepped out onto a flat grassed area outside the wooded thicket that stretched between the reservoir and the road. They made their way across to the police vans and were met by Sergeant Lok. Mann knew Lok by reputation, although he'd never met him before. He held the honor of the most corrupt policeman ever to get away with it in the New Territories.

'Did this couple find the bag?'

Mann pointed to a stupefied-looking couple in their early thirties. Wearing matching tracksuits, they sat huddled together on the grass, next to their matching bicycles.

Lok nodded, Mann introduced himself to them. 'You were looking for a picnic spot?'

'Yes.' The man answered for them both. 'We parked our bikes and were looking for somewhere to sit. We smelt it first. Then the noise – a droning. We went to investigate and saw the bag resting at the bottom of the tree. It was partially hidden by twigs and debris and covered in flies. As we approached we saw the arm hanging out.'

The woman began to cry.

Mann turned back to Lok. 'How far away is the road from here?' He looked behind them away from the thickest part of the wood.

'Three hundred metres.'

'Does the road afford good access?'

'Yes.'

'So how close could someone get to this spot before dumping the body?'

'I would say twenty metres.'

'It's still quite a way to carry it. Look for signs of dragging, Shrimp. Look for tyre marks.'

'Yes, boss.'

Mann looked over towards where the white-suited SOCOs were photographing the remains and searching in a grid system.

'Is Daniel Lu in charge?' he asked. For a minute, Mann couldn't see the man he was looking for. Then he came into view. Daniel Lu stood up, paused in his searching, and acknowledged Mann. Mann had worked with him on many occasions. He was a brilliant Crime Scene Investigator. He was scrupulous and meticulous and found clues when others gave up.

Mann inched closer to the red and white exclusion

tape. His eyes focused on the bag and all else in his vision fell away.

'Do you want to get a little nearer?'

By the time the question was asked, Mann had already done so. He had crossed the exclusion zone. He was contaminating the crime scene. He walked straight across to the bag.

Ng shouted to him.

Daniel Lu looked up as Mann approached.

'Mann . . . what the fuck! Get the hell away! Get back!'

Mann didn't hear him – he just kept walking. His eyes were focused on the bag – nothing else mattered. Like walking into a huge mirror and having it shatter around him, piece by piece his world disintegrated – until all that was left was the arm hanging from the bag. The arm that was wearing Helen's bracelet.

60

'You shouldn't be here, Genghis. You need to get away – anywhere but here.'

Ng and Li stood beside Mann in the mortuary. Mann didn't answer Ng. He hadn't said anything for hours, all through the agonising time it had taken for the SOCOs to give the okay for her to be moved. All that time Mann had stood apart, watching and waiting, never taking his eyes from her.

Kin Tak was unusually quiet as he attended to the tasks of washing and weighing, measuring and finally laying the parts of Helen's body out on the mortuary slab.

Mr Saheed arrived. As he stepped into his boots and pulled on his latex gloves he looked at the policemen. They looked at Mann. 'Gentlemen? Something I need to know?' They all looked at Mann. 'Inspector Mann?'

Mann didn't answer, he just shook his head.

'Okay.' Mr Saheed picked up his notes. 'Found this morning. Is that right?'

Ng nodded.

'Do we have an ID for her?' He looked over his glasses at Mann.

'Her name is Helen Marie Bateman,' Mann said, without taking his eyes from her face.

Saheed looked questioningly at Ng, who replied by rolling his eyes towards Mann. Mann caught it and shook his head. 'I'm okay.'

'Let's begin then. Helen Bateman – torso and head are still attached, arms and legs have been dissected from the body at the hip and shoulder joints. She was frozen after death. There's a bluish tint around her mouth. She was probably killed by asphyxiation. No signs of a ligature, or bruising around the neck. No signs of asphyxial haemorrhaging, probably suffocated using a bag. She has several small wounds on her torso, concentrated on the buttock and upper-thigh area. I would say that they have all been made by the same instrument. Not sure what yet.' He took a swab from one of the wounds while Li photographed and measured them.

'A metal-tipped whip,' said Mann. Although he kept his eyes on her face, he had noted her injuries while Kin Tak had been laying her body out for examination. He had done it subconsciously. He hadn't even registered he was doing it. Even if the lover didn't want to see it, the policeman in him had no choice.

'We'll see what the lab comes back with.' Mr Saheed paused as he looked over his glasses at the three officers. Li and Ng remained silent.

'She looks very thin,' Mann said quietly, almost to himself.

The pathologist paused and looked at him. 'Yes, skin is slack, indicating rapid weight loss. There is a wound across the lower abdomen, and there's this.'

Mr Saheed turned her arm over, and the needle marks were plain. Mann was fighting for breath now. He could see nothing but Helen's beautiful face: laughing, smiling, crying, screaming, pleading for mercy. It was as if he had murdered her with his own hands. He felt so much pain that it made him want to crumble, to dissolve into the ground. He also wanted to run as fast and as far as he could from her dead body. At the same time he longed to take hold of her, even now, even when the stench of her rotting body stayed on his hands. He wanted to protect her. But he was too late.

He couldn't stay to watch Saheed cut her. He knew the man had to do it, but he wouldn't have allowed him to touch her while he watched. Not his Helen.

He stood outside the mortuary door and put his hand against the wall for support.

Ng came out to find him when the autopsy was over. He placed a hand on Mann's shoulder.

'You all right, Genghis?'

'She looked so . . .'

Ng patted his back. 'I know what you want to say – *It is the beautiful bird who gets caged.* I am sorry, Mann.'

'You know the wheel of life, Ng? Well, whatever I was in the last life, it wasn't nice.'

'*The gem cannot be polished without friction, nor man perfected without trials*, Genghis. You'll be okay.'

'I'm not being perfected, Ng – I'm being punished.'

'Don't even think that. Helen's life was not dictated by you. She chose her own path, it was just unfortunate that there was someone waiting for her along it.'

Li caught up with them, and Mann turned to him as he drew level.

'What else did you find out, Li?'

Just as Li was about to answer, Ng put up a hand behind Mann's back to silence him before he could say it. There were some things Mann just wasn't ready to know.

Meanwhile, Kin Tak waited till everyone had left, then he slid Helen's body out from the fridge, wheeled it to the centre of the room, unzipped it and put it back onto the slab, piece by piece.

61

Back at Headquarters there seemed to be a distinct lack of policemen in the building. Those who were there quickly averted their gaze from Mann and made themselves busy with anything that involved walking the opposite way to him.

Inside room 201, David White was waiting. He came around from behind his desk.

'I am sorry, Johnny, truly sorry.' He put his hand on Mann's shoulder.

Mann slumped. 'You should have seen her, David. She was emaciated. Her body was covered in wounds. She suffered such a lot. Who could have done this? And why Helen? She had no connection to Club Mercedes, or to the nightclub world any more. She'd been working as a PA for the last two years.'

'I don't know, Johnny. I wish I did but I don't.'

'God help him when I find him, David. His last minutes will be filled with more pain than he can imagine.'

'We'll double our efforts, I promise you. We'll have an answer for you, but you must go home now. I'll come around later to check on you. I'll bring a bottle of something. We'll get drunk together.'

'The only thing I want to do now, David, is find the bastard who did this. I don't want to go anywhere.'

'I know you don't, Johnny, but you have to. You can't investigate your own girlfriend's death. You just can't. I won't allow it. Rest for a couple of days, then we'll talk about what you *can* do.'

'Don't pull me off this case, David. Don't do it.' The blood returned to Mann's face.

'Go home for now. Rest. I'll be around in the evening. We'll talk it through then.'

But when White got to Johnny Mann's apartment later that evening, Mann wasn't there.

Mann was waiting for Mandy in the smoking room – the alley at the back of the pub. He sat in the half-light, tucked against the wall. He had been knocking back the vodka for hours but he seemed to have drunk himself sober. Nothing helped numb the shock or the pain. Nothing could turn back time. He had come to talk to Mandy. He had to talk to someone else who knew Helen well. He had to understand what had happened.

'You knew her, Mandy,' he asked when she joined him. 'Did you think she meant to leave me?'

'Johnny, what's the point in all this? She's dead. She was in the wrong place at the wrong time. There's just no point in torturing yourself.'

'Did she, Mandy? I need to know.'

'All right, Johnny, I'll tell you. She loved you. She

wanted to stay with you. But she was tired of waiting for you to commit. She came to see me a couple of weeks before she left. She said she was going to go back to England if you didn't try to stop her. At least, she intended to disappear for a few days and wait to see what you did. I warned her that pretending to leave you wasn't a good idea, that you'd never been one for emotional blackmail and that it might backfire on her. Anyway, she obviously went through with it. She phoned me just after she left. She was in the taxi. She said that you'd been there when she'd left. She said you didn't try to stop her, and she said she was going to lie low for a few days and then decide what to do. I waited for a call from her to say where she was staying. When it never came I just presumed she had gone through with it after all and had returned to England. That maybe she did want a clean break after all. I'm sorry, Johnny. Maybe I should have said something before. I never dreamed that . . .'

'I know, Mandy. That she was being held somewhere, tortured, starved, and finally murdered. It's not the kind of thing you could imagine happening to someone you know.'

Mandy placed a hand on his shoulder and gave it a squeeze.

'She loved you, Johnny. That's a rare and precious thing in this world. You threw it away. But you didn't kill her.'

He got to his feet unsteadily and walked back down the alleyway. Mandy watched him disappear before going back inside. Georgina looked questioningly at her as she returned to the bar. Mandy just shook her head, wiped her eyes and went back to work.

Mann went home. He didn't want to. He was ordered. White had caught up with him in one of the bars in Wanchai and frogmarched him back. He didn't want company. The Superintendent made sure he was safely inside his front door and then he left.

Mann didn't bother drawing the curtains. He slumped in the armchair, drank his vodka, and thought about Helen. He needed to think about Helen. He needed to take the responsibility, the remorse and the regret full on his shoulders. He needed to wallow in it, just for a while. He got up and walked around the flat. He felt her presence in every room. Normally he tried to ignore it, but tonight he drank it in. He went into the kitchen. He could still see her, hand on one hip, the other resting on the work surface, recounting her day to him while he pretended to listen but was really looking at her and wondering if she could get any sexier. He went into the bathroom. Her perfume, Miss Dior, was still there on the side of the bath. He unscrewed the top and held it to his nose. He closed his eyes and remembered how he always smelt it on her neck when she tilted her head to one side and waited for his kisses. She would be laughing because she knew it would tickle, and they would end up in bed and she never refused him. He replaced the bottle and went back to his vodka.

Two days later he surfaced. Superintendent White sent him home again. He needed a shave and a shower. Instead, he went to the gym. He ran for an hour solid. He ran and he sweated and he cursed the whole of the human race. He felt that anger intensify. His defensive wall was building itself back up. But he wasn't quite there yet. He needed the comfort of a woman. Just for a while he wanted to hold another human being, soft and warm in his arms and fall asleep touching another living person. He wanted to forget all his sadness and he wanted to put his head somewhere else for a while. He rang Kim's number. It went straight to answer phone. He phoned Honey's number. It was engaged. He scanned down the page. His eyes stopped – now that was someone to give him comfort; make him forget his troubles . . . He rang it. She answered. She had the night off. No, she didn't mind skipping the meal, having a drink at his place. She understood he was upset. She would be glad to keep him company. She would call a taxi and be with him in half an hour.

The next morning he awoke and saw Georgina lying next to him. She smiled and reached for him. He just couldn't. He felt sick with guilt, vodka and regret.

Mandy called him the next day.

'How the hell could you? She's such a sweet girl. Why didn't you just go and find yourself some tart for the night? Why did it have to be Georgina?'

'I'm sorry, all right. I'm not pleased with what I did. I don't want to make excuses. I like her. I do.'

'What? So you don't even take her out on a date, you trick her into bed, screw her, then drop her off the next morning as fast as possible? Just a "thanks very much"? "See you around"? That's caring?'

'How many times, Mandy? I am sorry.'

'Yeah, well, it's not me you should say it to. She's a decent girl. When are you ever going to grow up, Mann? It's almost as if you don't want to find happiness with someone. As fond of you as I am, I have to tell you – you're a self-destructive bastard! For Christ's sake let go and let yourself feel something for someone before it's too fucking late!' She slammed the phone down.

He went into the Operations Room on the ground floor. When he walked in, the animated voices of police officers on computers and telephones became instantly hushed and a sudden busyness developed that meant no one had time to look up and make eye contact.

He stood in the middle of the room and waited until they stopped their pretend chatting and looked at him.

'Okay, I want every one of you to hear this. My ex-girlfriend has become the latest victim to be found. This investigation has just become personal to me. But it doesn't stop me from being a professional. Don't for one fucking second think that I am not here. I want to be brought up-to-date with any new developments and I want to be briefed NOW.'

There was a shuffle and a muffled chorus of 'Yes, sir'. Mann walked out and down to his office.

62

'Ng?'

'She was probably held for several months. Weight loss, systematic torture. Extensive bruising and deep wounds around the wrists. Measurements indicate that she was tied at the wrist and suspended for long periods of time, certainly in the last twenty-four hours of her life.'

'Was she dissected by the same man, Li?'

'Yes, boss.' Li kept his head down while he answered.

'Trophies?'

'Yes.'

The three detectives were finally alone, inside their office behind closed doors. Mann could ask the questions he didn't trust himself to ask downstairs in the Operations Room with so many eyes on him.

He stood at the window, opened the blind, and filled his eyes with the last of the day. A whisper of purple cloud edged the bold and orange streaks that stretched themselves across the sky. The sun set beautifully on a truly horrible day. Mann watched it in silence as Li and Ng sat waiting at their desks. He felt the anger in him dive deep into his soul. He felt it settle into a growling magma layer of hate. Welcome to the world of raw emotions. Mandy was right – it wasn't a world he chose to visit. Since the death of his father he had avoided it at all cost.

He let the blind slip and fall as the last of the sun died. Then he turned back to Li and Ng.

'I want you to picture in your head exactly what happened to these women from the minute they said hello to the murderer to when they were found in the bag. Ng – reopen Beverly Mathews' file. See if there's any forensic to rework now. See if they ever pulled anyone in for questioning in the original investigation. Shrimp – start swotting up on your torture and find out as much as you can about the sites where the bodies were found, link them up for me and see about tyre prints. When you're working out scenarios tell me how the bodies got to where they ended up – dragged, thrown?' Li was writing it down as fast as he could. 'I want you in the clubs, posing as a tourist – shouldn't be too difficult – you talk like a Yank. Find those films that Annie talked about. Ask for the foreign girls, or girls that specialise in S&M.'

'Yes, boss.'

Mann took copies of everything with him and headed home. The police station was not the place for him to be. He needed peace and seclusion. He was going to devote the next twelve hours to getting inside the heads of dead women.

He called in at the supermarket. He loaded up with two carrier-bags of decent food and carried them up to his floor. He found his key, opened the door, jammed his foot in it to stop it shutting and picked up his bags. He went straight into the kitchen to unload.

Then, he took a shower, poured a large vodka and made himself a stir-fry. He switched on the news while he ate his dinner. There were pro-democracy riots on the horizon. Mann didn't blame them. If he wasn't a policeman he'd be out there demonstrating as well. The region was being shafted. The Chinese government was working its way down its list of promises, pre-Handover, and reneging on every one. There was a group of visiting Russians, mafia types, being entertained by top triads – a great combination. The only difference being that the Russians liked everyone to know they were gangsters. The triads liked to keep it a secret.

He switched the television off, took his plate out to the kitchen and realised he was stalling.

Understandable, but not acceptable.

He opened his briefcase and took out all the files, exhibits and photos and set them out in neat groups over the lounge floor.

Victim one . . . He placed her photos in the far right corner of his lounge room, under the window. Victim two underneath, clockwise, against the window, and so on – neatly laid out to afford space to walk between them. He arranged them in a circle until he came back to Helen – victim six . . . he put her at the top, next to victim one, but tucked slightly back from the others.

He stood and looked at the photos. Then he walked around among the victims. His eye lingered on each group of details as he tried to picture the victim's death. He started with Gosia – victim three. Gosia's torso was found in the first bag. The bag on the building site at Sha Tin. There'd been a hundred trucks a day going in and out of that site, so there were no tyre tracks to examine.

What kind of woman was she? He picked up the photo of Gosia that her brother had sent and placed it in the centre of the group. She looked Eastern European, dark blonde – she was very pretty in an austere, hard way. She was an independent traveller, a loner, a wild child, otherwise she wouldn't have ended up working in a club in Hong Kong on her own. She only had her brother and yet she fell out with him. She bore grudges. She had issues. She came from a tough background, orphaned. She was strong. She would have fought hard against her attacker. She was held for several weeks. She had been systematically tortured. She'd had electrodes applied to her nipples and she'd been burnt with cigarettes over her chest. Her wounds were made over a period of days. The person who had done this was into humiliation; there was nothing to gain by torturing her except his own sexual gratification. And there was the trophy taking . . . Mann studied the picture of the abdominal wound, made by a sawing action – *carefully made* – but not by a surgeon.

Mann picked up her file and scanned the notes. Traces of heroin. How did she die? Guess – asphyxiation – bag over the head. If her killer was into taking his time, he might have brought her to the point of death many times before finally leaving her there.

Victim two. All he had to go on was the upper right thigh and right arm. She had been tethered with rope. Mann pulled out the sample from the exhibits box. Tiny threads of common rope with a myriad of uses. But the wound was deep. She had been kept tied up with the same piece of rope for some time. It had worked its way deep into the flesh on her wrists. She must have pulled hard against it, caused friction. The skin on her limbs was slack. She'd been held a long time too.

There were no obvious signs of torture. The bite mark didn't count – that was made several hours after death. Mann took out the cast of the bite from the box. There were a lot of uneven teeth in that cast – too many. This person's upper jaw never met his lower. This person's mouth wouldn't meet. He would have a problem eating, talking.

Ng called.

'The file – Beverly Mathews. Nothing, sorry. No forensics at all.'

'Anything else come back?'

'We're having no luck tracing the F brand on Roxanne Berger. We looked at all the pig farms in the region. None of them have any branding even similar. Wherever it comes from, it's not here.'

'Did you trace the licence plate from the pig lorry we saw?'

'It doesn't match anything on our records.'

'Okay.'

'You'll be pleased to hear that the Shrimp is working hard on his assignment.'

'I bet he is.'

'He left word for you to meet him at "The Lips" in Kowloon, just past the . . .'

'I know where it is. Thanks but no thanks. I've messed up enough recently.'

63

Lucy was feeling the pressure. She worked every hour that she was able. She turned punters around so fast that she was in danger of losing her prestigious place in Mamasan Linda's mercenary heart. Mamasan had always picked the wealthiest men for her – those with *special need*s. Now Lucy was choosing her own clients and they were not paying Mamasan their dues. They were quantity rather than quality. But Mamasan Linda was fond of Lucy and knew that she had money problems and that her and her sister's relationship was strained with the arrival of Georgina. She had seen the way Lucy reacted when Chan was in the club. Even though Mamasan Linda provided Chan with information on the girls, Lucy had brought her in a lot of money over the years and she had to protect her assets.

She was not pleased when three Chinese men from the mainland asked for Lucy by name. She did not know them. 'Low-life triad types', she called them. Lucy didn't like them either, they looked as if they had clawed their way up the ranks and still hadn't reached the dizzy heights of the sewers. But she needed to pull every punter at the moment.

Two of the men left five minutes after Lucy sat down. She was quite relieved; they hadn't been the greatest conversationalists. Just a few minutes after that the third made advances to buy her out. Mamasan Linda looked at Lucy and shrugged disparagingly. Would she like to go? Yes, she would. Mamasan Linda came back to the Dressing Room to tell Lucy to be careful. She told Lucy she would see her when she returned later in the evening.

They drove to an apartment block in Causeway Bay. Lucy knew it. She had been there once before. It was a place that let apartments to tourists or travelling businessmen who did not want to stay in a hotel. She followed him in. No doorman. Just a pass code.

'Nobody here tonight, hey? Got the night off?' she joked. He didn't answer.

Lucy walked behind him, staring at his shoulders. He was nervous. She could see the tension in the way he walked, bristling, hackles up, looking twitchily from side to side, starting at any creak or squeak. In the elevator he avoided her gaze.

Alighting at level thirty-two, they walked down a quiet corridor; her heels thudding on cheap carpet. He stopped at an apartment door and knocked. *Why had he knocked and not opened it with a key?*

The answer came to her just as the door was opened. It was then that her heart began racing, and her mouth dried. Her instincts told her to run but he was blocking her exit. Then she knew: *Not his apartment, someone else there.* Too late! She was pushed inside as the door opened, and into the waiting arms of his two companions from the club.

Lucy turned to run. There was no chance – the door was already shut behind her. She bolted for the bathroom and tried to lock the door but they were on her. They pulled her around the apartment by her hair, smashing her face into the walls as they went. She closed her eyes and covered her face with her hands in an attempt to minimise the damage. Finally, trapped back in the bathroom, one held her by the throat, pressing a knee onto her chest, while another removed her trousers and knickers and they took it in turns to rape her. Just when she thought she would definitely die, they gave her a last kick for good measure and left.

For a few minutes she stayed absolutely still, waiting for their return, but there was only silence. Then, blinded from her injuries, she crawled along the floor and found her bag. She fumbled inside for her phone and called Max.

He was at her side in minutes. She had managed to find her clothes and dress herself. She crawled to the door and opened it for him.

'Max, are both my eyes still there?' Her hands shook violently as she held them up in front of her face, not daring to touch.

Max bent down to look at her. Lucy felt his breath on her face.

'Yes.'

'Sure?'

'Yes, I am sure. Lots of blood. You need stitching.'

'Get me to a hospital, Max.'

He did as he was told.

Lucy was allowed to go home the following morning. She had come off well, considering. She had some bad cuts to her face and two cracked ribs, and she had extensive bruising. She needed stitches to the cuts around her eyes and forehead.

'I knew this would happen to you one day.' Ka Lei's voice was shrill. She was shaking uncontrollably. She couldn't look at her sister without physically crumbling. 'Please, Lucy, don't go back there. Find some other job. We can manage, we'll be all right.'

Georgina was equally as wide-eyed and dumbstruck as Ka Lei. Looking at Lucy's battered face made her feel sick. Lucy didn't answer; her lungs were bruised and it was painful to talk or breathe. She shuffled around the flat, resting every few steps, and, after pausing for a few minutes at the entrance to her bedroom, she moved inside and eased herself onto the bed.

She squinted at the bright blanket of sunlight that stabbed her eyes as it blasted through the windows. Ka Lei went round to pull down the blinds, before joining Georgina and Lucy on the bed. Max stood in the doorway – waiting for her to tell him she didn't need him any more.

'Why did they do it, Lucy? Do you have any idea? Did you recognise them?' Georgina asked. Lucy didn't answer. She closed her eyes and shook her head miserably.

Georgina turned to Ka Lei. 'We should call the police.'

Lucy groaned and shook her head.

'I know you don't want to, Lucy, but we can't just sit here and do nothing, can we?'

Georgina turned to Ka Lei for support but Ka Lei shook her head.

'I don tink we call police, no goo, dey do nudding,' she said.

Lucy started to cry. Silently, one tear at a time squeezed out and negotiated a difficult downward path between the swellings.

It was not *just* the memory of the beating and the rape that made her wince, made the blood pound in her face and the swellings tighten around the stitches. She wasn't crying because of the pain. Lucy was thinking about the debt and the fact that she would have no chance of paying it back looking like she did.

64

It would be several weeks before Lucy would be able to return to work. While Georgina and Ka Lei were out earning the money to stay afloat, Lucy took on the role of housemaid. She stayed in the flat all day and drifted in and out of shock-induced lethargy that made her sleep for several hours in the day and stay awake all night. In between resting periods she shuffled about the flat, slowly and deliberately carrying out mundane tasks. She folded blankets, smoothed sheets. She arranged clothes into neat piles. She spent an hour on a task that would normally have taken her a few minutes.

Ka Lei and Georgina tiptoed around the flat. They tried to stay out of Lucy's way. At night-time they lay wide-eyed in the darkness and whispered to one another. They looked towards the wall where they knew Lucy would be listening: Lucy – the bringer of evil, the spoiler of everything. As much as they sympathised with her, she had thrown them into a world they had never asked to enter. The happy home that they had created was ruined. Now they had to get out of the flat to find any privacy. Lucy was always there.

Their favourite bar was Bar Paris. It was a small bar in Causeway Bay.

Georgina sat beneath the peeling Parisian posters, picking at the wax that spilled from a wine-bottle candleholder, while Edith Piaf warbled from the speaker. The bar was empty except for a delivery man and the bar manager, who were deep in animated conversation, gossiping about other patrons on the delivery man's rounds. It was still only five o'clock and too early to expect much custom. Ka Lei arrived flustered and anxious. Georgina had left her an urgent message about meeting.

'Waz wrong?' She dropped into the seat opposite. 'Is it Lucy? Something new happen?'

Georgina calmed her. 'No, it's all right, Ka Lei, nothing new,' she reassured her. 'It's only that I wanted to talk to you about what we are going to do.'

Ka Lei screwed up her face and nodded.

Georgina continued: 'I've been thinking, I think we should talk to him. I'm going to tell Mr Chan that Lucy is sick and she needs more time . . .'

The bar manager and the deliveryman stopped their gossiping to listen. Georgina lowered her voice. 'We have to think of a way to help Lucy. We must do everything we can.'

'Yes, no juz Lucy ploblem now, is *family* ploblem. Tese very bat men, you unnerstan?' Ka Lei tried to smile. 'Maybe better you go back to England, more safe dere. Maybe better go home now, huh?' She looked away as she spoke, dreading the answer.

'No way! This is my home now. *You* are my family.

274

Where else am I going to go, hey?' Georgina smiled and squeezed Ka Lei's hand. 'You know I would never leave you.'

'I am glat. Very glat. Ten we muz pay him.'

'But how? None of us have that kind of money. How are we going to get it?'

After a few minutes Ka Lei broke the silence. 'Maybe I star workin at te club, just till te money is finished.'

'No, Ka Lei, you mustn't. You would hate it. And what about your nursing?'

'Tese men will kill Lucy, or me, maybe you. Everyting is different now.'

'Is there no one who could help us?'

'Tere is no one. We muz get money. Tat's te way it is here in Hong Kong: nobody care – nobody help you – only money.'

They trudged their way home from the bar and talked it through endlessly. It took them nearly an hour, but by the end they had raised each other's hopes slightly and steeled themselves for whatever lay ahead.

They stood outside their mansion block, pausing to gather their resolve and comfort one another. They hugged.

'We will face it together, right . . . anything . . . Yes?' said Georgina. Ka Lei nodded and smiled bravely. 'Then I will talk to Mr Chan.'

65

The next day Lucy was the only one home when the call came.

'Hello, Ka Mei. I was sorry to hear about your accident. I understand from your mamasan that you were hit by a car. You must be more careful next time. Meet me at the paper stand in Admiralty MTR station in fifteen minutes.'

Lucy found a large pair of sunglasses to hide her face, and set off immediately. It would take her a few minutes to reach the Wanchai MTR station, then about three minutes to walk to the platform. The next stop was Admiralty. She was there on time. He sent his chauffeur down to find her.

'Poor Lucy.' They sat in the back of his car while the chauffeur drove them around. Chan reached out to touch her face. 'Still, you're used to pain, aren't you?' He smiled smugly. 'You won't be able to work for a while, though, will you?'

She gave a small shake of the head.

'Pity.' He stared out of the window. 'How is your sister?' Lucy saw the corner of his mouth tug. 'You know, Lucy, I have been thinking and I would like to see her again.' Chan turned back to look at her and waited.

'I don't think so, Mr Chan.'

He leaned over to pat her leg. 'Your mamasan tells me that yours is not a happy home at the moment.'

Lucy searched his face incredulously.

'You see I know all about your life.' He grinned. 'I know that things have not been easy for you, Lucy. I know that you have been a very good sister to Ka Lei, like a mother. You have had to bring her up and you have done a good job – she is a lovely girl.' He leaned closer. 'This English cousin of yours, I hope she isn't coming between you. That would be a terrible shame. Ka Lei needs you and I am sure you wouldn't want to lose her.' He paused to see what effect his rhetoric was having on Lucy. She wasn't looking at him; she was staring at her lap. 'Maybe I haven't helped the situation. I have been a little hard on you.' He sat back to observe her. 'Never mind, maybe I can make it up to you. I have an offer for you, Lucy. Come on, a smile, things are not so bad, are they?'

She looked at him and smiled with a nervous sweetness.

'Lucy, how would it be if we were to start again? If we forget all about the debt?' He swiped the air. 'No debt, gone! Would you like that?'

Lucy nodded warily.

'This is my offer: I have been thinking a lot about you and Ka Lei recently. I have plans for you both. I want you to take good care of your sister. Look after her – she is special to me. You should stop working at the club. I will help you financially.' He took out a wad of notes from his pocket and pushed them across the seat to Lucy, where they stayed untouched. 'I would also like you to move. I have a vacant apartment.'

Lucy was lost for words. She stared at him, expecting some awful twist to this strange new turn of events.

'From this day on, Ka Lei is mine. I own her. I will keep her. She will become my concubine. Your job will be to see that she stays safe – stays . . . contained. She is not to leave the house without supervision. Do you understand, Lucy?'

Lucy was afraid that she did.

'But there is one more thing, Lucy. One more thing I demand from you before the debt is finished.'

Not even Lucy was prepared for what came next.

66

Georgina emerged wet from the shower. Her phone was ringing.

She was hoping it would be Mann. Despite what had happened, she still held out hope it would be the start of something between them. But it was Lucy. She wanted Georgina to do her a favour. Georgina was doing her best to be kind to Lucy – even after what she had done to Ka Lei, she felt sorry for her. She and Ka Lei were just waiting till Lucy felt better, then they would think about moving out.

'Will I be able to find the shoe repairers, Lucy? I don't want to be late for Ka Lei. I'm meeting her at Bar Paris at two, after she finishes her shift at the hospital. We're going to spend the rest of the day together. She needs me at the moment. She's still so upset about . . . everything . . .'

'No problem. I tell you how to get there. It's on the way. Got a pen? It's no problem, right?'

'Of course it's no problem, Lucy. If you need it done, I will do it for you.'

* * *

It was one thirty. The sun was high in the sky. It blasted down onto the busy street and began burning the top of Georgina's head. She scratched her head as the sweat tickled her scalp. She longed to be out of the heat.

As she stepped onto a narrow cobbled street she paused to listen to a strange noise coming from a dilapidated building above her. It was the click-clack of a mahjong game that had been going all night. By now, the players' irritability had reached its peak. Their eyes were scratching with tiredness and their manners were raw. They shouted above the clacking pieces, slamming them onto the table.

Georgina stood in the road and listened for a while. Her eyes were searching all the time for the exact source of the noise. She had never heard the sound of a mahjong game before. She was lost in thought when an open-backed truck passed within inches of her.

The driver was Man Po. He had just taken delivery of a consignment of pig carcasses and was delivering them to a restaurant across town. Georgina smelt the truck in the same second as she saw it: salted meat and animal faeces drenched the air around it. In the back of the truck were piles of split-throated pigs. She watched them pass – their stubbly blond hairs shone in the sunshine and their sad opaque eyes stared up at the sky. Man Po turned his head back to look at her, not smiling, just staring in his lolling fashion. The pigs' black throats gaped and their trotters bounced as the truck jolted over the cobbles. Then he turned the corner and was gone.

Georgina stumbled, reeling slightly from the near

miss with Man Po's pig lorry, and slipped on the uneven road. Looking down at the ground she saw that water filled the cracks between the cobbles under her feet. It was coming from market stalls just across the street. She crossed the road, entered the market area, and was immediately swallowed by stalls and livestock. It was a typical Chinese market, a place where all creatures alive and dead were being offered for sale (anything that lived beneath the sky certainly *could* and definitely *would* be eaten, according to Chinese belief). The smell in the air was flesh and fish, perfumed with incense.

Georgina felt lost and disorientated in the market, but she had no inclination to leave. Tiredness had stolen her ability to reason, and, anyway, there was shade from the stalls to bring relief from the hot sun, and the water from the fruit stalls was cool underfoot. She felt it through the soles of her sandals.

She stopped by a small group of people gathered in front of a fat stallholder who had a flat face and an enormous head. He stood behind a chopping board, a long knife in one hand, while the other rested on a bag on the table in front of him. The bag held his merchandise, bulging, spreading, heavy with a weight and too dark to define its contents. It twitched with an irregular pulse like some massive heart dumped there – collapsing over the wooden slab, but still beating.

The fat stallholder addressed the crowd excitedly. He beckoned to the people to come and watch this imminent spectacle. Then, after a few minutes, when sufficient people had gathered including Georgina, he held the knife aloft with the one hand and reached into the net bag with the other, pulled out a tiny pair of dark green legs, stretched them, then sliced them clean through at the thigh. He pushed the torso to the back of the board and offered the legs forward for sale.

The small group of people turned as one unit to stare at Georgina as she gasped, and the fat stallholder stopped his work. Looking up, he smiled.

'Don lok so sat, Missy, fill no pain.'

She smiled, embarrassed, as the stallholder and onlookers stared at her. She wanted so much to walk away but she was unable to move, riveted by repulsion as more frogs were taken out, sliced at the thighs, their torsos pushed to one side of the chopping board creating a grizzly mound of wasted life, and their legs scraped shivering into a bag. Then she turned and, with great relief, saw a familiar face. Max was standing behind her.

67

In Bar Paris Edith Piaf crackled away as Ka Lei picked at the candle wax around the old wine bottles and sipped her warm Coke. She checked her messages again and again. She didn't know where Georgina could be: Georgina was never late. In fact, she was usually early.

Every time the door at Bar Paris opened, Ka Lei searched the faces of those entering, sure that one of them would be Georgina. But, as each stranger stepped inside and closed the door behind him, a small panic surged upward in her chest and a voice in her head said:

Georgina isn't coming . . . Georgina isn't coming.

But Ka Lei couldn't bear that thought: she needed Georgina so badly; she had waited all day to be able to see her. Georgina was the only one who could make her feel better. And now it was over an hour and a half since they were due to meet and the panic inside continued to squeeze her. Caught like a rabbit in a boa constrictor's grip, she couldn't breathe, and she couldn't swallow the scream that was wedged in her throat. She instinctively knew something awful had happened.

She left Bar Paris and ran all the way home.

Georgina wasn't there. Lucy was. Ka Lei ran into the flat calling: 'Where is Georgina?' She stared wide-eyed at the scattered belongings in Georgina's room. 'Why are all her things in such a mess? Where is she?'

Lucy came towards her with her arms outstretched, tears welling in her eyes. Ka Lei fended her off. 'What's wrong, Lucy?' She looked past her into the bedroom. 'Where is she?'

'Ka Lei, I think Georgina must have gone.'

'Gone where? What do you mean?'

Lucy walked across the room to the dressing table. 'Look – this is the place she always kept her passport, and now it's gone – see! And her things are in such a mess, as if she left in a hurry. She took just what she needed and left the rest. Sorry, huh?'

Ka Lei stood in the middle of the room, shaking her head in disbelief as Lucy showed her the empty box that had held Georgina's passport. She took the box from her sister and stared into it, willing the passport to reappear.

'And her toiletries, her papers – other important things, they are all gone.'

Ka Lei's hands shook as she held on to the box and her saucer-eyes froze with panic as she surveyed the evidence of Georgina's departure.

'Did you know she was leaving? Did she say anything to you, Ka Lei?'

Ka Lei shook her head and, as she did so, swollen tear drops spilt down her face. She began searching for her phone.

Mandy was setting up for the evening when the call came.

Lucy stood poised, just outside the bedroom door, listening – straining to hear the one-sided conversation.

'Mandy? It's Ka Lei here. Georgina cousin. Please – have you see Georgina? . . . Oh no . . . not here also . . . I see . . . no . . . I solly . . . yes please . . . yes . . . okay . . . I will . . . thank you. Bye bye.'

Then Ka Lei went into the bathroom and locked the door behind her.

As soon as Mandy got off the phone to Ka Lei, she called Mann.

'No, she doesn't know where she is . . . no . . . no idea. It's unthinkable that she doesn't know where she is. The two are always together and Georgina's just not like that, and with the murders going on . . . I thought I'd better call you.'

Mann put the phone down. A cold cramp spread out from the pit of his stomach. It turned his blood to ice. Had Georgina become the latest piece on the killer's chess board?

He went straight round to the flat. Ka Lei was in such a state of shock and panic that she couldn't speak.

Lucy explained. 'Only Georgina would take these things. She has taken the only possessions that matter to her,' she told Mann.

'She didn't take *all* her things?'

'No, maybe she just didn't want the rest. I hope she's okay. Maybe she just went back.'

He turned to Ka Lei, who was slumped on Georgina's bed and hadn't moved since he'd got there.

'Was there anything worrying her?'

Ka Lei looked at him and then at Lucy. He thought she was going to say something but then she shook her head and went back to staring at the floor.

Mann finished going through Georgina's belongings. He didn't find her passport, but he found something else – a small photo album. Photos from the beginning. Georgina as an infant, wrapped in white, nestled in the crook of a very proud-looking man. Underneath was written: *Me and Dad.* Her mother, *me and Mum*, a photo of a small woman standing beside Georgina, a tall teenage girl, her arm around Georgina's waist. Then there were countless photo-booth montages of Georgina and Ka Lei.

He knew there was no way that Georgina would have left either the photo album or Ka Lei behind. No way.

68

'It's broad daylight, Mann. Her passport's gone. She packed up and left. I don't know why you think any different. In any case we wait forty-eight hours, like you've been doing, see if she turns up like the others have done.' Superintendent White walked back to his desk, sat down heavily and leaned back in the chair.

'She didn't.'

'Didn't what?'

'She didn't just leave.'

'Okay. Let's look at the facts. So far as we know, Bernadette, Roxanne and Gosia were all taken at night. This girl was last seen in the day. The others disappeared from Club Mercedes. This one wasn't working at the club any more.'

'That doesn't mean there isn't a connection,' said Mann. 'And she lived with Lucy.'

'Yes, Mann, and we come back to the passport, and the fact that she packed up and took what she needed, left the rest. Her cousin seems certain . . .'

'Her cousin's lying. I asked the other occupants in the building, shopkeepers, street vendors outside, and they remembered seeing her that day. She left on foot, walking towards Causeway Bay. She wasn't carrying anything, just her handbag. She wasn't on any of the passenger lists of flights out yesterday. I checked.'

'She could have left on a ferry. I can't afford to waste man hours. She might well have just decided to leave. I still feel we ought to wait forty-eight hours to see if she turns up.'

White looked at Mann. He knew it wasn't what Mann wanted to hear. The rest of the team looked at Mann as well. They knew he was trying his best to stay calm, but those of them who had ever seen him angry before were also aware that he didn't give much warning when he blew.

'She could be lying on a beach somewhere, Mann, sunning herself. She could be with a boyfriend. She could be anywhere.'

'And she could be being tortured and be minutes from death.'

'I am going to pull rank on you with this one, Mann. I think you are too involved – your judgement is not as sharp as it should be and I need you to see things clearly. There is a system in place – we need to follow it. We wait forty-eight hours.'

'I see things crystal clear.' Mann was hanging on to his temper by a thread. 'I will find her myself. Fuck the system!' He grabbed his jacket and stormed out of the office.

69

Georgina came to, semi-awake, on a cold stone floor. She was aware that she was naked. At the same time as she reached to cover herself, her arm gave way and she slumped to one side. She felt the rough cold stone against her skin. Her body was too heavy to move and she could do nothing about it.

She heard the sound of men's voices in the room with her – Chinese voices. Through a nauseous semi-sleep she heard them talking. Her head thumped against the side of her skull. She tried hard to open her eyes but they were too heavy – they stayed open for a second then dropped shut.

Someone switched on the shower above her head. She flinched as the jet of cold water hit the back of her head.

'Wakey, wakey, SHOWER!' A man's voice.

She struggled to sit up, managed to straighten herself a little, then stopped. Her head fell forward onto her chest. Two men watched her from the corner of their eyes as they chatted.

One of the men walked over to her.

'UP. STAND UP!'

She tried to lift her head but the weight of her wet hair forced it back against the wall. Her hair stuck to her face. She stared up at the men for a few seconds then her eyes slid closed.

'Fuck. She looks ill.'

'He gave her too much. If she dies we'd better be ready to cover for each other.'

'She's not going to die.' The man nearest Georgina nudged her with his foot.

'Hey, wake up. STAND UP, I said.' He kicked her thigh with his foot. Georgina groaned and slid further down the wall.

'Watch. Cover for me. I'm going to wake her up,' he said to his companion as he unzipped his flies and took hold of Georgina by her wet hair, dragging her head upwards. Her eyes were closed, her mouth hung open.

'Let's see if she likes Chinese dick,' he said, turning to his friend and grinning.

At that second Georgina vomited.

'Fucking bitch.'

He threw her back against the wall and turned the shower on himself to wash the vomit from his trousers.

The next thing Georgina heard was a loud knock at the door and a woman's cockney accent shouting, 'Open this fuckin' door.'

70

Mann went back home to think. Somewhere, amid all these images on his lounge floor, there was the answer. He had to get Georgina back. He had to find out who killed Helen.

He stared hard at Roxanne's photos. The person who had killed Roxanne was walking around now. This wasn't two years ago, or twenty, this was now.

He closed his eyes, leaned back in the chair, took a large swig of his vodka tonic and let his mind drift.

Roxanne: the picture he had in his mind was electric-blue eye-shadow; short, stumpy legs; permed frizzy hair. She wanted fame at all costs, but she was a tough little woman. She had put up with a lot of abuse in her life and had come out the other side. She knew that she was lucky compared to others. She also knew you had to make your own luck.

Mann reread the notes on her – on her death. The autopsy was more detailed than the others because she was the most recent and hadn't been frozen. What had she had to eat on that last meal again? He read that she'd had steak and potato. That wasn't a Chinese meal. He'd been starving her up to that point, then he gives her steak. Did he make her eat it with him? She had heroin and a trace of Rohypnol in her urine. Someone wanted Roxanne to look like she was enjoying it, or at least not to care. Someone wanted her to last the distance. Why?

Electric-shock torture? A cattle prod? He must have neglected to put something in her mouth because she bit her tongue, and that was careless. Dressing her up? Role play? Why? The fantasy aspect of the death was important to him. Serial killers tended to re-enact the same fantasy, look for the same type of victim. Were all the others dressed as cave girls, like she was? It didn't appear so. Only Roxanne had traces of calf skin on her. Maybe the fantasy was broader than that, maybe the calf skin wasn't the crucial part of this fantasy? Maybe it wasn't always the same man?

All this time that Mann contemplated Roxanne's death he couldn't look at Helen. Her photos remained at the top of the room, obscured from his view. He would take time to come to them. He wasn't ready to know what Helen had to tell him.

He looked again at Roxanne and imagined her last minutes. He saw her dressed in a calf's hide. *Cave girl* . . . She died by a ligature applied around her neck. *She was hung, most likely*. Mann closed his eyes for a few seconds and imagined the scenario. He saw her dressed up, rope around her neck, but she wasn't hanging. *No – she wasn't*. Roxanne was *lassoed*. The cave girl was dressed in an animal skin to *become* an animal. She was cattle-prodded and she was lassoed and she was dressed as a calf because that's what she was to someone, an animal to be branded and slaughtered . . . branded with an F. Who or what did the F stand for?

71

Ng was in the office when Mann arrived the next morning.

'What did you come up with, Genghis?' Ng asked as Mann walked in.

'Roxanne Berger.'

'Me too. Cave girl. Hung and electrocuted. We want to look at the others again – they may all be the same.'

'She was dressed like an animal, she was treated like one, not a cave girl. The person who did this, he gets off on pretending she's one of his herd. She wasn't hung either, she was lassoed. The more she struggled, the tighter the noose got. But he didn't let her die. He kept bringing her to the point where she passed out. He brought her round with the cattle prod, that's how she came to bite her tongue. He raped her in between. She must have been submissive with the Rohypnol.'

'Why did he give her that?'

'It has the effect of making a woman become sexually abandoned, but at the same time it is a powerful sedative. I haven't had one case of it here before. The drug is just becoming known here.'

'Not a thing your average rapist or murderer would bother to get, even if he knew how to source it.'

'Or your ordinary pig farmer. This man takes his pleasure very seriously and he's willing to pay for it.'

'Any news on your friend? Has she turned up?'

'No. Georgina's not going to turn up, Ng. This may represent a new twist, but she is definitely a victim of the Butcher. CSI have been around to the flat to see if they could find anything. I am going to visit Lucy again later. She has an infinite ability to lie, and I think that's what she's doing now. Haven't figured out what's in it for her yet, but I presume it has something to do with money.'

Ng picked up his papers and tidied them into a pile. 'What about the other women? What about Helen?' He didn't look at Mann as he asked.

'I'm working my way through them. I haven't looked at Helen's case yet. Have you?'

'Just briefly. I think it should be done urgently. We only have two complete victims, after all. She is one of them.' His eyes finally met Mann's. 'We have to get as much information from her death as we can.'

'Of course. I am going to look at it tonight. Definitely.'

Li walked into the office. He'd been out in the clubs all night, but he'd still had time to think about the way the women died.

'Any more on any of the others, Li?'

'Gosia. The cigarette burns on her. They form a pattern.'

'What do you mean?'

'They look like the Islands – Lantau, Lama, Cheung Chau.' He pulled out the photo and set it on the desk. 'See!' He traced the outline of the Islands.

Ng squinted at the photo. 'Well, what's that? A passing ship? A shoal of tuna? And that? What is that?' asked Ng. 'You need to get some sleep, Shrimp, you're hallucinating.'

Li blushed and giggled, embarrassed.

'Anyway, Shrimp, you're sure there are sixty-eight, right?' said Mann. 'Keep working on it – there is something significant about these burns. Some role play, some clue. Some fucking game or other. It's good to keep looking at it and trying out ideas. Even if some of them are shit.'

Ng patted Li on the back. 'What else?' He could see Shrimp was bursting to tell.

'I was with a girl last night. She said she'd seen a film. She said it was a snuff movie. She said it had a white woman in it.'

72

'Did she say where she'd seen it?'

'No. She wouldn't say. She disappeared on me after that.'

'Okay, Shrimp. Concentrate on finding these films. Ng – get every officer we can spare out there looking for these tapes. Any more results through from the path lab?'

'I have them, boss. They just came through a minute ago. Victim six . . . Helen . . . definitely asphyxiated, probably with a bag . . . no obvious signs of pressure or crush injuries. Traces of metal in the wounds across her body, definitely looking at a metal-tipped instrument of some kind.'

'What else?'

'Nothing else,' Li mumbled.

'Say it, Shrimp.'

'She was sexually mutilated.'

'How?'

No one spoke. Li looked at Ng, but Ng couldn't save him. He was treading water in the middle of the ocean and he was about to drown.

'How, Li?'

'Her uterus and ovaries are missing.'

'Give me the file. I'm going home – call me if you need me.'

Mann took the file from Li and left the office. He had to face the photos, and he had to face Helen.

They were still waiting for him, spread out over his lounge floor. They hadn't moved. His eyes scanned all the pictures but missed out Helen's. He stood in the middle of them: Roxanne, Gosia, Beverly, and the three others – two still without a name.

He stood and forced his eyes towards Helen's pictures. He focused on her face. He loved that photo. He had taken it himself. It was a black and white shot. The sun was on her face; she was laughing. The wind had blown her hair across her face and she'd put up a hand to brush it away. Her eyes were sparkling and her whole face was full of love, of happiness. She was looking right at Mann.

He picked up all the other photos and pushed them to one side. He collected Helen's and laid them around the chair. He sat in the midst of them, leaned back and closed his eyes. The cool-season effect was about to hit him. The tornado was about to pick him up by his heels and spin him through time – to somewhere he really didn't want to go. The dream came back to him. Helen was packing her bag again, throwing everything into a small suitcase, and it wouldn't fit and she was getting frustrated. He helped her shut it. They pushed together and forced it closed. Mann picked it up. It hardly weighed anything. They walked to the door in silence. Already, an anxiousness was creeping into the dream. Mann was trapped in it now. He'd have to fight to get out of this one. He was being held back. Helen was walking far ahead of him. He couldn't catch up. Helen was almost out of sight then ... *BANG* ... Helen's voice, not speaking – screaming, with pain. And someone else was with her.

73

Mann rocked on his feet as he held on to the cold porcelain bowl and steadied himself for a few seconds. He wiped the bitter bile from his mouth before turning on the shower and undressing. He looked into the mirror. He was wet with sweat, and his face was blotched from the exertion of vomiting. He stood for a few seconds and tried to see Helen as he wanted to remember her, not as he had just seen her. He wanted to forget that image as fast as he could, but he knew the dream was not done with him yet. It had more to show him.

He stepped into the shower and turned the massage jet on. It blasted his back with needle-thin jets of water. Tipping his head back he felt his scalp tingling as the water pelted him like hard rain. He reached out his hand and steadied himself against the cold white tiles, closing his eyes. He bowed his head. He so wanted to escape. But he knew he had not finished yet. He must go back into the lounge and face Helen's suffering again. He must relive it and find whoever did it. And he must find Georgina. He owed her that. He owed it to Helen as well.

He towelled dry, slipped on some boxers and a T-shirt and went into the kitchen to make some tea. No more alcohol for him for a while. He needed to stay focused, plus it made him morose and he didn't need any help with that at the moment.

Back in the lounge the photos were around the base of his chair where he had left them. He walked past them and went to stand at the window. He wished he could see the sea, but he couldn't. He could just look at the other tower blocks in the development. But the sea was out there somewhere. He looked for it to help him now.

If we ever make enough money, that's what we'll do with it . . . buy ourselves a little shack on Lama Island. Lie on the hot sand, sleep on the beach, get drunk and make love under the stars.

He pulled down the blinds and adjusted them to allow just enough light through, but to take away all distractions. He turned back to the chair.

There were fifteen photos from the autopsy, a lab report and a plastic bag containing her bracelet. He took the bracelet out and held it in his hand and turned it over a few times. Then he placed it next to the black and white portrait and moved the photo and the bracelet away from the rest. Those two items belonged to Helen alive. The rest were from Helen dead.

Mann grouped the photos into the different sections of the body. He picked up the report. She had been frozen approximately twelve hours after death. Her uterus and ovaries had been extracted shortly before that. Her stomach was empty. There was heroin in her system. She had severe bruising around the wrists, consistent with having been suspended by them. There was evidence of rape.

Mann looked at the photos. He kept coming back to the photo of her head. Her face looked swollen and empty but still serene. He stared hard at the photo until his eyes stopped seeing it and he went back to the dream. He went back to Helen packing the case. Mann picked it up. It weighed nothing. He had come back to sort things out with her. He knew she was leaving, she had told him the day before. He had watched her pack her case. He had left for work, but he had come back. When he'd arrived she was already loading her things into the taxi. It was too late. *If she wanted to go, then he should let her*. But he had come back to ask her to stay. Pride got in his way. He watched her give her case to the taxi driver. Mann could see him now. He'd looked up at Mann as Mann arrived. The files in Mann's head rolled and flipped, matching images, fitting noses to faces, to expressions, to flashes of frozen memory – searching, searching, until they found what they sought. And then Mann saw Max with Helen's case in his hand.

74

It was early evening when they set off for the club. Chan was accompanying three of his new clients: Mr Sun Yat-sen and two other newly recruited triad brothers.

The helicopter flew over the ancient walled cities of Kowloon and the small fishing villages of the New Territories. Instead of heading towards Shenzhen, they skirted around it and flew over the reservoir and into the Special Economic Zone. Then they followed a line of disused quarries that pockmarked the land below. Just when the fat trio were beginning to exchange curious looks, they saw it. The men whooped and clapped. There, at the bottom of one of the redundant quarries, two buildings shaped into the numbers sixty-eight dazzled in the last rays of the sun, like diamond-studded birthday cakes.

Chan told the pilot to take his time so they could get a good look at the place. He was immensely proud of his creation and more than willing to show it off. The helicopter circled around a few times and Chan pointed out the various buildings below. The two main buildings, Sixty-Eight, were connected in the middle. They stood four storeys high, coming halfway up the quarry-side, and were surrounded by lush green garden. There were small lakes dotted around the grounds and a golf course that flowed from that quarry into the next.

In all, the complex took up about a square kilometre. The men were obviously impressed, especially when Chan told them about his special attraction for golfers:

'I keep wild boar in the woods around the golf course, so that if you lose your ball, it is up to you whether to risk finding it, or concede defeat. You are welcome to do a spot of hunting while you are here. This is the place where you only have to ask and it will be arranged.'

The pilot circled around a few times, hovering above the swaying palms and rippling rooftop pools before landing. Four security men met them and took their luggage. It would be returned to their rooms after being checked. They were led to the palm-lined entrance, which was in the Eight building.

They stood in the reception area. It was a classy mix of crystal and black marble with antique Chinese furniture mixed with modern paintings and swathes of hanging silks. Above their heads the building spiralled upwards to its four floors. Two young girls dressed as Korean brides served them tea and hovered over them with warm towels. Checks completed, a receptionist approached to escort the men to their rooms. They took the lift up to the fourth floor and walked down the plush-carpeted landing till they reached the first of three rooms. The receptionist opened the door and bowed as she stood back for the most senior man – Sun Yat-sen – to enter.

'Please enjoy . . . your fantasy-maker will be along in a minute.'

She shuffled backwards, bowing as she went. Sun Yat-sen closed the door and looked about him. A bottle of scotch was waiting for him on the glass coffee table. He poured himself a generous one and took a slug, undoing his tie and stripping off his jacket. He threw it across the zebra-skinned bed. As he did so there was a knock at the door. A man in a tuxedo brought in his leather holdall and placed it on the rack. He bowed and left. Sun Yat-sen took another swig of the scotch and waited. He was excited, anxious even.

Another knock on the door. A young man waited outside, briefcase in hand. He was immaculately dressed, if a little too carefully, and to the feminine side: his eyelashes were too long, and his mouth was slightly too wide with a smile that required a tilt of the head and a pursing of the lips to perform.

'Mr Sun Yat-sen?'

'Yes.'

The young man entered. 'How do you find the room?'

'Good. Very good.'

'Let me refresh your drink for you.' He poured out another scotch and placed it in front of Sun Yat-sen. Then, with a small bow, he sat perched on the edge of the leather sofa, knees together, legs tucked to one side.

'Now, Mr Sun Yat-sen, I have been looking at your requirements.' He looked up from Chan's letter, which he had in front of him. 'I believe that you are more interested in the fantasy side of Sixty-Eight rather than the gambling?'

'That's right.'

'Normally our clients like to have the full experience of earning their fantasy – *but*, when you come with *this* sort of recommendation...' he fluttered Chan's letter, 'we don't tend to argue.' He giggled as if his voice had never broken. 'As you know, we do not use currency here – clients pay a fee to enter and earn the rest. Your benefactor has, of course, provided unlimited funds for you. So, you may have whatever you desire. Although...' he smiled his wide smile and batted his inch-long lashes, 'you may find it more *fun* to earn the points needed in some other way...'

The young man shifted his legs to the other side and waited for an answer. Sun Yat-sen just stared at him.

'Well, let's see now, your fantasy is pretty straight anyway, isn't it? I believe that you wish to have some intimate time with one of the girls, preferably foreign.'

'*Must* be foreign.'

'I see, well, that can be done. And no other requirements, sir? Believe me, you can ask me for *anything* you wish.'

'I don't think so, but thank you for the thought,' Sun Yat-sen replied, growing tired of the young man.

'It's my job.' He stood and bowed. 'See you later, Mr Sun Yat-sen, enjoy your fantasy, she will be waiting for you in the nightclub.'

75

Big Frank had decided to update his image. He had hair extensions glued onto his own white-blond strands of thinning hair. The hair once belonged to a fourteen-year-old Bangladeshi girl named Sonali. In order to achieve the look that Big Frank required, the hair had been bleached till it was ruined. Sonali had been paid enough to buy her brother some shoes so that he could walk the five miles to school each day. Sonali never went to school – there wasn't one for girls.

Big Frank had bought himself a pair of tight leather trousers and a Harley Davidson motorbike, which he kept beneath the stilts of his Captiva house. He wasn't able to ride it yet. Occasionally he flicked back his long hair, hoisted his creaky leathered leg over the saddle, and straddled the Hog, making engine noises. He kept a helmet for Lucy on the back. He had decided to ask her to marry him. There was some quality in her that he just hadn't found elsewhere. Whether it was her devotion to her work, the pleasure she took from it, or just that she knew which of Frank's buttons needed pushing – he had decided he could do a lot worse than spend the rest of his life with a willing whore. He caught a plane back to Hong Kong to seal the deal.

Lucy had accepted Chan's deal, and she wouldn't be returning to work at the club. She had a new job – looking after Ka Lei. Soon Chan would want them to move into the flat he had in mind for them. Then Lucy would have to tell Ka Lei that she had a new life ahead of her. That her nursing career meant nothing. It was over before it began. She would have no more money worries but she would have no freedom either. She would be owned by Chan.

Lucy dreaded telling her. She couldn't do it yet – Ka Lei was deteriorating daily. She went from pacing around the flat to sitting on her bed for hours, staring at nothing. She was going mad, Lucy was convinced of it. She spent much of her time talking to the bathroom mirror: *I love you, Georgina. Come back to me, Georgina. I can still see you in my eyes, Georgina* . . . She repeated it endlessly. Lucy asked her what she was doing. She was talking to Georgina, she said. She could see her in the mirror, in her eyes, in her soul. Lucy despaired.

Ka Lei was sleeping when Big Frank called. Lucy was delighted to hear his voice. He wanted to see her straight away. She told him she couldn't. Maybe tomorrow. But Frank was adamant. She *must* come over – he had one helluva surprise for his good little Hong Kong girl – something really special.

Lucy knew she shouldn't go but she was sick of hanging about the flat looking after Ka Lei. She would love to get dressed up, go out and have some fun . . .

So she agreed to go. She'd see him in his hotel room in one hour.

She left Ka Lei sleeping. She didn't intend to be more than an hour – Ka Lei would be fine until she came back.

The rain woke Ka Lei. She listened out for Lucy. There was only silence and she knew she must be alone in the flat. She lay in her bed and watched the light change in the room as evening came, and she watched the shadows stretch out around Georgina's room. Outside it was raining hard: tropical, pouring, soaking rain, streaming down the dirty windows.

Ka Lei began to feel panicky. She looked at her watch – Lucy had been gone for at least two hours now and Ka Lei had no idea where she was. She tried ringing her sister's mobile, but it was switched off. She felt that panic again, like the day Georgina had disappeared. It squeezed her heart in a tourniquet. She couldn't breathe. She listened to the rain and her mind went back to the happy days when she and Georgina had been caught in the downpour. Laughing and splashing like children, they got soaked. They didn't care about the people who watched them, thinking they were mad. They didn't care – they had each other.

Ka Lei cried so much that her stomach hurt.

Finally, exhausted by her grief, she wiped her face with her dress. Looking up from her lap she saw that darkness had descended. She watched the rainfall stick in large globules to the oversized windowpanes and she felt suffocated, imprisoned. She got out of her seat;

her tiny frame was agitated now. The memories of Georgina that made her smile were the hardest to bear. The sadness weighed her down, but the happy memories cut so sharply that they made her want to scream with despair. She went to the bathroom for the hundredth time that day. She needed to look into Georgina's eyes. She switched on the bathroom light and stood in front of the mirror, touching its cold surface, tracing the outline of her face with her fingers. Her eyes flicked back and forth, endlessly searching.

76

In the centre of the room was a king-sized bed, draped in purple silk. A red velvet pillow was laid at the top of the bed and on it rested the sleeping head of Georgina. She wasn't actually asleep, she had been given a dose of Rohypnol and was merely inert. Her hair was brushed and laid out artistically over the pillow. Her cheeks blushed a rosy pink. Her lips were painted red. She was naked. She remained very still as all around her lights were adjusted. She heard the voices of the technicians but could not open her eyes to see their faces. Above the sound of equipment being adjusted and technicians communicating, she heard the sound of people: voices and laughter, but she could do nothing but listen. She was an inanimate object, fully aware of her body but unable to communicate to it.

Then she felt the man's breath on her face. She felt the crush of his body. She felt him inside her. From some faraway place she felt it – the pain and the hatred. She saw it accurately, recorded it, but could do nothing to reach it. She couldn't breathe.

Squeezing hands were around her throat. She was drowning.

At the same time, at the other end of Hong Kong, Ka Lei stared into the bathroom mirror and began to hyperventilate. Her breath steamed the mirror. She wiped it furiously. Her arms tingled as she gulped the air down into her throat and her legs buckled beneath her. She hit the edge of the sink as she fell, cutting the side of her head. She didn't notice. Heaving herself upright, she gripped the sink for support and swayed unsteadily on her feet as she wiped the glass with frantic hands and screamed:

Georgina . . . Georgina . . .

She stood, reeling, breathless and panting as she stared into terrified eyes – her own eyes.

Wait for me, Georgina, wait . . .

She ran out of the flat to the landing and yanked open the French doors that led to the balcony where washing usually hung, but which was empty now. A cold sheet of torrential rain momentarily blinded her as it hit her in the face, and she stood for a few seconds, disorientated. Then, shielding her eyes with her hand, she saw the railings. She came to the edge of the balcony and placed one foot at a time onto the first rail. She became unbalanced as a gust of wind almost tipped her over before she was ready. She swung backwards. Then she stepped up again, in control this time, and inch by inch she let her weight tip forward until she fell. Over and over she tumbled in the air.

Back on the silk-covered bed, Georgina slipped into

unconsciousness and fell with her. They fell through the bottom of the world, arms outstretched, holding on to one another. They turned around and around in the rain and laughed so hard. Georgina had never felt so happy. But then her hands lost their grip and she was slipping away from Ka Lei. Suddenly the distance between them was too great, and all around her was darkening. She watched Ka Lei grow distant at the same time as she saw the room reappear. She hovered above her own body and watched it being brought back to life.

77

Lucy switched her phone back on as she exited the MTR station. There were five missed calls. She held a piece of card over her head to shelter from the storm and ran towards home. The pavement was awash with rainwater. Her legs were soaked as she ploughed through the puddles, making no attempt to avoid them. She didn't care; she needed to get home as fast as she could. She had an anxious feeling that had been growing for the last two hours. She'd never meant to leave Ka Lei for so long. She knew in her heart that she shouldn't have left her at all, but she also knew she must reel Big Frank in now that he was on the hook. And she had been right. He had asked her to marry him. She couldn't just say 'thanks very much, and I'll be off now'. Still, she had felt very uneasy in that last hour; it had become torturous for her to stay. In the end he had let her go, with the promise that she would return the next day.

The cardboard over her head dropped, soggy and useless. The wind and rain battered her face. She was panting with exertion and there was a small wheezy noise like the squeak of a frightened animal in her lungs as they fought to keep pace with her legs. She wished she hadn't worn heels, but she didn't dare stop, she was nearly there now. Just around the corner, a few more strides and she would be able to see their block, make out their balcony, see the light glowing from within, and see Ka Lei just where she had left her.

She rounded the corner and slowed down. There was a group of people, standing with blown-out umbrellas, pieces of card, flapping plastic bags held above their heads. All gathered around an object on the pavement outside the supermarket entrance. Some of the people were talking about which balcony it must have been. Lucy listened. What did they mean? She didn't know. They were looking at her balcony, and at the French doors swinging in the rain and catching the light. The crowd parted as she walked towards them.

78

Mann ran down the corridor and burst into the Superintendent's office.

'We're ready to leave.'

'How many are you taking?' The Superintendent was on his feet. The place was buzzing with adrenalin.

'Twenty.'

'Is now the best time?'

'Yes. We want to get there when the brothers are at work. I want to have a look around first.' Mann's heart hammered and his eyes burned with impatience, but he knew it had to be done right. He wanted to find Georgina alive.

Mann, Ng and Li parked outside the four-storey building situated three-quarters of the way along Herald Street, at the lower end of Sheung Wan, Western District, where the Fong family lived. Normally it was a peaceful, dusty old street with a permanent smell of rotting vegetation and an aura of general decay. But this evening there was a pink pre-storm light. The air was charged.

Mann looked up and down the street. It had once been busy – thriving with shops – but now it was waiting to be knocked down. There were only a few shopfronts still in use. A few kids were tinkering with their mopeds at the far end of the street. An old tramp sat waiting for nightfall.

They walked up to the house. A woman was coming downstairs. She was a resident of the top floor, on her way to the market. Mann showed his ID. He asked her about the Fongs. The brothers were not at home, she said, only old Father Fong was upstairs. They occupied the apartment on the first floor and they still rented the surgery and shopfront on the ground.

'Is this the surgery?' Mann pointed at the door just inside the entrance.

'Yes. It used to be where the old man held his practice and sold his herbs. I haven't seen anyone go in there for years. I don't know why they keep it.'

Mann thanked her and sent her on her way. He radioed to the rest of the team waiting further down the street. They split into pairs and spread out along the road.

'Ng, you and Li go on up and try to get the keys to this room for me. Don't let the old man out of your sight.'

Mann went outside to check the metal shutter at the shopfront. It had been a long time since it had been opened – it was completely rusted up. There was no noise coming from the old surgery.

Ng returned with a set of keys.

'How was the old man?'

'A bit confused – agitated. He's housebound – sick. He thinks it's one of these keys, he doesn't know which.'

'When does he think his sons will be home?'

'He expects Man Po at any time now. Max, not till the morning.'

'Don't let him out of your sight.'

'Shrimp's with him.'

The fourth key fitted. Mann nudged the door with his foot. It opened a fraction. He stood in the doorway. There was absolute darkness – thick and stagnant. There wasn't a sound. But there was a smell. Herbs, disinfectant and something else. He knew, without entering, that this was *the* room. This was where the women had been kept. The air inside was rancid with a musty heat – the smell of fear and sweat trapped within the walls. This place had been a prison.

Someone had been held here recently – he felt their presence, smelt their adrenalin. He nudged the door a little further. Directly opposite him was a mattress. On the mattress was a discarded piece of duct tape and a length of rope, one end still attached to the wall.

He stepped further in and shone his torch around. At the far end of the room, twenty feet away, were the old metal shutters. He flashed his torch to the right of them and saw a shelf stacked with specimen jars. Inside one of the jars, something glittered. A black wig that was hanging from a hook beneath the shelf caught his attention. He looked at it again. It wasn't a wig, it was a human scalp and next to it hung bunches of skin, taped together. It was then that he felt the hairs on the back of his neck prickle and he knew he was being watched.

79

From behind the mattress a wall of death stared at him. He flashed his torch over the images. Lolling heads and blanched faces stared out in flaccid colour from cheap glossy Polaroids. He searched methodically, left to right, along the rows. He paused at each one, looked hard, tried to see past the distortions of death. He searched for anyone he knew. He recognised Gosia, defiant-looking, even in death – her features hard and lean. She glared back at him, her lightless eyes accusing. He flicked across the photos, searching, straining to recognise the dead women. Looking for Helen. Praying he would not find Georgina.

There was the head that had slipped onto the waiter's foot – Roxanne Berger's. It was as he had seen it that day in the car park at the New World restaurant, but someone had taken time to try to hide the wounds made from the rope that had nearly decapitated her. Her blonde curly hair was placed neatly around her severed neck to cover it. Someone cared about the way she looked in death – wanted her to look her best.

As Mann looked at the pictures he could see that all

the women had been posed – their hair brushed, their faces cleaned. Some of them had had their pictures taken several times from different angles. He stepped closer to the wall and squatted above the mattress. He looked hard at each image – searching. Halfway along the fifth row he found what he sought.

The street was cleared of loiterers. Twenty officers were in position. Three of them were on the second floor. Ng and Li were on the first-floor landing, outside the Fong apartment. They were sweating profusely in the heat. It ran down their faces, poured down their arms and backs, but they held absolute silence as they waited in the dark. Up and down the street, officers sat it out. Inside the old surgery, Mann crouched and waited. He didn't feel the heat. He wasn't bothered by the sweat. Every pore in his body was listening, breathing, poised ready. Every sensory receptor was activated. He listened, he watched. His hands itched to get hold of the brothers.

80

Man Po arrived home. He parked his truck outside the house and walked leisurely around it, inspecting its tyres, making sure he had locked the back. He looked around and it occurred to him, momentarily, that the street was very quiet. Usually there was a group of youngsters standing around mopeds at the far end of the street. They weren't there. Neither was the old beggar who came to sleep in the doorway opposite at about this time. But Man Po did not dwell on it. He went back to lock his truck – for the second time. Eventually, checks done, he walked towards his front door and stood searching for several minutes for his key. Just as he turned, as if to go back to the truck and look for it there, he dug deep enough in his pocket and found it, and lumbered over to his front door. Key in hand, he stepped through into the unlit hallway and hovered there for a few seconds staring at the old surgery door. Something wasn't right, it was ajar. He called out to Max, thinking he must be inside, but he got no answer. He walked straight in and stopped a foot from Mann. He looked frantically around for an

321

explanation. Where was Max? Ng and Shrimp raced down the stairs.

'Man Po, you are under arrest for murder. You have the right to remain silent. If you do not . . .'

Man Po turned to run. Ng stood with Shrimp and two other officers and attempted to block Man Po's escape. He threw them off with the strength of a cornered rhino in his first charge, dragging them with him as he made for the door. Ng brought a rubber baton down on his head, which threw him off balance for a second as Mann kicked his legs from beneath him and brought the big man crashing down.

Mann took Ng's baton. It shook in his grip. He wanted to kill Man Po. He raised the baton above Man Po's head. Just one or two heavy, hard shunts, that's all it would take. No. He took a deep breath and lowered his hand. He wanted this man alive. He held Man Po facedown on the floor whilst Ng sat on him and cuffed him. Man Po began blubbing then bellowing.

Max heard it as he drew up outside. He had come home to make sure his father was all right. He hadn't been well recently and Max had taken a few fares then returned to check on him. The sound of his brother wailing gripped Max by the heart, just like it had always done. He got out of his car and was immediately surrounded by ten officers and thrown onto the bonnet, where he was held and cuffed. Then he was dragged inside the surgery. He screamed at the policemen to get off his prostrated brother.

'Tell him to calm down,' said Mann.

Man Po twisted his head and looked at his brother.

He was wet-faced from sobbing and he was stuck, chest down, on the floor.

'Stop crying now, you're all right,' Max said, still shaking with anger at being held.

Man Po stopped sobbing and looked about him. 'Do we have to go?' he said to his brother.

'Yes,' replied Max. 'We have to go.'

Ng got off him and helped him to his feet.

'Can I take my photos with me?' Man Po asked, staring lovingly at the wall of dead women.

81

While the SOCOs moved in to take the old surgery apart, Mann headed back with the brothers. He sat with them in the back of the van. He wasn't going to take his eyes from them for a minute. Max stared at the floor while Man Po cried. At Headquarters they were separated and taken to opposite ends of the cell accommodation.

The noise of Man Po's bellowing resounded through the lower floor of the building. He was inconsolable: he wanted his father; he wanted his brother; he wanted his photos. He was getting nothing.

Mann ordered Max to be taken to an interview room on the ground floor.

The room was dark and claustrophobic. There was no air-con in the small room and no natural light. It was never meant to be comfortable.

A table and two chairs had been left in the centre of the room.

Max sat at the table. Ng and Li watched him from opposite ends of the room while they waited for Mann. Max looked every inch a worried old man. He wrung his hands and fidgeted and constantly looked nervously about him.

Mann was taking his time. He needed to prepare himself. He must stay calm, clever, and, above all, he must stay focused. White had ordered him to pass the interviewing over to someone else. But no one seriously expected him to do that.

He paused outside the room, took a deep breath, shut his eyes for a few seconds and then he opened the door. Ng and Li looked up from their stations as he entered. Ng raised an eyebrow. Mann nodded. *I'm all right, Confucius – better the devil you know . . .*

Max turned his head at the sound of the opening door. When he saw it was Mann he looked frantically around the room, as if assessing his chances of escape. Then he sank back into his seat and covered his face with his hands.

Mann sat down in the chair opposite Max. Max's eyes flicked everywhere but on Mann's face. Mann's expression did not change. He stared at Max until Max stopped looking at his lap and started making eye contact. After ten minutes Max reached for a cigarette. Mann flicked the packet off the table. It landed at Li's feet.

As Max looked at him, the image of him loading Helen's case into the back of his taxi returned. That second when Max had paused, turned and seen Mann.

'You ready to talk, Max?'

Max didn't answer.

'You ready to tell me about the things we found in your place?'

Max looked at his lap again.

'You want to explain to me how all those pictures of dead women came to be up in your house? You want to talk about the jars full of human remains? You want to talk about the scalp? The lengths of skin?'

Max shrugged and turned his face away and shook his head.

'Okay, then I'll tell you. I think you had quite a system going, you and your brother. *You* kidnapped – your brother disposed of the bodies. You want to tell me what happened in between?' Mann sat back on his chair and rocked on its back legs. 'Okay, maybe I should concentrate on your brother. We have a lot to link *him* to the murders. There's the evidence of pig hairs and blood on the women. There's the knife used to dissect the women, the same knife over the last twenty years. I have a hunch we are going to find out that it's Man Po's knife.' Max shook his head. 'He's not right in the head, is he? He's got a temper, your brother. He's down there right now raging like a bull, and he bites . . . doesn't he?' Mann grabbed Max's arm and lifted up his sleeve. Max tried to pull away, but Mann held it in a vice-like grip. 'He gave you this, didn't he?' The scar was still visible – the bite mark that Mann had seen outside the Albert. 'Do you know how I know he bites?' Mann pulled out the photo of victim two's injury from the first autopsy – the bite mark on the thigh. He placed it in front of Max.

'We made this from the wound.' He pulled out the cast. 'We could have a dentist come in and take a cast of your brother's mouth – see if it matches. I think I'd prefer to pull out each one of your brother's teeth instead, and *then* see if they fit.'

Max looked anxiously towards the door and tried to stand. Mann stood up and pushed him back down. 'It was *you* who made the initial contact. It was *you* they trusted. You gave them lifts in your cab. You befriended them.' Max tried to squirm away but Mann leaned over him. 'Then you waited for your chance: when they were a bit drunk, a bit vulnerable, when they needed your help the most . . . and then . . . *BANG*.' Mann slammed his hand down on the desk. Max jumped. 'You seized the opportunity to kidnap, rape, torture and kill. Sound familiar?' He leaned so far over the table that wherever Max looked he could not escape Mann's scrutiny. 'Strange, Max.' Mann got up and walked around the room for a few minutes. 'I wouldn't have put you down for a psycho.'

He came to stand behind Max's chair. Max shrank at his approach. 'But we saw the photos – quite a collection. Some familiar faces there, Max. Some people I know personally.'

Max's shoulders stiffened. Mann got out the photos and placed them one at a time on the table. Max turned away – he didn't want to see them.

'Look at them, Max. Here's Gosia. Do you remember her?' Mann picked up the photo that her brother had sent, taken in happier times, and pushed it into Max's face. He tried to turn away. 'Look at it! She's sitting in a park in the sunshine – smiling. Pretty girl, isn't she? And here she is again.' He showed the picture of her torso. 'Not so pretty now, is she, Max?'

Max began to whimper and writhe in the chair. Mann sat back and resumed his staring.

'Li, get Max a cigarette.'

Li threw a packet over. Mann lit one and handed it to Max. He took it gratefully.

'There – better?'

Max tried a half-smile as he dragged hard on the cigarette.

'Nothing like a cigarette to calm the nerves.'

Max stared blankly at him. Mann picked up the photo of Gosia's torso and flicked it across to Max. 'These are cigarette burns. There are sixty-eight of them.'

Max's eyes flicked up at Mann and for a moment Mann thought he would say something but he didn't. He sank back and stared at the photos as they continued to flash past him in lurid colour.

'All these women did was to get to know you and trust you, wasn't it, Max? That was their big mistake – they accepted a lift in your taxi and they trusted you.'

Max shook his head and stared at the table.

'I have nothing to say.'

Mann went back to walking slowly around the room, just out of Max's vision.

'Tell me . . . not everyone's photo is up there, is it, Max?' Mann looked across at Ng. He could sense his colleague watching him. Ng would understand how Mann was feeling right now. He was willing Mann to stay in control – stay calm.

'Huh?'

Max twisted his head to see where Mann was, but

he couldn't: Mann was standing directly behind him. Mann placed his hands onto Max's shoulders and squeezed.

'Where is the Irish girl, Bernadette? Where is Georgina?'

He wasn't ready to know about Helen yet. He still had a chance of finding Georgina alive – that's what he must concentrate on.

'Huh?'

'You liked Georgina. She liked you. She wasn't in that prison at your house. She wasn't one of the photos on the wall. But someone had been there recently, hadn't they, Max? Who was that? Where is she now?'

'I don't know where she is.' Max stood almost involuntarily. He wanted so desperately to escape.

'You want to leave, Max? I bet those women wanted to leave too? They didn't get the chance either.'

Mann pulled Max's chair out from beneath him and picked him up by the collar. He drove him backwards to the wall, knocking the table over in the process. He pinned him there – gripping him by the throat. Max hung from his hand like a rag doll. His eyes bulged and his face turned blue.

'You ready to talk, Max?'

Max looked straight into Mann's eyes, as if he willed him to end it for him. Mann waited an extra second until Max's eyes grew distant, then he dropped him.

'Do you think I would make it that easy for you, Max? Oh no! You and your brother have lots to come. Of course, I have the power to make things *slightly* more comfortable – better treatment, maybe even get permission to allow you to stay together if you co-operate. Tell me where Bernadette and Georgina are right now. Are they alive?'

Max wheezed and coughed and shook his head fiercely from side to side. He was still fighting for breath. His arms flailed as he banged his hands on the stone floor, trying to force the air past his squashed throat.

Mann walked away, picked up the table and chairs and sat down again.

Ng picked Max up roughly and sat him back in the chair opposite Mann. Max shrank into the seat and began fiddling with his fingers, while sweat poured down his face and arms.

'I don't know where she is. I'm not saying any more.'

Mann turned to Ng. 'I'm leaving.' He'd achieve more by leaving Max to ponder his fate for twenty minutes. Meanwhile, he'd go back downstairs and check on the idiot.

'Let me know when he wants to talk. I'm going to find some pliers – there are some teeth that need pulling.'

82

'How is it going, Georgina?'

She stood before him. She had lost weight. Her collarbones jutted above her neckline. Her skin was sallow and papery and her dark eyes were lightless. 'Come and sit here.' He patted the chair beside him. She wavered for a moment, then gave in and sighed heavily as she sat beside him.

'How long will I have to stay?' she said, with such weariness and sadness that, if he had been capable of feelings, it would have moved him.

'Why? Are you in such a hurry to leave me? You know, I have become very fond of you, Georgina.' He laid his hand on her thigh. She felt the heat of his hand through the fabric of her dress, the warm heaviness of it, and she wilted. The faintest smile appeared on her sad face and she shivered.

'You are cold. Come here.' He sat her on his lap. She was heavy and limp, like a child.

Georgina lost track of time as the days fused, and she stopped counting them. She stopped fighting and rolled up her sleeve. She felt them tap her vein and tighten the tourniquet. She felt the rush that started in her abdomen and spread warm relief throughout her body. Hours passed like days as she lay on her bed staring through pupils the size of pinheads – days came and went like years. She was sure she would die there. She would die and no one would ever find her. She knew in her heart that Ka Lei was dead. She felt it and she saw it sometimes. She lay on her bed and slipped into a dream zone and she saw Ka Lei walk around the room in no man's land, waiting for her Georgina. She saw her own life in celluloid snippets. Hours and lives played out in slow motion. She heard others talk about her. She heard her own heartbeat in her ear. She saw her hands move and wondered who they belonged to. The earth turned and the earth's core roared beneath her. She listened to it. She heard the women talk Cantonese in the Golden Dragon restaurant. She looked out, with a child's eye, from within the folds of her mother's skirt. And she stared deep into her mother's eyes and relived the last minutes before Feng Ying's death – listening to the life departing and to the breath that says: *I am not the last, not quite, not yet . . . here I am.* She turned her body inside out and sent her blood to the perimeters of the room, in a loop, opening and closing valves, each squirt of blood pumping its way to the room's corners, smashing into the walls and splintering into a million red droplets, then reforming, back to beat loudly inside her eardrum.

I am a fox . . . *Boom Boom* . . . caught in a snare . . . *Boom Boom* . . . and the hunt is coming . . . *Boom Boom* . . . The hunt is coming . . .

83

Man Po was sitting cross-legged on the floor, his big stomach spread out in front of him. He was crying, convulsing, not with remorse but with anger and fear.

'Just deliver meat,' he said as Mann approached. 'Just feed pigs. Did nothing wrong.' Then Man Po crawled forward on his hands and knees and shouted obscenities at Mann.

'You want to see your father again?'

Man Po stopped shouting and nodded, his face covered in tears and snot. Saliva drenched his shirt front.

'You just have to tell me what happened to the women in the photos.' Mann showed him the pictures, one by one.

Man Po shook his head. 'Poor, pretty women – just died.'

'How did they die?'

'Don't know. Just dead.'

'You killed them, Man Po, didn't you?'

'No. No. NO.'

'What about this one?' Mann showed him the photo of Beverly Mathews taken at her cousin's wedding. Man Po stared at it, and his face crumbled. He started to cry.

'Didn't mean to kill her.' He shook his head miserably.

'But you did, didn't you? You killed her. What about the others? Your brother kidnapped them for you, didn't he? You and your brother held them captive in the old surgery. Did you kill them there?'

Man Po sat down on the floor and covered his face with his hands.

'You took their bodies to your workplace and cut them up. You kept some of the bodies there a long time, didn't you? You kept them in the freezers at work. But then you had to get rid of them because you were going to lose your job, weren't you, Man Po? It is all going to change.'

Man Po looked at Mann, wide-eyed, and nodded. His shoulders started heaving again as the crying resumed. His nose was running. He sniffed loudly and forgot to suck the saliva back up through the lazy side of his mouth.

'What about your last victim?' Mann dreaded the answer. 'What about Georgina? What have you done with her? Where is she now?'

Man Po looked at Mann with a blank expression.

'Miss Geor-gi-na?'

'Yes. Georgina, staying at Lucy's flat. The Eurasian girl. Where is she?'

Man Po shook his head and cried louder, then he

started to bang his head against the cell wall. 'Just delivery man – that's all.'

Li appeared beside Mann. 'There are photos of twenty-two different women up on the walls,' he whispered.

'What about the jars? What's in them?'

'Human organs: ovaries, breasts, that kinda thing. Oh yeah . . . and there's a jar *full* of fingers and toes.'

'Did they search the rest of the place?'

'They're doing it right now. So far they've found nothing.'

'What about the Ho Young Dim Sum Manufacturers?'

'Yeah, they're out there – the SOCOs. I've heard nothing back from them yet.'

'I want a list of pig farms that supply them with meat. I want all of them searched and all their meat production halted till we get a look at them.'

'Okay. What about him?' Li pointed at Man Po.

'He's starting to talk. How is Max doing upstairs?'

'Smoking one cigarette after another and pacing about the room.'

'Has he said anything?'

'No, but he looks like he wants to.'

'Okay. I'll be back up in a minute.'

Mann went back to talk to Man Po, who was still banging his head rhythmically against the wall. 'You can see your brother, Man Po. But you have to tell me how you killed the women first.'

Man Po stopped crying and wiped his face with his hand. He looked up at Mann.

'She was so pretty. She liked me. I didn't mean to

hurt her. Never hurt them – just like them when they are dead. Never hurt them. I'm just a delivery man.' He repeated the last sentence over and over and sank back to his corner of the cell, sobbing.

84

Lucy was packing. It was a slow job. She just hadn't the energy to do it fast. The funeral had drained away her last gram of strength. She had not been able to take Ka Lei's ashes. She'd never realised that there was so much left after cremation. She had opted to have the ashes made into diamonds, and Frank had bought her a necklace with a locket attached. When the stone arrived she'd have it set into a golden heart.

It shouldn't be taking so long. She only had a few items that she really valued, and anyway, Frank had offered to buy her anything she needed when they reached the States. It should have been an easy job, then, but whole lives had to be condensed and crammed into one suitcase. Sorting Ka Lei's belongings was the most difficult. It was so hard to know what to leave behind, what to shut the door on and say goodbye to, and what to take with her to her new life.

The weather didn't help, it was sticky and hot. It didn't occur to Lucy to put the air-conditioning on – years of frugal living had taught her to live without it.

So, a job she knew that she must hurry had taken her all day so far.

She pushed aside the half-sorted piles of belongings and slumped into misery, sighing more and more until that became her mode of breathing – big, deep, regretful sighs. Occasionally she stopped and wept. It was not often Lucy wept. The noise wrenched from her – an alien sound. It filled the flat, the noise of her sorrow. Then, gradually, it subsided.

She stared out of the window. The glass was dirty from all the mucky rain that seemed to have fallen non-stop that summer and was hanging on longer than it should. The room had taken on a foggy quality, as if she were sitting in a dream, or in a cloudy memory. Just for a few seconds Lucy allowed her eyes to fill with tears again, let her breath fall on a sob before she caught it midair and snatched it back. Snap out of it, she scolded herself. She had gone through it all a million times and nothing would bring Ka Lei back. She must pack her bags, pack up her life and move on. But her eyes were magnetically drawn towards the flat door and to the balcony on the landing beyond, daring her to retrace her sister's steps on that evening.

She got up and started towards the apartment door, but didn't dare open it or stand on the balcony, gripping the railing, and look over. She didn't want to see the last image her sister had seen that night. She didn't want to know what her sister had thought of last as she prepared to tip herself over the edge. What was it? *Georgina* came into her mind like a lightning strike. Like a migraine flash. It distorted her vision and tugged as a tic at the corner of her eye – *Georgina*. Then Chan came into her thoughts. He was to blame for all of it. She could not fool herself. And Lucy had played a major part in it, and she would carry her guilt forever.

She stood abruptly and brushed the creases out of her skirt. Enough! She had had enough of guilt and pain. She was so tired of recriminations. She was full of life. She wanted to live. She wanted to start again with Frank. She wanted this chance to be happy. She deserved it as much as anyone.

She smiled when she thought of Frank. He was waiting for her at the Hilton. He would be so excited right now. He was doing some last-minute shopping – 'secrets', he told her – things she would find out about in time! Lucy was to spend just two more nights in Hong Kong, then they would leave for the airport and catch the evening flight to Miami, and she would be gone, starting their life together in Florida. Frank said they would pick up a car and drive to the Captiva house on the beach. They would make that stilt-house shake! He would take her out on his Harley (once he'd learned to ride it) and she could have as many leather outfits as she wanted.

Frank was becoming more attractive to her every minute. She loved his new image – especially his hair extensions – he looked like a movie star!

But where was her lovely Ka Lei? Where was her baby sister? Lucy dabbed her eyes carefully with a tissue. She could do without the red-eyed look. She needed to look at her most attractive for Frank and she couldn't risk any upsets now. Feeling slightly better, she continued her packing. She would soon be out of the flat and away forever. She would carry her sister in her heart (and around her neck), but she had her own life to live. For the first time in her life she was having a lucky break.

She went into the bathroom and retouched her make-up. She was going to Club Mercedes for the last time. She had some things to sell and the foreign girls were the only ones who would buy any of Georgina's belongings. The Chinese would never wear second-hand and, anyway, the clothes were too big for the local girls. She had no need to call Max because she would hail a taxi from the corner of Johnson Road, just as easy. Anyway, there was something strange going on with Max these days. He seemed not to be looking after himself and he was acting oddly. Lucy finished dressing and left the flat, promising herself that she would tackle the rest of the packing when she got back.

Club Mercedes looked the same as it always did. It was in its usual bubble, existing in its own time and space. Although it was early there were a lot of punters in. The Dressing Room was packed with hostesses, all in various stages of readiness.

There were a lot of new faces that Lucy didn't know. There were some missing, though: Candy had finished funding her boyfriend's deli and left, and Bernadette had still not been found. There were a bunch of new Europeans, a couple of English girls among them, doing the rounds of the Orient. Lucy didn't feel too inclined to be friendly but she wanted to sell her things. She went over to introduce herself and make small talk. She was just about to produce her wares when Mamasan Linda came to find her.

85

'Good girl, Lucy. There are plenty of men for you tonight. Your face looks like it healed well.'

'Sorry, Mamasan,' Lucy laughed. 'I can't work any more. I am engaged.' She flashed the huge diamond Frank had given her. Mamasan Linda grabbed her hand and held it closer to get a better look.

'Very nice. Good diamond. Good girl. Very clever, Lucy. Who are you marrying?'

'You remember the big American – Flank?'

'Aye! Big Flank! Such a good man, lucky you! But it's not so good for me. I lose you.'

'Sorry, Mamasan, but here is a gift from Flank to you.' As was the custom with hostesses who made a good catch, Lucy handed her mamasan an envelope containing a generous amount of cash, to ease the blow of losing a good earner. Mamasan Linda took it graciously and inclined her head respectfully.

'I wish you much happiness, Lucy.'

'Thank you, Mamasan.'

'And Lucy, so sorry to hear about your sister, very sad.'

Before Lucy had a chance to respond, Mamasan Linda's name came over the tannoy.

'Aye! be back in a minute . . .' She was called to the floor, leaving Lucy to sell her things to the *Gwaipohs*. In the end she managed to sell Georgina's CD player, nearly all of her clothes and some of her jewellery that Lucy didn't want for herself. She'd made a few dollars out of it, enough to buy herself some new lingerie. She estimated she wouldn't need much more than that in Florida.

She was chatting to some of the hostesses when Mamasan Linda re-entered the Dressing Room.

'Lucy, I need you, come, juz for one minute.'

'What for?' Lucy felt her pulse quicken.

'There's an important guest asking for you. I told him: Lucy's getting married, no more boyfriends. But he said he just had to see you for a few minutes. . . Come on, I'll take you there!'

Lucy's heart raced. She knew who it must be. She could try and run for it. But how far would she get? He was bound to have his men in the club some-where. She would be caught before she got as far as the elevator. She had no choice. She had to face him. She had to do just enough to be able to get on that plane and get out.

She finished up in the Dressing Room and reluctantly followed Mamasan Linda.

Chan was alone in one of the small VIP rooms at the back of the club. He was very tired – worn out by his whistlestop tour of the frozen North, where he'd been sent on a menial business trip by CK. But Chan knew it wasn't wise to push CK too hard. Not even *he* could expect to get away with it. He still had to do what he was told, for now.

'Ah, Lucy! How nice to see you. Please, sit down!'

He motioned for her to come closer. Lucy was about to choose the chair furthest away from him, until he pulled the nearest one towards him and patted it.

'I was just leaving when Mamasan Linda told me your news. How lucky that I happened to come in today, and that you happened to be here?'

Lucy smiled, tight-lipped. Mamasan Linda deemed it best to leave; she made some excuse about being needed somewhere else and promptly disappeared.

As soon as they were alone, Chan leaned back in his chair and stared hard at Lucy, his large, dark eyes focused with anger.

'When were you going to tell me about Ka Lei? Was I supposed to find out from your mamasan that she is dead?'

Lucy looked around her – the room seemed uncomfortably small. 'Nothing to say for yourself? You were supposed to be looking after her; that's what I paid you for.'

She looked towards the door. She wanted to run.

'That was the deal, wasn't it? All you had to do was devote yourself to looking after my new concubine. All you had to do was stay at home, look after Ka Lei. Too much, was it, Lucy? Couldn't resist the temptation to go out and earn some extra, huh?'

He leaned forward accusingly. She held her breath as she waited for the inevitable execution of her character.

But it didn't materialise. Just when she had steeled herself for the worst, he seemed to soften. He shook his head deliberately. 'It is very bad news. She was so young and pretty and I had hoped we might have a life together. Such a shame.' He sighed, pouring himself a large whisky as he did so, and sitting further back in his seat. Then he turned to her and smiled. 'And now *you* are leaving us too, Lucy, is that right?' His face was taking on a tight appearance, his fake smile overtaxing it.

'Yes, I am going to live in America.'

'In America? Good girl, Lucy!' He leaned over and patted her leg. 'I am glad it has turned out so well for you. We can exchange news.' He paused and added ice to his glass before continuing. 'You might be interested to learn how your cousin Georgina is?'

86

'Georgina?' As guarded as she had meant to be, Lucy's reaction betrayed her panic as she grappled to understand what game Chan was playing. Lucy couldn't think how it could possibly benefit him to bring Georgina into it.

'How is she?' she floundered.

'She's well. Considering what she has been through and what has happened to her. Can't be easy knowing that you were betrayed by your only family – sold.'

Lucy's face reddened and her heart pumped.

'I was left no choice, if you remember. It is hard to think straight when under threat.'

He laughed. 'Funny, Lucy, I don't remember it like that. You had plenty of choices.' He held out each hand in turn, as if weighing the evidence in a hammy gesture. 'To gamble, not to gamble. To sell your sister, your cousin, or not to sell them. See! Plenty of choices.'

Lucy fought against the instinct to run.

'I hope Georgina will forgive me, when I explain it to her.'

'I really wouldn't count on it. And you won't be able

to explain it to her. You won't be seeing her again. At least I keep to my side of the bargain. She's sick and she's sad – she has no one now and soon she'll be of no more use to me. That's what you wanted, wasn't it, Lucy – to be rid of your cousin? You sold her to me, remember?'

Lucy thought how ugly and mean he looked, as he sat opposite her, shrivelled by his malicious character, delighting in his triumph. She thought about Frank, how kind and generous he was. Soon she would be his wife. She would be as good as anyone then. Chan could go hang himself then.

He continued. 'It seems you have managed to lose what little family you had, all in the space of about a month. Impressive.' He leaned forward and rested his hand on her thigh.

She knocked the hand off her leg. 'I didn't cause the death of Ka Lei,' she snapped. She was growing dangerously close to being angry enough not to care about consequences.

He smiled and continued: 'That's why you sold Georgina to me in the first place. You were jealous. Ka Lei loved *her* more than she loved *you*. Your mamasan filled me in on the details.' He sat back to watch the outcome of his words. 'Quite clearly, for Ka Lei there was nothing, and no one, worth living for after Georgina was gone. You weren't enough, Lucy, were you? You couldn't even be bothered to look after her properly. You were ultimately responsible for your own sister's death.'

'Not just me.' Lucy fought to contain her anger and

lost. The words spat out like venom across the room. 'You could have done it gently, but you hurt her. She lost something the night that you bought her – not just her virginity – she lost her smile – she didn't want to live any more. All the harm came from you – all of it.'

Chan laughed. Lucy had to get out. 'You made me do it all,' she said, standing abruptly. 'Now I must go.' Smoothing her skirt down, she composed herself. 'Goodbye, Mr Chan.'

'It's not goodbye for us, Lucy. We have unfinished business. I might let you leave Hong Kong – *might*. But, remember, the world is a small place. It doesn't matter where you go in it – if I want to, I will find you. So, dear Lucy, my advice to you is to keep looking over your shoulder. Oh, and give my regards to your fiancé. Tell him he's a very lucky man. But then he knows that already.' Chan laughed.

87

David White sat back in his chair and grinned broadly at Johnny Mann as he walked into his boss's office.

'Well done! You've done it! We have our killers, Johnny. ' Superintendent White was in jubilant mood until he caught sight of Mann's face. 'What is it?'

'I'm not convinced. I will feel happier when we get the forensics report. I want to know exactly what was in the brothers' place.'

'You can't possibly doubt that they are responsible? It couldn't fit better, Johnny. One a butcher by trade, and the other a taxi driver and a friend of the girls. What more do you want? I'll get a unit out to Man Po's workplace straight away. We've closed all the farms, stopped all movement of animals.'

'I know they played a major part. I am just not sure that they were working alone. Several things don't add up.'

'Such as?'

'There didn't seem to be the equipment for torture in that room. It was bare except for the mattress, the restraint and the specimen bottles. If the girls were held in that room for weeks at a time – tortured and killed there – there would be some evidence of that. It is definitely a short-stay place.'

'Bloody hell!' David White rubbed his bald head vigorously. 'All right, it's worth considering. Maybe one of the farms? We might find a second location in one of those?'

'We might. We haven't seen anything like that yet, but we have teams out looking.'

'Did you get anything out of Max?'

'At the moment he fears something a lot worse than us. I'm going to change that.'

Ng knocked on the door. 'There is a small trace of human blood in the brothers' place. Not enough to mean the victims were killed or dismembered there. Another thing . . . There's some unusual activity in the New Territories. Someone's been buying a lot of land up past Shenzhen . . . through a bogus company.'

Mann left the Superintendent's office, closely followed by Shrimp, who was waiting for him.

'Boss . . .' Shrimp handed Mann two DVDs. 'I got these from a stall on Nathan Road. The woman said they are snuff movies. She was very nervous, but greedy of course. They cost me five thousand dollars.'

'Have you looked at them? Is it one of our women?'

'I thought I'd better wait . . . . in case.'

'In case Helen is in one, you mean?'

88

The three men were crowded into the office, huddled in front of a laptop. 'It's not Helen,' said Mann. 'It's too difficult to say whether she's one of the women on our list but it's expensively shot. Nice décor. Professionally produced. Believe me, this cost big money to make.'

They watched the screen as a young blonde woman in her early twenties, dressed in bra and panties, cavorted drunkenly around on a purple-silk-covered bed. She was drinking from a champagne flute held up to her mouth by a man. His face was blurred but his body was clear to see.

'The man who's pouring drink down her throat, he's definitely Caucasian,' said Ng.

'Definitely: pot-bellied, skinny-legged. I would say he is about sixty,' answered Mann.

'What's his accent?' asked Ng. 'He's saying something I can't make out – but I know that accent . . .'

'He's Russian,' replied Mann.

After a few minutes of foreplay the man undressed the girl and tied her hands together. The girl giggled drunkenly. He lifted her into a kneeling position. She was still laughing as he hoicked her arms above her head and onto a restraint hanging from the ceiling. The first camera focused on the girl's face as she twisted around to see where her partner had gone, then the second camera viewed the back of the kneeling girl. She continued twisting and giggling – waiting. The man's back came into view.

'Pause that. Look at his right leg. Deep lacerations. Old scars. Some of those wounds go to the bone. Okay, play . . .'

The man reached for something off camera. When he pulled his arm back in shot, he was holding a whip in his hand. He began to beat the girl violently.

Her body jerked at each contact and her legs thrashed around the bed as she tried to escape the pain. After three minutes she was covered in bloody welts. The man then stopped and lay down on the bed. He was exhausted from the exertion. His pigeon chest rose and fell as the girl's body shook violently with the shock and the pain. The only noise was his heavy breathing and the small, sharp intakes of breath from the girl as she tried to talk.

'*Bitte*, no more. *Bitte. Ich habe ein kind. Bitte. Nicht mehr.*'

The view changed to the front. Her head was dropped to her chest. She began whimpering and pleading for mercy. The man knelt behind her. His hands held on to her hips and he lifted her onto his lap as he began forcing himself inside her rectum. As she tilted her head back and screamed in pain, he slipped a length of silk around her neck, took up the slack, wrapped the excess around his fist, and twisted.

The camera zoomed in on her face. He brought her to the moment of death five times before finally letting her go. It took him forty minutes to kill her.

During those minutes Mann went quiet. He was counting the camera angles, listening for background sounds, watching for any mistakes that the filmmaker might have made. He tried hard not to imagine someone he cared for going through what he could see on the screen. The anger inside him was boiling his blood.

Shrimp returned. 'Will we be able to trace him from this film, boss?'

'Perhaps . . . It won't be easy.'

'What about the girl?'

'She is German. She said she has a child. She had a family somewhere – find them. And get me a list of the Russian mafia bosses who have been spending time here in the last few years, ones that were injured from a landmine.'

89

Chan stood before CK. He bowed his head before his Mountain Master, his Dragon Head.

CK indicated to Chan to sit. He was in no hurry to say what he had to. But Chan was tired and wanted to get home. He had just arrived back from Russia, had come straight from the airport, but not from choice. He had been summoned. He was tired and he was angry. He had been sent on yet another menial task that any one of a hundred people could have done, but he had to suffer his father-in-law's humiliation yet again. He wondered how much longer he was going to be able to take it.

'I will be able to brief you more thoroughly on the results of my trip in the morning, CK. I need to check some figures . . .'

CK interrupted him with a wave of the hand.

'I do not wish to talk about the Russians.' He pressed his fingers together, sat back in his chair and stared hard at Chan. Something was definitely amiss. Chan had seen that look before, though never directed at him. Suddenly there was dryness in Chan's mouth and his heartbeat quickened. He tried to think of which one of a number of misdemeanours had been discovered.

'I always hoped that we were of the same understanding, Chan, that we saw eye to eye, as it were. But it appears that I have been blind, while you . . .' CK smiled sarcastically, '*you* have been seeing all sorts of things.'

'I am not following you on this one,' Chan said, sounding a little too contrived.

CK banged his fist on the desk. 'I should have your eyes taken out, that you can insult me in this manner. You went behind my back to senior members of other societies. You have been courting allies for your own gain.'

Chan could not control his indignation. He retorted: 'I have made a lot of money for Wo Shing Shing.'

'Yes, but your methods . . . underhand – snake in the grass . . .'

'I was not aware that the Wo Shing Shing was a society with ethics. The porn industry would be a much poorer place without Wo Shing Shing money.'

Chan's bravado had overstretched itself. CK was furious. He sprang out of his chair and marched over to the window to regain his self-control. Chan stared at his back, watching his shoulders rising and falling and seeing the tension in his slight frame – how his head dipped and lifted as he ran through his thoughts. At last, he turned around, and Chan could see that he was still at bursting point.

'*I* am the Dragon Head, the Master of the Mountain,

not *you*. It is *me* who decides what this organisation stands for, and what it puts money into, not *you*. You have betrayed me, gone behind my back and humiliated me. People will know.' CK leaned across the desk and glared into Chan's face as he sat unflinching. 'I don't think you fully understand what you have done, my worthless son-in-law. You have caused me to lose face, and that is unforgivable. When you first came to me – a strong, brave young man – a newly trained lawyer, educated in England, people told me you had betrayed your own family, killed your own family members to advance yourself. I did not listen. They told me you had betrayed a friend. I didn't believe them. They told me that you were a snake. A snake who could change his skin but whose blood would always run cold. They were right.'

Chan stood to attention and bowed slowly. His fists were clenched to his sides and his face was ashen. He glared at CK.

'Forgive me, my Dragon Master. I am your humble servant.' He stood and walked backwards out of the room, his eyes fixed on CK all the way.

Once outside, he unclenched his fists and looked at the imprint of his fingernails in his palms.

'You have looked into the eyes of your successor, old man,' he said under his breath. 'Never again will you talk to me like that.'

90

'Two snuff movies. Made at the same location – different covers on the bed, different camera angles, but definitely the same place. In the first film the woman was killed by an old Russian soldier. In the second it was an oriental – possibly Japanese, maybe Korean.'

'So we have our second location?' David White did not look pleased.

'Yep! We certainly have that! A film set that cost a lot of money – professional and slick. That would explain why they are manicured, prettied up, David. They are used for big-budget snuff movies. Four different cameras for a start, and professional lighting. That was an expensive set we were looking at. That takes massive money. And, most importantly, all for the enjoyment of one man. I'd say, if I wanted to buy myself into a movie like that, I'd be looking to pay two to three million US. There's the girl to find: pretty, foreign, alone, disposable. It takes time and work to handpick girls like that. Then they must be held somewhere for a long period – we know that by the state of the bodies, tortured and filmed, until the final scene in their sad, wasted lives – to ultimately be the vehicle of some rich, twisted bastard's fantasy.' Mann shook his head and gulped his drink.

'Did you find a match for her among the photos taken from the old surgery?'

'Shrimp is looking for that right now.'

Li knocked and came into the office.

'We have it, boss. The girl in the first film? We found a photo that matches her on the wall in the brothers' place. Interpol have an open file on her. Her name is Claudia Weiss. She was a German girl working as a topless waitress in Kowloon. Been missing since April 2000.'

'She had a child?'

'Yes. A little girl. She lives with the grandmother in Bavaria.'

'Okay, so I accept the killings don't end with the brothers, but they wouldn't have a photo of Claudia Weiss up in their house if they weren't involved in it all somehow.' David sighed heavily and seemed to sink into his chair. 'This is all we bloody need . . .'

'Bernadette and Georgina – their photos weren't on the wall. It could mean they're still alive at this second location.'

'We have a whole new investigation going on,' said White, head in hands.

'. . . And we have a whole set of new players in it,' Mann added.

91

'Was there a clue as to the production company?' David asked.

'No chance. But I'm having Ng analyse the film to see if it resembles any legit work we know of.'

'There must be more films.'

'Yes, Shrimp's going back out to see the contact again – see if he can find out more. I think there's going to be a lot more of these films, David. You know Hong Kong. We'll copy anything. But this is going to involve some of our big guys. You know – the guys we can't touch?'

'We can only *hope* to bring justice for her and the others in the end.'

Mann looked at him – he knew that tone.

'Save your bullshit for someone else. I can hear it in your voice – you're already thinking, if Mann's right and these are some big guns having themselves some fun with women with *no* family, *no* connections – in other words, *no value* – then we have *no* hope of getting justice for these women. The men who did this are untouchable. They will have enough power and enough money to buy their way out. I can't live with that, David. I failed Helen. I failed that young woman in that film, and all the others like her. I owed them my protection and I failed them. We all failed them.'

'This is Hong Kong – it isn't all black and white, Mann.'

'No, it's all the colour of money, isn't it, David?'

'If that were true we wouldn't be standing here, would we? I know you are frustrated, Mann, I know you would like things done differently. But don't lose sight of the goal. Things don't always come right when they are supposed to, but eventually people get what they deserve. A few years down the line they have to account for their misdeeds – even if they end up punished for something different, they get it in the end.'

Mann laughed – hollow and cynical. 'Now *that* bit I do believe. But sometimes you have to hurry the process of retribution. Sometimes it doesn't come quick enough and you have to give it a hand.'

'What do you mean?'

'Today, after I saw the way that girl suffered, I know that I won't be able to watch these men walk free, David. I just can't do it.'

'Mann . . .' White held up his hand to speak, but Mann wouldn't let him.

'Listen to me, David. I just *won't* do it. I won't let those killers off the hook. If the Hong Kong police force can't get justice for them, I will do it – my way.'

92

Mann left Headquarters and headed along Hollywood Road. He needed some head space and he knew where he'd find it. Past the antique shops and curio stalls he found Man Mo temple – the oldest temple on the Island, green tiled roof, the colour of oxidised bronze, red calligraphy on the doors. It epitomized the heart of Hong Kong – no matter how many Westerners came and went it would always be Chinese. The place was still an everyday place of worship for Taoists and Buddhists alike.

Mann slipped through the doors as the last rays of the sun were just hitting the roof of the temple. Inside the air was blue with smoke and the smell of sandalwood from the large incense coils that hung suspended from the ceiling. He walked up the stone steps to the altar and stood for a few moments before the statues of the gods – Man Cheung, the God of literature, dressed in green, and Kwan Yu, the God of war, dressed in red. A few worshippers were offering up their gifts of fruit and flowers and others were knelt in prayer. Mann lit an incense stick and placed it in a large brass urn before kneeling beside one of them.

'Hedging your bets, Johnny?' Stevie Ho finished his prayers and reached up to place his incense in the urn in front of the God of war.

'I wouldn't call it hedging, Stevie. Looking at life from every angle, that's all.'

'Why did you ring me? What is it you want from me, Johnny?'

'My ex-girlfriend, Helen, turned up as one of the victims of the Butcher. Now another friend of mine has gone missing.'

'I'm sorry to hear that. I ask again what do you want from me?'

'We think the Butcher doesn't only kill the women himself; he sells them to the highest bidder to be used in snuff movies.'

'Why did you think I would know anything about this, Johnny?'

'Because the Butcher has friends in very high places – triad friends. Your friends.'

'It could be anyone. There are many powerful triads.'

'That's where you're wrong. The Butcher is a very special type of man. A man who doesn't mind breaking every rule in the book as long as he can make money from it. It's all about money and power, Stevie, isn't it?'

Stevie looked at him. 'I don't know anything, Johnny.' He looked riled. He stood, bowed to the deities and turned to Mann. 'I will give you this piece of advice, Johnny: stay away from Chan. He's growing tired of your persecution.'

Mann stood up, picked out the stick of incense that

Stevie had placed in the urn and turned it upside down in the sand.

'Thanks for the advice, Stevie. Now let me give you some – try and remember what's *right* and what's *wrong* because when the day of reckoning comes no amount of incense is going to save you.'

Mann walked out of the temple, leaving Stevie at the altar. He started the steep descent down Ladder Street. He wasn't ready to go back to the office yet. He was sick and tired but his heart raced with adrenalin and anger. Mann checked his phone. Five missed calls. Unknown caller. He put it back in his pocket – it could wait. He was still trying to make his brain function methodically. It was a mess – a jumble of loose cables sparking off one another.

His phone rang again. He put his hand in his pocket and pressed the busy button. At the other end of the phone Kim crouched beside her bed, out of sight, and cursed Mann for not answering his phone. She estimated she had just fifteen minutes before the guard realised his phone was missing. She'd already used up twelve of those minutes trying to make Mann pick up.

A moped nearly ran Mann over. He cursed it as he jumped out of the way. His phone rang again. *Whoever it was they could wait five fucking minutes* . . . He fumbled in his pocket. He couldn't find the busy button – he'd have to switch it off properly. He pulled his phone out of his pocket and pressed the answer button by mistake. Then he heard her voice.

'Johnny?'

He stopped dead and cupped his ear over the phone.

'Kim? Where the fuck are you?' He felt enormous relief at hearing her voice.

'I am some place that I wish I wasn't, that's for fuckin' sure.'

'You all right?' She sounded petrified.

'No, not really, Johnny.'

'So, where are you?'

'I have no fuckin' idea. I am in a club called Sixty-Eight, Chan owns it. He conned me into coming here. He said he had this club with foreign hostesses and he needed me to look after them, be their mamasan. But there's such weird shit going on here, Johnny, they're not telling me about most of it. He has us all prisoners here. There's no way to get out, believe me – I've tried.'

'How long did it take you to get there? Did you drive?'

'We helicoptered in – took about forty minutes. It's in the middle of fuckin' nowhere, Johnny. I have no idea. All I know is that we're in mainland China.'

'Do you remember what you saw on the way?'

'We flew north over Kowloon, small villages, reservoirs, country parks. Then we turned towards the west. We flew over old industrial sites, great big craters, no one workin' in them. We could be anywhere.'

'It's all right, Kim. I'll find you. Is it heavily guarded?'

'Yes.'

'How many men are there? Are they armed?'

'There are two dozen security officers here – at least – and all carry guns. Plus, there are about ten of Chan's personal bodyguards that come and go. The whole place is a fortress.'

363

'Are there any other foreign women there at the moment?'

'There's an English girl here . . . Georgina . . .'

'Is she okay?'

'Yes and no. They won't let me see her. I don't know whether she's still alive.'

'What about an Irish girl – Bernadette – ?'

'She was here – I don't know where she is right now. I have to go, Johnny. I can't stay on the phone. I stole it from one of the guards. He's going to miss it anytime *now*.'

'You watch yourself now. You be careful. I will get there as fast as I can. I want to see you safe and sound, Kim, do you understand?'

'You get here, Johnny. I'm gonna luv you forever. But be quick.'

93

'Kim said she flew west over an old industrial site. She said there were craters. Find me some disused mines – about forty minutes' helicopter ride from here. That's where the girls are.'

Ng's finger hovered above the page.

'Here.' Ng traced a line of pock marks on the map.

'Kim says they have Bernadette and Georgina out there. That's where our girls will have been going, for sure.' He stopped in the doorway. 'I've already told the Super. He's organising transport. I'll go and tell him we're almost ready to leave. And Ng . . . guess what it's called?'

Ng shook his head.

'I'll give you a clue. How many burns on Gosia's chest?'

'Sixty-eight.'

'Yep – the two luckiest numbers in Hong Kong. Club Sixty-Eight.'

He arrived in David White's office. As soon as the Superintendent put the phone down Mann asked: 'Have we got the permission we need to cross over into the mainland?'

White looked up.

'You're not going to like what I have to say, Mann.'

'Then don't say it.'

'We've been denied permission. Until the proper paperwork is completed – permits granted.'

'Until they have time to hide all the evidence, you mean?'

'I tried, Mann. They want it to be investigated by the local police over the border in Hicksville. We have already received orders to stay out.'

'Well, they can *want* all they like. I'm not staying out.'

'I know better than to waste my breath. I'll help as far as I can. Who are you going to take?'

'I'll take Ng and Li and five men from the Police Tactical Units. See if we can find a sniper as well.'

'Is that going to be enough?'

'It will have to be – I don't want to involve anyone else. Shrimp will brief the PTUs. While he's doing that I need to find out all I can about this place before we get there. Can you get me a helicopter?'

'Yes. But for Christ's sake don't prang it. I'll be in enough trouble when they find out I authorised this.'

Mann got up to leave.

'And Mann . . . For Christ's sake, come back alive.'

94

Georgina lay on her bunk. Her eyes were gill-like slits. Her face was the colour of cheap jade. Her body barely registered breath.

'Amber, I got good news.' Kim sat down beside her. She used the name the club had given Georgina, in case they were overheard.

'You got a client – we need to get you ready.'

There was not a flicker from Georgina. Her eyes did not change track.

'Come on, Amber!'

Finally, Georgina stirred. 'Now?' She winced as she spoke; her cracked lips were Sahara-dry. She hadn't worked since the night she'd had to be resuscitated and her heroin doses had been upped to keep her sedated.

'Yeah, you have to get up right now. I'll help you, but you have to hurry.'

Georgina raised herself up super-slowly from the bunk and swung her legs off the side, one at a time. She struggled to sit upright and then, that achieved, sat swaying unsteadily.

'Come on, you can do it.' Kim leaned in and whispered in Georgina's ear: 'Be brave, be strong – you are going home – but for fuck's sake hurry up!' Kim tried getting her to her feet.

'Come on now, Amber, I will help you get into your costume. Tonight you are a Geisha.'

Georgina groaned and slumped back down onto the bed.

'No, it's all right, Amber, don't worry, it's not like last time.' Kim leaned closer again while pretending to brush Georgina's hair from the side of her face, and whispered: 'Georgina, listen to me! I am trying to get you out of here. Someone is coming to help us – we must get ready.'

'Leave me alone – please. Leave me alone.'

The words cracked in Georgina's throat. Kim stroked Georgina's back, speaking in hushed tones.

'Don't give in to people like Lucy and Chan: they are just fuckin' leeches – low-lifes. Don't let the bastards do it to you, Georgina. Fight it! Find the strength inside to live, not for anyone else, but for yourself. But right now we have to get out of here. I need you to be ready.'

'Please leave me. I don't want to go anywhere.'

'Stand up! Don't be a victim, Georgina. Don't let anyone use you as a fuckin' punch-bag. Stand up! Get the gloves on and start fightin' back! Believe me, your life is not over yet ...'

Kim stopped abruptly. Chan was standing behind her.

'But yours is, Kim. Punch-bag – dartboard ... Good idea; my men need a bit of knife-throwing practice ...'

95

Mann checked his watch. It was one a.m. The five PTUs were led by their commander, Ting – a senior police officer with many years' service. They had picked up weapons and flak jackets from the armoury and driven to Central police station where there was a helicopter waiting on the roof. Mann knew the pilot, Peter Wong. They had been on many a dawn raid together at the OCTB. Mann was glad to see him. Not only was Wong the best pilot in the force, he was also a firearms expert and an expert sniper. Mann needed all the help he could get. Plus, he had Mann's brand of bravery – business as usual – job done. When David White had asked Wong if he'd be willing to fly on this mission, he hadn't hesitated.

Mann sat next to Wong to help navigate. He gave him the co-ordinates and spread the map out on his lap. They had an approximate idea where it was, but they could not be sure. They were relying on a visual when they got that far. The helicopter rose, hovered, picked up more height, turned, and flew north.

The bright lights and blazing neon soon petered out

to sporadic clusters of brilliance as they flew over Kowloon and the small fishing villages of the New Territories. Soon there was only dense, dark woodland below and visibilty was down to nil. Skirting Shenzhen, they flew over the reservoir and the country parks. They had been flying for thirty-five minutes when the terrain below transformed from green lush countryside into wasteland. They were flying over a redundant, ransacked former Industrial Economic Zone. Old quarries, plundered and now deserted, pockmarked the darkness below in ugly black holes.

Mann knew that they were looking for a large complex somewhere in the vicinity. He consulted his map and signalled to the pilot to head north-west. A few minutes later he saw it – half a mile ahead – a glow coming from the ground, as if from a buried town.

There was an air of reverence in the helicopter as each man watched the halo of light grow on the horizon.

Li broke it. 'Awesome! What is it? It's like a volcano.'

'Be alert. We could be expected,' Mann shouted back from the cockpit. Perimeter lights appeared below.

Li's face was glued to the window. 'It *looks* like a golf course.'

'It is,' said Ng. 'I had time to find out a bit about it before we left. The whole thing is about four square kilometres.'

'He must have had a heck of a job building this,' Mann said, looking down at the neat lawns, dotted lakes and illuminated bunkers.

'The grass, the trees – it's all imported,' said Ng.

Li leaned across Ng to get a better view. 'Look at that – in the next quarry . . . it's like a giant birthday cake!' he screeched.

Ahead of them, as one quarry led into the other, a building stood four storeys high, coming halfway up the quarry-side. It was made primarily of glass. As they neared, they could see that it wasn't one building, it was two – connected in the middle and forming the numbers Sixty-Eight. They flew towards it.

'Smoke! I smell smoke. Anyone else?' said Mann.

'Yes. I can see it,' replied Ng. 'It's in the air below us . . . but I can't see any fire.'

They hovered directly over the Eight building, blasting the rooftop palms and rippling the surface of the swimming pools.

'Awesome!' Li grinned. 'I've never seen anything like it.'

'Let's hope you never will again,' said Mann grimly.

96

'They know we're coming, otherwise they would have come out by now. They must have been tipped off somehow.' Mann felt that knot in his stomach, the one that told him he'd missed something important and it was too late to alter it now. 'Okay, let's set her down.'

They readied themselves, and checked their guns. The PTUs attended to their own preparations with precise calm. They all carried police-issue Glock 9mm handguns and standard police-issue HK MP5 sub-machine guns. Ng carried just a handgun. He was a good shot, he'd had plenty of practice over the years. Mann carried both a handgun and a sub-machine gun. Shrimp carried a surprise.

Peter Wong set the helicopter down on a landing pad one hundred metres from the palm-lined walkway leading to the main entrance of the Eight building.

'We'll cross in pairs. Get to the main entrance. Use the trees for cover. We stick together until we find out what and how many people we are up against. Wong will use the helicopter as cover and pick off what he can. Agreed?'

There was a grunt of agreement. Wong killed the engine. It was two a.m. The night was warm and sticky in the quarry base. So far there'd been no sound of a reception committee, but Mann knew it was just a matter of time.

One by one they stepped out onto the tarmac. Commander Ting and his men were first to sprint across the runway, with Shrimp in tow.

Mann watched the men secrete themselves behind the palms. He and Ng were the last to run across. Midway, the firing began. A volley of gunfire passed millimetres above their heads. Wong retaliated. The shots echoed around the quarry base. Mann reached Ng and Li. He saw what Li had in his hand – it wasn't police issue.

'Shit, Li! Where did you get that?' Li was carrying a Colt M16 rifle.

'Off the Internet.'

'Can you use that thing?' Ng whispered.

'Sure can, sir! Three-round bursts or fully automatic?'

'Shut up and just do it. Over there – to the right.' Ng gestured towards the second quarry. Li flicked the fire-selector catch forward for automatic and fired a round into the darkness. There was a silence for five seconds then fire was returned from five different stations around the edge of the runway and to the far side of the Eight building.

'Fuck! That pissed them off!' Li sank back behind the palm.

'Least we know where they are now,' said Ng.

The sound of feet running across tarmac and a single shot passed over their heads, fired into the undergrowth behind them. Wong was finding his mark. There was a thud of weight on tarmac and the skittle of a dropped gun. A body lay on the runway. Another burst and Wong took out another and another. No sound for five minutes, then, from somewhere at the back of the Six building, they heard a door close.

Mann judged it time to move and signalled to the PTUs to make their way around to the back of the Six building, while the rest of them made their way towards the main entrance, twenty metres ahead. They could see the reception ahead of them lit up by one huge tiered chandelier hanging just inside the glass doors. There was no sign of life. Mann, Ng and Li edged forward one at a time until all three stood on the black marble floor of the reception area. Above their heads ornamental swathes of silk hung down as the building spiralled in glass layers, fossil like, upwards to its four floors. All was still and silent except for the click and whir of unmanned electronic equipment.

The air-con was working, blasting them with cold air. Further into the building an acrid smell hung in the air and there was a thin veil of smoke in the atmosphere. Mann signalled to Ng to watch the door as he edged forward towards the large black marble reception desk to get a look behind it. He peered over the top. Hiding, as far into the corner as she could get, her knees tucked up under her chin, was a young woman dressed in a traditional Korean bridal outfit. She let out a startled scream when she saw Mann. He put his finger to his lips for quiet, smiled reassuringly, and flashed his warrant card. She stared back at him, shaking, her face frozen into a petrified smile. She tucked her legs even further beneath her and shook uncontrollably.

'Where is Kim?' he asked her as she blinked up at him. 'The black mamasan. Where is she?'

At the same time as she shook her head, her eyes flicked upwards to the stairs.

'Which floor?'

She didn't answer. Mann picked up a set of keys from a shelf beneath the desk. 'Are these the master keys?'

She nodded.

He bent down. 'You need to work on your reception skills, young lady. Now, which floor shall I start looking?'

The girl hesitated, saw the look on Mann's face, and then spluttered 'Fourth'.

Ng hung back to cover any unwanted guests while Mann and Li took the stairs. The place was deserted. Cautiously but quickly, they passed the landings, one, two and three, and stopped on the fourth. They walked along separate sides of the silent corridor, straining and listening as they went. There was no sound except the soft pad of leather-soled shoes on expensive carpet.

There were twelve doors on the landing. It was difficult to know which to try first, and Mann didn't have time to waste. He scanned the corridor. There was something different about the last three rooms – the doors. They were double in size – *for getting large equipment in and out.*

Mann sprinted to the last door on the right, tried his keys, gave up. He stepped back a few paces and charged at the door. His shoulder thudded into it. It rocked slightly, but it didn't give in. He took a few extra paces back towards the wall behind and charged again. Better. The door creaked, splintered slightly. The third time it flew open.

Li glanced inside then instantly backed away from the door.

'Stay here, Li,' Mann said, as he stepped inside and saw a sight that would haunt him forever.

97

In the far right-hand corner of the room, Kim was on her knees, tied at the wrists and suspended from two posts. She was naked and badly beaten. Where her knees touched the floor, they rested in pools of blood.

Mann went over to her and lifted her head gently. She was still breathing, just.

'Kim?'

She didn't answer. Her face was swollen and battered. He reached inside his jacket and took out a knife, flicked it open, and cut her arms free. She coughed and groaned in pain as her body fell against him.

He laid her gently down on the floor, took off his jacket and covered her. He shouted to Li to fetch the emergency aid pack from the helicopter and to hurry up. Kim heard his voice; she stirred and tried to open her eyes.

'Johnny?'

'All right, Pussy?'

'I'm fucked, Johnny.'

'You'll be all right, Kim. You'll be okay. Stay calm.'

He looked her over. She was covered in small-slatted

puncture wounds everywhere on her body. Some of the wounds looked deep, but it was impossible to see how deep.

Kim tried to smile, but coughed instead and blood splattered across his face. Mann looked down at her ribs . . . *Must have hit a lung.*

'Hang on, Kim. Stay with me.' He wiped the blood from her mouth and cradled her.

'Sorry, Johnny . . . Should have listened to you,' she whispered.

'Did Chan do this to you, Kim?'

She shook her head and flinched again. 'He ordered it. His men did it.' Her voice trailed off and Mann felt her body grow solid and heavy. 'He took Georgina. I don't know where. Sorry, Johnny.'

'That's all right, Kim. I'll find her. Just stay with me now, Kim. Stay here. Hang on. You're going to make it.'

'I'm dying, Johnny.'

'You're not fucking dying! Stay with me, Kim! For once in your life do as you're told! You're going to be fine. I got plans for us. I've just upped my job offer to live-in housekeeper, uniform, the works.'

She smiled. 'I'm gonna miss you, Johnny.' She lay heavy in his arms, and then she was gone.

Ng appeared at the doorway.

Mann didn't turn around. 'Just give me a moment, please, Ng.'

Ng stood and waited. Mann pulled Kim closer to him and cradled her for a few minutes before he kissed her on the forehead. Then he laid her gently back down.

*How many more women was he going to have to lose?
No more*, he vowed. He wasn't going to attend one more fucking autopsy and see someone he cared about lying on the slab.

'Sorry, Mann, I know she was a friend,' Ng said.

'Yes. She was. A good friend.'

Mann stood up. He looked around. 'There are four stations by the look of it . . .' He glanced at the ceiling. 'And each one has a camera trained on it.'

'There's a water hose here.' Ng stood next to a table with leather straps at its four corners. 'This must be for tying the victim down. And this . . .' he picked up a length of wire hanging from the wall, 'looks like an animal snare.'

'The hose is probably to wet the victim down prior to electrocution. This must be where Roxanne Berger met her death.' Mann looked at the cattle prod and clamps. He saw the image of the young woman from Orange County dressed in animal hide with the lasso around her neck. He saw the cattle prod forcing her further into the tightening noose, and then he remembered something else – the branding iron. He looked up and saw it hooked onto a shelf above the snare. Mann looked along the set of interchangeable heads – the F was missing.

'This is a two-way mirror.' Ng pointed behind him.

Mann looked above him. 'And we're being filmed.' A light blinked at him from one of the cameras. 'Let's take a look behind the mirror, Ng.'

It was a small, dark, rectangular room. Its main feature was the mirrored window directly ahead, which

379

took up half the room and afforded 360 visuals into the torture chamber next door. In front of the mirror, a bank of six computers were housed on an oval desk area. They were black-screened and vacant, except for one PC – it was on and linked to the camera trained on the station where Kim had been. It was still running – filming the empty space where she had been left hanging. Around the rest of the room were shelves and cupboards.

Mann touched the screen and tracked the camera down and left. He turned to Ng.

'Ever seen anything like it, Ng?'

'Once. On a sex-trafficking case – some women from Thailand were promised good jobs here. When they arrived they were being used for live porn shows. Some of them were underage. I was part of the raid. This looks like similar equipment. You don't need a lot to make your own films these days.'

Mann looked around the room. The cupboard doors hung open, revealing emptiness – not tidy, sorted, cleaned-up emptiness, but the left-in-a-hurry, no-time-to-sort-anything-out, just-take-everything-you-can-carry kind.

'It looks like the place has been stripped. Whatever films were made here, the hard evidence is gone. They left in a big hurry. Can't have been more than a couple of hours ago. Still, they might have left some evidence.'

'Whatever there is will be in those.' Ng pointed to the computers.

'And on the walls of that room in there.'

On the screen they saw Li cover Kim's body with a sheet, before he joined them.

'Down the corridor I found the bedroom set used for those snuff movies we saw. This whole floor seems to be where they do the film production. There are sets and storerooms full of expensive equipment.'

'Call the Super for me, Ng, and get him to send a team out here right away. They can't argue with *this* evidence. They'll have to do something. Then let's finish here as fast as we can. I want to catch that bastard before he gets too far. We'll briefly sweep the rest of this building then we'll head over to the Six – see how our friends are doing.'

Mann returned to Kim. He pulled the sheet back and leaned over to kiss her forehead. 'Be seeing you, Pussy.' Then he pulled the sheet back over her face, stood up and wiped his eyes.

Ng was waiting at the door for him. He handed Mann his jacket.

'There was nothing you could have done to save her, Genghis.'

'Not now – no. But a long time ago I had the chance to rid the world of Chan and I saved his life. If I have any regrets, that's the one.'

'Maybe one day you will get to correct that mistake, but for now Kim had her own path to tread and you could not alter it. Look to help those who can be helped now.'

98

Mann, Ng and Li walked briskly through the corridor that connected the two buildings together and into the main section of Six. They radioed to Commander Ting. He told them they'd found a bit of resistance.

'There are twenty of them altogether, sir, mainly women. They weren't expecting police. They knew something was going on when Chan had a massive clear-out and took half the security with him. He had to scramble three helicopters to get all the clients out. Apparently he tried to torch the place but these people here put the fire out. They aren't going to answer any questions about Chan. They might be scared of the police, but they're much more frightened of *him*.'

'Bernadette?'

'Not so far.'

Mann led the way into the tail section of Six. There were rooms with bunk beds, clothes, a few personal effects: make-up, jewellery, feminine things. The place still felt warm. There was the smell of people.

'There are kids here, boss.'

Li stood back from the entrance to one of the staffrooms. As Mann looked inside about twelve children stared back at him. They were a mixed bunch, mainly Chinese but there were some Filipinos among them. Some were asleep on mats, while others lay on their backs, staring into space. One little boy was rocking in the corner of the room.

Jesus Christ! thought Mann. *What's the matter with this world?*

'We're not going to hurt you. It's all right, children. You'll be safe now.'

One little girl stepped forward, attached her hand to Ng's and smiled up at him. Her grip was tight, her eyes desperate.

'Take me,' she said. 'Please, take me.'

Ng looked at Mann. He was a sucker for kids, and already his puppy brown eyes were melting as she held tightly to his hand.

Mann answered for him. 'We can't take any of you now, but help will be coming very shortly for you all. I promise.'

'Please. Don't leave me here.' Her grip intensified on Ng's hand. She wouldn't take her eyes from his face. Mann knelt down to talk with her. She tried to hide behind Ng's legs.

'We cannot take you with us, there isn't room, but help is coming and some men will stay here to look after you until we can get you out. No one will hurt you again, I promise.'

Ng knelt down and she wrapped her skinny arms around his fat neck and held on tight.

'I promise to come and find you as soon as you get back to Hong Kong,' he said. 'I promise. Now, be brave.' He pulled a bar of chocolate from his pocket. 'Share this out and stay put. I'll see you very soon.'

They met up with the PTUs at reception.

'We've found Bernadette,' said Commander Ting.

'Alive?'

He shook his head. 'Been dead for several days. There's a cold storage place in the other building. It's laid out as a morgue down there. She was on a trolley.'

'Any idea of the cause of death?'

'She looked like she'd been strangled, tortured. What do you want us to do? Shall we come back with you or shall we stay here and help the teams when they come?'

'Stay here. Protect the kids. Keep looking. You shouldn't have to wait long. Ng has phoned the Super – there's a team on the way.'

The three detectives walked back across the tarmac one at a time, towards the waiting helicopter. Peter Wong was ready to take off. Mann was three-quarters across and Ng was halfway when they heard the young girl's shouts. The child who had latched on to Ng's hand was now running at full speed to catch them up. As her young cry echoed around the quarry-base, so did a flash of gunfire and a volley of bullets a millimetre from their heads.

Mann and Ng ran towards the child. Ng pinned her to the floor just as a further volley of shots was returned by three rounds from Li's M16. Then there was silence.

'Okay, Ng, we can move now. Li must have got him. He's getting better with that thing.'

Mann touched Ng on the shoulder. He didn't move. He'd been hit.

99

'How is he?' Superintendent White stopped Mann on the stairs on the way down from his office.

'We don't know yet. They're working on him. He was hit twice: once in the shoulder, once in the stomach. We'll go down and see him in a few hours when he comes round. Are the teams on their way to Sixty-Eight?'

'Yes, they are there now, but Mann . . . we need to talk. I will do what I can, but it's not going to be straightforward. I had a difficult job getting permission to send the rest of them in, over the border. It's not in our jurisdiction. There were stipulations – concessions.'

'But these women are our responsibility. They were kidnapped from Hong Kong and taken to mainland China, where they were murdered. Plus, we have child-trafficking charges, added to the murder of an Irish citizen. Surely that's enough to get some attention?' Mann was descending the stairs as he spoke.

'It's not the kind of attention that's wanted, Mann,' Superintendent White called after him.

'Sorry, David. Got to go. Can you get Li to brief you

further? I need to interview the brothers. If I am to have any hope of finding Georgina alive and getting Chan, I have to move fast.'

Mann disappeared, leaving the Superintendent halfway up the stairs and only a fraction of the way to telling Mann what he wouldn't want to hear. White stood for a few minutes, listening to Mann's footsteps, then he swore under his breath and walked into his office, slamming the door behind him.

100

It was late, but then there was no clock to watch in the cells. Man Po was slumped in the corner, his head resting on his chest. His T-shirt was saturated with dribble. He was heavily sedated. They had had to. He cried all day long. He wanted to see his brother. He wanted to see his father and he wanted to see his photo collection of dead women. Because he didn't get any of those things he had spent the previous twelve hours hitting his head repeatedly against the bars of the cell. One side of his head was a mush.

Mann looked at him. He had better get used to it, he thought. He was going to spend the rest of his life tied up, knocked out, and kept in conditions befitting an animal.

Mann called to him. He didn't answer. He couldn't even lift his head. So Mann went to talk to Max, who was housed in the opposite side of the building to his brother. When he got there, Max was sitting on his bunk, his head in his hands. One bare lightbulb shone down into the cell. He didn't move or look up as Mann approached him.

'You ready to help, Max?'

Max didn't answer.

'I know about Club Sixty-Eight, Max. I know that at least some of the women met their deaths there. You want me to help you and your brother, you need to talk to me now.'

Max shook his head miserably and wrung his hands as he stared up at Mann from his bunk.

'What have you got to lose, Max? What are you afraid of?'

Max blinked up at Mann.

'I don't know how you came to be involved in all this, but I don't see you as a killer, Max. But you and your brother played an important part in it, and you will stand trial and go to prison for it. I can't alter that, but I can help you make some recompense for what you've done.'

Max's eyes stayed fixed on Mann's face.

'Nothing is going to save you or your brother now, but you could help me save Georgina.'

At the mention of her name, Max grew agitated. He turned away.

'You liked Georgina, didn't you?'

Max's head sunk to his chest.

'Where is she, Max? Where will Chan have taken her? You know him, Max. He's your cousin. He would trust you more than most. Where would he go to hide for a few days and wait for transport?'

'I don't know. I don't know these things.'

'Tell me what you *do* know, Max.'

'I never killed anyone.' Speaking softly, he stared at the floor, wringing his hands.

'And your brother?'

Max looked up at Mann. His eyes were darting all around the cell, alighting on Mann's face then flitting past.

'My brother didn't mean to. It's not Man Po's fault. He's a simple man. He never meant to hurt anyone.'

'I'm listening.'

'Twenty years ago, Man Po was driving along in his truck in Stanley, delivering meat. It was early morning. A white girl flagged him down. She was drunk. She starts coming on to my brother like a bitch on heat. She has no shame. She lifts up her top, exposes her breasts. She hikes her skirt up, shows him her legs – he's never seen a woman's legs like that before – and she takes his hand and starts rubbing it between her legs. I told you she was a bitch on heat, shameless – an animal. He didn't mean to squash her. He put his weight on her. He doesn't remember how long it was, but when he turned her over she was dead.'

'What did he do with her?'

'He put her under the pigs, in the back of the lorry, and he brought her home. For a couple of days he hid her. He didn't tell me.'

'Hid her where?'

'Inside the old surgery.'

'And when you found her, what did you do?'

'I asked my father. He said he knew someone who could help. Someone in the family who owed us a favour. He would tell us what to do with her.' Max shook his head. His shoulders heaved as he sighed heavily. 'We went to Chan. He was a young man then

– ambitious, mean. He'd just joined the Wo Shing Shing. We asked him for help.'

'He was your cousin, after all?'

'Yes, he was – and my father paid for him to go to school in England. He *owed* us.' Max looked at Mann, his eyes sharp, shining in the gloom of the cell, eager to share the injustice of the situation. 'He was supposed to help us dispose of it. Hide the evidence. He was supposed to do all that to repay his debt to my family. He was *supposed* to help.'

'What did he do?'

'He told Man Po to take the body to work, cut it up and feed it to the pigs when he went to the farms. He said he'd go to Stanley, to the place where it happened, and make sure there was no evidence there to convict Man Po.'

'And then?'

Max got off the bunk and started pacing agitatedly around the cell.

'For ten years, *nothing* – then it started. He came to me and said he wanted me to kidnap a girl he knew from a club. He said he would get her drunk, put her in my cab, and I was to do the rest. I had to keep her in the old surgery for a few days, then he would call me, tell me where I was to take her.'

'Why did you go along with it?'

Max's arms flapped in the air. 'Huh? He said he had evidence. He said one word from him and Man Po and I would be arrested. I had no choice.'

'So, you did what you were told. Then what?'

'He called me. I had to give her a sedative, get her

in the cab again . . . drive out into the New Territories. I had to take her to him late at night. He had a different club then, not Sixty-Eight – small, just beginning. We met in a car park. I gave him the girl. I thought it was all finished. Then, after a month, he called me again – told me to get Man Po to pick up her body and dispose of it the way he had the other one. Man Po didn't want to. We had no choice. Chan made us do it. He used us. We had no choice.'

'You had a choice.'

'No . . . no . . . no!' Max dissolved into a heap in front of Mann and clung to the bars as he slid down to his knees. 'He said we owed him a *lot*. It was never enough – one girl, ten, twenty, never enough. I had to keep bringing them to him. I had to keep them in my house, in the old surgery, make them nice, make them scared.'

'How did you choose the girls, Max?'

'Huh? Sometimes Chan told me to pick someone up. Sometimes I got to know them myself.'

'How?'

'Through Lucy – the girls who stayed in her flat. They rode in my taxi to work. I got to know if they had family. Chan always asked me. "Any new ones?" I had to keep looking for them for him, more and more. He always wanted more.'

'Why didn't you tell him you'd had enough?'

'Huh? I tried. He threatened to put all the blame on me and Man Po – for all of them. He threatened to kill my father. He said that Man Po had been hiding the bodies, not doing as he was told, and it would be easy for it all to be pinned on us.'

'He was right about that, wasn't he? The trophies?'

'Yes – the trophies. Chan told Man Po to cut the bodies up and feed them to the pigs on the farms, but Man Po didn't do it, not every time. He cut them up and hid them in freezers at his work. It wasn't always easy to get to the farms every time. He had to wait sometimes, so he had to store them in the freezer. Then they had to defrost somewhere so that he could give them to the pigs easily, cut up small, no trace. It's not always easy, huh?'

'He liked the dead girls.'

'Yes. He liked them a lot.' Max shrank away from Mann. He edged back towards his bunk. 'Sometimes he just kept a part. Small parts that he put into jars. Big parts in freezers. Until there were too many in the freezers. Then we heard that the company was changing hands, selling up, and soon Man Po would have no job. So he started emptying the freezers at work. He panicked.'

'Got careless.'

'Yes! He left the bags all over the place! So stupid.' Max sat on the bunk, shoulders hunched, swinging his head monkey fashion. 'So stupid.' He turned sharply towards Mann. His eyes were burning in the gloom of the cell. 'See! We're not so bad. We didn't kill them, except that girl. And that was an accident. Man Po is just a delivery man. He cuts up the carcasses and disposes of the meat. That's his job. Nothing more. Just a delivery man.'

'But it isn't meat, is it, Max? It's people. And you don't *always* get them through Lucy, do you, Max?'

Max looked up and waited. He knew that Mann would come to it. Mann had saved the question until last. He had steeled himself for it. But Mann knew, whatever Helen had suffered he must suffer it now too.

'That day you picked up my girlfriend from my flat.'

Max started writhing. He didn't want to look at Mann. He didn't want to answer this question.

'That day, Max. Was she a random choice? Or were you ordered to pick her up?'

Mann's heart was breaking. He felt near to collapse. He was tired, sick. He was trembling with grief and anger.

'I am sorry. I did not want to . . . I did not know her.' Max stood up again and came back to stand at the bars, but not too close – not close enough so that Mann could reach him.

'Answer me, Max! Were you ordered or was it something that just happened?'

Mann's anger made Max flustered. He was squirming. 'He showed me a photo of her. He told me where you lived. I was ordered to watch her. I was told to wait for my chance.' Max wrung his hands, looked everywhere but at Mann. 'I was ordered to pick her up. I didn't know her. He did.' Max glanced at Mann. 'For six months I watched and waited. That day – she called a cab. My controller told me the address. I knew it was my chance. She came out with her suitcase. I saw you come. You drove up. I thought you had come to stop me. I wanted you to stop me. But you let us go.'

Mann fought an overwhelming urge to reach between the bars and drag Max through them like they were a cheese-grater. At the same time he thought he would throw up.

'I will regret that day forever, Max – till the day I die. But my death is some way off. Yours is almost here. You deserve to die, Max. And, when they kill you, please let the last image you see be of Helen. A life for a life, Max – you are truly damned. But, if it's any consolation, I'm damned if you're the only one.'

101

'I've never seen the like of it, sir – kids as young as five.'

Li was speaking to the Superintendent as Mann walked in. Mann needed to get the meeting over with as fast as possible if he had any chance of catching up with Chan. Time was slipping out of his hands.

He stood next to Li, waiting impatiently for him to finish his account of Sixty-Eight. He could see he wasn't the only one agitated. Mann looked at David White. The Superintendent had been listening to the account of Club Sixty-Eight without interrupting, but Mann could see that he was distracted. The late-morning sun was irritating his eyes. He looked ashen-faced and exhausted. His restless hands continually smoothed back the ghost of his hair.

'Mann – summary, please?'

'These men will have paid big money. They are going to be some of the richest men, not just in Hong Kong but across Asia. Maybe even worldwide. They will have paid millions to fulfil these warped fantasies of theirs, and Chan is the man who made it all possible. This is what we've been waiting for, David – now we finally have him!'

White sat back in his chair and looked towards the window. His eyes lingered there and he sighed heavily. The room went silent except for the whoosh of the ancient ceiling fan and the sound of voices in the corridor outside. The atmosphere in the room bristled with tired irritation and raw emotion. Shrimp looked at the Superintendent and then at Mann, and he waited. He had no idea what for – he just knew something was about to kick off.

'Thank you for your help, Officer Li. It's the Inspector I need to talk to.'

The two were left alone.

'Sit, Mann.'

'I'd rather stand.'

'Mann, please sit down before you fall down. We're all exhausted – none of us has slept for days. I know this is the last thing you want to hear, but sit down and let's get this thing done.'

'I'm standing, David, until I hear what I want to hear, then I'm walking out of this office and getting on with my job.'

'We've been told to leave Chan to his own – let the Wo Shing Shing deal with him "inhouse".'

Mann took one of his deep breaths, which sometimes helped to calm him. This time the fuse was already lit and the breath merely gave fuel to the explosion.

'I don't want to fucking hear it!' Mann's voice leapt up several decibels. 'Don't even come close to fucking saying it!' He stood rigid with anger. 'No . . . fucking . . . way.'

Superintendent White held up his hands to silence him – he wanted his turn.

'You're right about these men. I am sure some of them will turn out to be among the wealthiest in Asia. They are all triad-connected – if not actually belonging to a society they will be affiliated somehow along the back-scratching, favour for favour route. They will certainly be under the protection of the Wo Shing Shing. CK will know most of them personally and his reputation will be at stake here. He won't want to lose face. Chan got these men into this mess. CK will have to get them out of it.'

Mann leaned in over the big oak desk, past the grand-children's photos, past the rugby trophy and cigar-box.

'We can't allow it to happen, David. Just to save CK from loss of face we have to let Chan escape? No fucking way! Loss of face is the least of his problems. Chan is involved in the deaths of all these women – he must come to justice. What about Helen? Is no one to stand trial for her murder? No one?' Mann took a step backwards, stood tall. He looked David White straight in the eyes. 'Let's not waste any more time here. He's already got a head start. He'll make his way to the Philippines. There's a big triad network out there on Negros. He will be protected there. If we don't get him before he reaches Manila we've lost him for good.'

'Mann, you are not listening to me – CK will have every expensive lawyer on the planet working on this

398

case. I've already had one of them on the phone. He says he can prove that these girls went willingly to Sixty-Eight. That their deaths were accidents as a result of sexual games that they entered into willingly. Their histories as hostesses, prostitutes, will come into it. The films will be discredited in court. The identity of the men is unproven.'

'Unproven? I can tell you who some of these men are. We just need to look through the *Who's Who* of the world's richest perverts – we'll soon identify them.'

'And what jury will convict them, Mann? Who's going to stand up in court and condemn their whole family to certain death by convicting a highly connected triad? No one – that's who.' The Superintendent shook his head wearily as he slumped in his chair and sighed. 'It wouldn't get to court anyway. It would be thrown out by a judge, who's probably in one of the bloody films. We have to swallow this, Mann. We have – no – choice.'

'And Georgina, is she supposed to swallow it too?'

'I am sorry, Mann. If she's not dead already then she soon will be.'

Mann paused and shook his head slowly and sadly. He never thought that he'd see the day when the man he had looked up to all his life would sell out.

'I never thought I'd hear you talk like this, David. I thought you had more balls and more integrity than this. Now that you're about to retire, none of it means a damn to you any more.'

Superintendent White leapt up from his chair. It rolled

back and crashed into the window frame. 'Don't ever talk to me like that. Not ever. Do you understand?'

'Then tell me it's not true, David. Tell me there's not about to be one almighty cover-up, a trade-off, a pay-off?'

White went to stand by the window. He pulled angrily at the louvre blind, shutting its slats with a snap before turning back into the room.

'Do you think I like it, Mann? Don't you think I feel the same as you? I am disgusted with it all. I have given my life to upholding justice here in the region, never compromising, always putting my own life second. My reputation and credibility comes first for me – it's para-mount. You know that, Mann. But now integrity counts for nothing. Scum like CK are in charge – not us.' He sat down heavily in his chair. 'I had a call from someone *very* high up, Mann. There are to be no charges brought against any other individuals concerning the deaths at Club Sixty-Eight. Only the brothers will stand trial. The women went to the club willingly, consenting adults and all that bullshit.'

'They consented to what? To being tortured to death? And the brothers are to take the rap for all the murders?'

Superintendent White nodded.

'And I suppose they're wanted in China on similar charges?'

He nodded again.

'So, we have our two fall guys nicely stitched-up and facing a firing squad, while the money men walk free.'

'That's about the strength of it, yes. There will be no charges brought against Chan. CK will be responsible for keeping tabs on him from this moment on. Chan will stay in hiding until it all blows over. Then, *when* he returns, he will take a background role in the Wo Shing Shing from now on.'

'Yeah, right! This whole thing might even work in his favour. CK takes the rap. CK has to watch his step – Chan escapes to start building a new life in the Philippines. Nice work! Well, David, you and the rest of the so-called justice system may have made a deal with the devil, but I haven't. You may have sold *your* souls, but you didn't sell mine. I am going to find Chan and make him pay, one way or another. I'm going to get Georgina back, safely. Then I am going to track down each one of those women's murderers and bring them to justice. W*hoever* they are and *whatever* form justice takes.'

David White glared at Mann.

'Don't be stupid, Mann. You can't win this one. You know what it's like here. Money rules. Money is God. Money can buy anything, even justice.'

Mann had heard enough. He thumped his fist down on David White's desk, upsetting the family photos and sending the rugby trophy flying.

'Money might buy *your* type of justice, David. It's never going to buy mine.'

102

If he was to secure a smooth path in his search for Chan and Georgina, Mann had to try and stay alive long enough to find them. Not an easy task when he was without police protection and surrounded by Wo Shing Shing. He knew it was time to up the stakes.

Two minutes after it opened, he joined the throng of people pushing through the revolving glass doors of the Leung Corporation building. He went through with the first rush of appointments and slipped into the stream of pencil-skirted, clicky-heeled secretaries tottering across the Italian marble floor, preparing for another day of money laundering. The whole building was dedicated to legit ways of using illegitimate triad funds.

Mann flashed his badge and slipped through security. He was hoping to make it up to the penthouse, where CK Leung had his office, without being stopped. It worked until he tried stepping out of the elevator on the top floor and was ejected straight back in. CK's PA was flanked by half a dozen Wo Shing Shing gorillas, all flexing their muscles for a chance to hit someone so early in their working day.

'Take it easy. I just want to have a chat with CK.' He held up his hands for peace.

'Mr Leung is a very busy man. You need to make an appointment,' the PA – a slight, thin-faced, effeminate man – said before stepping back behind the gorillas.

'This . . .' Mann flashed his police badge, 'usually makes up for the lack of invitation. Tell him I want to see him.'

The gorillas started grunting. The PA put his small hand up for silence. He ushered Mann forward, and Mann grinned at them. 'All right, boys? Nice suits. I didn't know they made them in kids' sizes. Cute!'

'Follow me, Inspector. I will see if Mr Leung is free.'

They padded along on the thickest pile carpet Mann had ever trodden on. His leather soles sunk into it as he walked and he felt as if he were floating. It was over-the-top plush, with eye-popping décor that left you feeling slightly woozy with its purples and reds – like being inside a womb.

'Please wait here.'

The PA left him sitting in the lounge area outside CK's office for ten minutes, then he returned. 'CK will see you now, Inspector. Follow me.'

As Mann entered, CK was standing by the window, looking out at his panoramic harbour view. He was in his customary Prince Charles pose – his hands clasped behind his back, his body leaning slightly forward, shoulders stiff. He was a slight man, elegantly dressed in a traditional Mandarin-collared dark suit. His luxuriant silver-grey hair was perfectly groomed and just touched the edge of his collar. There was an aura of calm menace about him, simmering just below the surface. Mann could feel it in the way he stood, the practised position of the all-powerful.

CK turned to acknowledge Mann – no smile, just a flicker of curiosity in his eyes. His face looked pale, thought Mann – tired. No, not exactly tired. More like white with anger.

'Please, make yourself comfortable, Detective Inspector. Do you require some refreshment?'

'No, I'm fine, thank you.'

CK nodded to his PA, who backed deferentially out of the room.

'What is it, Inspector? How may I help you?' He was frosty, curt, as he came back from the window to sit behind his desk, which was empty except for an antique jade dragon placed at his left side and a black phone console on his right.

'Sorry. I know you're a busy man, lots of arse-licking to do.'

CK looked up at Mann, shocked for a second, then he smiled – thin-lipped and mirthless.

'Some of your English idioms don't translate correctly into Cantonese. We quite enjoy arse-licking, it is thought of as one of life's pleasures here. We are not so . . . anal as you British.'

'That's handy because you must have blisters on your tongue, the amount of people you've had to keep sweet since Chan's little enterprise got discovered.'

'If you are referring to Club Sixty-Eight, my son-in-law merely provided a service that others enjoyed. You have nothing on him – nothing that can be proven against him – and you have the case so cleverly wrapped up, with those brothers in jail.'

'I think the term is stitched up.'

'Anyway, I have cleared it with your superiors. Chan has been working so hard recently that he is going on holiday for a while. When he returns I will deal with any problems that may have arisen from his . . . enterprises. Now, if you'll excuse me . . .'

'Are you aware of *exactly* what type of business your son-in-law was involved in?'

'It was a complex: nightclub, golf course, film studio and so forth, quite magnificent!'

'Did you go there?'

'No, I didn't. Now, what is your point, Inspector?'

'I went there. I saw it all: the torture chamber, I saw the Irish hostess laid out on a slab – tortured to death. Sixty-Eight was a prison for sex workers. Films were made there that involved the rape, mutilation and murder of women and children. I saw it and I have evidence.'

No one had mentioned children or torture to CK, and yet he knew it was probably true. He felt a momentary stab of self-recrimination – he knew he should have watched Chan more closely. He should not have let him take such a gamble. To make the films was one thing – to be found out, quite another. Now it appeared that CK would be left to take the blame. Others would think he had authorised it. Chan was impatient to take over as Dragon Head, and now he had influential friends to back him up.

CK rested his elbows on the desk and pressed the tips of his fingers together while he thought. Finally, he looked up. He tried to keep the anger out of his voice.

'I grow tired of this conversation and of you. I am sure that your superiors will be surprised to learn of your insubordination.' He reached for the phone.

'Before you do that, CK, I think you might like to get a look at these.' Mann threw the two DVDs onto the desk. 'I bet you'll recognise at least one of the people in these films. I only know a few people in the Russian mafia, but you know what? As luck would have it, I remember seeing him the other day. He was with Chan, here to drum up business. Then I saw him again, a few days later – on television – relaxing by a pool. The man has massive damage to his right leg. He stood on a landmine in his terrorist years. Some of the injuries are to the bone. He was lucky not to lose his leg. He takes it for granted, doesn't even think about it any more. But it's quite shocking when you see it. It sticks in your mind. So useful for identifying murderers in snuff movies.' Mann leaned forward in his chair and smiled. 'I have made copies of each.'

CK stood abruptly. He locked his arms and spread his fingers on the desktop.

'What is it you want?'

'I want Chan. I want him brought to justice in some form or another, and I want the witness Georgina – alive.'

'No court will convict Chan. He is a clever man. He will slide through your net, Inspector.'

'Not the net I have in mind. I'm not looking to bring him to court.'

CK studied Mann for a few minutes, a curious expression on his face. Mann returned his scrutiny with a hard-man stare. Then CK slowly rose and went back to stand at the window. Mann watched his narrow shoulders rise and fall as he weighed up this new information.

After a few minutes CK turned around. His eyes burned and his mouth betrayed a faint smile.

'Okay, Inspector Mann. I will play your game for now. But do not cross me – you will not do it more than once. I am not an enemy you should choose. You can have Chan if you can find him, but I have no idea where he is – he was careful not to tell me. The girl may remain alive as long as she remembers nothing of her time in Sixty-Eight. But . . .' he paused and stared hard at Mann, the smile still present, 'if you find Chan, don't bring him back. I will not allow it to go to court. I will not allow him to stand trial and incriminate others to save his own skin. Of course, I will deny all knowledge of this conversation.'

'Really? So sentimental, CK? One would think you didn't like your own son-in-law. Or is it just a trust issue?'

CK had grown tired of the conversation. He sat down at his desk.

Mann stood up. 'Thanks for your time. Happy viewing. But, before I go, one more thing . . .' Mann leaned in a few centimetres from CK's face, 'tell your friends that their time will come. I will watch and I will wait and I will have justice for those women, in or out of the courtroom. Be sure of it.'

CK smiled at Mann, unfazed.

'If ever you plan a change of career, Inspector, come and see me. I like a man with integrity.'

'I thank you, CK, but your brand of integrity will never be mine.'

103

Mann found Li waiting for him in the office. He looked pale and tired. He looked lost. Papers and photos were scattered across his desk. He was staring into the space above them when Mann entered.

'You should get some rest, Shrimp.'

'Will you, boss?'

Mann smiled at the young officer. 'I will get a few hours, *after* we go and see Confucius. You ready?'

Li jumped to his feet. 'Ready.'

The hospital was in sleep mode. Voices were hushed, lights turned down. Electronic equipment beeped down the empty corridors. Nurses shuffled on the linoleum.

Mann and Li were shown to Ng's room by a petite Filipina.

'He is breathing on his own now, but he is still very weak. Just a few minutes with him, okay?' She opened the door and stepped back to let them in before shuffling her black-stockinged feet back down the corridor to the nurses' station.

Mann and Li approached Ng's bed and stood at either side. It was hard to get close to him – he was surrounded by bleeping, blinking machinery. They stood in silence, waiting. Li was the first to speak as he whispered across the bed to Mann:

'He looks bad, boss.'

Ng's eyes opened a fraction and flicked from one man to the other. 'I wasn't shot in the ear, you know. I can hear.' He attempted a smile. 'All right, Genghis? he said to Mann, then turned to Li and winked. 'How you doin', Rambo?'

Li grinned, flattered. 'I'm fine, thanks, Confucius. How are you feeling?' he asked with a little too much enthusiasm.

'Great!' Ng grimaced, rolling his eyes.

Mann smiled, relieved to see his friend on the mend. 'It's a good job you're so fat. The bullet just couldn't cope with the layers it had to go through.'

'Sure, sure. Ha fucking ha.' Ng grinned. 'Tell me . . . ?'

'What?'

'Something's going on. I can tell by your face, Mann.'

'It's the investigation, Ng. It's going nowhere. The women were killed by wealthy, high-up, untouchable men. We've already been told that the brothers are taking the rap for it – and they were involved, definitely, but they weren't the ones to kill our women. It's a big cover-up.'

'And Chan?'

'I've been warned to leave him alone. The top brass have tied the Super's hands.'

'Cut off his balls, more like,' said Li.

'Yeah, that's about the strength of it. Although I did go and see CK personally, took him a present of a couple of films, and I got the distinct impression that he would have loved to have told me where his son-in-law was.'

'It figures. Not the easiest of relations. Chan has Georgina?'

'He has her. Insurance, I would say. Just until he feels safe enough to get rid of her. I'm thinking of taking a bit of leave, starting now. I fancy doing some sightseeing. Might even make it to the Philippines. What do you think?'

The nurse reappeared at the door. 'Time to leave, gentlemen. Your friend is tired.'

'Okay. Okay.' Mann started to go. Ng called him back.

'Mann . . . try to get him before he leaves Hong Kong. Find him. Find her. Make your peace, Genghis. Remember – *a man who commits a mistake and doesn't correct it is committing another mistake.*'

They got outside the hospital.

'What did he mean by that, boss? A man who commits *what mistake*?'

Mann smiled and shook his head. 'I have no idea,' he said unconvincingly.

'Where now, boss?'

Mann looked at Li – his face was flushed with energy again. Mann knew Li wasn't going to settle for Mann telling him to get a few hours' sleep. They were both alike in that way. The race was on, and although Mann had intended to run it alone . . .

'I am taking that leave, Shrimp. I am going to find Chan. I should warn you that I will be working without orders. Actually, I will be working against orders. I have been ordered to allow Chan to escape. You run a big risk if you stay with me tonight, Shrimp. You should think about it. You are at the start of your career.'

'I have thought about it, boss. It's not a career I want if there's no integrity attached. We are supposed to get the bad guys, aren't we?'

Mann grinned. 'Yes, we damn well are.'

104

Georgina sat in the back of Chan's car, feeling sicker than she had ever done in her entire life. Withdrawal had kicked in. Every bone ached. Every muscle hurt. She sweated with the pain. She thrashed around on the back seat while Chan sat in the front next to Stevie Ho, who was driving. Chan was waving his phone around as if it were another hand. Occasionally he turned his head and nodded towards Georgina in the back.

'She's my insurance, in case our minister decides to cut a deal.'

'He won't do that. He's a sworn brother.'

'I made him swear allegiance to the Wo Shing Shing as well. CK could get to him, CK will have a difficult dilemma. I'm his son-in-law, after all. I'm family. I can always insist and prove that everything I did was for the good of the Wo Shing Shing. You must go ahead, Stevie, make the arrangements.'

'I will. I will wait for you in the Philippines. Negros will be your new home.'

'Just until the time is right, then I will return. But send someone else to Negros. I need you to track Johnny

Mann. He is the only one I fear. He hates me more than anyone else. By now he will know about the death of his girlfriend. He will come looking for me, I'm sure.'

'Even he wouldn't risk everything for revenge. All police activity around the case is halted. They're not looking for you. They've decided to let the brothers take it all and let you go.'

'Kill him anyway.'

'He's a policeman – it's not going to be easy.'

'If I expected it to be easy I would do it my fucking self! You know Johnny Mann. You worked with him. You're the best person to kill him. Don't let your old loyalties get in the way.'

'I was only in the force for four years, and three of those were undercover. I have no loyalties to anyone but you and the Wo Shing Shing.'

'Then do as I command. This man has pursued me my whole life. We are opposite sides of the same coin, but he will never admit it. He stands for everything I cannot abide. He spends his whole life in pursuit of justice.' Chan laughed. 'Fucking justice! He knows there is no such thing in the world – only greed and disappointment. He sits on my shoulder like my fucking conscience. Kill him.'

They drove to the ferry terminal in Central and parked up. Georgina struggled to get out of the car. She was feeling worse by the minute. Chan was anxious to get undercover. He pulled her out of the back seat and propelled her down the jetty and towards the waiting ferry. They left Stevie Ho at the car.

'Remember what I said – find him fast.'

He pushed Georgina forward towards the boat. Once inside, he led her towards the back. She sat in a corner and tucked her legs up onto the bench. For the next hour she dozed, flitting in and out of restless sleep. Periodically she opened her eyes and watched Chan. Sometimes he was texting or talking on his phone; other times he was just staring into space. He looked scared, she thought. She peered past him, through the darkened glass to the glistening ocean beyond. Small green islands, dotted with fishing pontoons, came and went. White-rimmed, they sat proud on the water. She lay down on the bench and slipped into a deep sleep. As she drifted deeper the ferry drone was replaced with the sound of laughter. She was spinning in the rain with Ka Lei. She was so happy. Then her hands lost their grip and she was falling; slowly she fell through thickening darkness, as through water; she sank away from the light at the surface until her knees scraped on the bottom of her consciousness and there she found the memory. Hands gripped her throat. She tried to scream but no sound would come. She tried to breathe, but there was no air. Her assailant's hot breath was on her face, his greedy eyes watching and willing her to die. She tried to fight him but her arms and legs wouldn't move. She felt herself begin to fade; now she could hardly see his face and she heard Ka Lei laughing again. She awoke with a jolt. Chan was jabbing her with his elbow. He took a packet of tissues from his inside pocket and tore one open.

'Wipe your face. You look like shit. People are staring at you. Sit up and stay awake now. We are there.'

She sat up and peered through the window.

'Where?'

Chan stood up and motioned to Georgina to get up from her seat. 'It doesn't matter where. We are going to a holiday chalet. It's not very salubrious, but we won't be staying there long. Now get up.'

'I feel so ill.' Georgina struggled to stand but couldn't, and sank back onto the seat.

Chan's patience was becoming stretched. 'You don't have to stand for much longer. There's a nice bed waiting for you. Let's go.'

'But . . .'

Chan leaned in, out of earshot of the handful of other passengers who were gathering at the front of the ferry ready to disembark. He took hold of her arm at the elbow and pulled her to her feet, hissing into her ear:

'I want no fuss. Do you hear? Get up. Get off this boat without attracting any attention – otherwise, you know those children back at Sixty-Eight? They'll all be burnt alive. Would you want that?'

Georgina shook her head.

'I have left instructions. One signal from me that things are not going well, and poof! Up they go! Are you listening to me, Georgina?'

His hand twisted her arm. She flinched and nodded.

'That's a good girl. Be nice to Daddy and he'll be nice to you.' His mouth turned into a smile but his eyes didn't. 'We are going to stay here for a night, then we will be moving on. That's all you need to know – now look alert!'

Georgina walked down the gangplank and stood reeling in the glare of the sun. Chan steered her straight ahead.

In front of her she saw the long low island of Cheung Chau. Directly opposite the ferry terminal was a dilapidated parade of two-storey buildings with striped awnings in faded colours of green and ochre – all bleached by the sun. Rubber rings and children's toys spilt out onto the sandy pavement. No high-rise buildings were allowed on the island and no cars – just bikes and walkers – dodging each other on the narrow lanes.

They walked across the tumbledown promenade and down a lane that started opposite the ferry terminal and ran the breadth of the island at its narrowest point. It took them straight to the windsurfing beach, the most popular on the holiday island.

They walked for five minutes at a fast pace. Chan dragged Georgina along. He talked on his phone as he walked. He looked about him nervously. They passed seafood restaurants and bars, market stalls and beach shops. Georgina longed to stop and rest awhile. A woman serving food in one of the restaurants beckoned to her. Georgina wanted to sit down so badly but Chan hurried her away.

At the end of the road, concrete steps dropped down to a narrow semicircle of yellow sandy beach. They turned right at the top of the steps and past a beach café – with cheap metal chairs and spindly-legged tables, still covered in the rings of congealed beer from the night before. Chan walked on ahead. Georgina halted. She watched a family – the only people on the beach: grandmother, proud young parents and a chubby little girl who had fat pink cheeks and black plaits that swung back and forth as she ran from parent to parent.

Georgina looked at the sea with longing. She wanted to walk into the static mass of cool blue. She wanted to feel the rough sand ease her itching skin and the cold water fill her ears, creeping over her hot scalp and easing her throbbing head. She longed to slip out of her skin and swim away and keep swimming forever. But, at the same time, she saw the shark nets and wondered what lay beneath. She shivered, turned her back on the sea and followed Chan.

Chan or the sharks? Not much of a choice.

105

Chan was in a hurry to get undercover. He'd taken an inordinate amount of risks lately. He knew if he wasn't married to the boss's daughter he'd be dead by now. As it was, he couldn't rely on it much longer. He hadn't seen his wife in days. He'd heard she had moved back into Daddy's. She must be waiting to see the outcome – hedging her bets. Chan wasn't surprised. There was always something distant about her – something he could never reach. But he had destroyed his chance of promotion within the Wo Shing Shing. He knew it, it had been written all over CK's face.

He'd have to wait till the old man died. But that could be speeded up, especially with his new friends on board. He'd go to Negros as soon as his transportation turned up, but not to hide. He would use the time to build up his strength and his allies. He had made many in Club Sixty-Eight. So many rich old perverts were very grateful to Chan for having fulfilled their twisted dreams. They would not forget him. Plus, in case they contemplated it, he had a copy of each of the films to serve as a memory jogger.

When the time was right he'd launch a takeover of the Wo Shing Shing. His wife could divorce him and remarry. They were never more than a business arrangement anyway. And she had proved barren like the rest of them. He would take Georgina – not only would he need some company in his new home, he had taken a liking to her in Club Sixty-Eight. Even though she wasn't willing, she was compliant, and that made a refreshing change from the usual greedy whores. And when he grew tired of her she could disappear as easily as the others. Perhaps she would even bear him a child . . .

They reached a little chalet not far from the sea. It was a single-storey basic holiday beach let: concrete floors, bare stone walls, barred windows. Chan unlocked the door and pushed Georgina inside. It was then that she turned and noticed Chan's men – four dark suits. They didn't come closer than nodding distance. Georgina saw them for a second and then they were gone.

Chan locked the door behind them and put the doorkey in his jacket pocket. He placed his briefcase onto the low coffee table directly in front of the door in the lounge area and threw his jacket over the back of the rattan sofa. The chalet hadn't been properly aired for weeks and was unbearably hot. He began opening all the doors and windows.

'Bathroom, bedroom, kitchen,' he announced like an estate agent as he marched briskly through the small chalet, opening the rusted-up metal windows as he went.

Georgina stood just inside the front door, by the coffee table. As he re-emerged from the bedroom he caught her looking at his jacket.

'Don't even think of stepping outside, let alone trying to run away. I have armed men surrounding the chalet. They will shoot you and anyone else that I tell them to.' He picked up a newly starched cellophane-wrapped packet of bedding from the breakfast counter and threw it at her. 'Make the bed up, have a shower and get some sleep. I have to make some phone calls.'

Inside the bedroom was a small double bed and one scruffy wardrobe with its door hanging on by a rusty hinge. It was full of old metal hangers.

Georgina placed the packet of bedding down, sat heavily on the bed and pressed her bare feet onto the cold tile floor. She lay back and looked at the ceiling. A breeze trickled in and did its best to disperse the build-up of heat in the small room; it touched Georgina's face as it passed and she turned her head to see where it was coming from. Through the bars of the window she could see the small side-street leading to the beach and hear a bike's bells and the people chatting. She could smell the sea. *Not a bad place to die*, she thought. Then, with an enormous effort, she stood up and steadied herself against the wall. She flicked the sheets out of the packet and laid them loosely across the bed. She longed to lie down but she knew she wouldn't be able to lie still – her body was shaking with a fever, her skin crawling. Before she slept she needed a shower to cool her. Moving silently past Chan, who was sitting at the lounge table shouting his instructions down the phone, she passed the kitchen and went into the bathroom.

She held her hand against the stone shower wall for support and stood for several minutes, head bowed, eyes closed, beneath the lukewarm water as the hard jet blasted her face and shoulders. Then she soaped her body. Lathering up the small white deposit of soap, she scrubbed her skin hard. After ten minutes she turned the water off and stood, eyes shut, feeling the water cool on her skin. Shivering, she reached for a towel. Chan was suddenly there, and he handed her one. She tried to cover herself.

'Don't bother. I've seen it before – remember?' He watched her as she dried herself. 'Poor baby.' He slipped his arm around her waist and pulled her to him, nuzzling into her moist neck. 'Are you in pain?' Georgina was shaking so much that she was barely able to keep upright. 'Don't worry,' he said, licking the drops of water from her neck. 'Daddy is going to look after you from now on. I'm getting you something. It's on its way. You'll feel better soon.'

Georgina said nothing. Clutching the towel to her, she waited for him to leave. He stood watching her for a few minutes, delighting in her humiliation, then he closed the door and went back to his phone calls.

Georgina leaned against the wall. Her naked body shook with anguish as she began to cry, silently. She pressed the towel to her mouth and bit into it so that she would not make a sound. She cried for the frustration of it all, and with so much sorrow. She wanted to smash the wall down with her fists, to kick and scream. She wanted someone to help her. She was sick and she was frightened. She wanted to be rescued. She wanted Johnny Mann.

106

She finished drying and went back past Chan to lie down. She felt his eyes follow her but he was busy on the phone. She crawled into bed. The cool cotton sheet soothed her sensitive skin and calmed her torn flesh where she'd been scratching. All day she lay on the bed, drifting in and out of sleep. She had fitful, horror-filled dreams when she slept, and crazed, pain-filled minutes when she awoke. All her senses were heightened. She listened, wide-eyed, to a beetle scuttle back and forth across the stone floor. She smelt the sea and the hot sand as it drifted in through the bars of the window. She watched the shadows dip and fall on the grey, pock-marked walls of the bare room, and she drifted in no man's land.

After a particularly long doze she awoke to find that the room was dark and there were voices coming from the lounge. Chan was talking to several other men. They argued back and forth. The bedroom door opened and Chan came into the room. Georgina watched him. Just her eyes followed his movements. He didn't look at her. He hadn't come to see her. He had come to pace and to gather his thoughts. He smoked a cigarette. It lit up his face and reflected in his dark eyes. Georgina watched him in the gloom of the evening. He didn't look at her. He didn't notice her at all. She was just a ghost in the corner of the room, silent, observing. She thought about how it would feel to kill him.

107

Ten p.m. Mann sat opposite Max in the interview room. Max looked dishevelled and exhausted. Shrimp leant against the far wall.

Shrimp had brought Mann some fresh black coffee, although he needed very little more wiring – he hadn't slept for three days. He was going to get more out of Max, one way or another. He had a hunch that if anyone would know where Chan would run, Max would. Max had spent years catering to Chan's subversive tastes. He must know more about him than even he realised.

Mann's eyes were on the clock on the wall to his right. He was waiting for fifteen minutes to pass. He sipped his coffee and sat back in his chair and looked at the clock. Max went to get a cigarette from his packet on the table. Mann flicked the packet away; it landed in the corner of the room. Max looked at Li, whose feet it had landed at. Li stared back, unblinking. Every few minutes Max lifted his eyes towards Mann, waiting for the interview to begin and for it to be over with; waiting to be allowed to return to the seclusion of his cell. Mann tapped his pen on the tabletop as he watched Max sweat. Fifteen minutes was up.

'Okay, Max, that's fifteen minutes off your brother's life.'

'Huh?'

'That's right. Every minute you waste my time in here comes off your brother's life.'

'Huh?'

'Now, that may not seem like a big deal to you, Max – after all, you are going to die anyway.'

'Huh?'

'You and your brother are to stand trial on the mainland. You know what that means, don't you, Max? It means they are going to shoot you. So, maybe you think – okay, at least my brother and I will be shot together? You and your brother, side by side against the firing squad? Well, you will have to stand next to his corpse for fifteen minutes now. Want to make it a day standing next your dead brother? Want to watch the fly infestation begin while you're waiting to die?'

Max swung his head from side to side, confused.

'Then tell me what I want to know.'

'I do not know any more. I have nothing more to tell you.'

Mann looked at the clock. 'Twenty-two minutes. Buzzzzz. It doesn't take long for flies to start laying eggs. They start laying in wet places: eyes, nose, mouth.'

Max looked at Li for help. Mann slammed his hand on the table. Max shrieked and turned back.

'No one can help you, Max.'

Mann sat back and drank the rest of his coffee. He rolled the coffee cup in his hands.

'The thing is, you deserve to die for your part in all of this, but you're not the only one. Chan deserves it too. Nothing can make a difference to you dying or not, now, Max. Chan can't cut your life any shorter than it is.'

'What about my old father?'

'How much longer do you think he's going to last now without his sons to look after him? He's as good as dead anyway. You did that – you, your brother, and Chan.'

Max started to whimper. Mann nodded towards Li, who picked up the packet of cigarettes and threw it over. Mann got one out, lit it, and placed it in Max's shaking fingers.

'The thing is, Max, after they have shot you and your brother full of holes, Chan will drink a toast to you. You will be dead and he will have escaped justice. Is that what you want? The man who reneged on his promise to your family? The man who used you and your brother? He walks free and leaves you both to carry all the guilt for him. That's all right with you, is it? Chan cares less about what happens to you than he does about, say, Georgina.'

Max looked up.

'Remember Georgina, Max?'

'One of the nicest *Gwaipohs* I ever met.' Max shook his head miserably and looked accusingly at Mann. 'Good manners, always polite. Not like some.'

'I'm not a *Gweilo*, Max – remember that. I may look

like one, but inside I am all Chinese. Chan has her and he will kill her. Do you want that?'

Max shook his head – large despondent swings that took him seconds to complete.

'There is still time to help Georgina,' Mann persisted. 'Do one good thing in your miserable life before you die . . . Now tell me . . . where would he take her, Max?'

Max looked at Mann. Looked away; looked back.

'Where, Max?'

'Find Miss Mad-arh-lin?'

'Yes, Max. Find Miss Georgina. Try and right some of the wrongs you and your brother have done.'

Max looked at the floor, then back at Mann. He spluttered something.

'What, Max?'

Max repeated it. This time he looked at Mann as he did so. 'Maybe Cheung Chau. He has a cottage there.'

'How do you know that?'

'Once, he stayed there for a week. He got ill. He rang me. I had to deliver some herbs from my father. I had to give him acupuncture. I went there.'

'Do you remember where it was on the island?'

'Straight across from the ferry, near the beach, a chalet. I don't remember anything else.'

108

'How are we getting there?' Li asked as he appeared, carrying a backpack.

'I have the keys to a boat.' Mann held up a set of keys. A gold tag hung from them with the initials DW on it. Li looked at him. 'It's a friend's.'

They drove down to the Hong Kong Yacht Club. Mann flashed his badge at the gates and they were ushered through. They headed towards the marina, parked up and walked along the line of expensive boats until they reached the mooring. Gently lapping against the side of the jetty, a white, fibreglass, twenty-one-foot Sea Ray Cruiser was waiting patiently for her first outing.

'He must be a very good friend – to just give you the keys,' said Li.

'He is.'

'Can you drive it?'

'More or less. Stop asking questions now, Shrimp, and get in. Find a knob with BLOWER written on it.' Mann switched the battery on, en route to the helm.

'This one, boss?'

'Yeah. Hit that one.' Mann turned the key and put the throttle into reverse. 'Cast off, Shrimp.'

'What?'

'Undo the rope that's stopping us from going anywhere.'

'Okay, boss. Awesome!'

Mann turned the boat and headed for the islands. The waters were quiet: the large ships were laid up for the night, all the ferries finished. Their small boat cut through the still water effortlessly as it glided between the huge ships like a cleaner fish on patrol.

Li pulled out a pair of board shorts and a surfer's T-shirt from the backpack.

'Where are you going to put your gun, and how many more outfits have you got in that locker of yours?'

'Just a few.' Li came to join Mann at the helm. 'Got my handgun where I keep my board wax. What's the plan, boss?'

'We avoid using guns if we can. We don't want to attract attention. If possible we want to get the girl, get Chan, and get out. Fast and slick.'

'Awesome!'

'Yeah, well, that's the plan, but I'm not sure how we are going to achieve it yet. And another thing, Shrimp – Chan will be guarded by his most loyal. They are the men who killed Kim, back at Sixty-Eight. They don't take prisoners and neither will we. Are you okay with that?'

'More than that, boss – I am trained in empty-handed combat – I won't let you down.'

Mann looked Shrimp up and down and resisted the

urge to smile. Li had finished his outfit off with a peak cap.

'I can believe it. Good man.'

'Boss, if you're not carrying a gun, what are you packing?'

'These . . .' Mann opened his jacket to reveal a custom-made knife belt with three pockets for throwing stars.

'What the heck! I've never seen some of those before.'

'Over the years I have confiscated various weapons from triad members, and some of them I've had customised. I'll show you what they do later.'

109

Chan came into the room and threw a small package onto the bed. He reached into his pocket and took out a hundred-dollar bill and a lighter and threw them down with it.

'You'll have to chase it. There are no needles here. Now take it and shut up. No more screaming.'

He left.

Georgina shuffled forward into a corner of light at the end of the bed, and laid the ingredients out in a line in front of her. So neatly did the packet contain its dusty block of China White that its corners unfolded like an origami puzzle. There would be enough in there to have several hits. She knew how to do it. She'd watched the amah who came to clean her room take it on the days when she'd lain on her bunk staring at the walls. She'd seen the ritual it involved.

She picked up the foil, and stretched it gently on her thigh. She needed to smooth out the creases so that the liquid heroin would not snag and fizzle to nothing too quickly, or run a ragged path and be too difficult to chase. She tapped out a small amount of heroin onto the smooth sheet of foil before setting it carefully to one side. She picked up the hundred-dollar bill and rolled it into a tight tube between her fingers, and then picked up the lighter and paused.

Her thoughts went to Ka Lei. If she took the heroin there would be no going back, no point in being rescued. She would be back, spinning in the rain with her Ka Lei. It would mean that she had accepted her fate and that she was prepared to die one way or another – by Chan's hand or by her own. But it would be so nice to feel better for a while. She placed the note in her mouth, flicked the lighter and picked up the foil. It would take no more than a few minutes to go into her bloodstream, then she would be back in the no-feeling zone. Back among the living dead – untouchable – unreachable. She would be lost forever.

She paused. Ka Lei would not have wanted her to do it. She would have expected her to stay strong, to weather it. It wouldn't be long now before she would feel better – the withdrawal couldn't last forever.

She owed it to Kim, to Ka Lei. She owed it to herself to fight back. *Leeches*, Kim had said they were, and she had been right. Georgina was worth more.

She picked up the envelope and tiptoed over to the window. Taking the neatly folded packet between finger and thumb, she pushed her arm between the bars, as far as it would go, and shook the packet. The heroin flew away like ash – like death on the wind. It disappeared. She was damned if she'd give up the fight yet.

She stood for a few moments, leaning her head against the cool bars, then, turning her head away from the light, she listened. For a second she thought she heard someone call her name.

110

It was midnight when they docked. Mann and Li left the boat in moorings and headed inland. They stopped at the busiest-looking restaurant on the road that cut across the island to the beach. The bulk of clientele were sat at tables and chairs outside. Groups of foreigners with their rented girlfriends were noisily demonstrating their inability to hold their drink. Mann and Li went inside. Just a few elderly Chinese were enjoying a chat with the proprietor – the rest of the place was empty. It wouldn't be long before they shut, and they were taking a rest at the end of their busy evening. Mann spotted the owners – a husband and wife team who looked like they'd been in business there for a long time and knew both the island and its people very well. If anyone knew of strangers arriving, they would.

Mann and Li sat at a central table and waited for the wife to amble over with the menus.

'Menoo Engleesh?' she asked, looking at Mann.

'I'd prefer it in Cantonese. Unless, of course, you only speak English?' answered Mann.

'Ha ha!' The rotund proprietress held her stomach

with her small fat hands and laughed. She turned to share the joke with her husband and the other three old people sat with him at a table by the bar.

'See! I told you I speak good English – this man didn't think I could speak Chinese!'

The whole group fell about laughing.

'Come and join us. Come!' The proprietor made space around the table.

'Is this your son?' the proprietor asked Mann, pointing at Li as they sat down. Before Mann had time to answer, the wife spoke. 'You need to loosen up, like your son . . . get your shorts on . . . you still young . . . enjoy yourself . . . you're on holiday here on Cheung Chau.'

'My son has aged me prematurely.' Mann patted Li's cheek. 'That's children for you.'

The fat proprietress tutted and giggled as she stood and went to fetch a bottle of rice wine, and returned with seven glasses. She poured them out and handed them round before disappearing again to return with an assortment of noodle dishes and rice bowls.

'How long are you staying on Cheung Chau?' she asked.

'We really wanted to see about hiring a cottage by the beach. Do you know if any are free?'

One of the old women spoke up. 'There is one that's always free. I clean it, but the man who owns it doesn't usually let it out.'

The proprietress stopped, midway through refilling Mann's glass.

'He's here at the moment – your man. I saw him. He passed by here this morning.'

'The man who owns the chalet? I wasn't told to expect him.' The cleaning woman looked bemused. 'I am always informed when he's coming. I open it up for him, get it ready. He's only ever been here once before, mind you. He lets others use it sometimes – business friends – not very friendly types. Was it definitely him?'

'Yes. He passed by this morning with a young woman – tall, beautiful. She looked so pale and tired, I felt sorry for her. I asked her if she wanted something to eat and drink but your man pulled her away – he was in such a hurry.'

'Yes,' her husband added. 'And then more men arrived, dressed in suits. Must be his friends.' The old people nodded knowingly to one another. 'And one man arrived alone, just an hour ago. He passed by here – looked inside – did not stop.'

'What did he look like – the man on his own?' asked Mann, pushing his bowl aside having left a small amount inside to signify he was full.

'He was tall – he had a small beard – bald headed, Chinese.'

'Where is that chalet?' asked Mann.

'Down to the end, turn right, follow along to the first lot of chalets, it's last on the left. But it's no good if he's there. You better look for somewhere else. Where will you stay tonight? You can sleep here. We have a room upstairs you can rent for a night.'

'Thank you, that's very kind, but we will sleep on the boat. In fact, I'd better get my son to bed. He looks tired out. Come on, sonny!' Li finished eating hastily.

'But who shall we say wants to rent his chalet – if he asks?' The fat old proprietress followed them out and stood with her hands on her hips – a mischievous look on her face.

'There's no need to mention anything.' Mann peeled off three hundred-dollar bills and pressed them discreetly into the proprietress's fat hands.

She smiled gratefully and inclined her head. 'You know – your Eengleesh so bat, I can't understand you. I think you never here.'

111

'Do you know the man they're talking about? The one who arrived on his own?'

'Stevie Ho – he's an old acquaintance.'

Mann and Li turned back towards the ferry terminal.

'What's his business here? Is it us?'

'Yes. I would say so.'

'Does he work for Chan?'

'Yes, but his loyalties are split between CK and Chan.'

They turned left and then headed inland. Mann wanted to approach the chalet from the busy side of the island. If Chan was expecting trouble at all, he would expect it to come from the ferry side.

It was now two a.m. and as dark as the night could get. Except for a couple of die-hard bars where there were still a few girls and a bowl of rice to be bought, most of the restaurants were shut. The island had taken on a blanket of stillness. Just the gentle sound of the sea, the whisper of the breeze in the vegetation, and the vibrating-bellied cicadas whose noisy call disturbed the night air. Added to that, there was always the odd whoop of laughter and click-clack of mahjong pieces.

Mann and Li crept silently along the narrow streets that ran as a grid across the centre of the island. In the daytime these roads were filled with street vendors and market stalls, but now the smell of freshly steamed seafood was rapidly being replaced by the stench of the day's prawn shells left too long in the sun. Two bleary-eyed bar girls sat on stools at one of the bars, head in hands – they had not quite given up hope of making some money. There was a group of tourists asleep at their table, who would remain there until the sun came up.

They turned from the main market square and zigzagged down the middle section of the island. Joining the cats and rats and dodging the piles of dumped rubbish, they made their way through the tiny alleyways that ran between the buildings, parallel to the beach. Between them and the ocean was a two-storey accommodation block, a few guesthouses and a couple of bars. They turned a corner and came out a hundred feet away from the last line of chalets.

Crouching in the darkness they heard the low voices of several men talking, and they could see lights emitting from the front of the single-storey chalet at the end of the line of holiday cottages. The only window they could see was the barred one that overlooked the lane.

It was then that Mann saw her. He watched Georgina empty something through the bars of the window and lean her head there for a few moments. Then he saw the outline of a man emerge from between Chan's chalet and the next. He was returning from toilet relief, zipping up his fly. As he stepped out into the lane, another man joined him. There followed some discussion about food. The second man was taking orders. He was going to one of the all-night bars to get them something to eat.

Mann looked at Li and gestured towards the man taking the food order. Li nodded and crept backwards until he disappeared out of sight, to cut back along the way they had come and head the man off.

Silently, Mann opened his jacket. From a leather pocket he extracted a four-pointed throwing star measuring six inches in diameter. Made from steel, each of its four blades was razor-sharp and reinforced with steel rivets to give added precision, balance and performance. It was also, quite simply, a thing of great beauty.

Just as the two men finished their discussion, and one turned to go, Mann crossed the lane, keeping close to the chalet walls and sheltering beneath the vegetation around each building. He made his way to within twenty feet of where the man was standing and watched him reach inside his pocket for his cigarettes. Mann waited till the man tapped a cigarette from the packet, put it to his mouth and held up his lighter. He waited until the man brought the lighter in front of his face. Then he stood, drew his hand level with his chest, and, holding the star at the apex of one of the rivets, he balanced it between finger and thumb. Then, with one sharp, hard flick of the wrist he sent it spinning through the air. A second later the man's lighter went out, there was a faint rattling sound, then a pause and a thud as his headless body dropped to the sand.

112

Mann's eyes flicked towards the door. He heard voices – raised but not rowdy – four, probably five. They hadn't heard him or they would have been out by now. Mann crouched across the lane from Georgina's window and listened. It seemed like the conversation had sunk back down to conspiracy level.

He picked up a small amount of sand and threw it between the bars of her window. He threw some more and some more, pausing between each throw to see if she had heard.

She appeared at the window slowly, as if summoned there by some ghost on the wind. It took her a few seconds to make out the figure standing across the lane. He looked at her and smiled. She gripped the bars, gasped, and almost said his name. Mann held his finger to his lips and ducked down at her window. Reaching up, he squeezed her hand.

'You okay?' he mouthed.

She nodded and smiled. But he could see that she was not. Her face was skeletal, and as pale as the full moon – so sick and sad. She had lost so much weight that only her long, curly hair and her smile reassured him that she was still in there somewhere. She held tightly on to his hand. She didn't want to let go. She jumped as Li reappeared and crouched by Mann's side.

'It's all right, Georgina, this is Shrimp – Detective Li. Did it go all right?' he asked Li.

Li nodded.

'I saw your guy, Stevie Ho. The guy I was tailing stopped to talk with him. I heard him say there was no sign of us.'

'He is walking a dangerous road.' Mann's eyes searched the darkness. He knew Stevie was bluffing. He wasn't sure why yet. 'Let's hope he's chosen the right path.' He turned back to Georgina. 'A man was sent for food; he's not coming back – we are. As soon as you hear me knock, slide anything you have across the door, as quietly as you can – then, as fast as you can, get back over here by the window and get down.'

Mann pulled out a small handgun from inside his jacket and handed it to Georgina through the bars. 'If you have to – shoot.'

'I don't know how to . . .'

'Just point the trigger and squeeze. It's all ready for you. Okay?'

She nodded – small, sharp, brave nods – and Mann's heart went out to her. 'Remember now, be ready – put anything across that doorway you can, and then get down quick.'

Mann signalled to Li to follow him.

'You ready for this, Shrimp? There are five men in there, and one of them is Chan. You've seen the photos. You know what he looks like – leave him alive. I'm going to be the guy who went for food. You're going to be the nasty surprise that came free with the order, okay?'

'Got it, boss. Ready to rock and roll . . .'

Mann took off his jacket and revealed five throwing spikes that were strapped into a harness on his arm. Each one was a six-inch, hardened steel, needle-sharp, red-feathered dart – perfectly weighted for throwing accurately and penetrating deeply. He pulled out all five.

Li stood to one side while Mann knocked at the chalet door. There was a sudden hush from inside the chalet, then a man put his hand to the lever and opened the door a fraction. 'Hello?'

Mann kicked the door wide open. The four men darted in different directions. The man who had opened the door was already dead. He had a throwing spike embedded into his left eye, the red feathers sticking out from the socket, shivering. He remained standing for a few seconds, eerily still, as if he hadn't realised he was dead, before dropping to the floor.

The two men who had been sitting on the sofa lunged in either direction as they tried to reach their weapons in time, but they couldn't. One had a throwing spike embedded in his heart and the other had one in his temple.

Li was over the sofa in one leap, and a kick to the fourth man's throat sent him unconscious, slumped against the wall.

Mann looked around. Chan had gone.

113

As Mann entered the bedroom he saw the shadowy figures of Georgina and Chan facing each other a few feet apart. They were side-on to the window, both standing absolutely rigid and still. The only things moving were Georgina's hands; they were trembling as she clenched the gun and pointed it at Chan's face.

'It's all right, Georgina. I have him covered. Give me the gun now.'

Mann took a few steps forward and signalled to Li to find something to tie Chan's hands with. Georgina still didn't move, and she didn't take her eyes from Chan. Mann inched closer – he was within a few feet now.

'He can't hurt you any more, Georgina. Give me the gun.'

She wasn't listening. Her shoulders rose and fell with her rapid breathing.

'I want to kill him.'

Her hands shook. Not for one second did she take her eyes off Chan, and not for one second did Mann doubt that she was capable of shooting him.

'No, Georgina – you have suffered enough. If you kill him it will only make it worse. It's not your job, believe me – it's not yours.'

Keeping his eyes on Chan, Mann walked the last few paces and gently prised the gun out of her hands. He held her to him for a few seconds before steering her over towards the door and out of harm's way.

Li had returned with a length of fisherman's cord he had found outside. 'Tie his hands tightly, Shrimp.'

Chan began to laugh at Georgina as she retreated. 'I can't believe you would do such a thing, Georgina, after all we've meant to each other!'

'Leave her out of this, Chan.'

'Why should I? She belongs to me. I own her. Besides that, she likes me really. She needs me. Don't you, Georgina? We are quite a couple, even though we have our ups and downs, as you can see.' He laughed at her again. She turned her head away. He turned back to Mann. 'I don't know what you think you are doing here. I know for a fact you don't have enough evidence to touch me. The brothers have confessed to most of it, and the rest, unfortunately, has gone up in smoke.'

'The staff didn't feel like burning to death. Sorry, but the place is still standing. We have a team of SOCOs out there right now, going through it with a sieve. They will find enough to have you shot.'

Chan laughed. 'I don't think so, somehow. I do believe I'm cleverer than that, Mann. For a start, it's on the mainland – can't see the Chinese government being awfully helpful, can you? As you probably realise, many of them know about it already. Never mind what

449

you find out there, none of it will be enough to get me to court, let alone convict me – and you know why, Mann? Because I am untouchable. I have the world's richest perverts looking after my back, and they know that one day I will be Dragon Head of the Wo Shing Shing. Everyone knows it – even CK can't stop it.'

'You will have to be alive to enjoy it.' Mann turned to Li. 'Stay here. Look after Georgina. Watch out for anyone else.'

'You don't want me to come?'

'No, Shrimp – stay here. I will be back shortly. Chan and I are going to talk about old times – we have some catching up to do.'

Mann pushed Chan through the adjoining room and out before him onto the sandy lane, down towards the boat. He looked behind him as he did so and saw Stevie in the shadows. He saw the way he carried himself; saw the way his right shoulder was raised, his arm steady – ready to fire his gun. But he didn't.

Chan kept looking for him too. He had expected Stevie to rescue him by now. What was he doing? Waiting till the last fucking moment?

It was when they reached the water that the first real signs of panic crossed Chan's face. Since the incident back when he and Mann were boys, he had hated the water. A big ferry was bad enough, but a small boat was something he'd never been able to get into. He turned, ready to run, but Mann anticipated it, held on to him tightly, as he climbed into the boat. Mann cast off, sat Chan in the seat beside him and started the engine.

Mann throttled the boat, reversed it, eased it round and headed out to sea, leaving a gentle ripple in their wake. He looked behind him. Stevie was edging away from the shoreline, his way forward now clear. He had chosen his path.

Chan sat back and smiled at Mann, pretending to enjoy the ride.

'This is all very pleasant, but we both know you can't do anything to me.'

Mann steered the boat out into open water. Nothing but the blackness of the still ocean lay ahead.

114

'You won't kill me. You'd be the most wanted man in Hong Kong. The whole of the Wo Shing Shing would be out to get you.' *Where the hell was Stevie Ho?* Chan thought. *Surely Stevie wouldn't let him down?* 'You can loathe me all you want, Mann. I am what I am.'

'You had choices just like everyone.'

'Did I? Even when we were kids you never understood what it was like for me. At school in England we lived as brothers. We were inseparable. But there was one big difference – when we came home in the holidays you went back to your parents' nice home in the Mid-levels. I went back to government housing – ten to a room. I suffocated in the heat and dirt. One hundred and fifty people shared four open toilets. I saw the violence and the depravity of living without dignity, without money. Going to England showed me I could be anyone as long as I had money. Being sent to the UK for my education was the one piece of luck I had –'

'It wasn't luck, it was paid for by your hard-working relatives and you repaid your benefactors by joining the Wo Shing Shing?'

'I had no choice. In my neighbourhood you did as you were told. I was recruited the summer I was fifteen. I hated it, but it brought its rewards. I accept I could have led a more honourable existence. But you never understood how it was for me. I had to take every opportunity I could in my life. I had to make it at any cost. You didn't have that terrible weight of poverty and desperation hanging over you. All you had to deal with was being mixed race. It didn't hold *you* back. You had the best of both worlds. You could choose to step effortlessly into either world, whereas I belonged to only one – a world that will get you if you don't get it first. I had to climb my way out of the gutter.'

'Yes, you had it tough, but you didn't have to turn your back on everything decent. Life is full of choices, Chan, of roads to walk. You chose the lowest path you could find.'

'The night of my father's death. You were ordered to keep me away from the house until a certain time.'

'Yes, I was ordered to.'

'My father was a good man. He treated you like a son.'

'Huh! He treated me like a poor relative. He kept me at arm's length, made it quite clear he didn't want his son mixing with me.'

'You checked your watch so many times that night. I remember saying, "What is it? You late for a date?" You laughed and all the time you knew that my father was being tortured.'

'I could do nothing to prevent it.'

'Then, at the allotted time, you left me at my gate and you knew they were waiting for me.'

'I told you – I had no choice. Triad orders.'

'I was made to watch his execution. Do you know what that did to me? It didn't make me fear the triads. It made me determined to wipe every one of you out.'

Chan looked about him. The water was closing in. He was becoming frantic now – Stevie was leaving it very late.

'For friendship's sake, Mann, take me back to shore. Let me disappear. You'll never see me again. For the boys we once were?'

Mann didn't answer him. He kept his eyes ahead and steered the boat further into the darkness. 'Do you want to know how Helen died?' Chan said, desperation in his voice. 'Do you want to know the man who killed her? If I tell you, will you let me go? I have a film of her death. I will give you that film if you take me back to shore.'

Mann cut the engine. The boat bobbed on the still water. The only sound was the distant horns of passing ships and the lapping of the water around the boat's hull. Behind them, just a few lights from Cheung Chau's seafront restaurants and bars winked at them from the shoreline. Mann thought of Helen. Her calmness, her strength, her beauty. He knew what he must do. Across the darkness, their eyes reflecting the iridescent white of the boat's hull, they stared at one another.

'I know all I need to know. I will search till I find the man who physically killed her and I will bring him to justice, one way or another. But I know that you are

454

the person who is ultimately responsible for her death. I will have to live with my part in it. I will regret letting her get into that taxi till the day I die.' Mann took out a knife and reached over to cut Chan's bonds. 'But I can undo something I have done. I saved your life years ago, Chan, saved you from drowning when we were boys.' *A man who has committed a mistake and doesn't correct it commits another mistake.* 'Sink or swim, it's your choice.'

115

'How long have I been asleep?'

Mann stood at the entrance to his bedroom, watching her.

'A few hours. You fell asleep in the car on the way here. I carried you in and put you to bed. How are you feeling?'

'Better.' Georgina smiled sleepily. 'What time is it?'

'It's nearly ten.'

'What about you – did you get any sleep?'

'I dozed a bit.'

Mann came to sit next to her on the bed. She found his hand and held it.

'Thank you for rescuing me, Johnny,' she said but her eyes were sad.

'Please don't thank me. I am sorry that it took me so long to find you. How are you feeling?'

She didn't answer; she just shook her head. Her eyes filled with tears. She gripped his hand tighter.

'Is Ka Lei dead, Johnny?'

'Yes she is, I'm sorry.'

She gasped. A sob cracked from her throat. She sat

up and Mann rocked her in his arms. Gradually the sobbing abated.

'How did she die?' she asked, her head still buried in his shoulder. His T-shirt was wet from her tears.

'She jumped from the balcony.'

She pulled back and looked at him. Her eyes were filled with anguish and pain. It hurt him to see it. 'I knew she was dead. I felt it, Johnny. I saw it. I was lying on this bed. I couldn't move. A man had his hands around my throat. I couldn't breathe. Then I saw her. It was raining. I held on to her hands. We were laughing and spinning around and around in the rain.' Georgina smiled at the memory. 'Was it raining the night she died, Johnny?'

'Yes it was.'

'Where is she now?'

'She's gone. She's been cremated.'

Georgina rested back against him.

'I so wanted to see her – one last time. What will happen to me now, Johnny?'

'The fallout from Sixty-Eight is going to be around for a long time, and in a lot of places in the world. Lots of men will be very nervous for a while. CK says that you will be safe in Hong Kong, as long as you do not talk of what happened in Sixty-Eight. With Chan out of the way, that's probably true.'

'Why does CK care so much about me?'

'You are a witness to things that happened at Club Sixty-Eight – the people who were there. *You* may not know who they were, but *they* know. And CK will feel responsible to them because of Chan's involvement.'

She hugged his neck. 'Do you want me to stay, Johnny?'

'I can't tell you what you should do. If you stay I will help you to start again. The first thing we are going to do is find an island.'

She smiled. 'Become castaways?'

'Yes. Just you and me – hide from the world. Get the colour back in your cheeks. Work on those freckles.'

'We can't hide forever, can we, Johnny?'

'No. And I have to go and show my face at work now.'

'Don't go yet!' She held on to him as he sat up.

'I will come back. Then we'll plan, okay?'

She smiled a watery smile and nodded.

'I will be gone a few hours. If you need something to eat – take the keys with you. I'll leave you some money on the table, there's a supermarket a couple of blocks down. Otherwise I'll get us something when I get back.'

Mann didn't want to leave her but he had some things that just wouldn't wait. Two of them were about to face a bullet.

116

He arrived at Headquarters and went straight in to see Superintendent White, to find him packing his belongings into boxes. The photos, the rugby trophies, memorabilia of forty years of service were all coming down and being neatly wrapped in newspaper and packed away.

Mann stood at the doorway and watched him for a minute. 'Bit premature, isn't it, David? You've got a few more months yet.'

'They decided to let me go early.' White looked up and smiled ruefully.

'When are you off?'

'I'll be here for another week or so. They added up all the holiday I might *not* have had and decided it was time to go now. I have the house to pack up and the cat to find a home for. Do you want it?'

'I'd love to, David, but I'd forget to feed it. Give it to my mother, give her something to fuss over.'

'Okay. I'll do that.'

Mann glanced around the empty room. 'I'm sorry, David.'

'Don't be, Mann. I've had enough. I'm ready to go, believe me.'

'What did they say?'

'Oh, you know. The usual. Didn't seem to be able to keep command of the troops any more. Best to hand it over to someone else.' He paused in his packing, shook his head and sniffed. 'And maybe they're right. But I don't want to follow some of these new orders and I don't want my men to have to.' He put down his box and turned to face Mann. 'I am bloody proud of you, Johnny. Of course, it's highly unlikely you're ever going to make more than Inspector now. I think you can kiss promotion goodbye, but you will make a difference to the force and to Hong Kong, and that's more important. And Mann . . . your father . . . he would have been very proud of you. Very proud indeed. He would have expected no less from his son, mind you. He was a good, honourable man, a real gentleman. But you could not have saved him from his fate, Mann, no one could. Live your life now. Don't try to change the past any more. Draw a line under it and walk your own road. Keep on doing what you think is right, Mann, but try to work within the perimeters of the law. If you step outside too often, even to do good, you become like the men you hunt. There's a thin line, Mann. Be careful not to cross it. And now, take some leave – you deserve it, plus it would be better to lie low for a bit.'

'I will, David. Just want to tie up some loose ends first. What's happening about the brothers?'

'They'll be gone in the next day or two, to Beijing

and a bullet. We are still getting results back from the lab – we know who the skin and the scalp belong to.' He handed Mann the sheet of paper with the lab results.

'Jesus. They must have hated her.'

'Yes. A bullet is no more than they deserve.'

'But there are others who deserve it just as much, David.'

'They will get it in the end, Mann. Karma and all that.'

'Does karma come with laser sights?'

David White laughed. 'Just watch it, Mann, and try to stay alive for Christ's sake. Come and visit me. Maybe you'll end up back in England one day.'

'Visit, yes. But Hong Kong is my home. I couldn't live anywhere else.'

'Okay. Well, take good care of your Hong Kong. She's a heartless whore at the best of times.'

'Yes, and a beguiling mistress at others. But I can handle her.'

'I have no doubt of it . . . her and her daughters. By the way, where's my bloody boat? It better be in one piece?'

'Back safe and sound at the yacht club.' Mann fished in his pocket and pulled out the keys. He threw them across to White who threw them straight back.

'You keep it. Leaving present.'

Mann walked down the corridor to his office to see Li.

'Did you get your copy of the report into last night's disturbance on Cheung Chau, boss?'

'I did. The report was good, Shrimp. The drug-smuggling theme was brilliant. Exaggerating the heroin stash from two grams to twenty kilos was maybe a touch too much, though.'

'Sorry, boss. I got carried away. But, boss – Peter Farringdon – the surgeon – he's clean. Can't find a thing on him.'

'Keep looking, Shrimp. Everyone's got something on them.'

Mann stepped outside into the corridor and made his way down the stairs. He was going to see the brothers for the last time.

Max didn't move as Mann approached his cell. Only when Mann called his name did he slowly turn his head.

'Did you find her – Miss Geor-gi-na?'

'Yes. I found her, Max. She is safe. We also found your stepmother.'

Max grinned, and nodded his head, satisfied.

'She came back one day, to demand more money from my father. We argued. She had a heart attack and died right in front of me. After she was dead, I let Man Po skin her.' He looked up sharply. 'They won't let me see him – my brother!'

'He's all right. You'll be moved soon.'

Max nodded. 'I know.' He had accepted his fate. He turned away from Mann and lay down on his bunk. He was finished with conversation.

On his way out, Mann stopped to speak to the sergeant in charge of the prisoners.

'Move Max in with his brother. Make sure they stay together now, and pass on instructions that they should remain so till they face the bullet, till the last minute – together.'

117

Big Frank awoke with a smile on his face. He bounced out of bed and sang his way into the shower. The maid came and put his breakfast tray on the table. He shouted his thanks from the bathroom and emerged, his hair extensions dripping and a flapping hand towel slung around his waist. He just missed the maid as she disappeared at bullet-speed out of the door.

Big Frank was in the best of moods; everything felt right about the day. He strapped himself into his corset and, while humming the Wedding March, sat down to eat his hash browns and grits and wait for Lucy.

Lucy gave up packing. She called Max's number again – he didn't answer. She hadn't seen him since she stopped working at the club. *Where was he? Sleeping?* It wasn't like him not to answer her calls. She would have liked to have said goodbye to him, but it wasn't to be.

She called another cab and while she waited she sat back, staring out of the window at the Hong Kong she would not see again for a long time. She was moving to Florida with Frank. She would be his wife, and they would have children and she would be the best-kept hostess on the planet. She shook her head sadly. How ironic: the dream – marry a passport, get a ticket out – only now it wasn't a ticket for two; her beloved Ka Lei was dead and now she must go alone.

She sniffed, wiped her nose, stood and straightened the creases from her trousers. She looked towards the door. For a moment she thought she heard a key turn. She listened again. Nothing. She was getting jumpy. The sooner she got out of Hong Kong, the better.

Frank was waiting for her. His bags were packed – he was ready. He squeezed her so hard that she squealed in pain. She was still feeling the effects of the attack.

'Flank, you gonna kill your little Hong Kong girl before we get married?'

'I'm gonna eat you, honey.' He scooped her up and carried her into the bedroom.

'We gonna miss the flight, Flank!'

But he didn't answer – his mind was elsewhere . . .

They arrived at the airport late. Lucy raced Frank through to check in. She stood nervously by Frank's side, tucking herself as close to him as she could get, as they waited for their tickets and passports to be checked. She looked furtively around her. She didn't want to make eye contact with anyone, but she was searching for small groups of smart-looking men. It didn't even have to be a Wo Shing Shing member. Rival triad societies made pacts with each other in order to carry out a crime more effectively. She might never be safe from Chan. Wherever there were Chinese businesses there were triads.

Lucy hurried Frank through to Departures and straight to the boarding gate. She clung to his arm the whole way. They wouldn't dare take Frank out too, she thought. They would have to separate them first, and there was no way she was going to let that happen.

Twenty minutes later they boarded an American Airways flight to Miami. Lucy's eyes were fixed on the window. The minute the plane took off she knew she would be able to relax. They fastened their seatbelts and Lucy sighed gratefully as the plane began its taxi down the runway. *Phew – that was it.* She smiled at her reflection. She was safe, for now at least. She turned back from the window and smiled sweetly at Frank.

'Not long, Flank. We gonna be husband and wife. Did you make the arrangements?'

'I sure did, honey, you gonna be mine forever.'

Lucy smiled at him. 'You're so sweet. Yes, I am, Flank. I'm never gonna leave you.'

'I know that, honey. You know why?'

Lucy shook her head.

'Becoz,' Big Frank slid his massive hand beneath Lucy's fleshy bottom, 'I'm gonna brand you. That'll stop you runnin' off. I'm gonna put a big fat F brand here.' He pinched her hard.

Lucy tried to wriggle away. 'Oooh! That's enough, Flank! You're hurtin' me.'

Frank leaned across. 'Enough? Enough, honey? I'm just gettin' started.'

Lucy noticed that Big Frank's left eye had gone into spasm again.

118

Georgina awoke three hours after Mann had left. It was lunch time. She got up and showered. She was starving. She rummaged through his kitchen cupboards and found a lonely Pot Noodle and a pack of Earl Grey tea. That would do for now. She sat in the lounge and waited for Mann. She really hoped that he would come back soon. She wanted the chance to talk to him properly.

The mid-afternoon sun stretched in through the lounge window and warmed Georgina through. She waited. Mann would be back soon, she was sure, and yet the day was trickling away. She turned on the TV and waited.

Dusk came, and she found herself still sitting alone. She began to feel panicky. Surely if Mann wanted her to stay he would be back soon? She got up and walked around the flat. The evening's shadows made her shiver. The flat felt suddenly cold and unwelcoming. Then she realised it wasn't just the flat. She didn't really belong in Hong Kong. Hong Kong hadn't been kind to her. It had chewed her up and spat her out. Maybe, she thought, it was time to go home. She wished Mann would come back and reassure her, provide her with the answers, tell her what she should do. But then she wasn't sure he could or would do that.

Mann called in to the Albert. As he walked into the bar he saw Peter Farringdon. The surgeon didn't see Mann – he was in the midst of greeting an elderly Chinese. The way they clasped one another's hand struck Mann as slightly awkward, and then he saw it – the surgeon tapped his little finger three times on the outside of the other man's hand.

'How is she, Johnny?' Mandy left the busy bar and came around to see him.

'Georgina has been through such a lot, Mandy. It's going to take time but I think she'll be all right in the end. I have faith in her.'

'Is she going to stay in Hong Kong?'

'It's for her to decide.'

'Do you want her to?'

'She knows I will be there for her if she needs me but she must make up her own mind. She's a grown woman. She's been through a lot but she's survived. Her strength will see her through, I'm positive of that.'

'But what do you want her to do?'

'I want her to be the woman she is meant to be.' He stood and kissed Mandy goodbye. As he made his way out he turned back and nodded in the direction of the surgeon who had been watching him. Mann held his gaze a few seconds longer than was comfortable for the surgeon. Did he know what he'd got himself into? Mann doubted it.

He who rides the tiger is afraid to dismount.

119

Mann had to make one more stop – back at the office. He needed to pick up some things if he was planning to take time off. Headquarters was relatively quiet. Shrimp had gone home to rest. David White was still packing up. As soon as Mann walked into the office he saw it – a small brown package on top of his desk. He picked it up and turned it over in his hands – no sender's address. It had been hand-delivered.

He looked around the office as if something might tell him where it had come from, but Ng's and Li's desks were empty. Mann held the package in his hands for a few more moments before carefully slitting it open. His heart began to beat faster. He reached inside and slid out the contents – a black plastic DVD case. He opened it: a DVD, no title.

Mann watched his fingers perform the ordinary task of preparing his laptop, flipping it open and firing it up as if in slow motion. Smoothly and slowly, these familiar actions were taking him to the point he dreaded. His heart was racing now, his palms were sweating.

He inserted the DVD into the drive and waited. He heard Helen's voice before he saw her – begging for mercy. There she was – her arms tied together at the wrists, suspended from a hook in the ceiling. It was in Sixty-Eight, at the same station where Kim had died.

Helen's arms were pulled high. Her feet barely touched the floor. A black cloth bag was over her head. He knew it was her. He knew every inch of her body. Even as it looked now, thin, bruised and battered, he knew it was her.

A man came into view, his back to the camera. He was European, of slight build, short, his skin saggy with age, his shape testimony to years of debauchery and bad living. His spindly legs were overhung by a flabby gut. He started whipping her.

It killed Mann to watch but it was worse to look away. He pulled his laptop closer to him. He had to be with her. He had to feel the full weight of it in his heart.

For minutes she screamed, twisting her body away from the pain. Then, the man paused. His shoulders heaved with the exertion. He wiped the blood and sweat from his face. Mann caught his profile. In that second his death became a certainty.

The man removed her hood. The camera zoomed in on her face. It was blotchy and swollen. Her eyes were petrified. Mann's heart was breaking. The man unhooked her hands and dragged her across to a table. Helen was trying to get away – screaming. Mann would hear that scream – the sound of pure terror – for the rest of his life. The camera angle changed. Now Mann was down directly above the table. Helen was strapped down. Only her head was moving now – thrashing wildly from side to side as she tried to get away from the man's hands and the polythene bag he held in them. But, she couldn't. The camera zoomed down onto her face. Mann found himself looking through the mask of clear plastic into the eyes of his beautiful Helen. He watched the light in them slowly extinguish and he listened to the background sound of a man grunting. Helen died at the same second as James Dudley-Smythe ejaculated.

120

Georgina refolded the same T-shirt again and again, hovering over her small bag. She didn't want to leave like this, but she didn't think she should wait any longer for Johnny. She didn't know why he hadn't come back. She felt more alone now than ever. All her instincts told her to go home. She stood at the window and watched the lights go on in the block opposite. People appeared in illuminated windows like in an advent calendar. She wrote him a note.

My plane leaves just after midnight. If you want me to stay, come and find me. X

She took the MTR to the airport. She had hours to spare. When she got there she ambled around, changing seats now and again and staring blankly at unfamiliar faces. She wasn't feeling well, she was breathless and anxious. She felt better when she kept moving. People brushed past her, children spun around her feet. She didn't move through passport control into the departure area; she had no baggage to check in, just a small bag which she carried with her. She did not have the resolution needed to cross over to the other side, from Hong Kong into no man's land. She looked at her watch. There was still plenty of time for him to come – if he wanted.

121

Superintendent White had just about finished his packing when Mann walked into his office.

'Jesus, Mann! What the hell?'

Mann slumped straight into a chair and put his head back and closed his eyes. He was nauseous and tired. He felt the cool of the overhead fan on his face.

'Are you okay?' Mann heard Superintendent White stop in his tracks. He opened his red-rimmed eyes and stared at a stain on the ceiling. The fan was turning – whooshing rhythmically.

'I could do with a drink,' he said, without moving or blinking.

David White unpacked one of his boxes and took out a bottle of vodka for Mann and a bottle of scotch for himself, and two cut-glass tumblers. He set them on the desk and poured out two large ones before walking over and handing the vodka to Mann. Only Mann's eyes moved – his head remained glued to the back of the seat. He looked at his old friend's troubled face and smiled ruefully.

'Sorry, David. I must look a state.'

David White stood, vodka bottle in hand, waiting for Mann to dispatch his drink before he refilled it. 'Bloody awful.'

'I feel better than I did a few hours ago.'

'What happened, Mann?'

'I saw a film of Helen's death . . .'

There was a knock at the door. 'Go away!' Superintendent White bellowed. A young officer, who didn't dare put more than his nose around the door, answered.

'Sorry, sir. I know you said you didn't want to be disturbed, but there is an important call for you.'

'Okay, okay.' Superintendent White picked up the phone and pressed the extension number. Mann watched him as he listened intently for several minutes. His only contribution to the conversation was: *When . . . ? Where . . . ? Witnesses . . . ? Anything taken from the scene?*

After a few minutes he put the phone slowly and deliberately back onto the receiver. Then he walked over and refreshed Mann's drink. Mann watched him as he paced mechanically around the room, piecing his thoughts together. Mann waited. After a few minutes White came back to sit at his desk. He poured himself another scotch, put the bottle back into the drawer and drew the air in through his nose in a cleansing gesture of having finally reached a decision. He didn't look at Mann while he spoke.

'There's been another death,' he said matter-of-factly. 'It's a man this time. James Dudley-Smythe was found hanging in his wine cellar this evening. Found by his maid – hanging – naked – severely beaten. We don't need to look for the weapon. A metal-tipped whip was found implanted in his rectum. He probably died of a heart attack in the midst of it all. The maid seems to think there's nothing missing.' White glanced at Mann.

Mann sat up. 'That's what I was going to talk to you about, David.'

David White put his hand up to stop him.

'I don't think we need to waste police resources on this. The officers at the scene have found all sorts of apparatus in his house. It's most likely he did this to himself. One of those weird sex rituals. Open and shut. He got what he deserved in the end. As you said – karma with laser sights.'

122

Georgina took out her photo album. She smiled at the pictures of her and Ka Lei, squeezed into photo booths, laughing and making faces at the camera. Then she closed the album and put it back in her bag. She didn't need to look at photos of Ka Lei to remember her. She would carry her cousin in her heart forever.

She would always miss her and she would always wish things could have been different, but she would never regret coming. She looked up at the screen:

Now boarding . . .

She closed her eyes for a few minutes. Inside her stomach was a solid weight of trepidation. But she knew she had to go. She must repair herself and rest. She needed to do this on her own. She was a grown woman now, she had to stand on her own two feet and find her place in the world. She would return one day. Maybe Johnny Mann would still be around. She hoped so. She stood and made her way through to Departures.

123

'Hello, Kin Tak. Sorry it's late.'

'Of course, I don't mind, Inspector. I wanted to see you. Please, come with me.'

Mann followed him into the long storage section, even colder than normal. He could see that Kin Tak was nervous. He looked like he hadn't slept, or if he had it was fully clothed. Kin Tak stopped at a fridge and checked the list.

'I am glad you called, Inspector. Just bear with me. I have something to confess. Something to show you.'

Mann began to feel decidedly uneasy. This wasn't a good place to have a lengthy conversation. It was never going to hold fond memories for him.

Kin Tak opened the fridge and wheeled out a trolley. He unzipped the white body bag and for a moment stood in front of it, shielding it from Mann's view.

'What is it, Kin Tak?'

'Helen Bateman was a special friend of yours?'

Mann felt a surge of anger. He almost pushed the young mortuary assistant aside. *What the fuck had he done to her?*

Kin Tak stepped out of the way. And Mann saw that Helen had been lovingly washed: her hair was glossy and bright, her body reassembled with the neatest stitching that would have served a plastic surgeon well. Her face was serene, beautiful. She was dead and gone, but she was his Helen again.

'I thank you, Kin Tak.' Mann found himself unable to speak. 'Thank you very much. You have done a really good job.'

Kin Tak held his hands up as if to say there was no need to thank him. 'I'll wait outside. Take as long as you like. I am not going anywhere, Inspector.' He beamed his baby smile.

Mann looked at Helen's face for the last time. 'See you on a beach somewhere, my love. Please forgive me.'

He zipped the bag back up.

124

He arrived back at the apartment. It was dark. It was empty. He saw the note on the table.

He checked his watch. It was nearly eleven – she wouldn't be lifting off for an hour. A night flight to Heathrow, care of Cathay Pacific. He had plenty of time to get there, if he wanted to.

His phone rang.

'Who else would know his way around Headquarters? I knew it was you who left it.'

'I felt you were owed it. I had no hand in her death, or any of the others, you know that?'

'I know.'

'I will deny being on the island when CK asks.'

'Of course. I never saw you.'

'See you around, Johnny.'

'See you, Stevie.'

Mann stood watching the night sky: glass in one hand, Georgina's note in the other. Finally, he put the note down. He respected her decision to leave. He hoped she would come back one day. He shrugged and smiled sadly – people and their paths. His was a lonely one sometimes. But he'd rather walk it alone – for now. In the morning he would go for a long run, clear out his head, focus on his future, think about what had to be done and how to achieve it. For now, he needed to get a good night's sleep.

But the morning seemed a long way away, and the night before him loomed lonely and long. He was restless. He had a need to forget everything for one night. He rolled the iced vodka glass around in his hand and searched the sky again. High up, a plane blinked its colours at him. He downed his drink, poured another, and drank a toast to Helen, to Kim, to Georgina, and to all the women he had known.

He was tempted to get blind drunk, but he didn't think it would work. It wasn't what he needed. He needed . . . He needed . . . Then it hit him. He picked up his phone. He needed Honey Ryder. At least it would be a good start.

Twenty minutes later he was stood by Ng's bedside.

'I thought you'd be in bed or out getting drunk somewhere?'

'Yes, well. Nearly was, then I got a better offer and here I am. How's it going, Confucius?'

'In a couple of days I should be able to pee for myself, which will be nice.' Ng rolled his eyes around the room. 'Getting sick of lying about. What's the news? Did you get Chan?'

'I got him.'

'I knew you would. *He who walks on snow leaves footprints.*'

'Snow, water, he wasn't very good at walking on either.'

'What else . . . ? I can see it in your face.'

'I took the law into my own hands, Ng. I crossed the line. Not just Chan. I found out who murdered Helen.'

There was a silence in the room, just the droning of equipment. After a few minutes, Ng spoke.

'Justice is not always written in stone or in the law books, Genghis. Justice comes in many forms.'

'There will be repercussions.'

'There will be some people who won't like it, but there will be many more who will back you. There are lots of policemen just like us who won't tolerate the triads any more. Enough is enough! Remember, Mann: *It is not the cry, but the flight of the wild duck that leads the flock to follow.*'

'We'll soon see. Hurry up and get well, Confucius. It'll be good to have you back.'

Mann got up to leave.

'I mean it, Genghis: *Set yourself as standard and others will fall in behind you.*'

'You know, Ng – you're full of shit. Take care of yourself. Leave the nurses alone. I'll see you in a couple of days.'

Mann smiled to himself as he walked quietly down the empty corridor, just the sound of his Prada loafers on linoleum. Ng was right – there were many roads to justice.

THE TRAFFICKED

DETECTIVE JOHNNY MANN IS BACK . . .

Missing children. An evil racket. A race
against time . . .

Nine-year-old Amy Tang is the third child to be
kidnapped recently and held for a vast sum of
money. While the other two children were released
after the ransom is paid – Amy is not.

Summoned to appear before his boss, Inspector
Johnny Mann expects to be told that, owing to his
insubordination, he is heading back to traffic duty.
Instead he is ordered to lead the investigation into
the kidnapping of Amy – who happens to be the
illegitimate daughter of a major player in the Flesh
Trade, CK Leung.

Mann's investigation takes him to London, where
he teams up with DC Becky Stamp. Within days of
arriving in London, there is an arson attack that
kills more than a dozen women and children. The
bodies of the victims are found chained to their
beds and are unidentifiable.

Mann must uncover the link between Amy's kidnap-
pers and the arson attacks before it's too late.

Prepare to be terrorised all over again with this
disturbingly addictive thriller, unleashed in
autumn 2008.

ISBN: 978-1-84756-083-4

Read on for an exclusive extract from
Lee Weeks's next novel,
The Trafficked, coming soon . . .

1

'Shhh, stop crying. The white man will hear you. What's your name?'

'Perla.'

'How old are you?'

'Eleven.'

'I'm Maya. I'm eight. You from Mindanao?'

'Yes.'

'Me too. Where are we?'

'Angeles City.'

'Why are we chained up? Are we in prison? Why does that Kano hurt everyone? What will happen to me?'

'You will be sold.'

'Sold?'

'Sold to a man.'

'What will the man do with me?'

'He will have sex with you.'

'I'm just a girl. I can't. I'm going to run away. Let's do it, Perla. Let's run home to Mindanao.'

Perla stated to cry again.

'Don't cry. Kano will come. He will hurt you. He will poke you with the electric stick again.'

'My legs are wet. I am bleeding.'

'Don't cry, Perla. I'll be your friend. I'll tell you a Mickey Mouse story.'

By the time Maya finished her story Perla was dead.

2

Detective Inspector Johnny Mann was at the end of the bar. He held on to a glass and rolled it in his hands, savouring the cool condensation, before allowing it to slip through his fingers and land in the centre of the barmat. He checked his phone – another message, same as the last one. He pushed his dark hair back from his sun-sore eyes and signalled to the barman that he was ready for another vodka.

Mann was one of nine men sat in the Boom Boom Bar – a palm-thatched, rattan-floored beach hut. Apart from a dozen stools, there was a tatty couch that had lost half its back and had two threadbare cushions to sit on. There was no fan in the Boom Boom Bar, only the breeze to cool it down and tonight there was not a breath of wind. Five of the ten men were watching a boxing match on a small television set suspended from the ceiling. The other three stared at their drinks, willing the alcohol to hit. Mann's t-shirt stuck to him in the suffocating heat, tracing the contours of his strong, lean frame.

A cockroach dropped from the roof and landed on the barman's back. It clung to his shirt.

'How's it goin', bro?'

Mann felt a hand on his shoulder. It was Jojo, the proprietor, a short, fat, fifty-year-old Filipino wearing a pink shiny shirt with *Boom Boom Bar* embroidered on the back. His soft afro hair ballooned over his shoulders.

'Good, Jojo. Place is busy, I see.'

Mann gestured toward the area of candlelit tables on the beach outside. Most of them were occupied.

'Yeah, pretty busy, man. We gotta real good singer tonight.'

A young brown-skinned singer, his hair in a wide ponytail, was wailing a Bob Marley song on a small stage pitched into the sand. Next to him, a young musician sat on a drum box with his back to the sea. His eyes were closed. His long bony fingers beat a rhythm on the box's stretched skin. His name was Rex. He was Jojo's eldest son.

The barman set another drink down in front of Mann. As he did so, the cockroach crawled onto his arm. He knocked it off and stamped on it hard.

'Stick around, Johnny, it's gonna be a good night. Plenty of people about.'

Jojo was about to walk away when Mann caught him.

'Thought about what I said?'

Jojo laughed uncomfortably. 'I told you, bro, this is paradise – you should know, you been comin' here for long enough. Best place on Mama Earth.'

He disappeared to play the 'happy patron', circling the bar and talking to his customers. After twenty minutes he came back to stand at the end of the bar. Mann proposed a toast to Boracay.

'To paradise – where every hour is 'happy hour'. You're right, Jojo.' He smiled. 'I've been coming here a long time. I've known you since I was a rookie and your son, Rex. . . .' He nodded in the direction of the youth on the drum box. '. . . was a small boy.'

'Long time, bro, long time.' Jojo nodded his head.

'Remember that time you were suicidal over a woman? What was she called?'

Jojo screwed up his face, struggling to remember her name.

'Janie,' Mann recalled, 'that was it. Then there was the time the local police shut you down when you didn't pay them enough. Never seen you so angry. But the worst was when I came here and there was nothing left. Typhoon Rosy took everything. You were devastated – remember?'

Jojo closed his eyes, put his hand on his chest and sighed.

'That storm was one I never forgot.'

'But do you know what? In all the years I've been coming here this is the first time I've ever seen you scared.'

Jojo wiped the sweat from his eyes with his shirt sleeve. He was smiling but he didn't look like a happy man.

'Listen to me, old friend.' Mann held his gaze. 'I know the Chinaman came through here. I followed him from Hong Kong. Tell me what he wanted.'

'You gonna get me killed, Bro.' Jojo looked around

nervously. The boxing was still going on. The others were still staring at their drinks, waiting to find that 'happy place'. Jojo turned his back on the bar and looked hard at Mann. 'I in enough trouble.'

'Tell me. I might be able to help.'

'A Chinaman come here ten days ago. He rent my house – real nice place I have behind here.'

'What did he look like?'

'Not as tall as you, but tall for a Chinaman – goatee beard, bald, mean-faced, thirty-five maybe?'

'That's the man. Anyone else?'

'Come wid five other Chinese – his monkeys. Same time as he arrive come four white guys. They stay up at the end of the beach. Come wid whores from Angeles.'

'What did he want ?'

'He wanted me to sell 'im somethin' – somethin' I own.'

'What?'

'I have businesses in Mindanao, down south. He want me to sell them to him – cheap.'

'What kind of businesses?'

'A bar, a small hotel. Nuttin big. Nice place – on de coast.'

'What did you agree to?'

'Not agree nuttin. He said he be back. He left wid white guys here. Bin here a week. Deese are bad fuckers,' he whispered. 'One of de whores is beat up nasty. Dey got money – plenty – pay off de police. I see them talking wid dem like *old* friends.' Jojo shrugged and shook his head. He stared hard at Mann. 'I tell you,

496

bro, I gonna be in big trouble when dat Chinaman come back.'

'Are they here tonight – the white guys?'

Jojo signalled for Mann to wait whilst he walked out of the bar and across the narrow sandy lane that ran the length of the mile-long white sugar beach'. Halfway across the lane he started swaying to the music . . . He began dancing with three of his sons who touted along the lane for him. As Jojo swang his hips to the rhythm, Rex on the drum box got a nudge from the singer. Rex opened his eyes. He stopped rocking his dreadlocks and began drumming faster. Jojo tried to keep up. He couldn't. He staggered back into the bar, amidst laughter and applause, clutching his hand to his chest as if he were about to have a heart attack.

'Bastards.' He laughed, talking to the men watching the fight and rolling his eyes in the direction of the beach. 'You give dem your name an' they treat you like shit. Kids.' He took a beer from the barman and waited for the fuss to subside before making his way back over to Mann. Jojo fanned his face with the bar mat.

'They here?' Mann asked again.

Jojo leaned in. 'One of dem is here. . . . sat left of de stage wid a young Filipina . . . Big white guy . . . peak cap.' Jojo turned away from Mann and leaned his back against the bar, pretending to be interested in the boxing match which had reached its fifth round. He kept his eyes diverted from Mann and kept smiling, 'Anuder ding, ' he whispered. 'Dat old white guy's got somethin' hard in his pocket an' it ain't his big old cock.

You gonna spoil my business you make trouble here, Johnny.'

'Relax, old friend. They'll be no trouble.'

Mann picked up his drink and walked across the lane. He sat on the end of a table of Dutch tourists, directly behind the man. It was hard to see the man's face hidden beneath the peak cap and with just the candlelight and crescent moon to help. But Mann could see he was big, strong and weathered, ex-military, with tattoos over his upper arms. He wore khaki shorts and a sleeveless shirt. He chainsmoked and was texting fast, impatiently. The young Filipina sat a little apart from him, waiting nervously by his side. The text messages came back every few minutes – no jingle from the phone, just a light and a vibration. His leg twitched with adrenaline as he read a new text. He called a number, said a few words, then finished the call abruptly and slammed the phone down onto the table. He pulled off the peak cap and rubbed his sweaty head. His silver grey short back and sides was indented with the outline of the cap. Mann saw his face, mottled and puffy, dominated by bulbous eyes that made him look what he was – angry. Mann recognised him straightaway. It was the man they called the Colonel – one of the biggest traffickers of women and children in the Philippines.

Enjoyed *The Trophy Taker?*
Prepare to be frightened all over again . . .

BLOOD LINES

Grace Monroe

Blood is thicker than water – and far more deadly . . .

A woman is lured to a remote spot in the Scottish Highlands and strangled almost to the point of death. As she begs for mercy, her tormentor begins to carve her face, before burying her alive.

In Edinburgh, unorthodox young lawyer Brodie McLennan becomes tangled up in the case. When it emerges that Brodie was the last person to see the victim and crucial evidence is found at her flat, she must fight to clear her name – and save her own skin.

Meanwhile in an asylum in Inverness, a deranged patient writes the name Brodie over and over in her own blood . . .

As another mutilated body is discovered bearing the same ritualistic markings, Brodie is running scared from unknown forces, eager to see blood on her hands . . .

Prepared to be shocked in this dark and gripping thriller, for fans of Ian Rankin and Mo Hayder...

ISBN: 978-1-84756-041-4

Coming in **June** 2008

LOST SOULS
Neil White

A ritual murder. Abducted children mysteriously returned. Why?

A woman is found butchered on a Lancashire housing estate, her tongue and eyes brutally gouged out. Ritual murder or crime of passion?

Children are abducted and then returned to their families days later, unharmed but with no knowledge of where they have been – or who took them.

DC Laura McGanity, having relocated from London to the old mill town of Blackley, quickly learns that life up North is far from peaceful. She needs to solve these mystifying cases – but keep the local police on side.

Her reporter boyfriend Jack Garrett – the reason for McGanity's relocation – is back in his hometown and finds himself entangled in the two mysterious cases. His investigations reveal murky connections and sordid secrets.

But when Jack meets a man who 'paints' the future – prophecies of horrific events which he then puts onto canvas – it's becoming terrifyingly clear that many people, including his own family, are in grave danger . . .

ISBN: 978-1-84756-018-6

Coming in **May** 2008

THE MURDER GAME
Beverly Barton

Are you ready to play . . .?

The game is simple – he is the Hunter. They are the Prey. He gives them a chance to escape. To run. To hide. To outsmart him. But eventually, he catches them. And that's when the game gets really terrifying . . .

Private investigator Griffin Powell and FBI agent Nicole Baxter know a lot about serial killers – they took one down together. But this new killer is as sadistic as they've ever seen. He likes his little games, and he especially likes forcing Nicole and Griff to play along. Every unsolvable clue, every posed victim, every taunting phone call – it's all part of his twisted, elaborate plan. And then the Hunter calls, wanting to know if they're really ready to play . . .

There's a new game now, and it's much more deadly than the first. A brutal psychopath needs a worthy adversary. He won't stop until he can hunt the most precious prey of all – Nicole. And with his partner in a killer's sights, Griff is playing for the biggest stakes of his life.

ISBN: 978-1-84756-059-9

Coming in **August** 2008.